UPSTATE
UPROAR

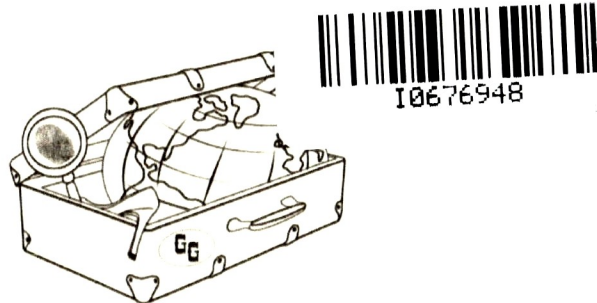

Joan Rylen

ALSO BY JOAN RYLEN

ISBN 13: 978-098567-3-6-5-9

Library of Congress Control Number: 2015934258

To Ashley – you're the sweetest, cutest, funniest, silliest goose ever.
I love you, Momma

This one's for you Big Lou – with love, Johnell

Prologue

Kate took one last sip of mango margarita, set her glass down on the dock and jumped into the lake. The cool water was welcome after the heat of the day, and it got cooler and cooler the further she went. A pain shot through her leg and she stopped swimming to rub her calf with one hand while treading water with the other arm. The pain struck again, this time in both legs, extending up her thighs, causing her to gasp and swallow water.

Help me! Help me, she thought as she coughed. "Help," she sputtered, but because of her coughing, it was barely audible. She knew she was in trouble. Her head was just above water.

She tried to swim to shore, but her legs wouldn't work. She attempted a couple of strokes, letting her legs dangle, but the pain moved up her back and into her arms. Her heart raced as she slipped completely under. *No! Have to get to shore!*

Kate kicked as hard as she could, trying to break the surface, but the cramping refused to yield. Beams of sunlight streaked through the water, providing no help as her lungs burned, yearning for the precious oxygen that floated in bubbles around her. Despite her efforts not to breathe, she involuntarily inhaled.

She coughed and spattered, water invading her nose and mouth. She reached down to feel the living being that had been growing within her for almost five months, but it was gone. A new panic and sadness embraced her, but she knew it was too late. The rays of light faded as she sank lower and lower.

1

Day 1

Vivian Taylor's heart pounded and she gripped the armrests of her middle seat. "Oh my god!" The sweater she had put on that morning in preparation for brisk autumn weather was now suffocating. *What was I thinking wearing this?*

Wendy Schreiber turned the page of the in-flight magazine. "Geez, Viv, it was just a little turbulence."

The plane shuddered again and Vivian whimpered, then groaned as the seat belt light flashed on and the captain's voice rang out. "We've got a patch of storms ahead, but we'll be through it in no time. Flight attendants, please take your seats."

From the back of the plane, Vivian watched as the passengers' heads jerked in unison as the 737 hit another rough spot. "I hate it when the captain says that!" She reached across Wendy and pulled down the shade.

Wendy tucked the magazine into the seatback pocket and pushed her long, brown hair behind her shoulder. "You're such a chicken, and it's so unlike you. I'm not excited about it, but it's just a little turbulence."

The plane dropped and Vivian's stomach lurched into her throat. "That was not a little, that was a lot."

"Okay, that was more." The right wing dipped, then leveled out. "But that was less."

"That was definitely NOT less. We're gonna die!" Tears leaked out of Vivian's eyes and ran down her cheeks. She lifted her blonde curls off her neck, trying to cool down.

Wendy grabbed the magazine and started fanning her. "Seriously, Viv, we're going to be okay. What is with you?"

The plane hit another hard bump, causing Vivian to scream, her green eyes round with fright.

An older man in business attire who was seated across the aisle leaned over and looked at them, then slowly leaned back against his seat and continued working on his laptop.

Vivian couldn't help but laugh, which is often how she dealt with fear. Her lack of control and not being able to see out the windshield was sending her over the edge. She wiped her clammy hands on her jeans, then white-knuckle-gripped the armrests. The plane hit another air pocket, dropping what felt like 500 feet. She leaned forward and closed her eyes. "That was more. A LOT more."

"No, that was less, definitely less than the one before," Wendy said and kept fanning.

"I don't want the swimming pool slut to raise my children," Vivian said. "She's such a bitch, it will ruin them."

"You're not going to die. But even if you did, they'd always have good memories of their fun mom." Wendy smiled sweetly. "I think the bad weather is almost over, Viv. Their evil stepmother won't have to raise them."

"Rick never stands up to her. He asks her permission to keep the kids if we ever have to switch our schedules, for god's sake. What's with that crap?"

"Maybe he's just being courteous, checking their schedule?"

"No, he's asking permission. She can't be inconvenienced."

"So did the kids get that backyard that Rick said was his reason for getting married?"

Vivian laughed. "You should see the money pit they bought. The house barely looks livable and the backyard is a joke. It's so overgrown, the weeds are taller than the kids."

"So much for that." Wendy shrugged.

The plane gave another shudder and Vivian winced, but soon the sun peeked through the cracks of the window shade.

"See, it's about over," Wendy said and lifted the shade. "We always have a little turbulence on our vacations. Let's hope that was the end of it." The smile in her brown eyes faded, but then she smiled at Vivian and went back to reading her magazine.

Vivian and Wendy, friends since elementary school, were on their way to Albany, N.Y., to meet two other childhood friends, Lucy McGuire and Kate Jameson, for their fourth girls' trip. From there, the girls were driving north to Lake Placid to spend a week hiking, enjoying the fall foliage and all-around relaxing. Kate preferred mountains over city after their last trip to New Orleans, no one was ready for the beach, and since Lucy lived in the Rockies, she wanted different mountains. The group had decided on the Adirondacks.

The four had grown up in funky-smelling Pasa-Get-Down-dena, Texas, a blue-collar suburb of Houston full of refinery workers who loved their line-dancing and Lone Star Beer. Two of the most notorious icehouses were right across from one another on Shaver Street, the "He's Not Here" and the "She's Not Here." The girls tried to go into "He's Not Here" once their senior year in high school but didn't make it through the door, so instead they went to Cherry's Liquor Store and ordered wine coolers from the drive-thru. No ID required.

The plane landed, and Vivian and Wendy were among the last off. Big hugs from Lucy and Kate awaited them at baggage claim. The girls chit-chatted and Vivian showed pictures of the kids while waiting for their bags to slide down the chute.

Kate turned to Wendy, concern in her brown eyes. "How are you? How are things going with Jake's investigation?"

Wendy shook her head. "I'll tell y'all about it in the car. It's not the best news."

"Darn, that's not what I wanted to hear," Kate said. "But it's good to see you, and I'm glad you decided to come on the trip. I know it's been a rough few months."

"I really needed to see y'all." Wendy took a deep breath. "Let's get this show on the road."

Lucy pulled the rental car keys from her purse. "We're all set. I got us an SUV that can handle all this luggage. We have a couple hours before we get to Lake Placid, so let's find a grocery store here in Albany and stock up on goodies."

"As long as Dos Equis is on the list, I'm in," Vivian said.

Wendy whipped a piece of paper out of her purse. "I'm all over it!"

The girls walked to the parking garage and Lucy led the way, her auburn ponytail swinging as she walked. Vivian butt bumped Kate and smiled. "So, you pregnant yet?"

Kate raised her eyebrows and pulled open her cardigan. "What do you think?"

2

Vivian pulled Kate in for a big embrace, then stepped back and rubbed her baby bump. "You're so cute!"

Kate smiled and patted her normally flat stomach, which now had a little pooch.

Lucy asked, "How far along are you?"

"Almost five months." Kate smiled. "I learned some moves on our last trip in New Orleans from all that strip club sleuthing. Shaun was impressed! Now really encourages me to take these trips."

"I can't believe you kept this a secret," Vivian said. "We should be planning your baby shower by now."

"It hasn't been easy to keep this from y'all, but I had to tell you in person. Now I can go public with my news."

"Boy or girl?" Wendy asked as she took Kate's bag off her shoulder. "And give me this. No more lifting for you."

"I'm fine, the baby's fine, everything's fine." Kate reached for her bag but Wendy refused to give it up. "We want it to be a surprise, so I don't know." She rubbed her belly again.

"You're carrying precious cargo and I got this," Wendy said, firmly clutching the bag. "What can we do special for you? Craving any certain foods, extra sleep, mommy massage?"

"I've been craving meat and I'm definitely hungrier than usual, so we need to find a grocery store. And even though I'm past the nauseous stage, I need to sit in the front seat. Otherwise, nothing special."

"We can accommodate that," Lucy said. "First stop, groceries. Do you want to drive?"

Kate took the keys. "Sure, and that way I can control all the windows." She giggled, then said, " 'Cuz I'm a little gassy."

Kate demonstrated just that, so the girls picked up the pace to the SUV. Lucy, the expert car packer, got everything loaded and with just enough space to see out the back window. Wendy rode shotgun and navigated Kate to the highway, while Vivian and Lucy tucked into the back seat.

Kate adjusted her seat belt and said, "Okay, so what's the latest on Jake's accident? Wait, do we call it an accident?"

"I call it his disappearance," Wendy replied. "There hasn't been any trace of him. I've spoken numerous times with Sue Garrett, the detective with the Las Vegas Police Department, but she hasn't been able to make any headway on what happened."

Vivian patted Wendy's shoulder. "There has to be some evidence. Vegas is the capital of cameras, for god's sake, either in buildings or traffic cams or in people's hands. Something has to turn up."

"It's like he got sucked up in the Bermuda Triangle. I keep waiting for the phone to ring and see his number, but it doesn't happen. I catch myself in the middle of the day thinking about him, wondering what he's up to, and then remember, he's gone."

"Don't give up hope," Lucy said. "Until we know something definite, you have to think positive."

Kate clicked on the blinker, pulled off the highway and soon parked in front of the grocery store. "Let's get our shopping done, then tell us the story on the way to Lake Placid. I want to hear the whole thing, start in detail."

Lucy opened her door. "We need to hit up the liquor store next door while we're here. I have a feeling we're going to need liquid therapy."

The girls piled out of the car and made their way through the grocery store. Kate bypassed the produce department and bee-lined for the beef jerky. "Vegetables repulse me these days. I need meat."

"Who are you?" Lucy asked. "Hadn't you given up just about all meat before you were pregnant?"

"Yep, 95 percent vegetarian, couldn't give up dairy, but now I'm all about the meat. Gimme brisket, bacon, beef tips, barbecue, anything animal."

"Good thing you live in the barbecue mecca of Texas," Lucy said. "I haven't found anything in Denver that compares to Franklin's Barbeque."

"I've become a smoked meat connoisseur, dragging Shaun around Austin and the Hill Country, trying 'em all."

The girls stocked up on snacks, bought a Styrofoam cooler and a bag of ice, then headed to the liquor store for red wine, vodka and beer, even though only three of them would be drinking on this trip.

The only place in the car to put the goods was the back seat. Lucy and Vivian did their best not to crush the chips, smush the bread or damage the donuts, and the only place for the cooler was smack-dab between the two of them.

"I'm in charge of the back seat bar, baby!" Vivian called as they pulled out of the parking lot. "Wait! Pull into that fast food restaurant."

"Need to use the restroom?" Kate asked.

"No, more important than that. I'll be right back." Vivian ran inside and returned less than a minute later with a plastic utensil packet. "I needed a knife to cut my limes!"

Wendy pointed to the back. "I have a Swiss Army knife in my big blue bag. But good luck with the plastic one."

"Ahh, should've known!"

As Kate merged onto the interstate, a light rain started to fall. "Okay, Wendy, I need you to start from the beginning with Jake's story. I know it's hard, but I want to hear the whole thing. Maybe we can help somehow."

"I'm just not ready to rehash it all right now. I need a beverage, or three, first. Can we talk about something else?"

Kate glanced at Lucy in the rearview. "Of course, we can. Lucy, what's the latest with you and Steve? Did you officially file?"

"Yes," Lucy said, the twinkle in her usually cheerful green eyes dimmed.

Vivian handed Lucy and Wendy both a red Solo cup filled with vodka and cranberry.

Lucy took a sip. "It'll be final in a couple of months."

"How's Steve doing?" Wendy asked.

"Oh, you know, he's his usual unemotional self. We've been friends forever, and I'm hoping we'll be able to maintain that when this is over."

"I hate that you're moving out of the townhouse," Wendy said. "You worked so hard remodeling it."

"The mortgage and homeowners association dues are way more than I can afford, even though he's been good to me in terms of splitting stuff and making sure I'm okay financially. I've found a little apartment in Denver, which at least cuts down on my commute."

"Who gets the cats?" Kate asked.

Lucy crunched a piece of ice. "One each. I hope they don't freak out."

"Will you be able to maintain your expensive shoe habit?" Vivian asked.

"Probably not. I'm kicking up my hours at work, promoting myself more and just trying to spend less." Lucy was a self-employed interior designer. Her income fluctuated with the economy and also how hard she worked.

"That sucks," Vivian said.

"It's okay, I'm stocked up on shoes." Lucy slowly stirred her drink. "I'm still able to take vacations, but thank goodness we have our Getaway Girlz trust fund."

In the Rocky Mountains, the girls brought a thief to justice and received a hefty reward. They split some of the loot and put the rest into a trust fund to be used only for their vacations.

"Enough about me, what about you, preggo? Any other news from Austin other than your new meat habit?"

Kate gripped the wheel and sighed. "Shaun's having an affair."

3

Vivian and Lucy shared the back of their rental SUV. The colors of the fall leaves whizzed by as Kate drove and Vivian almost spit out her beer at Kate's announcement. "What the hell? I thought y'all were madly in love. Shaun's having an affair? With who?"

Kate giggled. "Little Debbie, Sara Lee, and probably Marie Callender this week since I'm gone."

"Oh geez, you scared the crap out of me!" Vivian said.

"I was ready to go to Austin and kick his ass!" Wendy said. "But I can certainly understand the love affair with Little Debbie. Ummmm, Swiss Rolls."

"Those are the best." Kate looked at Wendy, then in the rearview mirror. "I think the pregnancy hormones are affecting him. He's always been a health fanatic, but right now, he's out of control." She turned off the windshield wipers.

"He'll get over it," Vivian said. "Rick went through the same thing with me. But he never was healthy to start with. At least Shaun has a base."

Wendy directed Kate off the interstate and onto Highway 73. "Yeah, Shaun introduced me to Bruce's sweet potato pancakes. Those are the bomb dot com with blueberries and pecans and smothered with agave nectar."

"I realize you're only on your first drink, but can you talk about Jake yet?" Kate asked.

The sun peeked through a break in the clouds as Wendy stuck her drink in the cup holder and pulled a tissue from her purse. "As y'all know, when we were at the New Orleans airport, I got the call that Jake had been in an accident. I changed my flight and went to Vegas instead of home to Houston. That morning the police found Jake's rent car burned up in the desert. There was a body inside, burned beyond recognition." Wendy wiped a tear and took a breath before continuing.

"The hotel's security camera showed Jake leaving his room around 4:45 a.m., then getting the car out of valet. He headed east out of the casino, and the police were able to get footage from a gas station about a mile away. He filled the tank, paying at the pump, and left." Tears ran down her face, and she didn't bother to wipe them away.

"What was he doing driving out into the desert at that hour in the morning?" Kate asked.

"No one seems to know why he'd be out there at all. The police talked to his friends and they have no idea about any of it."

Lucy took Wendy's cup and mixed her a second vodka and cranberry. "Were the police able to identify who was in the car?"

Wendy took the drink and gulped, then said, "Telling everyone the wedding was off was hard enough, but telling the Las Vegas PD who Jake's dentist was so they could get his dental records was one of the hardest things I've ever had to do in my life." She took a ragged breath. "Then, finding out there wasn't enough left of the teeth for the forensic dentist to identify the body, that was torture."

Vivian patted Wendy's shoulder. "It might not have been him, Wendy. Stay positive."

Wendy shrugged. "But who else would it have been? And why were they in Jake's car?"

"I'm so sorry you had to go through this," Kate said, slowing down as they approached town.

Wendy sniffled. "Right as I walked out the door for the airport on the way to New Orleans, Jake gave me a kiss and told me he needed to talk to me about something when we got back from our bachelor and bachelorette weekend. He was pretty serious and I thought maybe he wanted to talk about finances, but I've been wondering about this ever since he disappeared. What did he want to tell me? What?"

They were quiet while Wendy stared out the windshield, still crying. Kate drove past the Olympic complex and Wendy gave Kate directions to the bed and breakfast.

Kate stopped at a red light beside a police car. "Uh, girls, drinks down. I don't want to be the pregnant lady in jail."

This made Wendy laugh, and she looked toward the lake. "Look, a rainbow. You can see both ends."

"It's the most vivid rainbow I've ever seen," Vivian said. Every color was clearly defined against the next and almost seemed to glow and the yellow, orange and red of the trees made the scene all the more beautiful.

"The air is cleaner here," Lucy said, putting away her Solo cup. "And look, there are two rainbows."

Vivian rolled down her window and snapped a couple of pictures. "The kids will love this. And it's got to be a good sign for this trip, don't you think?"

Wendy, too, snapped a picture. "I'll take just about anything as a good sign right now. I need Jake to come home."

14

Kate squeezed Wendy's shoulder. "He will."

A stop sign and a few turns later, Kate pulled onto the dirt drive of Turlington Farms Bed and Breakfast. The humble, two story nineteenth-century farmhouse stood proudly in a grassy field, its cedar shakes long coated in a pleasant butter yellow hue. The house was trimmed in white and capped with a steep pitched roof and brick chimney. High in the gabled end of the attic, a narrow, arched window punctuated the siding. Lean-to porches flanked both sides of the house, and double-hung windows marched around the facade in a simple pattern.

A man in jeans and a red and black plaid shirt stepped out of the house and walked toward the car. He looked in his late 30s, in good shape, with unruly brown hair and a goatee. Once the car was stopped, he flashed a smile and opened Kate's door. "Welcome, I'm Brandon Holt, proprietor, wood chopper, sometimes cook, always handyman."

Kate got out of the SUV. "The cook part of that sounds really good right now."

Brandon helped Vivian out of the back seat, which was no easy feat with all the groceries in the floorboard. A Dos Equis bottle fell to the ground and rolled between his work boots. He laughed and picked it up. "I see you girls have had some refreshments, but come inside and we'll get you some more. You're here just in time for our afternoon wine and cheese."

"I'll drink to that," Lucy said and popped open the back hatch.

Brandon helped the girls get unloaded as they made introductions. "My wife, Tracy, is inside and will get you fixed up while I take your luggage to your rooms."

The girls walked up the steps to the porch and the painted deck creaked under their feet. White rocking chairs and a small wooden bench promised a restful and much needed getaway spot. Vivian pulled open the screen door and they stepped inside. The living and dining were on either side of the foyer and stairs led up immediately from the door.

A woman with bottle blonde hair and a gymnast's physique popped the cork on a bottle of red wine. "Hi, I'm Tracy Holt. Come on in, warm yourself by the fireplace. I'll be right over with goodies for you."

"Just water for me, please," Kate said, looking around the house. "Where's the restroom?"

The woman pointed under the stairs. "It's right down there."

A couple sat on the loveseat flanking the fireplace, and the man introduced themselves as Mitzie and Wendell Fincher, newlyweds. They wore matching pink polos with tan Dockers, except she wore the capri version. Mitzie's perfectly placed hair was cut into a bob with the ends curled up. Her sunglasses rested atop her baby blue visor. Wendell's sunglasses were tucked into the front of his shirt. They were from Wayne, Pa., and planned to stay five more nights before venturing to Vermont.

Vivian walked around the room, stretching her legs after the car ride. She stopped in front of the wooden sofa table covered in pictures and picked up a framed image of a younger Brandon with a tall, slender brunette holding hands on the front porch.

Brandon walked by on his way out the door.

Vivian showed him the picture and asked, "Who's this?"

He smiled ruefully, "My first wife, Mary Beth. This was her family's estate. It was her dream to open the bed and breakfast."

"Oh, what happened to her?"

He took the picture from Vivian and cleaned off an invisible piece of dust before setting it down. "She died."

4

Brandon walked out the front door and Vivian looked for Tracy but didn't see her. She turned to the girls, who were seated around the fireplace with the newlyweds. "Oh my gosh, did you hear that? Brandon's first wife died. How sad."

Kate, who had just returned from the restroom, looked at the picture and said, "Poor thing. She was so pretty."

Tracy walked out of the kitchen with three glasses of wine and Kate's water. "So happy to have you with us for the week. Let me know if I can help you arrange any activities."

Vivian took her wine glass and looked at the picture of Brandon and Mary Beth again. "So sad to hear about Brandon's first wife."

"I've tried to get him to put that picture away," Tracy sighed and put the picture back into place, "but he insists."

"How long ago did she die?" Lucy asked, swirling her wine.

"Guess it's been over six years ago now. She drowned out in the lake."

"That's horrible," Wendy said. "I've always had a fear of that."

"Yeah, and she loved to swim. It was a bad accident." Tracy turned away and went into the kitchen.

The girls chatted with the Finchers about what they'd been doing in Lake Placid since their arrival. The newlyweds recommended touring the Olympic complex and raved about the Michelin-rated restaurant in town. "Their escargot is phenomenal," Wendell said.

"And there's the cutest little boutique next door," Mitzie said between sips of her wine. "I bought the most amazing silk scarf there."

Vivian didn't take the Finchers for outdoorsy types and didn't ask about hiking trails. She asked them about spas instead.

The Finchers told the girls all about the Placid Place Spa until Brandon came in carrying the cooler. He set it down and asked the girls, "Do you want to keep this in your room, or would you like us to keep this stuff in the refrigerator?" He pulled out the bottle of vodka and wiggled his eyebrows.

"In the fridge is fine, or the freezer for the vodka," Lucy said.

"Will do. Now let me show you to your rooms."

The girls followed Brandon to their adjoining rooms.

"This is pretty," Wendy said, tossing her purse into a high-backed chair in her and Kate's room. "Is there anything going on tonight?" she asked Brandon.

"We've got great star gazing off the dock out back with an Orion StarSeeker II you can use. There are a couple of bars in town, but otherwise, it's pretty quiet around here. Let me know if you need anything at all," he said and walked out of the room.

"We can't sit here for hours," Kate said.

"Let's toodle around the lake," Vivian said.

Wendy looked out the window. "There are some kayaks down by the water."

Lucy walked up beside her. "Those are canoes. Kayaks are flat."

Wendy shrugged. "Whatever. Details."

"That sounds fun," Vivian said. "I could use an upper body workout." She jiggled the skin where her triceps should be.

"Indeed." Lucy laughed and flexed her bicep. Living in Colorado for the last several years, Lucy had become an athlete and outdoor enthusiast. From aerobics to Zumba, hiking fourteeners to rafting class fives, she embraced it all, and her muscular physique proved it.

Wendy turned to Kate. "You okay going out there being preggo and all?"

"Definitely. I swim at my gym all the time. And these arms could use some working out, too. I need to build up my mom arms."

"You look fantastic," Vivian said. "What've you gained, two pounds?"

Kate looked in the mirror and lifted her boobs. "I've gained seven, and I think it's mostly here." Other than her pooch and her bigger than usual breasts, Kate was as slender as ever. Her long, straight, light-brown hair was extra shiny, and her cheeks were extra rosy. Her almond-shaped brown eyes reflected her Taiwanese heritage and sparkled with happiness.

"So not fair," Vivian said. "I gained 53 with the twins! I looked like a submarine."

Wendy pulled a sweater over her head. "You were ginormous, it's true, but you did a good job losing it. Your submarine sank."

Lucy then slipped on her Northface jacket and stuck a brown newsboy hat on her head. "Let's grab some paddles and get up a creek!"

The girls traipsed downstairs, found Tracy in the kitchen and inquired about the canoes Wendy had seen from the window.

Tracy wiped her hands on a kitchen towel. "They're for you to use any time, but let me get you the life jackets."

"We're all strong swimmers," Lucy said. "And I don't think any of us plan on going for a dip, it's too chilly."

"I'd prefer you wore them, or at least had them in the boat. I don't want to lose anyone else I know to a drowning."

Vivian felt a little bad. "Okay, we'll take them with us."

One canoe was ready to go on the shore, two life jackets already inside. Tracy walked to the wooden rack that held three additional canoes. She picked up the end of one and set it down, grabbed the other end and got it off the rack, then flipped the canoe over and pushed it alongside the other. She went into the boathouse and grabbed two paddles off the wall.

Wendy admired the Chris-Craft powerboat resting on a lift, hovering five feet above the water. "Too bad it's too cold to ski, that'd be fun."

"I don't know why Brandon bought that thing. He prefers to go out in a canoe." Tracy looked at the boat in distain before getting two life jackets out of a built-in storage cabinet.

Ready to roll, the girls got the canoes close to the water before Kate and Vivian each jumped in and Wendy and Lucy shoved them off, then hopped in themselves.

Wendy started paddling and looked out over the lake. "Which way?"

The lake was surrounded by short, stubby mountains, the opposite of the Rockies and their sharp, dramatic peaks. The fall foliage and tall pine trees reflected a multitude of yellow, orange and red along the edge. The wind blew gentle ripples across the water, but with the occasional gust, the ripples turned into small waves.

Vivian put down her paddle and zipped up her neoprene jacket.

"Hey, no slacking up there," Lucy joked and smacked her paddle in the water, which splashed Vivian.

"You better watch it!" Vivian said, picking up her paddle and splashing her back. "I'll rock this boat and send you overboard."

"Yeah, yeah, good luck with that," Lucy said and looked around. "Let's go against the wind to start and head that way." She pointed to their right. "That way, if we get tired, we'll at least have the wind at our backs to return."

They paddled around the lake, taking silly pictures and admiring the beautiful colors.

"This is so peaceful and the leaves are gorgeous,," Kate said, laying her paddle across her knees. "So opposite of Texas where everything goes from green to brown quickly. Hardly any brilliant shades of red, orange or yellow for us."

"Last Thanksgiving when Jake and I went to North Carolina I was super impressed with their fall foliage," Wendy said. Their canoe drifted along next to the other. "Guess I won't have a reason to go there any time soon."

"Don't give up," Kate said.

Lucy asked, "Could Jake have gotten carjacked?"

"Maybe, but then where is he?" Wendy said. "They had no John Doe's that fit his description in any of their ERs or hospitals. He's not in jail. He just disappeared." Tears welled in her eyes. "He's not the kind of guy to just up and walk out of his life, leave his family and me. We were about to get married. I know him and something's not right."

Vivian leaned over and grabbed their canoe, pulling it even with Lucy. "Of course he isn't that kind of guy, Wendy. Somehow, he'll turn up." *God, I hope I'm not lying!* Vivian thought.

Wendy covered her face with her hands, crying. "I met his parents for a week in Vegas after it all happened, but there was nothing we could do. They stayed for a month, and nothing new turned up. It was so sad when they left. They felt so helpless, and so did I."

Lucy pulled her hat down, fighting with the wind. "This is going to sound crazy, but I've been to Roswell. Could he have been abducted by aliens?"

"Lucy!" Kate gave her a stern look.

"I know, but come on! How far is Vegas from Area 51? I mean, he just disappeared. That doesn't just happen. What other explanations can there be? Haven't y'all ever seen the *X-Files*?"

"I doubt it was aliens," Vivian said.

"Why would someone else be in his rental car?" Kate asked. "Maybe he picked up a hitchhiker?"

"I have tried to come up with a zillion different scenarios and have shared them all with the police," Wendy said. "No one seems to know anything."

The sun dipped low, getting closer to the mountain peaks, and the air was getting chilly.

"We better head back to the house," Vivian said. "It'll be dark out here soon. Don't want to run into the boogeyman."

Just then, a gust of wind blew across them, blowing Lucy's cap off her head. Instinctively she reached for it and flung herself right out of the canoe.

Vivian clung to the sides, desperately trying to keep the entire thing from flipping. She looked at her empty canoe and screamed, "WOMAN OVERBOARD!"

5

Lucy broke the surface of the lake, sputtering and shrieking. "Holy shit, it's cold! Vivian, hurry, get me out of here!"

Vivian leaned forward, reaching for Lucy's hands. "Don't pull me in with you!"

"Wait, I can touch," Lucy said, and she stood up. The water was above her waist and she was able to fling herself inside the canoe.

Kate was busy snapping pictures while Wendy took off her jacket, then tossed it to Lucy. Vivian followed suit.

"Have a nice dip?" Wendy asked.

"I'm freezing," Lucy said, grabbing both jackets and wrapping them around herself.

"You should get naked," Vivian said between laughs. "That's what Bear Grylls does."

"Who?" Kate asked.

"He's a survivor guy on TV. Any time he falls in cold water he gets naked. It's the only reason I watch the show!"

Lucy squeezed the water out of her hat. "Let's get moving before I become a cryogenics experiment."

They hustled across the lake, happy the wind was pushing them along. Lucy paddled like a mad woman, working to get warm.

As they passed the boathouse, Wendy indicated to the Chris-Craft perched above the water. "I wonder who Becky Lou is?"

The canoe hit land and Lucy jumped out. "Who cares!" She ran toward the house, leaving the other three behind.

Vivian carefully maneuvered herself to the front of the canoe and stepped out, then dragged it up the shore a bit so it wouldn't float off. "Becky Lou what?"

"That's the name of their ski boat," Wendy said, helping Kate onto land.

"I hadn't noticed," Vivian said. "Do you think we need to re-rack these things?"

"Nah, let's just drag 'em over."

They did, then the three walked to the house.

21

Tracy met them at the front door with a hot toddy. "After seeing your friend slosh upstairs, I thought you might need this." She passed the drinks out, then smiled at Kate. "Yours is virgin."

"Thanks," Vivian said. "Smells good."

They went inside and hunkered by the fire, showing off the pictures of Lucy flailing in the water to the newlyweds. They all laughed.

Mitzie snuggled close to her groom. "Would you have gone in after me?"

"Of course, my schmoopsy-poo." Wendell kissed her forehead then whispered in her ear.

Mitzie turned bright red and Vivian thought she heard the word "handcuffs."

Vivian giggled to herself. *Wendell might be wilder than he looks.*

Tracy walked in with a tray of deli meats, bread and cheeses and set it on the coffee table. "I thought you might be hungry so I wanted to offer a little something. Sorry it's not more elaborate."

Kate started creating a sandwich masterpiece of roast beef, corned beef and Swiss cheese. "Thank you so much, I'm starving."

Wendy and Vivian let Kate have first dibs, then Vivian piled hers high with ham, turkey and pepper jack cheese. Wendy munched on a couple of slices of cheddar.

Wendell asked, "Do you have plans for later? Mitzie and I went to the corn maze last night. They practically had to send out a search party to find us, but we weren't lost. We were doing the thing that lovers do."

The pink in Mitzie's cheeks spread to her chest, but she slapped at Wendell's knee playfully. "Oh, Boo-Boo Bear, don't tell everyone."

He winked at her. "Let's go get lost again."

She giggled and leaned in for a kiss on the cheek.

"I'm getting lost right now," Vivian said and stood up with her sandwich. "You two lovebirds have fun."

"I think y'all are adorable," Kate said between bites.

Vivian ran into a freshly showered Lucy in the hall. Her hair was pulled into a tight ponytail, and she had on several layers.

"I can't seem to get warm," Lucy said.

"There's a lot of body heat in the living area, compliments of the newlyweds. Good news is Tracy put a tray of sandwich stuff out. I'm losing myself at the breakfast table; feel free to join me."

"Okay, loser, see ya in a sec."

Vivian sat at the table and got a fresh napkin from the porcelain holder on the table.

Brandon emerged from the kitchen. He smelled like diesel fuel and wiped his hands on a blue shop rag. "Everything okay?"

Vivian gave him a thumbs up. "Yep, thanks. I'm a bit of a klutz and didn't want to make a mess in there. I require a table." She drummed her fingernails on the oak.

He tucked the rag into his back pocket. His checkered, flannel shirt was open and untucked, and his undershirt was streaked with grease and sweat. He had a childish look about him, unkempt, and his dark hair had fallen into his eyes. Below his eyes were dark circles, as if he didn't sleep well or carried the weight of the world on his shoulders.

Vivian wiped her mouth and asked, "What's this I hear about a corn maze?"

Brandon grinned. "Ah, yes, the Amazing Maize Maze. It's only around for a few more days. Then they'll harvest."

"Is it far?"

"Nah, not at all. I'm happy to drive you girls over if you want to go. I'd like to go visit with the owners, Bill and Jan, anyway."

"We don't have anything else planned, might as well. Thanks!" Vivian took the last bite of her sandwich and crumpled her napkin into a ball.

Lucy walked in carrying a four-inch mountain of meat and cheese. No bread. She sat across from Vivian. "I saw the body heat you were talking about," she said. "I think I'll pass."

Vivian smiled at her. "Nice mound of meat you have there."

"Gotta stay away from the carbs. Buns go straight to my buns." She wrapped a piece of cheese with a slice of ham and turkey and started munching.

Brandon laughed at their exchange, then looked at Vivian. "Around 9:30 sound good?"

"Perfecto," Vivian responded.

"What's the plan?" Lucy asked.

"Get ready to be amazed at the Amazing Maize Maze."

"Oh no, you mean like in *Signs*? That movie freaked me out. I'm not good with aliens, and I've already had my Area 51 paranoia dismissed today. And it was legit."

Brandon chuckled. "The most alien thing you're going to encounter tonight is Mrs. Zimmerman's square funnel cakes. Who the heck makes square funnel cakes?" He laughed, turned and went upstairs.

"I'll brave aliens for funnel cake," Lucy said and stuck a whole piece of ham in her mouth.

"Then it's settled." Vivian scooted her chair out. "We'll eat funnel cake while going alien hunting in crazy, creepy cornstalks."

6

The girls bundled up and walked downstairs to meet Brandon for their adventure at the Amazing Maize Maze. They had relaxed after canoeing that afternoon and were ready for some post-sunset excitement.

Brandon met them in the living room. "You ready to go? I have Fred pulled around."

"Fred?" Kate asked.

"My Expedition."

Tracy, wine glass in hand, opened the front door for them. "Scooter Bill likes to name his vehicles."

Vivian laughed and said to Brandon on her way out, "Scooter Bill?"

He rolled his eyes. "It's a long story, and don't you dare call me that."

Lucy hopped in the passenger seat while Kate, Vivian and Wendy shared the back bench.

"Don't you need to sit up front?" Wendy asked Kate.

"It's a short drive."

They started down the road and Brandon asked, "So what do you think of Turlington Farms? We've put a lot of work into it, but I'm always looking for ways to improve."

"I love how you've restored everything, it's so bright and airy," Kate said. "I know that's tough to accomplish with nineteenth-century farmhouses."

Lucy chimed in. "And good job on the updated furnishings!"

"You're last name is Holt, right? So who are the Turlingtons?" Wendy asked.

Brandon glanced at her in the rearview mirror. "This property was in my first wife's family for generations. They're great people. I'm still close with her parents, but it was too much land for them to keep up. The house is older, which can be a problem. They moved into a townhouse in Albany several years back and left us the farm."

"Did the farm actually ever farm anything?" Kate asked.

"Mary Beth's grandparents, and then her parents, grew all kinds of

24

vegetables and raised dairy cows. Keeping up with everything is tough work, and once Mary Beth and I did a financial analysis, we figured it'd be better to sell the cows, keep a smaller garden and open a bed and breakfast. She died just as we were getting ready to open." Brandon paused. "I've kept it going because it was our dream."

"Wow, that's a big commitment," Vivian said.

They drove along about three miles, talking about the town.

Brandon turned off the county road onto a dirt lane. Leaning against a tree was a hand-painted plywood sign with a big arrow pointing to the right. It was lit by a single spotlight and read "Amazing Maize Maze."

The SUV bumped along the dark dirt road until it opened to a field. Brandon parked between two other cars in a makeshift lot near the house and turned off the truck. "See you all at the end of the amazing maze." He got out of Fred and closed the door with a bang.

"That house looks JUST like the one in *Signs*," Lucy said and hit her lock. "I'm not getting out."

"I saw that movie," Vivian said. "This house looks nothing like the one in the movie."

"Yes, it does. It looks like it has the creepy window/door face." Lucy turned around to look at them. "Don't you remember when the kids are reading the book about aliens? They had on the pointy aluminum foil hats?"

Kate opened her door. "I remember that the humans won in the end." With that, she hopped out.

"Guess we're going," Vivian said and opened her door. "We can't let a pregnant lady wander the maze alone."

Wendy followed Vivian, and Lucy eventually pulled herself away from the safety of the car and joined them.

"I'd like to go on record as saying this is a bad idea," Lucy said, scanning the night sky as if looking for UFOs.

The moon shone above them, but clouds passed occasionally, making it darker and more difficult to see.

Vivian pulled her sweater tight as they walked along the edge of the cornstalks to the front porch of the house where a few people were sitting, standing and rocking, Brandon among them.

An older man in overalls sat on the steps wearing a booty bag. Vivian smirked at the sight, having not seen a booty bag in a while, and never on someone wearing overalls. He could have walked out of the "American Gothic" painting.

He grinned at them as they walked in his direction, showing a nice set of dentures that flapped a little when he spoke. "Greetings. Welcome to our home and the Lake Placid Amazing Maize Maze."

Wendy stuck out her hand and made introductions. "We're glad to be here. This is our first maze!"

Brandon spoke up. "They're staying with us, Bill, so give them a discount."

Bill thought about that for a moment. "How about buy three, get one free, just like they do in the five 'n' dime when you buy tube socks?"

"Sounds good to me." Wendy said and dug into her jacket pocket. "How much for three?"

"Fifteen smackers," he smacked.

She handed him a twenty and he counted out five ones.

"You start over by the three jack-o'-lanterns," he said, pointing to his left. "There are flashlights on that table. One per pair, please, got to have enough for the crowds."

Vivian didn't see any new cars pulling in. *Maybe eight cars is a crowd?*

They walked over to the table and tested the flashlights.

"Let's have a contest and see who can get to the end first," Vivian squealed, getting excited at the prospect of going into her first maize maze.

"I think we should stick together," Lucy said, banging a flashlight on the heel of her hand, which produced a solid beam of light.

"Nah, buddy system, but twosome buddies." Wendy agreed with Vivian. "Who's with whom?"

"I'll take scaredy-cat here," Vivian said. "You take preggo. Y'all go first. We'll give you a two-minute head start."

Wendy and Kate hooked arms. Kate held a large, rectangular, yellow flashlight.

"On your mark, get set, go!" Vivian yelled. She and Lucy watched as Wendy and Kate scurried off into the corn, giggling like schoolgirls. Vivian could hear them debating which way to go.

"I still think this is way too cliché," Lucy said, picking up a different flashlight and clicking it on and off. Satisfied with one, she shined the light under her chin and changed her voice to sound something like Vincent Price. "But since you've chosen the dark side, I'll be your corn companion. Wahahahaha. Waahaaahaaahaa haa."

Thriller flashed through Vivian's thoughts, along with images of zombies crawling their way out of graves. She laughed. "Corny companion is more like it."

7

Lucy lit the way through the rows of corn with the flashlight as she and Vivian tromped through the maze. The stalks rose above both of their heads and Vivian wished she was holding their single source of illumination rather than Lucy.

"This giant corn makes me feel shorter than I usually do," Lucy said, shining the light left and right, then up and down the stalks. At 5-foot-3 she was the shortest of the four friends.

"I know. Me, too," Vivian said. She stood 5-5 and couldn't see over the corn, either. "Can I be in charge of the flashlight?"

"Negative, no way, un-uh. I've got this bad boy," Lucy replied.

They walked along, making twists and turns, not worrying which way they were going. Occasionally Vivian would see the dim glow of another flashlight through the swaying stalks, but it always disappeared quickly.

Chatter and whispers swept across the corn. Vivian couldn't tell from which direction the sounds were coming. The wind increased, and she pulled up the neck of her sweater.

"My nose is cold," Lucy said. "Let's find our way outta here before we freeze or get beamed up on a spaceship."

"I agree, but not because I'm worried about beaming," Vivian said. She looked up to the sky anyway.

They followed the maze going toward what they thought was the direction of the house, but after a few minutes they turned around.

"How long before they send out a search party, I wonder," Lucy said. "They probably should have given us rescue flares, with our luck."

"What do you mean by that?" Vivian asked. " 'With our luck?' "

"Oh, come on! We can't take a trip that doesn't tank, at least temporarily."

"We have fun, though."

"We do, but someone's always ending up in the back of a police car or in handcuffs. Even you, Viv."

"And not the kinky, fun kind!" Vivian said, but Lucy wasn't joking.

"And now look at Jake. He's still missing from his last trip." Just then, the flashlight flickered and went out. Lucy smacked it with the palm of her hand, but nothing changed. "Oh my god!" She jumped up and down. "The aliens are coming! This is what happens, they take all energy from stuff!"

"Let me see it," Vivian said and took the flashlight from the bouncing Lucy. She whacked it on her leg but still no flicker or flash. "Guess we'll be mazing by moonlight."

"I need to pee," Lucy squealed, still imitating a kangaroo.

"No one will see you now, go for it. Trail pee." Vivian laughed.

Lucy reached for her pants but paused. "I can't do it out here."

"Come on." Vivian pushed her forward but stayed close, holding onto the back of Lucy's jacket.

"Why don't you lead the way?" Lucy asked.

"Nope! You broke the flashlight, you go first."

They went along the maze for several minutes, Vivian occasionally jumping up and yelling, trying to see lights from the house. "Hello? Anyone? Our flashlight died! Helllooo?"

A big gust of wind rustled the stalks around them and they both stopped.

A crunch behind her about caused Vivian's heart to jump out of her chest. She turned around in time to see a dark figure rush toward her making a crazy sound.

"Aaaaaaaaahhhhhhhhhhhhhhhhhhhhhh!" Vivian yelled.

The figure grabbed her, pushing her into the corn stalks. Vivian tripped and fell back, the figure falling on top of her.

"E.T., phone home!" Wendy yelled, laughing. "Poke her! Prod her!"

Vivian kicked and shoved Wendy off of her. "Not funny! Not funny!"

Wendy rolled over, cracking up, holding her stomach. "So funny!"

A flashlight flicked on and Kate appeared from between the stalks. "Y'all are hilarious. We've been following you for about five minutes. We were prepared to take pictures of Lucy's trail pee!"

Wendy rolled around on the ground, snorting with laughter. "Aliens taking the energy out of your flashlight! That was classic."

Vivian picked straw out of her blonde curls. "You'll pay for that one, Wendy. Just you wait!"

Wendy rolled over and picked herself up off the ground. "Totally worth it, I just wish I had video so I could put it on ellentube. She'd totally run that on her show."

Lucy spoke up. "Holy crap, I would never forgive you if Ellen DeGeneres ran a clip of that on her talk show. I almost wet my pants back there." She looked around and put her hand on her hips. "How do we get out of here?"

Kate turned around and started marching. "Follow me! I have an excellent sense of direction. Plus, I smell food."

They followed Kate's nose through the maze, laughing about aliens and crop circles, poking and prodding the whole way. They emerged at the edge of the field, near the makeshift parking lot.

"Told ya I'd find the way," Kate said as she clicked off her flashlight. "My nose knows no bounds these days."

They walked up to the house where Lucy headed in to find a bathroom. A group had gathered on the front porch, the front porch steps and in lawn chairs. A lady was selling food off to the side, and Kate walked straight to her.

"Hi, there! Whatcha got?"

"Corn on the cob hot off the grill, smoked turkey legs and pogos."

"What's a pogo?"

The lady held up a corn dog.

"I'll take a turkey leg, please," Kate said.

The woman handed her a bigger-than-her-face shank.

Kate greedily took it and sank her teeth in.

Lucy walked up, licking her lips. "I'll try a pogo-slash-corny dog. Got mustard?"

The woman reached into a vat of heat and pulled out a foil-wrapped foot-long tube, then handed over two mustard packets and looked at Vivian.

"Corn on the cob for me," Vivian said.

The lady handed her a foil-wrapped, fatter, shorter tube.

Vivian looked at Wendy as she unwrapped her cob and took a big-ass bite. "I can't spend that much time lost in corn and not make it pay!"

Wendy pulled out some money and paid, then the girls rocked on the porch while they ate. Kate was super-impressed with her turkey leg and only pulled off a few pieces to share.

"I'm feeding two here," she reminded, patting her belly. "Save the best bites for Little Plum."

"Is it a girl?" Vivian asked. "Is that why you call the baby 'Little Plum'?"

Kate licked her fingers. "The baby is the size of a plum. That's why I call her/him that. We had the opportunity to find out, but we want it to be a surprise."

"It's a girl, I just know it!" Vivian said as she watched people wander into and out of the maze. She noticed Brandon was sitting alone off to the side.

A middle-aged man in jeans and a green flannel shirt walked up to them. "So did you girls enjoy our upstate New York's finest maize maze?"

"Our flashlight died," Lucy said, finishing off her pogo.

"Yeah, that happens sometimes. Can sure mess you up." He sat down next to Wendy on the porch step. "So you have plans tonight?"

Joan Rylen

"Bed is my plan," she said.

"My kinda plan," he said, and he put his arm around her.

She gently picked up his hand, lifted it over her head and placed it on his knee. "I'm sleeping with preggo over there, buddy. You're outta luck."

He laughed. "Story of my life. Where are you staying?"

"Turlington Farms," Vivian said.

He gave a stern look. "Really? I didn't know that place was still open."

"It's nice," Wendy said. "Why wouldn't it be open?"

"You know," he said but didn't elaborate since Brandon walked up.

"Hey, Gus, how are you?"

"Doing fine," the man said, standing. "You enjoy your trip."

"Thanks," they all chimed.

"You ready to head back?" Brandon asked.

Kate finished off her turkey leg and tossed it in the trash from a distance of at least eight feet. "Our work here is done."

They made it back to Turlington Farms, said their goodnights to Brandon and got ready for bed.

Vivian had to floss her teeth twice to extract all the pesky corn kernels. She climbed into bed with Lucy, who was already breathing rhythmically, and drifted off.

Vivian startled awake, got her bearings and looked at the clock — 4 a.m. Covered in sweat, she threw the covers off and flipped her pillow to the cool side. As she lay there, she felt like someone was watching her. She didn't want to do it, but she couldn't help herself and clicked on the lamp next to her.

"You're awake, too?" Kate asked.

"Jesus, you scared me!" Vivian said, then she looked at Lucy, who rolled over but didn't wake up.

Kate stopped pacing and sat in the high-backed chair next to Vivian's side of the bed. "Sorry. I've been awake for a bit. I had a weird dream."

Vivian's stomach clenched. Kate's weird dreams often involved dead people. "When you say weird, do you mean…"

"No dead relatives visited me."

Vivian sighed in relief. "Oh thank god, I was worried you might have had one of 'those' dreams."

"A dead stranger visited me, instead."

Vivian stopped breathing.

"I know, I know," Kate said. "I'm a super-freak. But I have to say, this person was really interesting. She wanted me to find her killer."

"And you know this how?"

Kate took a deep breath and rubbed her baby bump. "She let me live her death."

30

8

Day 2

Vivian grabbed her pillow and held it tight to her ear. Chirp! Chirp! Chirp! Zzzzz….Zzzzz…Zzzzz…. She opened one tired eye and quickly squeezed it shut. The faint light of morning was way too bright. Chirp! Zzzzz.

Dammit! She threw her pillow on the floor and flung the comforter off, then padded to the dresser. She yanked open a drawer, pulled out jeans and a sweater, and headed to the bathroom.

"What the heck?" Lucy yelled to the slamming door.

"Sorry, sorry," Vivian said. "Stupid birds." After her morning routine, she followed the scent of frying sausage to the kitchen, where she found Brandon and Tracy working on breakfast.

"Morning," Brandon said. "You're up awful early, care for some coffee?"

"No, thanks," Vivian said. "I love the smell but can't drink it, even with tons of sugar and cream."

Tracy turned from the stove, apron on and tea kettle in hand. "How about some hot tea?"

"That sounds perfect. I'll take it to the back porch with me." Vivian prepared her tea and started out of the kitchen, then stopped. "Are the birds always this noisy in the mornings?"

The proprietors just laughed and continued making breakfast.

Vivian let the screen door slam shut, hoping to scare off her arch-enemy, her foe, the fowl. *I'm going to invest in a BB gun if this keeps up.* She sat in a rocker, sipped and enjoyed watching the sun come up over the water until the remnants of her hot tea were cold.

Lucy opened the screen door, closed it gently and sat in the rocker beside her. "We've got to document this, it's epic. Vivian Taylor, up before the rest of us! I'm impressed."

Vivian laughed. "Don't be. I didn't sleep well. I had a creepy feeling I was being watched, then Kate got up and told me about the crazy dream she had, and I was finally dozing off when the birds started chirping and you started snoring."

Lucy shook her finger at Vivian. "Oh no, I don't snore. You're the log saw– wait, did you say Kate had a dream? What about?"

"I'll let Kate tell you. It was pretty creepy."

Lucy bobbed her tea bag in the hot water. "Nothing's going to happen on this trip. No murders, stalkers, abductions, *nada*. We don't need Kate to have any dead relative dreams."

Kate's height came from her American father, but her superstitions were from her Taiwanese mother. Kate's dreams often starred deceased relatives from both sides of her family tree, and they often brought cryptic messages.

Wendy poked her head outside. "Morning, early birds, y'all hungry? I couldn't get Kate past the table. She's in there chowing down on bacon and sausage. I may need to encourage her to eat some fruit."

Vivian waved her off. "That's what prenatal vitamins are for."

Lucy laughed and got up. "If it involves bacon, I'm in. Besides, I've gotta hear about this dream."

"Kate had a dream?" Wendy asked, trailing behind Vivian.

"I did and it was awful," Kate said and washed down a mouthful of something with milk. "I woke up clawing at the air and gasping for breath. My legs still hurt from the cramps."

Lucy set a plate of bacon in front of Kate. "What relative visited you?"

Kate swallowed a big bite of wheat toast slathered in two kinds of jam. "It wasn't that kind of dream, it was worse." She reached for a piece of bacon, so Wendy took the bowl of freshly cut fruit off the sideboard and set it on the table with an "uhn uhhh."

Vivian took the bowl and scooped some pineapple onto her plate. "She's got jelly, she's fine."

"It was a warm summer day, perfect for a swim, then all of a sudden, my left leg started cramping," Kate began as Tracy walked into the dining room with a fresh plate of pancakes. "I reached down to massage it while I treaded water, but then my right leg started cramping, too, and it became impossible to swim. I tried and tried, but my legs wouldn't work."

Though Kate had told Vivian about the dream earlier in the morning, she still cringed inside.

"What'd you do?" Lucy asked. "Did the cramps wear off? Were you able to make it to shore?"

"No," Kate said. "But I tried really hard because of the baby. The really scary thing was in the dream, when I rubbed my belly, it was flat. I wasn't pregnant. Freaked me out."

Wendy reached for Kate's belly. "Gosh, is Little Plum okay this morning?"

Kate rubbed her belly and smiled. "Everything's fine. I felt her move shortly after the dream. I think she woke up when I did."

"I must have been completely zonked because I didn't hear a peep."

"In my dream, my whole body started cramping. It started in my legs and worked its way up. It was awful wanting so desperately to survive and trying so hard to swim but have my body fail. The last thing I remember was the sun shining through the water as I sank."

Crash!

Tracy dropped the empty porcelain platter she'd been holding. "Goodness, excuse me," she said and bent to pick up the mess. Her cheeks were flushed as she stacked the bigger pieces, and though her hands looked steady, she had a hard time scooping the shards.

Brandon rushed in. "It's not a party until something gets broken," he said, then looked to see what had happened. "Darn, hon, that was a wedding gift from Grandma Turlington. What'd you go and drop that for?"

Tracy looked at him, her eyes sharper than the remaining bits of Mikasa on the floor. "It was an accident. I've got butter on my fingers and the platter slipped."

Brandon bristled but held his tongue. He followed Tracy out of the room and returned moments later with a handheld vacuum. "Sorry for the noise. Enjoy the rest of your breakfast."

The girls did enjoy it, although bickering could be overheard from the kitchen and the Finchers, who arrived just after the platter faux pas, made goo-goo eyes at each other and spoke in baby talk.

I guess they got lost and found again last night, Vivian thought. *I can't take much more of this.*

Wendy took a bite of strawberry and a last sip of coffee, then glanced at Mitzie and Wendell before saying to the girls, "Y'all ready to go on our hike?"

"You're going on a hike?" Mitzie said. Her hairdo was reminiscent of a Shih-Tzu this morning, pink bow and all. "You should get a dog for the day to take with you."

Though Mitzie was annoying, Vivian was intrigued. "What's that?"

Mitzie explained that the local shelter would allow volunteers to take dogs out for exercise during the day. "They really want you to fall in love and adopt, but they'll take any help they can get."

Brandon walked in with a fresh pot of coffee and confirmed what she'd said. "My buddy Steve runs the program, and even though you're not likely to adopt a dog, he'll still let you take a dog, or four, for a day. It's good for them."

"I miss my dudes," Wendy said. "Let's do it. Shelter dogs need some fun."

Vivian missed her dog, Cooper. He had come to her rescue when an ex-boyfriend went extra-crazy. Plus, he was an all-around awesome pup. "Great idea. I'm ready to go as soon as I get my tennies on."

Tracy appeared in the doorway. "I'll pack a picnic lunch for you if you'd like. Same sandwich stuff from last night, if that's okay with you girls?"

"That would be great," Kate said. "Could you make me a BLT, with extra B and hold the L and T?"

Tracy laughed. "Sure."

"Where's a good hiking trail?" Lucy asked Tracy.

"This time of year it's hard to find a bad one." She left and returned quickly with a foldout map of the area. "This marks the most popular trails."

Vivian started to get up from the table but Mitzie stopped her. "Can you please step out on the back porch with me? I wanted to talk to you for a minute."

"Sure," Vivian responded and told the girls, "Y'all go ahead, I'll be up in a few minutes."

The girls left the table and Vivian followed Mitzie outside.

Mitzie stood with arms crossed at the edge of the porch, looking out at the lake. She turned to face Vivian. "Ummm, you seem nice and I really don't talk to my girlfriends about this kind of thing, so I hope you don't mind."

Vivian smiled, her curiosity piqued. "Okay."

Mitzie turned bright red, took a deep breath and started in, talking faster and faster the more she said. "I don't really have a lot of experience with… you know, and Wendell is wanting some things and I don't know what I'm doing and I could use some advice about s-e-x." She wrung her hands and then crossed her arms again.

Vivian covered her mouth and coughed to hide a laugh. "You're talking to a s-e-x-m-a-n-i-a-c, so let's sit down and have a chat."

Mitzie's shoulders relaxed as she and Vivian sat in rockers. After their talk, Vivian joined the girls upstairs in their room. Kate, Lucy and Wendy were pouring over a map spread out on the bed.

Kate looked up as Vivian opened the door. "What'd Mitzie want to talk to you about?"

Vivian didn't want to betray Mitzie's confidence, but it was too funny not to share a little bit. "Sex stuff. I gave her some pointers."

Lucy rolled her eyes. "Your favorite topic. We've about decided on a trail about five miles outside of town. You sure you're up for it Kate?"

"I'm good, let's go." Kate gave a thumbs up.

The girls geared up, grabbed their lunch from Tracy and got directions to the animal shelter from Brandon.

At the shelter, they met Steve and told him about staying at Turlington Farms and wanting to volunteer to take a dog for the day. "Would you like to take more than one dog?"

"I think one is all we can handle for the day," Wendy said.

Steve smiled at her and said, "I've got just the boy for you. He's been here a week and is about to go stir crazy. I'd take him out myself, but I've got a wife who's a lot farther along than you," he nodded to Kate, "and she wants me close by."

Steve led them to a mostly empty row of kennels. The few dogs they passed stood at attention, waiting for someone to take them home.

It broke Vivian's heart.

Steve stopped in front of a red golden retriever, opened the kennel and let the dog out without a leash. "This is Austin, well mannered, well trained. The family who turned him in was down on their luck. The dad lost his job and they had to make budget cuts. They just couldn't afford to feed him, keep up his shots, you know."

"Aw, that's sad," Lucy said.

Vivian let Austin sniff her hand, then she pet his head. He looked up at her with big brown eyes and smiled a doggy grin. Her heart melted. "You want to go on a hike with these crazy girls? You going to be a good boy?"

Austin panted, swished his tail and licked her hand. *Affirmative!*

9

C ome on, buddy." Steve gave the dog's chin a scratch, then walked toward the front of the shelter and got out a clipboard. Wendy filled out the pertinent info while the other three girls played with the dog.

Business out of the way, they loaded Austin into the SUV and Kate got into the driver's seat. "Which way?"

Lucy sat up front with Kate and consulted the map Tracy had given them. She gave Kate directions and they soon pulled into a parking lot alongside Highway 86. There was one other car in the lot but no one within sight. Vivian clipped a leash to Austin's collar and let him out of the car. He pranced around and turned in circles before homing in on the trail.

"This boy is ready to go," Wendy said, taking the leash from Vivian. "Y'all?"

Lucy looked at the posted trail map as she marched in place. Occasionally she bent over to touch her toes and stretched side to side. "I'm ready. I see our first blue dot."

Vivian looked up at the clear sky and let out a breath she'd been holding, then followed the girls and Austin down the path of fallen leaves.

They hiked along the clearly marked trail for about a mile before crossing a small stream. Vivian's ballet training came in handy and she easily leapt across it. The mud squished a little underfoot when she landed, but she quickly gained traction on firmer ground. Austin splashed through the mud, tongue and tail wagging.

Lucy hiked ahead for a ways, then did jumping-jacks as the girls caught up. She offered them the spout of her CamelBak. "Thirsty?"

Kate took a long drink of water, then sat on a fallen log. "I can't believe I'm about to say this, but I could use a snack."

Wendy put her hand on Kate's shoulder. "You can say that any time. You're building a person inside you, for goodness sake! That takes calories."

Lucy reached in her backpack for an energy bar and handed it to Kate. While she ate, the other three girls played fetch with Austin.

"Wow, this guy has been caged up for too long," Vivian said. "I think my arm will fall off before he's tired of playing."

Lucy wrestled the stick out of his mouth and threw it as far as she could. "I have to say that although the scenery is pretty, this trail isn't nearly as challenging as the ones in Colorado. I'm a little disappointed."

Austin came racing back with his prize, dropping it at Wendy's feet. She threw it for him, then said, "You're Ms. Fitness. I'm huffing a little!"

"I'm sweating." Vivian pointed to a trickle making its way down her face.

"These mountains are a lot different from the Rockies," Wendy noted. "Not nearly the elevation."

Kate stood and stretched, and the girls set off again, quickly catching up with the dog. A few minutes down the trail, the hairs on Austin's neck raised and he slowed down. As they rounded a curve, Vivian saw what had the dog upset. A porcupine ambled along the base of a tree, just off the trail. He didn't pay them any mind and Austin didn't bark, but it made Vivian's heart race anyway. After her last hike in Vail, she didn't much like surprises along the trail.

A short distance up the path from the porcupine, the ground started to incline and the leaves got thicker on the ground.

Lucy stopped and glanced around. "Have y'all seen a blue dot in a while?"

Vivian turned in a circle, looking for the trail marker. "No," she said after carefully looking on every tree around for the blue dot.

Kate also turned in a circle but looked at the ground. "It would seem the path goes this way," she said, pointing toward the northwest, "but with all of the leaves it's hard to tell."

Wendy looked at Lucy. "What does the map say?"

Lucy dug it out of her backpack but the image wasn't detailed enough to tell. She studied the terrain and trees a bit more. "It's this way. There's a half-dot on that maple tree."

Sure enough, once Lucy pointed it out, Vivian could see the partial blue dot. "That dot is so faded it almost looks gray and blends in with the tree. Maybe they should've gone with bright orange."

The girls continued as the path gained in elevation. Kate had to stop to catch her breath a few times. Vivian and Wendy both had to stop once.

"I'm not even pregnant," Wendy said. "This is ridiculous. That's it, no more chocolate. No wait, I can't give that up. No more queso at Chuy's."

"Don't be so hard on yourself," Lucy said as she did a few lunges. "The air is thinner up here. You have to get used to it."

They kept going, managing to find the blue dots, and soon reached a bigger, swifter-moving stream than the one earlier in the day.

Lucy walked back and forth on the bank and tested a few of the rocks before saying, "We'll have to pull up our pants legs, but this is the best place to cross." She looked at Kate. "You up for this, momma?"

Kate took a minute to study the stream, then said, "Yep, and I want to have lunch right over there." She pointed to a big rock across the way.

"You got it," Lucy said, then helped Kate across.

Vivian and Wendy splashed in and then joined Kate on her rock. Lucy set the CamelBak and the backpack on the ground and started pulling out an assortment of goodies. Trail mix, Kashi bars, Tracy's sandwiches. Austin rushed to her, wagging his tail. Lucy broke off a piece of her sandwich and fed it to him. He then ran to Vivian and she did the same.

He ran back to Lucy, wanting more. "I just gave you some," she laughed and threw a stick for him to fetch instead. "Maybe that'll distract him while we eat," Lucy said. "Such a beggar. Bad dog."

"Brandon sure made a big deal out of Tracy breaking that platter this morning," Kate said between bites of her turkey, ham and Swiss cheese sandwich. "He sounded like a bully from what I could overhear."

"I heard them arguing but couldn't make out the details over the crunch from my bacon," Vivian said and then took a sip of water.

Lucy juggled a handful of trail mix. "I couldn't hear what he was saying, either, but he sounded pissed off. He shouldn't have been too upset, though, that platter is replaceable and not terribly expensive. It's not antique."

"He said it was from Grandma Turlington," Wendy said. "That's the name of the farm. I bet that was a gift from his first wedding."

Kate swallowed a big bite. "That would explain it."

Vivian finished her sandwich and started playing fetch with Austin. She tossed the stick across the stream and Austin splashed through it with enthusiasm. He trotted back and shook off close enough to Vivian that she got a few drops. She threw the stick uphill as far as she could, then said to Kate, "So tell us more about your pregnancy. Any concerns?"

"None, everything really does look good." Kate handed Lucy her trash. "The first time I heard the heartbeat, I couldn't stop smiling. It made it real, this was happening! I've been in a nesting phase ever since."

"Wow! That's a long time to nest," Vivian said. "You still have four months to go."

"I want to be prepared, and there's so much to know. Are there any foods I should avoid while I'm pregnant and nursing, what kind of diapers are best, first foods, day care, schools, college savings?"

Vivian laughed. "Don't get too far ahead of yourself. All they do at first is eat, sleep and poop. You'll have time to figure it all out."

Wendy stood up from her perch on the rock and called Austin. Turning to the girls, she said, "Doesn't it seem like he's been gone a bit too long? I hope we didn't lose him."

Vivian looked in the direction she last threw the stick. "No kidding, we should go look for him."

Lucy zipped up her backpack. "I don't think we need to get off the trail. The blue dots are too hard to see to be wandering around loose out here."

Vivian called Austin, and a moment later, he came racing through the trees with a stick in his mouth, kicking up a flurry of leaves. He held his head high as he approached and offered his stick to Vivian but didn't drop it.

"We thought we lost you, silly boy!" Vivian scratched behind his ear. "What did you do to that stick?" It protruded from his mouth and wrapped around his nose.

Austin ran in a circle around Vivian, then circled Lucy before stopping in front of her, looking proud. Lucy reached for the stick, but he pranced over to Wendy and offered her his prize instead.

Wendy held her hand out and shook with Austin. "Oh, all right. I'll play with you as we hike." She tried to grab the stick out of his mouth but he held it tight. She tried again but he wouldn't let go. "I can't throw it unless you let go, goofy dog."

Austin loped back to Vivian. She finally relented and reached for the stick, and this time he was willing to give it up. She started to throw it, but a glint caught her eye and she stopped mid-toss.

"What the heck?" she said, looking at the object in her hand. Then it registered what she was holding. "Ew ew ew! Gross! He brought me a bone." Vivian tossed it on the ground, then jumped up and down, trying to shake the germs and the heebie-jeebies from her hands.

Wendy leaned over and looked at it. "He sure did. Nasty, it's got teeth."

"Is it from a bear?" Lucy asked from a safe distance.

Kate crouched down and poked at it with a real stick. "I don't think so." The sun glinted again off the jaw. She stood up slowly and took two steps back. "I don't know of too many wild animals that get silver fillings."

10

Vivian's jaw dropped as she and the girls looked down at the jaw. A chill passed through her. "I touched a dead person! Oh my god! I touched a dead person! I need hand sanitizer! STAT!"

Kate gathered herself, then used the stick to maneuver the bone as Austin pranced behind them, wanting to continue with his game of fetch. "It looks like it's a bottom jaw."

Lucy shivered and handed Vivian a small bottle of hand sanitizer from her backpack. "This is so wrong. I've had a weird feeling for a while, but I didn't say anything. I just figured it was because we couldn't find blue dots, but this… this is… ugh, I don't even know."

Vivian jumped up and down, rubbing her freshly alcoholed hands together. "It's disgusting! I just touched a piece of a dead person!"

"Calm down, Viv. It's not dripping in blood or anything." Wendy reached for Lucy's backpack. "We need to call the police. There's probably more of this body out here somewhere."

"Oh, please god, no," Vivian wailed and leaned against a tree, sliding down it. "I thought the double rainbow from yesterday was a good sign. This is definitely not good."

"It's going to be okay," Lucy said. "We don't have much of a story to tell. It won't ruin our vacation, just mess up our hike, which was already messed up because the trail isn't half marked. We would have probably gotten lost."

Vivian felt like Lucy was just trying to ease her nerves, but it wasn't working. Finding some person's bone, partially covered in dirt and now dog slobber, had Vivian on the edge.

Wendy's signal was weak, but she managed to call 911 and put it on speaker. It took her a few minutes to explain their location and situation, and she had to repeat "human jawbone" three times.

"Are you in a safe location?" the operator asked.

"As safe as can be out here," Wendy responded. "I don't think we're in any imminent danger."

"As long as the porcupine doesn't come back," Lucy spoke up.

The operator informed them that it could take an hour for the sheriff to reach them and to please not go anywhere. Wendy clicked off.

Vivian groaned. "Why us? It's always us! And now we're stuck here with it." She cringed and looked down at the u-shaped bone.

"I'm sure they need us to stay here so they know where to start looking for the rest of the body," Kate said.

"Rest of the — " Vivian's stomach flipped and she needed to put her head between her knees. "I'm gonna pass out."

Lucy sat next to her and handed her the CamelBak. "Have some water."

Wendy put her phone in the backpack and said, "We ought to go look for the rest of the skeleton. I don't like this stuff, but it could speed up the process later when the sheriff gets here. Get us back to civilization and our vacation faster."

Kate sat next to Vivian and leaned against the tree. "I'll be right here. Someone needs to stay with the jawbone. If y'all find something, don't touch it. Leave that to the experts."

"No way I'm going. Besides, buddy system," Vivian said, then looked at Lucy. "You're it."

Lucy threw her head back. "This is a bad idea. I'm only looking for blue dots. That's it. My eyes are not looking at the ground."

"Come on, chicken," Wendy said, then looked at Austin. "You, too, buddy."

He jumped up and ran in a circle.

She rubbed his head, loving the feeling of his soft fur. It reminded her of her flat-coated retriever, Radar.

Lucy caught up with Wendy as they walked uphill. "This is definitely a *really* bad idea. What if there are other scavengers, bears or something?" She looked around, eyes off the ground. "I'm pretty sure they have mountain lions up here. And bears. Big ones."

"Austin will fight them off for us," Wendy replied and watched Austin run ahead, nose to the ground. "He's on to something. Hurry!"

Austin weaved between the trees and definitely off trail. The girls lost him for a minute, then saw him in the distance at a shallow ravine. He paced up and down the bank but suddenly stopped and started digging at the base of a tree.

"Austin, stop!" Wendy shouted as she and Lucy raced to catch up with him.

No use. Austin had dirt flying everywhere and kicked it all over Wendy and Lucy as they tried to stop him. They finally managed to pull him away from the turned up ground.

Lucy led him a few feet away while Wendy took in the scene. The ravine meandered through the trees and only had a trickle of water. Leaves covered the banks and were bright red on the tree Austin had dug under. Flooding had washed away the dirt from the ravine side of the tree, revealing a tangle of roots and leaving a cavity big enough to bury a large treasure chest, or something much more sinister. If more soil were to wash away, the tree would topple.

Lucy released Austin and joined Wendy and pointed to the base of the tree. "Is this where you think he got it? How would someone wind up underneath there?"

Wendy looked at a tree across the bank. A pile of logs, leaves and mud partially surrounded the base. She hopped across the stream and kicked at the closest log. It gave way and rolled into the ravine with a splash. "Oops, I didn't mean to do that. The ground is really soft."

"You think someone got caught in a flash flood and this is where he was deposited?" Lucy asked.

Wendy hopped back across the ravine and bent to get a closer look at where Austin had been digging. "I'm no expert, but that sounds like a good theory. This tree could have had a pile of logs and leaves like the one across from it, and that could have packed in around the person and no one knew he was here until another flood washed away the pile."

"Or maybe no one is buried here and someone somehow died and his body was scattered to the wind, compliments of animals and, like you said, flooding," Lucy said. "Maybe, it wasn't a man who died. Maybe it was a woman."

"I swear to god, if you start talking about aliens and shit I'm going to FLIP out."

Austin splashed in the ravine and hadn't sniffed anything else out since they stopped him from digging. Wendy had a feeling that whoever there was to be discovered lay under the tree. She grabbed a stick, making sure first that it was, in fact, a stick, and scratched at the dirt under the tree.

"I don't think you should be doing that," Lucy said.

"Whoever's jaw that is, he's missing. Someone has spent hours searching, hours worrying, wondering if he'll ever come home." Wendy squatted down and started scratching a little faster. "What if this was your loved one, you'd want him out of here."

Lucy laid a hand on Wendy's shoulder. "Wendy, I understand you're upset, and I know why, but trust me, we should leave this to the experts."

Wendy kept scratching away at the soil.

Lucy squeezed Wendy's shoulder. "Wendy, you need to stop. Wendy." No reaction, so finally Lucy squatted down beside her and gently grabbed her hand and stopped her from digging. "It's not Jake. You'll find him, but he's not here."

Wendy sank to her knees and started crying. "I don't know how to help him. He's got to come home. He's got to."

"We'll figure it out, I promise," Lucy said and held Wendy's hand. "But for now, we need to leave this to the police."

Wendy wiped her tears on her sleeve and straightened up. "Let's go back to where Viv and Kate are." She dusted off her hands on her pants. "I know all too well what this person's loved ones went through, and it caught me off guard."

Lucy called Austin and then led the way down the mountain. Though they didn't have blue dots to mark a trail, the girls had no problem finding their way back to Vivian and Kate.

Vivian took in Lucy and Wendy's somber expressions and mud-splattered clothes. "What happened?"

Lucy pointed to Austin, who was sniffing the jawbone. "He flung dirt everywhere when he was digging under the roots of a tree."

"Did y'all find anything else?" Vivian asked and grabbed hold of Austin's leash before he could grab hold of the jaw.

Wendy and Lucy looked at each other before Wendy responded, "No, but Austin went crazy around a tree base up there."

"Maybe there was another animal's scent," Kate said, still sitting against the tree. She twirled a bright orange leaf between her thumb and pointer finger.

Wendy reached for Lucy's CamelBak. "It got me thinking about Jake." She started crying again and sat down, burying her head in her hands.

Vivian sat down beside her. "You need to cry about this. It's good for you to get this emotion out."

Wendy sucked in a ragged breath. "Y'all don't know everything." She really started sobbing and could hardly catch her breath.

Lucy dug in her backpack and walked over with a pad of gauze. "I ran out of tissues, sorry."

Wendy took the gauze and blew her nose.

Kate gave her a shoulder hug. "What else is there to know?"

Wendy sobbed a couple of more times before taking a deep breath. "I found something really weird when his parents and I were cleaning out his apartment last week. I didn't show them because I didn't want to freak them out, but I'm sure it has something to do with his disappearance."

"I'm sure whatever it is, it's totally explainable," Lucy said.

"All guys have porn, Wendy," Vivian said.

"It wasn't porn."

"What was it?" Kate asked.

Wendy looked up at the trees. "I think Jake had another identity."

11

Vivian, Kate and Lucy glanced at one another after hearing the shocking information about Jake. Wendy just stared at the trees, almost in a trance, and then wiped more tears from her eyes.

Vivian touched Wendy's arm. "Excuse me? Did you say Jake has another identity?"

"I know, crazy, right?" Wendy said.

"You need to tell us exactly what you found," Lucy said.

"It was when his parents and I were cleaning out his apartment. His lease was up, and they told us to come get the stuff or they'd put it on the curb. I was working in his bedroom, and I went to pack up his autographed basketball. It's in a Plexiglas display case and it felt way too heavy. Basketballs are full of air, but it shifted in the box funny. I opened up the case, took out the ball and found a slit had been cut into one of the back seams. I pulled it open and couldn't believe what I found."

"What was it?" Vivian asked.

"A passport with his picture but under another name, Paul Vaughn. Money from different countries, all in South America. A lot of money, based on the currency exchange."

"How much?" Kate asked.

"Close to $50,000."

"Holy cow," Kate said. "It's times like this I wish I could have a glass of wine."

"Did you tell the police?" Vivian asked.

"No, I didn't know what to do. I was so freaked out I hid everything at my house. I have crazy scenarios running through my head. Is he a spy? A criminal? I feel deceived." Wendy blew her nose again. "Maybe he wanted to start another life somewhere? Maybe his name isn't even Jake."

"We'll help you sort it out," Kate said. "Are you sure it's real money?"

"Yes, I went to the main branch of my bank and got some to compare it to. It's definitely real." She paused. "There's something else. I found another cellphone."

44

Austin jumped up and started barking. Vivian didn't hear anything at first, but a few seconds later she heard the buzz of engines. Soon after, two people in tan uniforms on dirt bikes raced up the mountainside in their direction.

They pulled to a stop 10 yards away, and the shorter of the two took off her helmet, revealing a French braid. "I'm officer Cheri Stokola with the Essex County Sheriff's Department. You the ones who called about a bone?"

"That's us." Vivian introduced herself and the girls, then pointed to the jawbone on the ground. "We haven't touched it since Austin dropped it."

Austin barked in confirmation.

The other deputy walked up and Stokola introduced him as Brad Young. He looked down at the jaw. "Yep, that's human." He reached for his walkie-talkie. "This is Deputy Young, we're going to need the coroner."

Vivian's heart sank at Young's request for the coroner, even though she knew that would, and should, happen. A gust of wind swirled around her, sending chills through her body.

Stokola removed her sunglasses, showing off inquisitive green eyes. A few freckles accented her face. She pulled a pen and a notebook out of a leather bag on her bike. "Can you tell us what happened?"

Lucy and Vivian gave her a brief explanation of playing fetch with Austin and him returning with the jaw, and then Lucy said, "Wendy and I followed Austin up the mountain where he started digging frantically at the base of a tree. We think that's where he got the jaw. We can show you."

The deputies looked at one another. Young said, "I think it's best we wait for the coroner and crime scene techs to show up. They get pretty pissed when it comes to people trampling their scenes."

"I've got to pee," Kate said and started to stand up. "I'll go down that way, so as to not trample anything." She pointed in the opposite direction from where Wendy and Lucy had gone.

"I doubt you'll be here much longer, but I do need to get everyone's contact information before you take off," Young said, helping Kate to her feet. She quickly gave it to him. "The coroner is usually pretty quick, so be on the lookout. He's a maniac on a bike."

"Thank you," Kate said.

"Vivian can give you my info," Lucy called to Young. "I'm going with Kate. Buddy system." The two headed downhill. "We'll be back."

Wendy gave Young her contact information, then Vivian gave him hers and Lucy's. As she finished, she said, "I can't imagine y'all have a lot of crime out here."

"We have the same stuff the big cities have, just less of it, but finding a jawbone and possibly more of the skeleton, now that doesn't happen every day. We haven't had anything like this in the 15 years I've been with the department."

"What about any missing persons?" Wendy asked.

Young knitted his eyebrows and paused before responding. "We had a teen go missing about eight years ago. Never found him. Then there was one woman who went missing about five years ago. We never could figure out if she just ran off and left her husband or if there was foul play."

Before Wendy could ask any more questions, the whine of more dirt bike engines could be heard. Stokola and Young turned their attention down mountain and waved when two more bikes were visible.

Kate and Lucy rejoined the group just as the bikes pulled to a stop alongside the others. The riders got off, both wearing backpacks. Stokola introduced them as Brian Moreno, the coroner, and Jamie Doda, crime scene tech and photographer. Moreno was briefed by the deputies while Doda listened and got her camera out of her backpack. She pulled her long, sleek brown hair into a ponytail, then both officers put on gloves and yellow crime-scene booties over their boots.

Moreno pushed a small, bright orange flag in the ground beside the jaw, and the photographer got to work taking pictures.

"Done," Doda said after several clicks. "I need to get video, too." She backed up and walked around the area, talking into her camera. Eventually she walked closer to the bone, zooming in, then turned and gave a thumbs up.

Moreno turned to the girls. "Can you take us to the spot the dog led you to earlier? We don't need you to stay, just show us the area."

Lucy reached to take Austin's leash from Vivian. "I think I could find it again, but it would be best if he led the way."

Vivian didn't want to be separated from her friends again, especially now that the cops were there, and she held tight to Austin's leash. "Is it okay if we all go?"

"Sure," Stokola said, so the group took off, leaving only Young behind with the jaw.

On the way up mountain, the coroner, Moreno, said, "I can't have my crime scene jeopardized, so please show us the tree but stay back. In fact, you're probably free to leave after this. Stokola?"

She nodded. "If we need anything else from you, you'll hear from Deputy Young or me."

Austin started pulling harder on the leash, dragging Vivian along. Kate lingered behind. The tree with its roots exposed stood out from the others, and Vivian could see where Austin had been digging. Goosebumps covered her arms, although the temperature hadn't changed.

Wendy pointed to the tree and stopped walking. "That's it." She looked at the coroner. "I hope you're able to find something." She turned to Stokola.

"Especially if the person has been missing."

"We'll do our best," Stokola responded. "You girls can go now. Thank you for calling this in. I know it's not how you wanted to spend your afternoon."

"It wasn't what we had in mind when we started out, but we're happy to help," Vivian said, and then the girls turned to leave.

"Just to confirm," Moreno called. "You didn't recover any bones from this site?"

Wendy sighed. "No, but do you mind if we stay over here and watch you work? We won't get in the way or interrupt you."

"You don't want to stay for this," Moreno said. "We'll do a grid search in addition to digging around the tree. It's a long, tedious process. You'll be bored to tears."

"You're probably right," Wendy said and turned to leave.

Vivian grabbed her arm. "I don't think we want to see what turns up. I'm done with body parts for the day, thank you!"

12

The girls hadn't gone twenty feet before a muscular, mid-thirties, sandy blond guy approached. He moved with agility, and his hiking boots looked well worn. His Red Hot Chili Peppers T-shirt was ripped on the side, and Vivian could see part of the six-pack that lay beneath.

He nodded to the girls as he passed. "Good afternoon."

Vivian stopped to look at his backside. Baggy, khaki cargo shorts hid his rear, but muscular calves indicated nice muscles farther north.

"You digging for dinosaur bones, Stokola?" he teased. "I heard Young's call on the radio and figured you could use some volunteers for this one."

Stokola greeted the man with a handshake and a shoulder hug. "Larson, good to see you. I think we can probably use your help. We've got a jaw with a silver filling, and I suspect there's more to be found." She tucked some stray strands of hair back into place and fluffed the back. "Could be scattered around. The dog was digging at the roots of that tree."

"So they found the bone?" Larson asked and glanced in the girls' direction.

Vivian gave a little wave and smiled.

Larson and Stokola talked a few more minutes before he wandered over to the girls, who hadn't left as instructed.

"Who was the lucky girl playing fetch with the golden retriever?" he said with a grin.

Vivian raised her hand. "Me, and I may never play fetch with my dog again. I'm too afraid of what I'll get back."

Austin loped up to Larson who bent down and scratched behind the dog's ears, flopping them around. Larson's voice turned playful. "Who's a good boy? Who deserves a treat for finding the bone?"

Austin started licking Larson in the face and almost trampled him to the ground.

Larson stood, wiping his face on his sleeve, and patted Austin's side. He looked at Vivian. "He was just doing what was natural, digging, chomping on bones."

"It's just best when they're not human," Lucy said.

The girls laughed and Kate made introductions, Austin included. "We're visiting and thought a hike would be just what we needed today. You know, take in the fall foliage, get some exercise, help with a police investigation, that sort of thing."

Vivian looked toward Moreno who was excavating the dirt under the roots with a small shovel, then looked at Larson, who was still petting Austin. "We got more out of this hike than we bargained for, but things are definitely looking up."

Larson laughed. "You never know what you'll find out here. I love to hike and I've found some interesting things over the years. You've got to heed the Boy Scout motto and always be prepared."

"So you heard Deputy Young's call?" Wendy asked. "Are you a police officer?"

"No, I'm a volunteer fireman. We're part of search and rescue, and we pitch in with emergencies or situations like this."

"What is there for you to pitch in and do?" Lucy asked.

Larson pointed up mountain to where the crime scene tape had been hung in a 30-foot radius around the tree. Doda was busy taking pictures while Moreno pulled tools out of his bag. Five more guys arrived and started setting up big spotlights and running extension cords to a generator.

Larson waved to the new arrivals. "They're going to lay out a grid in a few minutes and start searching by section. We'll probably be here all night."

"You'll work all night even though this isn't a fresh crime?" Vivian asked.

"It's freshly found, and we have to gather all of the evidence and info as quickly as we can," Larson said. "I'll probably go from here directly to work in the morning for a half day because I have an event tomorrow with the fire department. Good thing I'm off from both the day after that."

"What do you do?" Kate asked.

"I'm a line repairman for the electric company."

Vivian cringed outwardly and inwardly. "I can't function without sleep. I don't see how you do it."

"Doesn't happen often. I'll sleep in the day after tomorrow, although the weather should still be warm enough to take the boat out on the lake. Will you still be in town? Want to go?"

The girls looked at each other. "Sure, that sounds like fun!" Vivian said. "Wear your fireman outfit. I can't resist a man in uniform."

Larson looked at Vivian with a mischievous twinkle. "Give me your number and I'll get you details tomorrow." They exchanged numbers, then he said, "I'd better get to work. I might be here as a volunteer, but Moreno

49

treats me like he pays me a six-figure salary." He laughed, gave Austin a final pat on the head, then winked at Vivian as he walked off.

Lucy slapped herself in the forehead. "Unbelievable. Absolutely unbelievable. We find a piece of a decomposed body and you're ready to make out with the first hiker to come along."

Vivian grinned. "He wasn't just any hiker. Did you see his legs? I bet his ass is picture perfect."

Groans all around.

"What? I'm single!"

"Just making the best of a bad situation, huh?" Lucy butt-bumped her. "Come on, let's move."

The girls passed the crime scene techs who had begun to lay out a grid; two worked in one quadrant, while two others worked in another. Doda took pictures while Larson and the techs got started digging in another section. Two more sheriff deputies arrived along with three men in street clothes, and Moreno put them all to work on the grid. The girls watched the action a few minutes until Kate said, "I'd like to use a real toilet the next time I feel the need. Can we head back?"

Larson bent over as Vivian admired. He straightened and she turned to leave. She giggled as they headed down the mountain. "Did y'all see the size of his feet?"

Lucy rolled her eyes. "I didn't pay attention to his feet."

Vivian looked around at them and grinned. She just couldn't help herself. "I bet that fireman has a big hose."

13

The girls hiked past Deputy Young, who looked bored babysitting the jawbone, and down the mountain to the car without incident. No more porcupines, tricky streams or body parts, though Austin sniffed the tracks of several somethings and left his mark on the mountain more than once. Vivian didn't want to find out what the somethings were, so she held his leash firmly until they got to the trailhead.

"I'm looking forward to a long, hot bath," she said. "When the water cools, I'm going to drain the tub and fill it again."

"I'm ready for a nice, mellow bottle of wine," Wendy said. "At a minimum."

Lucy rubbed her cheek. "I can't wait to use my Clarisonic. Wash off the jawbone funk."

"You didn't even touch it, Lucy," Kate said. "I'm just looking forward to using a real toilet. Is that too much to ask?" She dug in the right-hand pocket of her red North Face jacket, then in the left pocket. She patted her pants pockets before saying, "Uh, guys, I can't find the car key. Did I give it to someone to keep track of on the hike?"

"I don't think so," Wendy said, patting her pockets.

Vivian and Lucy checked theirs, too, and Lucy checked her CamelBak and backpack.

"Nothing," Lucy reported. "Do you think you could have dropped it on the trail?"

"I hope not." Kate looked back at the trail and shook her head.

"Maybe it's in the car," Vivian said.

Wendy peered through the passenger window to their rental. "Yep, there it is. Right there on the seat." She tried the door handle. "Locked. We just need a slim jim or something similar. We can pop the lock."

"At least it's not lost," Kate said, relieved.

Vivian looked toward several sheriff cruisers parked close together. A deputy stood outside one of them. "I'll be right back."

The officer strode to Vivian as she approached. His name tag read

Dawson. She smiled and said, "Hi, there, we seem to have locked our keys in the car. Would you happen to have a slim jim?"

He looked over her shoulder to the other three girls standing outside the SUV. Kate turned to the side, showing off her baby bump. Austin wagged his tail.

"I sure don't, ma'am," he said and reached for his radio, "but let me call someone for you." He told dispatch he needed a locksmith pronto. He turned back to the girls. "We don't want you stranded out here. Strange things have been known to happen on this stretch of road."

Kate, who had been watching Austin sniff a pile of leaves, snapped her head toward Dawson. "What sort of strange things?"

He shook his head and sighed. "Oh, I shouldn't have said anything. It's just a legend, but I'd feel better if you were out of here before dark."

Vivian took a step closer to the SUV, wishing she could somehow transport herself through the door. "Is there a giant man-eating bear in these woods?"

"It's Bigfoot, isn't it?" Lucy asked. "There's a show on Discovery Channel, I've been watching it. I knew he existed!"

Dawson looked solemn. "No Bigfoot, but what I've heard is just as scary. Years ago a young woman was sexually assaulted, beaten, then dragged behind a car 'til she died. People swear her ghost runs up and down this stretch of road at night, screaming to get away from her attacker. No one in their right mind walks or bikes through here at night."

Vivian took in a sharp breath. "Oh my god! Did they catch the guy?"

"Yes, and he hinted, but never confessed, to murdering several others. Though they investigated some missing persons cases, the detectives were never able to prove anything."

Vivian shivered. "We won't be out here at night, you can count on that."

A white paneled van with JD Locksmith painted in navy block letters stopped behind the girls' SUV. A tall guy with a beer gut, brown hair and a scraggly goatee got out and walked over. "Did you call for a locksmith?" he asked.

He and Dawson shook hands. "Hi, Jeremy, this is the vehicle we need you to pop the locks on."

Jeremy peered into the driver's window, then opened the back doors on his van and dug around. He came back with a deflated bag with a tube coming off one end and a black ball on the other end to pump it up. In his other hand, he held a long, thin rod with a hook on one end. The girls stood back as he pried the window away from the frame enough to slide the flattened bag through. He then began pumping the black ball, and the bag separated the window and frame wide enough for him to slide the thin rod through. He hooked one edge of the driver's lock and gently pulled it back toward him. The rod slipped a few times, but he had the door unlocked in less than a minute.

"Wow, that's impressive," Vivian said. "I've never seen a thing like that. Good work."

Jeremy tipped an imaginary hat to her and opened the car door. "Hope you don't need my services again, but here's a card in case you do." He reached in his front pocket and handed a card to Lucy, who stood closest to him. "I perform other services as well."

Lucy turned red and took the card but didn't have a comeback other than, "What do we owe you?"

"Let's see, for 45 seconds work, plus gas, let's say fifty bucks."

"You take credit cards?" Lucy asked.

"Nah. I've been meaning to get that Square card swiper, but haven't. How about I give you my 'damsel in distress' discount. Shall we say twenty bucks?"

Lucy pulled a twenty out of her backpack and handed it to him. "You're sweet. Thanks."

Jeremy laughed and walked back to his van. "Enjoy your stay," he called, then got in his van and drove away.

The girls said goodbye to Deputy Dawson, and Kate got behind the wheel. She drove to the nearest gas station for a pit stop. Once back in the car, she said, "We'd better go by the shelter and drop Austin off." She put it into drive and pulled in front of the shelter a few minutes later.

The faint glow of a computer screen was the only light coming from the front window. Vivian hopped out of the SUV. "I'll go see if anyone's here, just in case." The door was locked, so she knocked and waited a minute. No answer. She got back in the SUV. "Guess we're bringing a boy home tonight. Hope Tracy and Brandon don't mind."

Kate pointed the car toward Turlington Farms. "He's so cute, I bet they won't."

14

Tracy greeted the girls as they got out of the car. Austin was the last to emerge. "Hi, there," she said. "And who is this?" she asked, scratching under his chin and rubbing his head.

Wendy explained that they'd ended up with the shelter dog a little longer than anticipated. "Is it okay if he stays the night?"

"Sure he can. I've got some scraps he'll enjoy. I'll go get him a bowl of water, too."

Before she turned around, she took in their appearance. "Are you girls okay?"

"I'm heading up," Kate said and started up the porch. "I need a shower."

"Right behind ya," Lucy said.

Vivian ran a hand through her blonde curls. "It was a helluva day. We've been surrounded by men in uniform. Unfortunately, we weren't at a strip club. They were the real deal."

"Oh, wow. Would you like a glass of wine? Or a beer? We have all that you brought in the fridge."

"I'll have one of my Dox Equis." Vivian sat in a rocker on the back porch. "Thanks."

"You got it," Tracy said and disappeared.

Vivian and Wendy sat rocking and tried to relax. In a few minutes, Tracy brought them each a beer. She set down a cup of hot tea and walked down the steps with a large plastic bowl. She filled it with water from the hose. "Come here, boy," she called to Austin, who trotted over and went to town slurping.

She picked up her tea and sat down beside Vivian.

Vivian and Wendy told her about the hike, and then about finding the jawbone.

Tracy's eyes got big, and she put her hand on her chest. "A human bone? Are you sure?"

"The teeth had silver fillings," Wendy said. "There was no doubt. When we left the coroner, crime scene techs and a bunch of volunteers were there

54

and looking for more, uh, pieces."

Tracy shivered. "Had they found anything?"

Wendy shook her head. "Not that we know of, but from what we understand, it sounded like a tedious process. I bet we'll know more tomorrow. I hope so, for the sake of that person and the family."

Tracy got up. "I need a real drink; this tea isn't cutting it. I'll be right back, and I'll bring us all a little something special."

Wendy took a long draw of her beer and looked around. "It's so nice out here. It's little things like this I was looking forward to sharing with Jake."

Austin lay at Vivian's feet. He sat up and she rubbed his soft ears while she thought about the Jake situation. "Why don't we call Antonio in New Orleans? Ask him to use his NOPD accesses to see what he can find out about the name on that other passport? We can trust him."

Antonio Robichaux was a detective with the New Orleans Police Department they had met earlier in the year. He was also the brother/brother-in-law of Adrienne and Al Russo, whom the girls met in Playa del Carmen on their first vacation. They'd run into them in NOLA where Al's contacts and Adrienne's street sense had come in handy during Wendy's bachelorette party.

Wendy brightened. "I don't know why I didn't think of that before. He would be straight with us, tell us if he found anything, even if it wasn't..." She couldn't finish.

"Pleasant," Vivian finished.

Wendy nodded. "Do you still talk to him?"

Vivian shrugged. "I haven't been to New Orleans to see him, but we still talk occasionally." She grinned mischievously. "I wouldn't mind seeing him next time I go. Maybe slip into his handcuffs."

Wendy laughed and seemed to relax.

Vivian was happy to see her smiling. The past few months had been really tough, and they'd thought about canceling the trip, so this made her feel better about their choice to come. "I'll call Antonio first thing in the morning."

Tracy pushed the door open with her foot and came out carrying three martini glasses filled to the brim with a reddish amber drink, a cherry resting at the bottom.

Wendy held up her drink to toast. "To that poor person up on the mountain. May they not only find out who it is, but bring to justice whoever is responsible."

The three women clinked glasses.

Tracy sat down and took a sip. "Mmmm, not bad."

Wendy took a sip, then another. "Wow. I've given up bourbon and the like, but this is delicious."

"I'm not one for whiskey at all, but this is yummy," Vivian said, fishing the cherry out. "What is it?"

"Let me guess," Wendy said, and took another sip. "It tastes a lot like a manhattan, but sweetened up." Wendy had tended bar through college at Morton's Steakhouse and made her fair share of manhattans and martinis. She'd even won a martini making contest, twice. "What'd you use?"

Tracy sat her drink on the porch railing. "This is made with Crown Royal Maple, extra cherry juice. My secret ingredient from my bartending days. Shhh. I call it the Upstate Uproar."

Kate pushed open the screen door and walked out in her jammies and pink, fuzzy house shoes. "Who's causing an uproar?"

They all laughed.

"I'm going to make another round. Kate, what can I get for you?"

"Just some water, thanks. Lucy'll be down in a second. She'd probably like something."

"I'll check with her," Tracy said and went inside.

Wendy and Vivian chatted with Kate for a few minutes, telling her about reaching out to Antonio for help with the Jake situation. Lucy, smelling freshly showered, walked outside and sat down in the rocker Tracy had vacated. "Did I hear the name Antonio?"

Vivian smiled. "That's affirmative."

"Why am I not surprised?"

Wendy finished her drink. "I think it's a great idea. She's going to ask him about Jake's passport. Or actually, Paul Vaughn's passport."

"Yeah, it's a good idea," Lucy agreed.

Tracy arrived with a cocktail tray of decadent drinks. Even Kate's water was gussied up with a lemon wheel. "I feel like I'm back at The Rumor Mill."

"What's The Rumor Mill?" Lucy took a cautious drink, then a bigger one. "Yum-ola."

"The place in town where I bartended for years," Tracy said.

Vivian took a long sip of her cocktail. *After today and finding that jaw, I could use a few more of these.*

"Where's Brandon?" Wendy asked.

"At work. He's had a job at the hardware store for years. The money helps when it's slow around here, and besides, we can get things at cost. He'll be home soon."

"Totally worth it," Kate said, rocking back and forth in a white wicker rocking chair. "It's not cheap to keep up a house like this."

Tracy gulped half her drink and changed the subject. "So I can't believe what happened to you today. Who all was out there?"

"We met a couple of sheriff deputies, then the coroner and the crime scene photographer," Kate replied.

"What trail were you hiking?"

"Haystack Mountain."

Tracy looked out across the lake and nodded. "That's a good one." She finished off her drink. "Sorry it didn't end up so well."

Vivian set her glass next to Wendy's empty on the rail. "On the contrary, we met a sexy blond fireman."

"Larson Doolan?" Tracy asked.

Vivian looked at Tracy, amazed.

"I'm married, not blind." She smiled. "He's very involved with the fire department. It figures he would be there."

Vivian raised an eyebrow. "Does he have a way with the ladies?"

Tracy laughed. "You could say that, though as far as I know, he's never had a longtime girlfriend and he's never been married."

"Lone wolf," Vivian said. "A renegade, a rebel. I like it."

"AKA horny. Totally Vivian's type," Lucy said and looked at the girls. "I'm getting hungry, what's for dinner?"

Kate propped her feet up on another chair. "I don't feel like going anywhere. I'm tired."

"We have a great pizza place that delivers," Tracy said and got up. "I'll go get their menu for you."

"Perfect," Vivian said.

The girls decided on two large pizzas, a meat lovers and a veggie. Tracy went inside to call in the order.

Wendy set down her martini glass with a heavy clank, hard to do with such a delicate glass. "I was interrupted by the sheriffs showing up earlier today," she said and blew out a long sigh. She twisted her long brown hair into an up-do and tucked it in so it stayed.

Vivian knew Wendy was back to business.

"There was more inside Jake's secret basketball than money and the passport."

15

"What else was in there?" Vivian looked at Wendy, almost afraid to know what else she had found in Jake's basketball, but dying to know just the same. Jake was not turning out to be who Wendy thought he was, and she felt bad her friend had been deceived.

"Jake, or should I say Paul, has an iPhone." Wendy pulled a black cellphone out of her pocket. "I bought a charger and it's good to go, but I can't get past the code."

Kate took the phone from Wendy.

Wendy nodded. "It's unbelievable to me he had a whole separate identity and life. I keep questioning everything I thought I knew."

"You can't live like that, Wendy," Vivian said. "Don't do that to yourself. I'm sure Jake loves you or he wouldn't have been marrying you." *That damn sure better be the case.*

Kate handed the phone back to Wendy. "I can't get into it."

Vivian reached for it. "Let me try." She punched in common codes like 1234, 9876, 4567 and a few others. Of course the code was more complex and she couldn't unlock it.

They watched the sun set over the mountains, a brilliant display of colors. Kate took pictures and posted to Facebook as Vivian feverishly tried to unlock the phone.

Wendy tapped her foot on the porch. "I've tried his birthday, variations of his Social Security number, his parents' birthdays, the birthday on the other passport. Nothing has worked."

"I want a turn," Lucy said and took the phone. She tapped buttons on it while the girls discussed theories of what could have happened to Jake.

After a while, Vivian heard a car pull up and the front screen door open and close. Tracy brought out the pizzas, paper plates and napkins a few minutes later.

"I'll be right back with a couple of beers and more water for Kate."

"Thanks, Tracy," Wendy mumbled through a bite.

Vivian picked up a slice. "When I call Antonio, I'll tell him about the phone, too. Maybe he'll have some pointers for breaking into it."

Tracy walked outside with beverages so the girls ended the conversation and got down to business. They gave Austin a slice and their crust, and the pizza was polished off in no time.

Lucy threw down her napkin, stood up, brushed off crumbs and walked down the steps toward the lake. She looked up to the sky. "Wow, I can see a lot of stars in Colorado, but the reflection off the water is amazing here."

Tracy was picking up the pizza boxes and said, "We have a high-powered telescope. You might not be able to see Martians on Mars, but you can see the man on the moon."

"Oooh, I wanna see," Wendy said. "Y'all want to go?"

They did, and Tracy brought the telescope to the water's edge a few minutes later. She set it up for them on a small table she'd pulled from the boathouse.

"You can see Jupiter over here." Tracy looked through the lens and positioned the scope for them. "It's the brightest star. You can tell planets from stars because the planets don't twinkle."

The girls took turns looking at Jupiter, and then Tracy repositioned the scope. "Mars is over here." She headed toward the house. "I'll leave you to it. Please bring the telescope inside when you're done. You can just put it on the dining room table."

The girls thanked her and said goodnight.

Vivian peered through the lens after the other girls had checked out Mars. "Oh, I just saw a Martian!" She giggled and panned the telescope to the right a little. "Just kidding, but I wonder where Uranus is."

"Stooping to Uranus jokes, huh, Viv?" Wendy said.

"You knew it was coming."

"Speaking of asses, any new men in your life?" Lucy asked.

"Not lately. I have a few friends with benefits I see from time to time, when the need arises, but I don't have much time to date anyone seriously."

"You need to get back out there, Viv," Kate said, stepping up to the telescope. "You're not getting any younger, and you need to find your soul mate. I don't want you to be alone when you're old and feeble." She looked into the lens and didn't see Vivian's eyes roll.

"I'm perfectly happy being single, thank you. I'm not worried about finding my soul mate. I thought I had one once and that didn't work out, so no need to rush into finding another one. My soul can mate with itself if it needs to." She giggled to herself. "In fact, I've been looking at selling sex toys!"

"Oh my god, are you going to sell dildos out of your trunk?" Wendy asked.

"Not out of my trunk, out of a magazine. There are some pretty good companies out there that offer a variety of sexual enhancement opportunities. I'm seriously looking into it."

"I'd be your best customer," Lucy laughed.

"I'll probably not do it because of the time involved, but I did seriously think about it." Vivian bent over and shook out her hair and added from upside down, "I could use the extra income."

Kate turned to her. "I'll support whatever you do, even dildos, but I believe everyone only has one true soul mate, and Rick wasn't yours."

Wendy sighed. "I thought Jake was mine, but now he's gone." She turned and started walking toward the woods just beyond the house.

Lucy ran to catch up with her. "Wendy, wait."

Wendy waved her away. "Little things out of nowhere get to me these days. I'm okay. I just need to pee. I'll be right back." She disappeared through the trees.

"Why don't you go inside?" Vivian asked her. "The house isn't that far away, you know."

"It's fine," Wendy called from beyond the tree line. "I can pee in nature."

Kate looked at Vivian. "I didn't mean to upset her. I don't know what I was thinking. But you do need to get out there, Viv. I don't want you to die alone."

Vivian snorted. "Oh geez, come on now. I really don't have time, and my friends make me feel special."

"Aaaahhhh! Aaaahhhh!" Wendy ran back to the lakeside but then turned and started sprinting toward the back porch. "It's going to eat me. It has huge fangs."

Lucy screamed and ran in a circle. Kate made a mad dash for the porch, and Vivian looked toward the woods where Wendy ran from but didn't see anything.

"You sure something was after you?" she yelled to Wendy.

"Yes! I was mid-stream when I heard this mad gnawing, thrashing sound. It kept getting closer and closer!"

Lucy stopped circling and took a few hesitant steps in that direction and then stopped as something shook a nearby bush. She shrieked and high-tailed it to the porch, joining Wendy and Kate.

The screen door banged open and Brandon ran out, followed by a policeman and the newlyweds.

"What's going on out here?" he asked and stopped to look at the girls.

Wendy pointed toward the woods. "There's something in there. It was big and it almost got me. It might be Bigfoot."

Brandon looked at the policeman. "What do you think, Adam, bear?"

Vivian still hadn't seen any animal come out but she inched closer to the house anyway.

"Could be bear," Adam answered. "Or wolf."

"Wolf?" Wendy whimpered. "Are there really wolves out here? They can see in the dark, right?" She didn't waste any time moving up the steps and onto the porch.

"Do y'all have chupacabras up here?" Lucy asked.

"No chupa-whatever, but we do have plenty of wolves, and they can smell fear a mile away," Adam said, pulling his gun out of its holster and walking down the porch steps.

"Careful, Adam," Brandon said. "I don't want to have to tell Angie that you were eaten by a pack of wolves." He laughed just as something rustled in the leaves again.

Brandon pointed to where the trees met the lake. "There it goes!"

Adam pointed his gun into the darkness.

The group looked to where he had pointed but no one reacted. Vivian couldn't see what Brandon had seen. She walked toward the porch.

"There!" he said and pointed again.

Vivian still didn't see anything.

Tracy hit Brandon with a dish towel. "Stop messing with these girls. They had a bad day as it was. Besides, it was probably only a raccoon."

Just as she said it, a masked, ring-tailed bandit scurried through the leaves back into the protective covering of the woods.

"Well, damn." Wendy said. "I could have sworn it was Bigfoot."

Adam holstered his gun. "Raccoons can be vicious little suckers. Be glad you didn't cross his path. Or her — the mommas are the worst." He looked to Brandon. "Let's go finish up."

Brandon held the door for Adam and they went inside. Wendell and Mitzie stayed outside with the girls.

"I don't know what's going on around here," Mitzie said, "but I don't like it. The police showing up here, animals going crazy. It's not my kind of honeymoon."

Wendell held her hand with both of his. "We will leave in the morning. It's not safe to go now, what with wild animals and such."

Mitzie pouted but then must have decided Wendell had done all he could. "Let's go into the city tomorrow, go shopping!" She winked at Vivian, then looped her arm through Wendell's and they went inside.

Vivian laughed, figuring Mitzie was more at home at Macy's in New York City than at the Turlington Farms B&B in Lake Placid. She turned to the girls. "What is the cop doing here?"

"Brandon didn't seem too upset by him," Kate said. "They seemed to know each other pretty well. Maybe he's just a friend."

"Is it her?" Brandon's raised voice carried through an open window. "I have a right to know if it is."

"I can't tell you anything yet," Adam replied. "I just thought you should know." Adam lowered his voice, and Vivian couldn't hear any more.

The girls were quiet, but whatever Brandon and Adam discussed wasn't loud enough, and Adam left shortly with a slam of his car door.

"I'm going to turn in." Kate stretched as she stood. "I'm pooped since I didn't sleep well last night. I hope tonight is better."

Lucy held the door open for her. "I'm going up with you. The more I think about it, the more unnerved I get. I mean, we found a person out there today. A person."

They walked through the dining room on their way to the stairs and said goodnight to Tracy, who was tidying up.

Once in their rooms, Vivian resumed the conversation. "Lucy, you said it earlier today, this wasn't going to mess up our trip, and we're not going to let it. We're going to get up tomorrow and have a good day, and with minimal involvement with the police."

Lucy said nothing.

In the adjoining room, Kate lay in bed, propped up on pillows at the top and the bottom. Her hot pink toes were up in the air. She started coughing. "Anyone else feel like they're having a hard time breathing? My chest feels tight."

Wendy was changing into her pajamas. "I hope you're not coming down with something."

Kate coughed again. "It's like something is sitting on my chest."

"It's probably your big momma boobs," Vivian said before going to run her bath.

"Allergies?" Lucy asked.

Kate shook her head and rubbed her chest. "No, this is different. It feels heavy."

"I've got Claritin in my toiletries bag in the bathroom," Wendy said. "Help yourself."

The girls went to bed while Vivian relaxed in the hot water and mulled over the day. She sure hoped she never wound up buried in the woods, nobody knowing where she was. She couldn't even let herself think about her kids that way. The water eventually cooled and she drained most of it, then ran it again, letting the heat envelope her. When it cooled again, she got out. As she was drying off, she thought she heard moaning in one of the bedrooms, but the water draining covered it. She thought she heard it again as she was rubbing lotion on her face.

"What the hell?" She poked her head out of the bathroom and listened again.

There was just enough light to see Lucy sleeping peacefully, with Kate and Wendy in the other room. Kate's foot twitched and she whimpered. Vivian walked to her side. Kate's breathing was rapid, and just as Vivian was about to reach out and touch her shoulder, she heard a deep moan and rhythmic thumping pulsing through the walls.

Vivian covered her mouth and snickered to herself. *Someone's doing the nasty!*

She held her breath and froze as Kate rolled over, her face relaxed and breathing returned to normal. Vivian headed off to bed. *Which crazy relative is visiting her now?* she thought as she turned out the light.

Day 3

In her dream, Vivian was being whisked downstream by a swirling cascade of freezing water. She awoke and shivered, then pulled the floral comforter around herself, knowing Lucy would be tugging it back any second, except she didn't.

Vivian slowly rolled over, thinking she'd let Lucy have the covers, but there was no Lucy. She felt over on the nightstand and grabbed her phone, checking the time — 7:23. Thirty-seven more minutes, she thought, and closed her eyes.

Four minutes later Kate shook her awake. "Vivian!"

"I'm up! I'm up!" She pushed herself up, dizzy.

"Lucy's gone! She left!"

Vivian rubbed her eyes. "What?" Wendy, wearing her black and hot pink, kitty cat flannel pajamas, leaned against the dresser holding a piece of paper. She pushed her glasses up.

"It says she's sorry, but she'd just be a downer on this trip and she's going to see a friend who will understand the loss she's going through." Wendy put the note down, then held up a smaller, yellow piece of paper. "Here's a check for her part of the room and the rent car."

"Is her luggage gone?" Vivian asked, getting out of bed and heading to the closet. "Where would she go?"

"I wonder if she got an early flight out," Kate said. She picked up the note and read it to herself.

Vivian opened the closet door to find it void of anything that was Lucy's, though she did see a door to a crawlspace she hadn't noticed before. She hustled to a dresser and opened the drawers Lucy had neatly occupied. Empty.

Wendy picked up her cellphone. "Let's call her."

The connection went straight to voice mail six times. On the seventh, Wendy left a message. "Hey, Lucy, it's us. We're worried about you. Call us back. Please."

Vivian sat at the edge of the bed and wrapped herself in the blanket. "I can't believe she left."

"Me, neither," Kate said, then her stomach growled.

"Let's get Little Plum fed," Wendy said. "Maybe Brandon or Tracy saw

Lucy leave and can give us some info. We need to find that girl."

Everyone threw on clothes and trekked downstairs.

"Morning," Tracy chimed.

"Morning," Vivian responded. "Did you see Lucy leave this morning by any chance?"

Tracy looked confused. "No, but Brandon was up before me. In fact, I'm a little late getting breakfast going. He's heading into town soon."

Vivian grabbed a powdered sugar donut. "Can I talk to him before he takes off?"

"He's on the front porch reading the paper, I think."

Kate ripped off a paper towel and wrapped up two sausage patties. "This will tide me over 'til we get back."

Wendy filled a Styrofoam cup with coffee, then threw in a dash of sugar and a bit of cream. "I need my go-go juice."

They went out to the front porch where Brandon was reading the paper and petting Austin. As soon as they walked out, Austin bounded over, thrilled to see them. His red coat looked shiny and healthy, and he wagged his tail like crazy.

"Morning," Vivian said to Brandon, but he didn't respond. "Morning," she said again.

Brandon snapped to and looked up. "Hi."

"Did you happen to see Lucy this morning?" Vivian asked, wiping the powdered sugar from her mouth.

"Sure did. I was sad to see her go."

"How did she leave? Do y'all have cabs out here?" Kate asked, digging through her purse.

Brandon chuckled. "Won't see too many taxis around. Nah, I took her to the bus station in town. She said she wasn't feeling well and needed to go."

"She needed to go?" Wendy repeated. "That was it?"

Brandon nodded. "Yep, that's what she said." He went back to reading the paper.

"Do you mind giving us directions to the bus station?" Wendy asked, giving Austin a scratch under his chin. "Maybe she'll still be there."

Vivian glanced at the headline of the paper:

Human Remains Found Near Haystack Mountain

Brandon stood and tucked the paper under his arm. "Sure, I'll be right back."

Vivian pointed to the screen door after he disappeared through it. "Did y'all see the headline? It was about our hiking discovery. We need to see that." She told them the headline.

Kate started down the steps. "We've got to go find Lucy. Let's get a paper in town while we're out." She stopped on the last step and dug through her purse again. "I think I left the keys upstairs."

"I'll grab 'em," Vivian said, wiping puffs of white off her shirt. "Breakfast of champions right there."

"I think they're on the nightstand," Kate called out.

Kate and Wendy played with Austin while Vivian hustled upstairs. She opened the unlocked door to what used to be her and Lucy's room. A sad feeling washed over her. She and Lucy had been best friends for almost 17 years. They could finish each other's sentences, kick butt at Pictionary and practically read each other's thoughts, yet Vivian had no idea why Lucy had left. She remembered how annoyed Lucy had been when she was being silly about Larson. *Maybe I do need to cool it when it comes to meeting men on vacation. I kinda can't help it, though. But Lucy knows that about me.*

Vivian found the keys in the adjoining room, on the dresser, not the nightstand. *Pregnancy brain.*

She closed the door to Wendy and Kate's room just as Brandon was opening a door at the end of the hall.

"I gave your friends the directions," he said.

"Thanks, we'll be back soon. Hopefully with Lucy."

He stepped into the room and turned around, holding the folded newspaper. "Call if you have any problems."

He closed the door, and Vivian thought she heard it lock. *Maybe it's a secret bathroom.* She smiled to herself and high-tailed it downstairs. Wendy and Kate were playing with Austin when Vivian pushed open the screen door. "Let's boogie."

They got into the rental, leaving Austin behind, looking sad.

Wendy gave Kate directions to the bus station, and as Kate parked, she said, "This looks more like a strip mall."

"I guess Lake Placid isn't a hotbed for Greyhound." Wendy got out of the SUV.

The strip had an insurance agency and a place called LPTs, both closed, and a place that looked like a convenience store. A sticker on the window said "Bus Tickets Sold Here." Benches lined the front of the store with metal dividers sticking up every so often. Vivian guessed it was to prevent people from lying down. "This must be the place," she said and opened the door for her friends. A small bell jingled on the inside doorknob.

The girls walked straight to the counter where a kid who looked all of 19 sat on a stool, staring down at his phone. His long, gangly legs were practically up to his chin, and unkempt, stringy black hair fell down around his face. A skateboard was propped up behind him.

The girls waited a good 30 seconds before Kate cleared her throat.

Skater Dude put the phone down. "Can I help you?"

Kate had a picture of Lucy at the ready and put it in front of him. "We're looking for this woman. We think she may have bought a ticket earlier today."

He squinted at the phone, pushing his hair out of his eyes, then flopped his head to the left. "Huh. I dunno. I sell a lot of tickets."

"Really?" Wendy said, looking around. "Really?"

"Morning is pretty busy. I usually sell eight or nine an hour."

"I see," Wendy said. "Booming bus business."

Kate waved her off, zoomed in on Lucy's face and stuck it in Skater Dude's face. "Please think really hard. We need to find her."

He squinted his eyes and looked again, then snapped her fingers. "Oh yeahhhh, I do remember her. She had pretty eyebrows. And eyeballs. I dig green eyes." He nodded goofily, like a chicken walking around the barnyard.

Vivian smiled. "Yeah, she does."

"She almost missed her bus, but I was able to ring her up super-fast and she made it."

"Do you remember where she was going?"

He looked up at the ceiling, concentrating. Suddenly he jerked, slapped his knee and yelled. "Buffalo! She went to Buffalo!"

The girls looked at each other, then Kate said what they all were thinking.

"Who the hell's in Buffalo?"

16

The girls asked questions of the laid-back convenience store guy for a couple of minutes, not getting much information other than Buffalo. They bought a newspaper from him and walked back to the car.

"Maybe she switched her plane ticket to fly out of Buffalo," Wendy said, checking on her cell which airlines used the airport. Lucy had flown into Albany on Southwest, and it had gates in Buffalo. "I bet that's what she did."

Vivian sighed. "It's my fault."

"Don't be silly. In her note she said she was leaving to be with someone who understands her loss. Is she talking about losing Steve?" Kate asked.

"I think so. What else could it be?" Vivian said. "And here I am, being Ms. Flirty McFlirt Flirt with Mr. Hotty McHot Hot yesterday."

"Whatever," Wendy said as Kate pulled out of the parking lot. "We all know that's how you are and guys eat it up. It's kinda disgusting actually."

"I *could* tone it down."

"You could," Kate said. "But that's not what this is about. It's about Lucy."

"Then it has to be the divorce and moving out of the townhouse," Vivian said. "She worked so hard renovating it, just to have to leave. That sucks."

"That's life, Vivian." Kate looked at her in the rearview mirror. "You know that better than all of us. Things don't always work out the way we planned."

"True. True." Vivian turned her attention to the newspaper. The cover photo was a picture of the trailhead where Austin had dug up the jawbone. Crime scene tape wrapped around trees blocked the entrance.

Vivian read the story, summarizing as she went along. "Essex County sheriffs responded to a call that human remains had been found by hikers near Haystack Mountain. Crime scene technicians, sheriff deputies and volunteers scoured a perimeter around the area." She scanned down the page. "Four people have gone missing from the area in the last 20 years. Timothy Walker, a handyman, left a job site in his truck and never went home. His roommate thought he may have chased down his ex-girlfriend in New York

68

City and decided to stay gone. Bobby McFarland, a sixteen year old high school student. Margaret Jackson, a pharmacy tech and avid hiker, left for work on a cold and icy morning and was never seen again. And then there was Rebecca Holt."

"Holt!" Kate said, stopping for a red light. "Did Brandon have a sister, or is this another relative?"

Vivian sucked in a breath of air and had to reread the last few lines to herself before reading them out loud. "Holy crap! Listen to this. 'Rebecca Holt, wife of Turlington Farms proprietor Brandon Holt, went missing almost seven years ago. Brandon left early in the morning to go fishing, and she was gone when he returned in the afternoon. None of her belongings were missing and her BMW was still in the garage. Continued on p. 4.' "

"Wife!" Kate turned up the air conditioning even though it was in the 50s outside. "What the heck? I wonder if it's her."

"A cop came to the house last night," Wendy said, drumming her fingers on the console between the front seats. "But remember he told Brandon he couldn't say more? Maybe something identifying, like a driver's license, was buried with the body and they're working to confirm it."

"Brandon was awfully relaxed this morning for a person who just found out his long, lost loved one might have been found dead." Kate looked morose and tightened her grip on the wheel. "I'm really beginning to get creeped out. I was okay at first, maybe I was in shock after finding the jaw, but now I think the whole situation is really creepy."

"It is creepy." Vivian flapped the paper down. "It could be the other missing girl, Margaret Jackson, buried up there. Or someone else completely."

"The remains might never be identified," Wendy said. "That is an unfortunate reality."

Kate slammed on the brakes and jerked the rental onto the shoulder, fishtailing to a stop. A car honked as it passed. Kate breathed hard.

She jumped out of the car and ran toward the trees lining the road.

Wendy and Vivian chased after her and made her sit on a fallen tree.

"She's hyperventilating. See if there's a bag or something she can breathe into," Wendy said, pointing at the car.

Vivian ran back to the car and grabbed the plastic bag from the convenience store that the newspaper had been in. "Will this work?"

"Better than nothing," Wendy said and took it from her. She handed it to Kate and gave her instructions for breathing in and out of the bag. She stayed next to her, rubbing her back and fanning her.

Tears streamed down Kate's face. "Those women, those women" was all she could say between breaths.

"Do we need to get you to a doctor?" Wendy asked softly.

Kate shook her head, lowered the bag and took a little deeper breath.

Vivian paced in front of them, feeling helpless. She had only been tested in the emergency action realm once when Audrey had fallen off the metal bleachers at one of Rick's softball games. Audrey cut her lip, and blood spilled from her mouth. Vivian handled the situation pretty well until she saw blood on her own T-shirt. Then she had to pass Audrey off to a stranger and put her head between her legs so she didn't faint. Rick came out of the game to help.

After a minute, Kate was breathing normal again, but she was still trembling.

"You better?" Vivian asked.

Kate nodded.

"Come on," Wendy said, getting up. She held out her hand to help Kate. "I'm driving. Let's get back and pack up. We're not staying there another night."

Vivian and Kate both agreed, and they got back in the car. Kate laid her seat back and closed her eyes.

They were quiet driving to Turlington Farms. In the back seat, Vivian tried to call Lucy two more times. Both went straight to voice mail. *She's probably on a plane.* She gave up with the phone and flipped through the paper to p. 4, finding the continued story on Rebecca Holt. Since Kate was so upset, she decided not to share with the other girls what she read.

Questions remained surrounding Rebecca's disappearance. Many in town suspected Brandon. They married less than a year after Mary Beth's death, and Rebecca disappeared less than a year into their marriage. Brandon had her declared dead after three years. People also wondered about Mary Beth being a strong swimmer and yet drowned.

Wendy pulled up to the house, and they got out of the car. Austin bounded up, excited to see them. His demeanor was a contrast to what the girls felt, but they each patted his head anyway.

Vivian's legs felt like they weighed 200 pounds each as she dragged up the porch steps. She opened the door and the aroma of breakfast meats and sweet rolls enveloped her, making her mouth water and putting a little energy in her step. Pans clattered in the kitchen.

"You stay here, Austin," Wendy said and gave him a gentle pat. "Be a good boy."

Vivian turned to Wendy and Kate. "Let's get one last breakfast out of this, then pack up."

"I'm going to lie down," Kate said. "Y'all go on ahead."

"Are you sure?" Wendy looked at her. "I'll go up with you."

"I'm okay," Kate reassured and started up the staircase but then stopped and turned around, patting her belly. "On second thought, that maple bacon smells too good to pass up. I think a plate of piggy will help us both feel better."

The girls went into the kitchen and told Tracy how they'd had no luck finding Lucy.

Tracy handed Wendy a big, steaming cup of coffee. "I'm sure she'll be fine. She just needs some space."

Wendy put a cinnamon roll the size of a softball on her plate, then scooped some fresh pineapple. "I still can't believe she bailed." She put her plate down to fix up her coffee the way she liked it.

Vivian smirked as Kate put six or seven slices of crispy bacon on her plate, then threw in a link of sausage for good measure. She turned to Tracy. "Where's Brandon?"

"He's in town. Had to go talk to his buddy who was here last night."

"Adam, the cop, right?" Vivian asked.

"He just had to clear a few things up. No big deal. He'll be back soon."

The girls settled around the table, and Tracy went back into the kitchen.

Vivian looked at the other girls and mouthed, "Police station."

Wendy choked taking a sip of coffee. Kate didn't react and kept her attention on her plate of pork.

Vivian smeared a big blob of grape jelly on a biscuit and took a bite. *Mmmmm, just like my grandma used to make.* She watched Kate, who looked lost in thought. *She needs a biscuit. That'll cheer her up.* Vivian held the bread basket out to Kate, but she passed. "These are the best ever, you've got to try them."

Kate didn't say anything, just shook her head, then stabbed a piece of sausage with her fork and smeared it in maple syrup.

Wendy leaned forward and waved the girls in close. She whispered, "When are we telling Tracy that we're leaving?"

"After we eat," Vivian whispered back, then took another bite of biscuit.

Kate set her fork down and looked at them. "There's something I need to tell y'all, and I don't think you're going to like it."

Vivian stopped eating and looked at her. "What is it?"

"I had a dream last night. At first I was scared, especially after hearing the story in the newspaper. But I've been thinking about this while I eat, and along with my other dream, I believe there are two women trying to send me a message." She paused. "I think we should stay."

Wendy's hand slipped and her coffee cup clanked onto the table, spilling coffee on the white cotton tablecloth. "Excuse me?"

"Yes," Kate said as she fidgeted with her bacon. She looked both of them square in the eyes. "I had a very vivid dream last night. I was the woman who was buried alive."

71

17

Kate sat silent, staring at Wendy and Vivian, who hadn't moved since her announcement that they should remain at Turlington Farms because of a dream she'd had the night before. A dream where she was buried alive.

Vivian broke the silence. "Kate, I realize you have a history of helpful dreams, compliments of your sweet, dead relatives, but you're talking about strangers. People you've never met. Not to mention dead people. Ghosts. Spirits. And other spooky shit."

Wendy spoke up. "I'm sure this is happening because of yesterday. I mean, it's not every day you run across human remains."

"Maybe, but let me tell you about the dream and you'll see why." Kate picked at her sausage link and took a small bite. "If we left now, I'd feel like…like…like I'm abandoning them."

Wendy dabbed a coffee splotch with her napkin. "Okay, tell us about your dream."

Kate leaned forward. "I was hiking in the woods when all of a sudden there was a pain in my head. Next thing I knew, I was trapped in a dark hole. The earth was all around me, crushing me. It hurt to open my eyes, burned my lungs, my entire body was being smothered. The weight of the dirt kept getting heavier and heavier."

The door swung open and Tracy walked in with a carafe of orange juice.

Kate continued. "I had dirt in my ears, my nose, my mouth. I tried to move, but it was useless. All I could do was wait until there was no more air, and it was over. I was dead."

Tracy stopped in her tracks. "I'm sorry, I didn't mean to interrupt. I thought you might like some juice."

"I'll have a bit more," Vivian said and pushed her glass toward her.

Tracy reached over and poured, but she overshot the glass, spilling juice on the table. Her hands were shaky. "I'm such a klutz these days, I swear."

Vivian tossed her napkin over the spill. "You'll need to wash the tablecloth anyway. Wendy sloshed her coffee earlier."

"Sorry," Wendy said.

Tracy's three-quarter sleeve inched up and a purplish-green bruise peeked out.

"Ouch, what'd you do?" Vivian asked.

"Who knows?" She tugged her sleeve down to cover it, but there wasn't enough material. "I probably ran into the doorjamb or something. There's no telling."

Vivian nodded but couldn't get the thought out of her mind that maybe Brandon had caused that bruise. Then a really ugly thought popped into her head but was interrupted as the front door opened.

Brandon walked in looking drained and tired. He glanced at Tracy and forced a smile. "Morning, everyone. Mmmmm, sure smells good in here."

"Hi, honey. Can I make you a plate?" Tracy set the orange juice on the table and turned toward the kitchen.

"That sounds good, I'll go wash up."

Vivian wiped her mouth with her napkin and picked up her plate. "I'm all finished."

Tracy stopped in the doorway. "Just leave the dishes. You're our guest."

Kate stood up and stretched. Her belly looked like it had grown during breakfast. Wendy patted it. "Little Plum is plumping up."

Kate drummed her fingers on her bump. "That she is."

"Let's go upstairs and regroup," Wendy said. "I'd feel better if we heard from Lucy."

Vivian opened the door and almost stepped on a piece of paper that lay on the floor in front of the door. *What's this?* Vivian unfolded the paper. "Thanks for the talk. You helped me put the honey in honeymoon. We don't like what's going on around here and think you should leave, too. Take care – M."

"What's that?" Kate asked as she sat in the high-backed chair.

"A note from Mitzie." Vivian smiled to herself, happy she could help with the "honey."

Wendy ran a brush through her long brown hair. "Did they leave?"

Vivian kicked off her shoes and lay down on the bed. "Yes, and she advises we do the same." She looked at Kate. "So you really feel like we should stay? Because I have to tell you, I'm ready to pull up TripAdvisor and find something else. I'm having second thoughts about Brandon. Did you see that bruise on Tracy's arm?"

"I saw it," Wendy said, looking at them through the reflection of the mirror. "He seems like an okay guy, but we have to consider... what if he killed his first two wives? Who was buried on Haystack Mountain?"

Vivian grabbed the newspaper and pointed to p. 4. "Apparently we're not the first people to think Brandon had a hand in what happened to his wives. Here it says that his first wife was a strong swimmer, and she *drowned*. Hello? That doesn't sit right."

"Let me see that," Wendy said and took the paper. "He had her declared dead? That seems harsh." She passed it to Kate.

As Kate skimmed it, she shook her head. "Look, I realize they were just dreams, but I never felt anger toward Brandon. Seems like I would have felt something."

"Who do you feel anger toward?" Vivian said.

Kate looked at her, annoyed. "It's not like that. Trust me, if I knew Brandon murdered Mary Beth and had something to do with Rebecca's disappearance, we'd be out of here already. I don't feel any threat from him toward us, but I feel like the women in my dreams are asking me for help. I can't shake it." She stood up and went into the bathroom.

Vivian heard water running and Kate brushing her teeth.

Wendy grabbed her laptop and sat on the bed next to Vivian. "What do you think?"

Vivian shrugged. "The breakfast rocks and my bed is comfy. He doesn't come across to me as a killer, but still... "

Kate leaned out of the bathroom door and pointed her toothbrush at Vivian. "I remember a certain short Mexican guy saying that about you not too long ago."

Vivian laughed, thinking of Shorty. "And he was right, so maybe we should give Brandon a chance."

"Let's do some Google-ing and see what we can find." Wendy booted up her computer and soon was tapping away at the keys. "After this, I hate to say it, but we've got to take Austin back to the shelter."

"There's a fall festival in town later today," Vivian said. "I read about it in the paper. Maybe we can go when we take him back."

"That sounds fun," Kate said, joining them. "I wish Lucy was here to go with us."

"I found something," Wendy said, pointing to her computer. "It's Mary Beth's obituary on the funeral home website. Says she was 27, a teacher, survived by her husband, Brandon Holt, and several aunts, uncles and cousins."

"Guess she was an only child," Kate said, looking over Wendy's shoulder. "She was really pretty. Kinda cute, you know?"

Vivian scooted over to see the picture. Mary Beth was smiling, at ease, wearing a polo shirt with a school logo. Brown, wavy hair fell below her shoulders, and she had a dimple in her left cheek.

"That was probably her teacher photo," Wendy said.

"Sad," Kate said.

Wendy recalled the Google results and pulled up the next link, an article in the *Lake Placid News* written by Earl Jones, two days after Rebecca disappeared. He reported about Rebecca basically disappearing into thin air. Her purse and house keys were gone, but nothing else was missing or out of place in the house.

The article asked for people with any information to come forward. A picture of Rebecca smiling as she stood at the lake's edge sent a chill down Vivian's spine.

Wendy clicked on more links from the Google search and found articles written in the weeks after the disappearance. Wendy read the interesting parts aloud, but much of it was the same as what they'd already read. She clicked on a link from the *Chicago Tribune* and pulled up Rebecca's obituary.

"Guess that's where she was from," Wendy said. "Says she went missing at the age of 43. Wow, she had a big family. In addition to Brandon, she was survived by her father, two brothers and four sisters, aunts, uncles, etc. She was a graduate of Northern Illinois University. Then there's a whole story about her life, things she was involved with before her first husband died. Then it says she married Brandon and moved to Lake Placid, New York."

"They must not have thought he had something to do with her disappearance, if he's mentioned in the obit," Kate said.

"I guess," Vivian said. "But did they even really know him?"

Wendy closed her laptop. "So what's the verdict? Are we staying or going? I personally think we should leave. It's too much. Something's not right here."

Kate walked to the window and stared out, then turned around. "I really feel like these ladies need my help. They're constantly on my mind. I need to stay."

Vivian looked from Kate to Wendy. "I would die if something happened to Little Plum. Are you sure about this, Kate?"

"Absolutely."

Vivian took a deep breath. "Okay, we're staying."

Wendy put the computer into her laptop bag. "I'm not leaving y'all. I'll just steal a knife from the kitchen and keep it under my pillow. Now let's get out of here. We've got to take Austin back."

Decision made, they dressed for the day in jeans, sweaters, boots, scarves and jackets.

The girls grabbed their phones and purses and headed downstairs. As Vivian opened the screen door she saw Brandon toss a stick across the yard for Austin, who bounded after it. She couldn't help but cringe as thoughts of yesterday flooded her mind. She shook off the willies and the burning desire to wash her hands as she walked to the car. Austin jumped around them in circles.

"Time to take him back to the shelter, huh?" Brandon asked.

"Yeah. This is hard," Wendy said. "I don't want to take him back."

"We have to," Vivian said. "Does someone want to take him home?"

"I would love to, but I can't," Wendy said. "Wish I could. Damn this dog for a day program!"

Brandon scratched Austin on the head and took the stick from his mouth. "See ya later, buddy." He turned around and cracked the stick in half over his knee, then tossed it into a bush and went inside, the door slamming behind him.

That's callous, Vivian thought. *Oh, god. I hope we've made the right decision.*

18

On their way to the animal shelter, Vivian called Lucy three times, and three times she got voice mail. It was tough to say goodbye to Austin, so only Wendy went inside to drop him off. When she returned to the car her eyes were red and watery. No one said anything. Then:

"So where's this famous Lake Placid fall festival?" Kate asked, trying to sound perky.

"I think the paper said it's at the community center," Vivian said, digging in her purse. "I wrote down the address. Aren't you proud of me?"

"Very," Wendy said. "I think I'm rubbing off on you."

Wendy was known to be the planner, prepared and practical. She usually had an array of medications, bandages, defensive devices, and other fun gizmos in her purse.

Vivian plugged the address into her phone and gave directions to the community center. They drove past the festival the first time because they were captivated by a beautiful, vibrant tree with orange leaves. They circled back and parked behind the small, gray metal building.

"Not many cars here," Kate said as she hit the lock button on the rental.

They opened the doors to the fall festival, and it was as if someone yanked the needle off the record. Time stood still. Everyone turned and stared at the girls.

"I get the feeling we're not in Kansas, I mean Texas, anymore," Wendy said under her breath.

"Maybe I'll find the kids a souvenir while we're here," Vivian said, walking up to a booth filled with journals and hand-carved wooden pens. A lady in overalls sat cheerfully awaiting customers. She was makeup free, and her ponytail was pulled tight.

"You're not from around here, are you?" she asked.

"No, we're from Texas," Kate said. "How can you tell?"

"We're a pretty tight-knit community. I've just never seen your face before."

Kate smiled and rubbed her belly. "I smell chocolate."

"There's a hot cocoa booth a few rows over."

"I love your journals," Vivian said, flipping through one.

"Thanks. I make them all by hand, even the paper and the binding."

"Wow. I can't make squat," Vivian said. "I used to be semi-crafty, but not anymore."

"I'm going to find the cocoa booth," Kate announced and turned on her heels.

"Me, too," Wendy said and trailed after her.

Vivian chatted with the woman awhile, then asked, "So how much?" The woman shared her price.

Vivian resorted to her Mexico-learned bargaining techniques. She ended up with four for the price of three, one for herself, Wendy, Kate and the absent Lucy.

The woman was very happy and wrapped the journals in tissue paper, then bound them with string. She gave Vivian a card. "I'm online, have affordable shipping and take PayPal," she proclaimed.

"Thanks, I'll spread the word," Vivian said, then went to find the cocoa booth. She walked past a small stage and heard Wendy and Kate before she saw them. The sound of laughter steered her to the next row.

"You have to try this one," Wendy said to Kate. "It's got a kick, but it's fantastic." Wendy poured Kate a tester into a small paper cup from a push-button thermos.

Kate took a sip. "Wow, that is good."

A handsome older gentleman behind the table spoke up. "That's my cayenne cinnamon mix. It's a best-seller."

"I'll take two bags," Wendy said. "It's delicious and I like things spicy!"

"I think I need a bag as well," Kate said. "And maybe a pack of Rolaids for later."

The man handed Vivian her own cup and told her to enjoy the flavors.

She had a few sips, then pulled her scarf off and stuffed it into her purse. "This is delicious, but it's making me sweat."

The cocoa guy looked at the three girls. "You're a little overdressed for the weather."

Vivian polished off the last swig and pulled off her jacket. "You're right, but I'll take a bag of peppermint chocolate, cayenne cinnamon and milk chocolate. Group gifts for my kids."

At that point, other booth owners began to beckon the girls over. "It's my turn," several of them said as the girls walked around with their goodies.

Vivian noticed a "Pumpkin Drop" poster on the wall with a big orange arrow pointing to a door. "This sounds promising," she said, and she went through it.

The girls emerged at the front of the community center, near the road. The tall, beautiful distracting orange tree was right in front of them.

A short man with glasses and a receding hairline called to them. "Come on over and pick out your pumpkin. The big drop starts in 15 minutes." Behind him, stacks of hay bales lined with pumpkins of all sizes were placed here and there.

"How's it work?" Wendy asked.

"You buy the winning pumpkin right here for entry into the drop." The short man stood proudly, arm outstretched showing off his pumpkins. "Our local firemen will load them in the cherry picker and drop them overboard, one by one. The pumpkin with the best splatter wins. Our distinguished panel of judges includes the fine mayor of Lake Placid Village."

Vivian's attention had been caught at the word 'fireman,' but her competitive streaked took over. "I'm in. Let's pick a pumpkin, y'all."

The girls browsed the hay bales and chose a fairly symmetrical pumpkin a little bigger than a basketball. Kate had a theory that the symmetry would increase the chances of an ultimate splatter. Vivian paid the $8, which included the entry fee, and the pumpkin peddler stuck a round sticker with the number 17 on their pumpkin.

"Thank you for your entry. Just take it over to the picker." He stuck the cash in a box and turned to the next customer.

"You wouldn't happen to have a marker, would you?" Vivian asked.

"Sure." He dug into his apron and produced one.

Vivian used it to write "Getaway Girlz" loud and proud on their pumpkin, then returned the marker. She turned to Kate and Wendy. "Now let's go find the firemen! Maybe Larson will be here."

Wendy picked up their pumpkin, and they walked toward the people gathered near a roped-off area. "This must be the place," she said. She excused herself as she made her way through the crowd to the drop-off spot, Vivian and Kate in her wake.

Two men, one gray-headed with a buzz cut and the other a twenty-something redhead with a rookie look and crooked smile, greeted them.

"Good day," Buzz said. "I see you've picked a fine pumpkin that is about to be smushed to mush."

"Yes, we have," Wendy said and handed it over.

Vivian stepped up. "Is Larson here?"

"Sure is. He's our picker operator," Rookie replied. "He went inside to get something, but he'll be right back."

"Oh yay!" Vivian said.

"You need to get back behind the ropes," Buzz said. "We're going to be heading up soon."

The girls did as instructed and found an open spot to the left of the crowd along the rope.

Vivian clapped, getting excited. "I hope we win!"

"What's the prize?" Kate asked.

"Beats me!" Vivian squealed. "But whatever it is, I want it!"

Larson came around the corner carrying a bottle of water. His T-shirt hugged his chest perfectly and had an image of a potato talking to a packet of French fries. It read, "Oh no! Is that you, bro?"

Vivian laughed out loud and hollered to him. He recognized them and jogged over. "I should have known you'd be here. And by the looks of it, you're making the locals happy."

Vivian held up her purchases. "Doing our part to help the local economy."

"Did you enter the contest?" he asked.

"We sure did," Wendy said. "Our pumpkin says 'Getaway Girlz.' Make sure she gets a big splat!"

A sharp whistle came from the direction of the other two firefighters. Buzz waved Larson over.

"Guess I need to go fire up the cherry picker. I'll pick you up tomorrow on the Turlington Farm's dock at 2. Good luck with your splat!" With that, he jogged over to the bright red picker.

Anticipation rose as the picker began to lift into the air. A lot of folks had their phones ready to take pictures, Kate included. A tall, confident, athletic woman with cocoa-caramel skin and short, natural twists lifted the rope that separated the crowd from the pumpkin-dropping zone. She wore a messenger bag across her chest and snapped pictures of the crowd, then turned her Canon toward the announcer, a balding, pudgy man holding a megaphone. He pulled the trigger and it chirped to life.

"Hello, Lake Placid pumpkin people, and welcome to the sixth annual pumpkin-dropping contest sponsored by your local Chamber of Commerce! We're happy to have you here! Our favorite firemen have loaded up the picker and are prepared to plop some pumpkins! Are you?"

The crowd cheered.

The man introduced the judges, including the mayor, then laid down the rules. "All pumpkins will be dropped from the same height by our fantastic fire department representatives in the sky. Judges will rule on which has the biggest, loudest and best splat."

The crowd cheered again.

The announcer got the thumbs up from Buzz, who was poised against the rail of the cherry picker with a large pumpkin. He squeezed the button on the megaphone and yelled, "Let's get pumpkin dropping!"

19

Pumpkins were splattering left and right as the girls waited for their number to come up. Firemen were poised on the cherry picker platform being manned by Larson, who kept one eye on Vivian and the other on the controls. The firemen, suspended 25 feet in the air, dropped pumpkin after pumpkin, and the Lake Placid crowd roared approval with every annihilation.

About 15 minutes into the festivities, the mayor announced the Getaway Girlz pumpkin. Kate was poised with her phone, taking video of the great pumpkin drop. The crowd counted down — three, two, one, pumpkin overboard!

The semi-symmetrical pumpkin hovered for a moment in the fireman's hands. Three seconds later a flash of orange clunked with a thud onto the pavement. The pumpkin cracked open and the guts spilled out, but there wasn't much splashage. The crowd clapped politely, but everyone knew it wasn't the winner.

"Our pumpkin sucked!" Vivian yelled. "We need our money back!"

"Maybe they have a consolation pumpkin prize," Kate said. "But yeah, that drop was a definite dud."

Larson looked at Vivian and gave her a thumbs down. She nodded but couldn't help but smile to herself. She'd noticed him glancing in her direction. *Suck in your tummy and try to look fantastic! That fireman may need to put out some female flames!*

The next pumpkin went overboard and smack, pieces flew everywhere. People on the front row of the spectator area got chunks thrown their way. Vivian watched as people pulled pumpkin parts off of their pants and shoes.

"Now THAT was a splat!" she yelled.

"Damn straight," Wendy agreed.

Soon after, all the pumpkins had been pummeled and the judges came forward to announce the winner. To no one's surprise, it was the spectator-splashing pumpkin. A skinny kid about 12 years old ran forward to collect his prize. He grinned from ear to ear and threw his arms over his head in victory.

"I saw that kid and his pumpkin," Wendy said. "He carved a small hole in it. I guess he knew the trick."

"Not his first pumpkin drop, I suppose," Vivian said, giving him the stink eye as the reporter took his picture.

Kate pondered this for a moment. "I guess letting air into the pumpkin gives it more explosiveness. Makes sense."

"Come on, I want to go to a few more booths," Wendy said. "I saw Christmas crafts I need to check out, find a gift for my stepmom."

The girls went back inside and toodled around, perusing the items on display. Vivian wandered to a booth filled with paintings and drawings. A thin guy, probably in his late 30s with dark, stubbly hair, sat on a stool sketching in a book. After a minute or two he looked up.

"I see you've been busy shopping," he said with a smirk.

"Hello." Vivian smiled and held up her bags. "Just a few things."

He sat the sketchbook on a table that displayed three paintings on easels. His brilliant blue eyes were piercing and a stark contrast to the dark clothes he wore. Head to toe, from his turtleneck to his Doc Martens, every inch of his outfit was black.

Vivian stopped in front of a charcoal drawing of a dragon. Wings spread and breathing fire, its claws grasping at rocks on a cliff, it looked ready to turn her into ash. "You're the artist?"

"I am." He stood and stuck out his hand. "Mike Grimm."

"Vivian Taylor." She shook his hand and looked at the various pieces. "You're very talented."

He smiled and shrugged. "Thanks."

"My son loves dragons, but he's pretty young and yours might scare him." She smiled. "He's more into 'Pete's Dragon' or 'Dragon Tales' on PBS."

The artist nodded and cracked a sideways grin. "Yeah, these are a little darker than Disney allows. I have more pieces at my studio, some not so scary. How old is your son?"

"Three," Vivian said.

"If you'd like to come by the studio, I'd be happy to have you take a look." He handed her a business card. "My number is on here."

She tucked the card into her purse. "Thanks, I just may do that."

Wendy came up behind her. "The newspaper lady wants to talk to us!"

"What? Why?"

"I didn't ask. Come on!"

Vivian turned to Mike. "Thanks again."

He sat back down on his stool and nodded. "See you around."

Wendy shuffled her toward the stage where Kate stood talking to the lady holding the Canon. As Vivian walked up Kate introduced Nicole Jones, local editor, reporter and photographer for the *Lake Placid News*.

"They worked hard on that newspaper name, huh?" Vivian joked.

Nicole laughed. "I think my grandfather was trying to keep it simple. He helped start the paper years ago." She flipped open a small notebook. "So I hear you came all the way from Texas to smash a pumpkin and support our local economy."

Vivian laughed and looked down at the bags slung around her wrists. "You heard right."

"You didn't win the pumpkin drop, but I think you win for traveling the farthest. I wanted to get a picture, if you don't mind, and your names. I can't promise you print, but you'll at least make the website."

"Cool," Wendy said.

They chatted awhile, told Nicole how they'd heard about the festival, and showed off their purchases. Kate gave her a good rundown of the hot chocolate booth and insisted she visit with her right that instant.

"I need another sample myself," Kate said.

The cocoa man was happy for their return and that Kate brought another potential customer. He doled out the samples and explanations.

Nicole tried a few, and at Kate's urging she bought a bag of cocoa.

"You sure you don't want two?" the cocoa man asked.

"I'm on a reporter's salary, so although I want two, I can't afford it." Nicole handed him the cash and thanked him. She stuffed the purchase in her messenger bag and pulled out her pen and notebook again. Back to business.

She took notes on where the Texans had come from, how long they were in town and what they'd been up to during their visit.

"It's been an adventure already," Kate said, "but it always is."

"Yeah, finding that jawbone really threw us for a loop," Vivian said. "We've had some crazy stuff happen on our vacations, but finding a piece of a dead person, that takes the cake."

Nicole looked up from her notepad in disbelief, unable to speak for a moment. Finally, she shook her head like she was waking up, eyes wide.

"You're THOSE girls?"

20

Nicole Jones, the editor, reporter and photographer from the *Lake Placid News*, stood in shock after hearing that Vivian, Kate and Wendy were the discoverers of the human remains on Haystack Mountain the day before.

"I'm sorry, I'm not used to being taken by surprise like that."

"Neither are we," Vivian said with a laugh. "And that was one heck of a surprise."

"I'm sure." Nicole looked around at the crowd bustling in the booths. "Can I buy you a cup of coffee at the diner down the street?"

"I'm not a coffee consumer," Vivian said, "but ice cream, that's another story."

"I do drink coffee," Wendy said, shifting her purchases from one arm to the other. "And I could use a cup."

"We might need some pie," Kate said.

"It's walking distance," Nicole said.

"Will walk for pie," Kate said and headed toward the exit. "We have fall festivaled long enough."

Nicole pushed open the door and they spilled into the sunlight. The day was perfect, a crisp 65 degrees, the wind rustling the trees and multicolored leaves floating down.

Vivian's phone rang, and she glanced at the display. "It's Antonio! Give me a sec." She stopped on the sidewalk and accepted the call. "How's my favorite police man?" She heard Detective Antonio Robichaux of the New Orleans Police Department smirk on the other end of the line.

"Hi, Vivian, I'm good. How are you?"

"I'm doing fine, in Lake Placid, New York, at the moment enjoying the fall foliage and chilly air. But I do need to talk to you about something."

She told him the news that Jake had gone missing five months ago and also about the phone and other identity Wendy had found. "I'm not sure what, if anything, you can do to help, but I thought I'd call."

"I'm glad you did. What's the phone number to the other cell?"

"We can't get into the phone to figure it out. It has a password and none of us can figure it out."

"Turn the phone on and then hold down the power button again until you can put it into emergency mode. You should be able to call 911 and it will display the number you're calling from."

Vivian repeated the instructions to Wendy, who immediately powered up Jake's secret phone and was able to get the number. Vivian relayed it to Antonio.

"I'll see what I can find out," he said.

They spoke a bit longer, Vivian asking about his sister, Adrienne, and he about life in Fort Worth.

"You really should hop on a flight and visit. I'll keep you busy," Vivian said.

"I'll bet!" He laughed.

Vivian gave him the name of Jake's other identity, and they disconnected soon after. She joined the others, who were next door waiting outside the diner. "He's got the info and he's on it," she told Wendy.

"Thanks," Wendy said, then she looked down, sadness creeping into her eyes.

Vivian hated it.

Nicole opened the door and they all walked in. The diner sported classic colors: A line of chrome stools with red seats invited guests to the black and white checkered tile counter. Black, square tables and chrome chairs sat in the middle of the restaurant. Nicole picked out a booth by the window, and Kate squeezed into the red seat and grabbed the paper menus tucked between the napkin dispenser and the condiments.

"This is fun!" she said, bouncing up and down.

Vivian bopped in to the beat of the Four Seasons' "Sherry." "Wheeee!" She was stuffing her bags onto the ledge of the window when a marimba beat played out of her purse.

"That's Lucy!" she yelled, snatching up her purse and digging. "That's her text sound!" She pulled her phone out and read the message aloud.

Hey, I'm fine. Just needed to get away. Enjoy your vacation and be SAFE. I mean that in every sense of the word, you sexed-up, "opportunistic," stumble into trouble tramp! Love ya!

Vivian responded, saying "it's about time" and asking where she had gone, then she sent a text telling Lucy that the jawbone they found belonged to Brandon's second wife (they thought). Then she put her phone on the bench seat between her and Kate, hoping to hear the marimba sound again soon.

Wendy explained to Nicole how Lucy had been with them at the beginning of the vacation but then took off after the body incident because she couldn't handle another vacation of death and destruction.

"Does this sort of thing happen often?" Nicole asked.

The three girls just looked at one another. Finally, Kate spoke. "Our vacations are always fun, but they tend to get sidetracked."

"Side*swipe*d is more like it," Vivian interjected.

Kate ignored her comment. "It's okay, though, keeps us on our toes."

Nicole nodded but looked uncertain.

The waitress appeared to be in her early 20s and could have stepped out of Mel's Diner off the set of "Alice," with her Pepto-Bismol pink dress, white apron and goofy little hat. She asked if they'd like to order.

"Indeed, I would," Kate said, closing her menu. "I want a piece of lemon chess pie, the pot roast plate with mashed potatoes and green beans. And a big glass of water, please."

"I thought we were just getting coffee and pie," Wendy said.

"We haven't eaten since breakfast. I need linner."

Nicole looked at the menu. "What's linner?"

"Too late for lunch, too early for dinner. I'll probably need a snack later, too."

"I just want a slice of chocolate cake," Vivian said, pointing to a triple-decker doozy that sat on the counter under a glass dome. "And a large glass of milk."

"Coffee for me," Wendy said. "Cream and sugar."

"Same," Nicole said.

"Did you grow up here?" Vivian asked Nicole.

"Actually, I grew up in Philly but spent a lot of time here in the summer visiting my grandparents. I didn't move here until Gramps got sick and asked me to take over the paper."

"Did you study journalism?" Kate asked.

"I went to Penn State and was a reporter for the *Philadelphia Daily News* after college."

Wendy, always prepared, put a napkin in her lap. "It must have been culture shock moving here. Big city to small town."

Nicole smiled. "It was, especially since I'm almost the only person around with an ebony hue."

"Wait, your grandpa was Earl Jones?" Vivian asked.

"The one and only."

"We read an article online this morning he wrote about Rebecca Holt."

"He was all over hear death, Brandon's first wife's, too." Nicole pulled out her notebook and pen. "I still can't believe you're the ones who found the bone in the woods yesterday."

"Technically, a dog found it," Wendy said, and she explained how they'd borrowed Austin for the day.

"That's a cool program," Nicole said. "I'll have to do that sometime." Then she went into reporter mode and asked all sorts of questions surrounding the discovery.

Beverages arrived, and she kept at it, leaning forward and jotting notes. When their food came, she closed her notepad. "I think that's about all I need. In case it's not, can I get your numbers? Where are you staying?"

"Turlington Farms Bed and Breakfast," Kate said, stabbing her pot roast and then taking a big bite.

Nicole made a face.

"Roo yoo not like meat?" Kate mumbled, ignoring her manners and enjoying her bite.

"Oh no, I'm a carnivore." Nicole took a sip of her coffee. "It's Turlington Farms I was surprised by."

"Why's that?" Vivian asked, digging her fork into the large slice of cake. "Anyone want a bite before I annihilate it?"

"Mmmm, mmmm," Kate hummed, indicating she wanted some.

Vivian sliced off a bit and placed it on Wendy's borrowed coffee saucer. "Hope that's enough."

Kate nodded yes and kept on eating.

Vivian looked at Nicole. "So what's the deal with Turlington Farms?"

"I'm not going to beat around the bush here," Nicole said and stirred her coffee. She set her spoon down and looked at the three women. "It's because, despite the notes I've read from my grandfather, I think it's owned by a wife killer."

21

Vivian didn't know if it was what Nicole said or the sugar pumping through her veins, compliments of the diner's giant chocolate cake, that perked her up. "You have notes on the deaths?" she asked, then took a long drink of her cold milk.

"Yes," Nicole replied. "But that's not the part of my sentence I thought you'd notice. Do you know what has happened to the women living at Turlington Farms?"

The waitress walked up and reached to refill Wendy's coffee cup but caught her breath and stopped.

Wendy looked at her and answered Nicole. "We know." Wendy said to the waitress, who was still frozen in place, "I'd like more coffee, please."

Nicole tapped on her notebook with her pen. "Then you know that Brandon had one wife drown who was a good swimmer and another disappear into thin air. He made a pretty penny off of it, and he sure didn't waste any time finding a third."

The waitress scurried away.

Wendy reached for a creamer and peeled the top off. "We've learned a lot about Mary Beth and Rebecca in the last two days." She glanced at Kate.

Kate used her butter-topped roll to lap up some gravy. "I don't think it's him, and I'll tell you why. I have kind of a sixth sense when it comes to people, and he doesn't strike me as a killer. Jerk sometimes and hot tempered, but not a squeeze-the-life-out-of-you, stick-you-in-a-hole-to-die murderer."

"My grandfather wouldn't have agreed with you," Nicole said. "I've read through some of the notes he had on both cases but certainly haven't been through all of them."

"Now might be the time," Vivian said.

"I dug the boxes out yesterday after the bone popped up. Gramps preferred paper to computers so it's all in handwritten notes. Let me tell you, there are files on practically every person in this town. But one box in particular was his heavy-hitters list."

Vivian couldn't help herself. "Can we see it?"

"I don't mind if you want to come by the shop and take a look. I need to run back to the festival and get a few more pictures. How about 7:30?"

"Sounds like a plan," Vivian said, scraping chocolate icing off her plate. "We'll be there."

Nicole threw $4 on the table and stood up. "I hope you know what you're doing staying there."

Kate gave her a thumbs up, then pushed her empty plate back and pulled the saucer with the lemon chess pie toward her. "We're good." Nicole turned and left.

Wendy tapped her fingernails on the tabletop. "That doesn't make me feel good."

Kate waved her off with her fork, then took a bite of cake.

The waitress stopped at their table and placed the check face down. She began to turn, but hesitated. After a beat, she sighed. "I hate to admit I was listening, but I heard what you were saying about that dead lady and her husband. Everyone in town thinks he did it. It's too coincidental. People in Lake Placid don't just up and die like that or disappear. And he's had two of them croak." She turned and sashayed away, then said over her shoulder, "You can pay at the counter."

Vivian finished her milk, wiped off her mustache, grabbed the check and paid with their trust fund account. *Thank you, Thai government. That cake rocked!*

Kate and Wendy scooted out of the booth, and they met Vivian at the door.

"Where to?" Wendy asked. "I've got a caffeine jolt and energy to burn."

"I need a wheelbarrow or something to haul me around," Kate said, leaning on Wendy. "I ate too much."

"There's a cute little shop across the street," Vivian said, adjusting the bags on her arms and adding Kate's to her load. "I need to get the kids something other than cocoa."

You Name It was filled with the usual touristy stuff, but most of the items — coffee mugs, necklaces, T-shirts, hats — could be personalized with a name engraved, embroidered or emblazed.

Vivian picked up a tom-tom and gave it a whack. "This is fun! Lauren would like this."

Kate nodded, then crawled into a yellow and green plastic, pop-up teepee and curled into a ball. "Wake me up when we're ready to leave."

The store had lots of stuffed animals, most wearing T-shirts advertising Lake Placid. Mini-moose, bears, horses, skunks, deer, squirrels, you name it, lined the rows, all in neon shirts.

Vivian wandered around the front of the store where a plump woman behind the register was talking to another woman wearing khaki pants, an olive green hoodie and carrying a canvas bag that had trees on it and said "Go Green." A blonde-haired, chunky baby in a stroller next to her was trying his hardest to grab the display of key chains.

Vivian smiled as she watched him, missing her twins. They'd graduated from the stroller phase, but there were times she wished she could strap 'em down again.

"Maybe this time the cops will get it right and arrest that bastard," the register lady said.

"Surely this will do it." Hoodie had a calming voice.

"Screw this waiting," Register said. "How many people does he have to kill before they put him behind bars?"

Hoodie looked down at her baby and said something, but Vivian couldn't hear.

The women chatted a bit longer before they said goodbye. Register's cheeks were flushed and she fanned herself with a Lake Placid brochure.

Vivian picked out seven moose magnets for her co-workers and took them to the counter. The woman continued to fan herself while she rung Vivian up.

"Bad day?" Vivian asked.

"I'm just frustrated with the lack of justice in this town."

"Who didn't get justice?"

"My poor sweet cousin, that's who. Her husband killed her years ago, and he's still out there, free as a bird, while she's stuck in a grave. Then he went and married that rich bitch right after Mary Beth died. We all thought there was a chance she'd wise up and leave him." She leaned in closer. "But I heard they found her body finally, or at least part of it."

Holy shit! "Yeah, I heard about that," Vivian said.

"Very convenient, if you ask me, since he'd had her declared legally dead a few years ago." The fan was going fast and furious. "I heard they even buried an empty casket. Anyway, I'm sorry to be blabbering on. All this news gets me riled up about Mary Beth."

"I can understand why," Vivian said.

Wendy walked up with two stuffed moose wearing different-colored T-shirts. "What's this I hear about Mary Beth?"

The woman stopped fanning. "She was my cousin."

Wendy plopped the moose down on the counter, their long legs splaying awkwardly. "Oh, we're staying out at Turlington Farms."

The woman's mouth plopped open and she was speechless for a moment, but not for long. Her eyes cut from Vivian to Wendy, and she crossed her arms. "Are you Brandon's little spies?"

22

Vivian was shocked by the question posed by the shopkeeper, Mary Beth's cousin. "Spies? Us?" she said, laughing and pointing to herself and Wendy. "Nah, we're just staying out at the bed and breakfast. Got a great rate online, actually."

The shopkeeper uncrossed her arms and began fanning again. "I'm sorry, I didn't mean to snap at you. This whole mess is making me crazy." Her eyes teared up. "It's just been so long. I feel like Brandon's connections with the police have kept him out of jail, but I know he's guilty."

"What connections?" Wendy asked.

"One of his best friends since high school is a cop. I swear, I think if it weren't for that they would have worked harder to show he killed her."

Wendy repositioned the two moose so they were sitting on their bottoms, front legs crossed. "Why do you think he killed her?"

"I don't know why. I mean, they had been together since high school. It's not like he got a lot out of the estate, other than Turlington Farms. But then when he married that other woman so soon after Mary Beth died, it started to come together. They claimed they met in an online chat room for mourning spouses."

"You don't believe that?" Vivian asked.

"Not for a second. A chat room? Just go to grief counseling at the church or somewhere. Don't troll the internet looking for a new wife."

Vivian thought about that. She could see someone reaching out for support through the internet. Maybe Brandon was too embarrassed to get help in town, or if he felt like people thought he killed her, then maybe he didn't want to go out. On the other hand, going through the internet seemed really impersonal, especially for something so tragic. "How long after Mary Beth died did they get married?"

"I think it was around six months, but she was already in the picture within two. That I know for sure."

That is awfully quick.

"What's that sound?" the shopkeeper asked, looking past Vivian.

91

Vivian turned around. "What sound?" She listened, then she heard it. "I think it's snoring." She walked back to the little tent and saw Kate curled up with a big, fluffy stuffed bear. She was sawing logs like a lumberjack in a contest and looked pretty and peaceful doing it. Vivian turned back to Wendy. "Are you finished shopping?"

"Yes, got the moose for Lizzie."

"How is she?" Vivian asked as they walked to the front.

Wendy's niece, Lizzie, had battled adrenal cancer since she was 6 months old. Her initial prognosis wasn't good, but with Dr. Stanislaw Burzynski's antineoplastons treatment, she was beating the odds by a long shot at 3½ years old.

Wendy beamed. "The last two tumors in her lungs are gone. Only a small bit of scar tissue remains, and Dr. Burzynski is keeping an eye on it. She's cancer free!"

Vivian gave her a hug. "I'm so happy for your family. Amazing."

The shopkeeper got busy ringing up their merchandise and both girls paid for their purchases. Vivian picked up her bag of magnets and walked to the tent to wake up Kate. "Rise and shine, sleepyhead."

Kate snuggled closer to the bear.

Vivian reached down and shook her gently. "Kate, time to go."

Kate opened her eyes. "I'm buying this bear. He's a great pillow."

"That's good because you drooled on him." Vivian helped her get up.

Kate swiped his fur. "So I did." She walked to the counter and paid for her new fuzzy friend.

On their way out, Wendy turned to the shopkeeper. "Sorry about your cousin."

The shopkeeper nodded. "Thanks, enjoy your visit. Feel free to kick Brandon in the balls for me. Twice."

Kate was shocked at that last bit. Vivian hustled her out of the store and explained what all had happened while she snoozed.

"Wow. I'm glad I was asleep."

"It was a little awkward, especially when she asked if Brandon had us spying on her."

Kate nodded. "I imagine it was." She moved her bear bag from her left arm to her right. "What time is it? I'm getting hungry."

Wendy looked at her watch. "Almost 6 o'clock. I could use a beer or a glass of wine. Y'all want to find a restaurant in town and then go to meet Nicole at the paper?"

A steak and seafood place down the street had a nice deck with lake views. Much to Vivian's delight, the restaurant brewed its own beer. The waitress let them sample the varieties and Vivian decided on the blonde ale.

Wendy went for the Hefeweizen while Kate ordered a hot tea.

Vivian looked over the menu. "I should probably have a little something besides chocolate cake for linner." She ordered a grilled shrimp served with a side of rice, veggies and house salad.

Wendy decided on a cup of clam chowder, as did Kate, who added a small salad as well. The air was almost too brisk, but still they enjoyed some down time and the view while they waited for 7:30 to roll around. Vivian walked to the edge of the deck overlooking the lake and called the kids.

Rick answered on the third ring and rounded them up to talk to her. She spoke to Audrey first, asking if she'd enjoyed the zoo field trip the first grade had taken the day before. Audrey told her all about the animals she had seen, and how she ran into a tree because she was looking down at her shoes while she was walking.

"I got a big bump on my head."

"I'm sorry, sweetie. I'll kiss it when I get home, okay?"

"Okay, Mommy. Bye."

Audrey passed the phone to Lauren, who said a policeman had visited her kindergarten class. She was excited because he had given her a police badge sticker.

"I stuck it on my wall at Daddy's house."

"I think that sounds like a great place for it," Vivian responded. "Do you want to be a policewoman when you grow up?"

"No, I want to be on American Idol."

Vivian smiled. "I bet you will be, Lauren. Just you wait." She heard some shuffling of the phone.

"Here're the twins."

Ben and Olivia sang "Twinkle, Twinkle, Little Star" together. Vivian applauded them, then Rick got on the phone and confirmed what day she was returning.

She walked back to the table as the other girls were paying the bill.

"Time to go see Nicole," Kate said. "I'm full and happy."

Back at the fall festival, vendors were loading up, firemen were spraying off the pumpkin remnants, and visitors were leaving. The girls hopped into the rental and followed Google directions to the newspaper office.

Only two cars were parked in the lot. The front door was locked, so Vivian knocked.

Nicole appeared in the front window, waved and unbolted the door. "Welcome to my home away from home."

They went in and Nicole closed the door behind them. She took them on a quick tour, showing them the two printing presses in the back. Tables covered in newspapers lined the wall; paper, ink and other supplies filled the shelves.

"Is that the paper?" Wendy asked, pointing to two huge rolls that lay against the front wall.

"Yep. Newsprint."

"That's practically as big as my car," Kate said.

"It's like a giant roll of calculator tape, but a million times bigger!" Vivian said. "I have a sudden urge to jump on top and ride it like those lumberjacks ride a log."

"I can't tell you what I thought you were about to say," Wendy said, relief in her voice.

"Uhm, yeah. Don't," Nicole said and shot an "I mean business" look around the room.

"Okay, okay," Vivian said, but she really wanted to.

"Our print circulation is 3,000 and the weekly edition comes out tomorrow. I update the website every day. In fact, I'm doing that now."

They walked out of the printing area, through a hallway and another door and into the office space. Nicole pointed to three white boxes sitting on a wooden desk. "Those are my grandpa's files. The one to the left, from what I can tell, were his main suspects. Brandon's file is the thickest."

Vivian wasted no time. "Let's take a look."

23

Nicole went back to her desk to finish updating the *Lake Placid News* website, while Vivian, Wendy and Kate tackled the files. Wendy opened the primary suspects box and pulled out a few folders. A cloud of dust followed, and Kate sniffled and coughed. The newspaper offices were quiet with the exception of buzzing coming from an overhead light.

The file on Brandon was at least three inches thick and filled with newspaper clippings and handwritten notes. Vivian tried to read one of the notes but handed it off to Wendy. She worked to decipher it since she had the worst handwriting of them all, therefore making her a good candidate for reading bad handwriting.

"Grandpa wrote down a timeline of events, going all the way back to when Brandon and Mary Beth were dating in high school," Wendy said, holding it up. "Brandon and Mary Beth started dating their junior year. They got married at age 24, and she died after their third anniversary, so she was 27. He received $100,000 in life insurance, plus a bit more from the school district, since she was a teacher."

"Well if he did it, it probably wasn't for the money," Kate said. "Because that much won't go too far."

Wendy continued reading. "Six months after Mary Beth died he married Rebecca. He was 28, she was 42."

"Got himself a sugar mama," Vivian said, and she started singing "Money, money, money," *For the Love of Money*, by the O'Jays.

"He does mention in here that they met on the internet," Wendy said. "Rebecca went missing when she was 43, they hadn't even been married a year. Grandpa made a note that the time to declare her legally dead started on that day and ended three years later.

"Brandon started seeing Tracy a year and a half after she disappeared. He worked at the hardware store and frequented The Rumor Mill Restaurant and Bar when he got off, which is where Tracy worked. The three years passed, he got a chunk of change from Rebecca's estate and life insurance, and he and Tracy got married. Apparently the wedding was a big to-do at the country club."

Wendy held up a picture of the wedding party. A sticky note on it read #3. Tracy's white gown was sparkly and puffy, and she stood with seven smiling bridesmaids. Brandon's smile seemed forced, and there was only one guy by his side.

"Is that the cop?" Kate asked.

Wendy squinted at the picture. "Kinda looks like him, hard to tell, but that's the last thing on the timeline." She lowered her voice. "Guess Grandpa passed away."

"Or the case went cold," Vivian said.

They flipped through the pages quickly, looking at the pictures, highlights and headlines Grandpa had accumulated over the years.

Kate closed that file and began looking at the names on the others. "I think Grandpa believed Brandon was the killer, but he couldn't prove it." She picked up the file on wife number two, Rebecca, which was very thin.

"Guess she wasn't around long enough to warrant a thicker folder," Vivian said.

Vivian was able to make out Grandpa's scrawl and read the notes explaining that Rebecca had received a large sum when her first husband died. He was the CFO of a Fortune 500 company in New York and died from brain cancer.

Kate shifted in the office chair. "My back hurts."

"You've been on your feet a lot today. Are you ready to go?"

"Yeah, I think I am."

Nicole popped out from around the corner. "Did you solve the mystery of the dead wives?"

"Not yet," Wendy said, "but we're working on it."

"I'm going to take these home with me tonight," Nicole said, putting the files back into the box. "Maybe something will jump out at me."

Kate stood and stretched.

"Want help carrying them out?" Wendy offered.

"You mind?"

"Not at all."

Wendy and Vivian each grabbed a box and followed Nicole to her Corolla. She popped the trunk and they put the boxes inside. "I've got to go back in and lock up. Thanks for the help."

"Let us know if you find anything intriguing," Vivian said.

"Will do. Good night," Nicole said and went inside the shop.

They got into the rental and Kate pointed the car toward Turlington Farms. "We're such wusses these days, going back to our room at 9:00. I feel like I'm bringing y'all down since I'm pregnant."

"Nonsense," Vivian said. "I'd rather go back, layer up and sit outside by the fire. Maybe make some s'mores. It's not like Lake Placid is booming with nightlife anyway."

"There are bars in town we can go to," Kate said.

"Nah, we're good," Wendy said. "I want to call Jake's parents and see if there are any updates."

They turned into the driveway at the bed and breakfast. The headlights crossed the front porch where Tracy was sitting alone in a rocking chair. She stood and went inside before they were out of the car.

"I'm going to take a hot shower and put on my jammies," Kate said.

They got out of the car and walked up the steps. Wendy sat down on a rocker and pulled out her phone. "Guess I'll make my call."

"You want anything?" Vivian asked Wendy. "Glass of vino perhaps?"

"Sure."

The light from the phone cast a glow on Wendy's sullen face, and Vivian could see tears welling in her eyes.

Vivian went inside, leaving Wendy on the front porch to make her call. Vivian wandered into the kitchen hoping to find a nice pinot noir. Instead, she found Tracy standing in front of the stove, staring into space. "Hey there, long day?"

Tracy turned around slowly, her face grim. "Yeah, sorry. I'm tired. Can I get you something?"

"I was hoping to spy some wine and a couple of glasses."

"Sure. I think I have some Merlot in here. Will that do?" She began shuffling around, opening cabinets.

"That'll do just fine, thanks."

"Where is Kate? Does she need anything?"

"Nah, she went upstairs to take a bath. Wendy's on the porch calling her..." *what do I call them?* "... her fiancé's parents."

"Oh, that's nice. Both Brandon's parents are dead."

Vivian didn't know what to say to that.

Tracy sifted through several bottles of wine and turned around with one labeled Goosewatch. "This is my favorite local winery. Let me open it up." She grabbed a flat waiter corkscrew and had the bottle open in 20 seconds. She poured three glasses. "Think I'll have one, too."

"I wouldn't feel right if you didn't!" Vivian said, taking two of the glasses. "You can join us on the porch if you like."

"I may in a few minutes."

Vivian had a sip and walked to the front porch. As she stepped out she heard Wendy wrapping up the call.

"I will, thanks. And please, please, let me know if you hear anything at all. I miss him so much."

Vivian handed her the wine and sat in the next rocker.

"Love y'all, too." Wendy's voice cracked a little. "Take care, 'bye." She put the phone on the small wooden table next to the rocker and dropped her head, trying to hide the tears.

"I'm guessing there's been no Jake news," Vivian said.

Wendy sniffled. "None at all. I feel like I'm in a nightmare."

"I wish I knew what to say. But I tell you this, if you want us to go with you to Vegas, we will. I don't know what we'll find, but you know we're willing to try to help in any way."

Wendy pulled a tissue out of her pocket. "Thanks, Viv, that means a lot. And who knows, maybe we should go. I was such a mess the first time I was out there, I barely knew my own name. If I went back, maybe I'd think of something I hadn't thought of before, or ask better questions of the cops assigned to the case. I'd like to go to the convenience store where they have video of him getting gas, stay at the hotel he had been in, stuff like that. I may be grasping at straws, but at this point, what else can I do?"

Vivian didn't answer because her cell started ringing. "Perfect timing."

24

Vivian looked at her ringing phone and then back to Wendy. "It's Antonio in New Orleans. You ready to see what he's got?" Wendy nodded so Vivian answered. "Hey, Antonio. I'm with Wendy, do you mind if I put you on speaker?"

"I don't mind as long as it's just you two."

She hit the speaker button. "Okay, you're on. What'd you find?"

"The cellphone is a burner. Not a surprise there, but I wasn't able to tell where it was purchased. I have someone with higher clearance working on that." Antonio cleared his throat. "As for the passport, I was able to pull up some information, but it's not what I was expecting."

"But you found something?" Wendy said, hope ringing through in her voice.

Vivian could feel tension on the other end of the line and scooted her rocker closer to Wendy.

Antonio cleared his throat. "Yes, but I saw some red flags, things that don't sit well."

"What do you mean?" Vivian asked. She put her hand on Wendy's arm.

The phone crackled as if it was being moved around but Antonio was silent.

"Hello?" Vivian said, looking down at the phone to make sure they were still connected.

"Is anyone around you right now?" Antonio asked in a hushed voice.

Tracy was nowhere to be found. It was just her and Wendy on the porch. "We're alone."

Antonio's words reverberated on the porch.

"I think you need to call the FBI."

"Excuse me?" She and Wendy quit rocking as his words settled over them. "Did you say Jake is in the FBI?"

"That is NOT what I said. I said you need to contact them. There were several things I found that feel off. Paul Vaughn has a bio with a long arrest record, some of which make me suspicious." Antonio sighed. "It has a

99

federal feel to it. Not just anybody can get a fake bio into the system."

"What's that mean?" Wendy asked.

"In my experience it means this is bigger than local. It kind of makes sense if you look at the South America connection."

"Wait. Wait," Wendy said, shaking her head. "Jake is a salesman. He's got nothing to do with South America. This has to be a mistake. The stamps in the passport have to be fake."

"I've got some connections in the FBI," Antonio said. "I'm reaching out."

Vivian spoke her thoughts out loud. "Look at the facts, Wendy. He had a passport with another name, money from another country. Maybe this is a good thing. Maybe he's like James Bond or something."

Antonio couldn't let that one go. "First, James Bond is fictional. Second, he's from England. Third, I didn't say Jake *worked* for the FBI."

"And fourth," Wendy stood and tilted her head back, frustrated, "fourth, James Bond was never engaged and never went missing for six months." She turned and started down the steps. "I'm going for a walk."

"Wait," Vivian said, getting up. "Antonio, thanks for the info, I'll call you back." She hit "end" on the phone and followed after Wendy. "Wendy, stop."

Wendy kept walking around the house and straight toward the lake.

Vivian hustled to catch up to her, but she was moving fast. About 10 steps from the water Vivian grabbed the back of Wendy's shirt. "Buddy system, remember."

Wendy melted to her knees, sobbing.

Vivian knelt down beside her, stroking her long, chestnut brown hair. She just kept repeating, "It's going to be okay, it's going to be okay," and waited until Wendy had gotten a lot of frustration and sadness out through her tears.

After a few minutes, Wendy pulled a fresh tissue out of her pocket and dabbed her face.

"You okay?" Vivian asked.

"I don't know what I am." Wendy's arms hung listlessly at her side.

"We are going to get to the bottom of this," Vivian said. "One way or another, I know we will."

"You say that, but I'm not so sure. He's been gone for 202 days, Vivian. Two hundred and two days!"

"I know, but they haven't found anything to suggest he's dead. The dental records didn't prove anything. That's something. And now we learn that there's a connection with the feds. That's something, too. More than we've had."

Wendy nodded.

"Maybe he's on a secret mission somewhere and isn't allowed to call you, like he's deep undercover and contacting you could be dangerous."

"Yeah, or maybe he's dead," Wendy said, and she started crying again. "Maybe he's *dead*, Vivian! No one seems to know anything! We keep getting the runaround from the Las Vegas PD. There's been no mention of the FBI until just now. I thought at least I would get closure with the dental records, but no! And then finding that stuff in his apartment freaked me out.

"I'm angry, I'm sad. I feel betrayed. I hate this! I hate this!" She banged her fists into the soft earth. "It's bullshit! I hate it!"

Wendy was usually so composed, so large and in charge. It killed Vivian to see her in such pain. Vivian had known pain in relationships, and thinking about how she'd found her husband in the swimming pool with another woman fired her up. She stood in front of her friend, hands on her hips, in her mom/Wonder Woman pose.

"You listen here, Wendy Schreiber. We are going to find Jake. There is an answer, and I promise you, we will find it. We are Texas girls, and by god, we grab the bull by the horns and wrangle the hell out of him until it's over. I can tell you this, this bull and his shit are going down."

Wendy looked at her, sniffled once more, then started laughing. An uncontrollable, fall on her side, roll in the dirt laugh.

Vivian didn't know what to make of it but was glad to see something other than what she had been witnessing.

Wendy laughed so hard she could barely breathe. Eventually she threw her arms and legs out, spread-eagle, taking a deep breath and staring up at the stars.

Vivian leaned over her head. "Feeling better?"

"Oh my gosh, Vivian, I feel sorry for your kids. They aren't going to get away with anything, are they?"

Vivian smiled at her friend and offered her a hand up off the ground. "Nope. My nickname's not Mean Mama for nothing."

Wendy took her hand and stood. "Wow. I think I've been holding in some of my emotions."

"Hell yeah, you have. But I understand. What you've been going through is unreal. And now to hear this news from Antonio, I mean, it's like a movie or something."

"Yeah." Wendy started walking toward the house. "Thanks for my kick in the pants."

Vivian saw a shadow walk out of the house and sit in a chair. "Pfffft, nonsense. That was no kick. That was just a nudge. You don't want to see my kick." She did an awkward roundhouse move that more resembled a dog shaking water off its foot.

Wendy laughed out loud. "I hope you never have to use that on anyone. Then again, they might laugh so hard you get away."

Vivian gave her a butt bump. "I'm not stretched out. It's usually better."

"Uh huh."

They were halfway back to the house when Vivian decided to go ahead and mention one more thing. "Did you hear Antonio offer help with his contacts at the FBI?"

"Yeah, I did," Wendy said. "We should definitely ask him to do that."

Vivian grabbed her arm and stopped. "I don't think so."

"What? Why not?"

Vivian looked at her with a sly smile. "We have a secret weapon. A really sexy secret weapon."

25

Vivian looked around, like she was making sure they weren't about to get into trouble. "We're going to call your former flame from Colorado. Our most favorite, sexiest man alive, hell-yeah-he's-a-hottie FBI guy — Agent Wade Nelson."

Wendy shook her head. "I don't know, Vivian. Not only will calling Wade be awkward, but he's in Colorado. A long way from Vegas and certainly a long way from this case."

"I know it's the right thing to do," Vivian said. "He would help you with anything. He's probably our best bet, if, in fact this has an FBI connection."

Wendy took a deep breath. "I'm not going to win this argument, am I?"

"Nope."

CRASH! They both jumped.

"I'm so sorry," Tracy said, hopping up from the rocker. "I dropped my wine glass. I swear, I need to only use plastic ware."

"I hope it was empty!" Vivian said, rushing up the steps. "Want me to grab a broom?" Just then the front porch light popped on and Brandon stood in the doorway.

"Sounds like things are getting rowdy out here."

"Can you grab the broom, honey?" Tracy called to him. "Watch the glass," she said to Vivian and Wendy, who walked over and sat in rockers.

Brandon turned and disappeared but soon emerged with a broom and dustpan. "Hope it wasn't the good crystal."

Tracy snorted. "Like I ever drink out of that."

He cleaned up the glass and then turned to Tracy, a frown on his face. "You coming up soon?"

"In a few minutes."

He turned and went inside, letting the screen door bang behind him.

"Would you like a refill?" Tracy asked. She had brought Vivian's empty glass and Wendy's partially drunk glass to the back porch.

Vivian picked up her glass. "I thought you'd never ask."

"I'll be right back."

Wendy polished off her glass just as Tracy came back to fill it up. "Just in time."

"What's the matter?"

"I'll be better after this," Wendy said and took a long sip. "Thanks."

Tracy poured Vivian a generous glass, then filled up a rocks glass she had brought for herself. "Only wine glasses I had left were the expensive ones, and I didn't want to risk it."

"At least you own expensive glasses." Vivian laughed. "Mine are from the dollar store!"

"Nothing wrong with that," Tracy said as she took a big drink. "I love the dollar store."

"To the dollar store!" Vivian said and held up her glass.

"Hell yeah," Tracy said and clanked her glass hard against Vivian's. "Oops, sorry. Good thing that glass isn't from the dollar store."

They laughed at that and chatted about their day, and the missing Lucy.

"I still can't believe she left," Vivian said. "It's so unlike her."

"Sometimes people leave," Tracy said. "Look at Brandon's wife, Rebecca. We all thought she left him, but it turns out, maybe not."

Wendy glanced at Vivian, then asked Tracy, "Did they identify the body already?"

"Yeah. Well, at least they think they did. Brandon had to go to the police station today because they found a ring. They showed Brandon a picture of the inscription. It was hers."

"Oh no, I'm sorry," Vivian said. "How terrible for him. And you."

"I didn't know her. And they had only been married about a year, but still. He's sad."

"Yeah," Wendy said. "I'm sure."

"It's nothing like his first wife, though. He was even sadder about her." Tracy took another long drink and sloshed a little on her jeans. "Mary Beth did no wrong in his eyes. They were high school sweethearts, you know. Personally, I think she cheated on him while they were married."

"Really?" Vivian asked. "With whom?"

"I don't have any proof, but I heard it was with a student. Some kid who played football. I can't even remember his name."

The screen door burst open, startling all three women. Brandon stepped out. "I think it's time to go to bed."

Vivian looked at Wendy, who looked back at her.

Tracy stood up slowly. "Okay, I'm beat."

Oh my god, maybe she's trying to tell us she's abused?

"Good night," Tracy said, walking past Brandon, who held the door.

"Good night," Vivian and Wendy said in unison. They looked at each other, eyes wide, and said nothing for a while, waiting for Tracy and Brandon to get out of earshot.

"Holy crap, what do you make of that?" Wendy whispered.

"Do you think he heard us?"

There was a bang from inside, like something heavy fell or a door slammed. Raised voices came from the house.

"He must have," Wendy said.

"I wonder if Kate's asleep," Vivian said.

"If she is, she may not be for long."

The yelling continued for a few minutes. Wendy and Vivian sat on the porch, not saying a word. An engine started and tires squealed, then a vehicle raced down the driveway.

"Somebody's in a hurry," Wendy said and stood.

"Probably a good idea," Vivian said, then she stood and tossed the remainder of her wine over the porch railing. "Let's go to bed."

They crept upstairs and found Kate snoring away.

"Guess they didn't bother Sleeping Beauty over there," Wendy giggled.

"I feel kinda bad," Vivian said, "like it's our fault Tracy and Brandon are fighting."

Wendy contemplated that. "He's under a lot of stress, I'm sure. Maybe it just touched a nerve that short-circuited, then went haywire."

Vivian shrugged and started to walk into the bathroom.

"Let me hop in here real quick," Wendy said. She emerged five minutes later in hot pink pajamas and wearing her glasses. "Goodnight."

"Night." Vivian went and brushed her teeth. Her tongue was a deep shade of purple from the wine. She ran hot water on her washcloth, squeezed it out, then lay it on her face to steam. She repeated the process two more times, then gave her face a good examination in the mirror.

A tiny little wrinkle marred the right side of her nose. *I've got to start sleeping on my back.* She was convinced it had developed because she slept on that side of her face most of the time. *I know that's it,* she thought and ran water in the tub. She soaked for 20 minutes, then got out and dried off. She considered pajamas but then decided against it since Lucy wasn't there. She crawled into bed naked, scooted to the middle and spread out.

She lay there for a while, thinking about the day. The alarm of Lucy being gone, the fall festival and seeing Larson, meeting Nicole, the print shop, Tracy and Brandon fighting. She went back to thoughts of Larson and how sexy he looked at the pumpkin drop. He was right up her alley. *I bet he knows the intricacies of putting out all sorts of fires.* Her hand slid down to her waist and lingered on her tummy. *I've got a bit of a fire going on.*

Lights passed through the bedroom and an engine sounded below the window. Vivian got up and peeked through the lace curtains.

To her surprise, Tracy stepped out of a Honda Accord and headed toward the house.

A cold breeze passed through the room, the chill causing Vivian to jump back into bed. She laid there, covers pulled to her eyes, listening to every step Tracy took, from the back door to the bedroom. Low murmurs passed through the walls, and soon after, the rhythmic thump of hard sex.

Vivian snickered as she rolled over and settled into her pillow. After a good half hour of listening to pants and moans, she grabbed Lucy's empty pillow and shoved it over her head.

Enough of the makeup sex already!

26

Day 4

The squawk of perky birds once again woke Vivian and she rolled over, pulling the covers over her head. She glanced at the clock, 8:12 a.m. She could just hear Lucy yammering at her to get up and get moving. She rolled over again and grabbed Lucy's vacated pillow and stuffed it between her knees. *Ahhh, that's better.*

The pillow helped align her back, which hadn't been the same since the twins. *Lucy's not here so I can steal her pillow. Damn... Lucy's not here.* The revelation propelled Vivian out of bed. She threw on pajamas, then shuffled into Kate and Wendy's room and started clapping her hands.

"Up and at 'em! Time to rise and shine!"

Kate threw off her covers and padded to the bathroom. "Mornin'! I'm already awake and hungry. I'll be ready for breakfast in 20."

Wendy pulled her eye mask down further and snuggled into her covers. "What's the rush? What are we doing today?"

Vivian leapt onto the bed and started jumping up and down. "In honor of Lucy, we should grab a quick, semi-healthy breakfast and then go carry rocks around or something, get some exercise."

"If Lucy wanted us to do that, she shouldn't have left us," Wendy said and made no move to get up.

Vivian hit her with Kate's pillow. "Wendy, get up!" Pow! She smacked her again. "You need to call sexy-beast Wade first thing."

Wendy threw off her eye mask, snatched her pillow and hit Vivian. "You sure we should call Agent Nelson and not Antonio's FBI contact?"

Vivian was tempted to smack Wendy again with the pillow, but grabbed Wendy's phone off the nightstand and handed it to her instead. "I saw the way Wade looked at you. He really cared about you. Antonio may have some pull, but Wade would be willing to help you more than some random FBI agent that's super busy."

Wendy sat up and cleared her throat before dialing. She put the phone on speaker when Wade answered. Vivian could picture his broad shoulders, green eyes and dark brown hair.

"Nelson."

"Hey Wade, it's Wendy Schreiber."

He paused. "Good to hear from you. How've you been?"

They chatted for a minute before Wendy got to the purpose of the call. Wade already knew she and Jake were engaged and now she filled him in on Jake's disappearance, the other cellphone, fake name and the bio behind it.

"I asked a cop friend of mine in New Orleans to look into this yesterday and he suggested I contact the FBI for help. I don't want to get you into any trouble, but could you look into any of this for me? Something is really wrong and I'm sick to death with worry. Jake is not the kind of man to just up and disappear, leave his family," she paused, "or me."

"There are a few avenues I can look into. I'll call you back as soon as I know something."

"Thank you, Wade."

"Of course, anything for you." Click.

Wendy set the phone on the nightstand and swung her feet off the bed but didn't get up. She gazed at the ground, then looked up at Vivian with misty eyes. "What if he can't find anything?"

"He will. I just know it. Now let's get ready to kick butt today." Vivian opened Wendy's drawer and threw a bra at her.

Wendy caught it with one hand and smacked Vivian with a pillow in the other. Wendy ran into the bathroom before Vivian could really get the pillow fight going. Wendy's feistiness was good, but Vivian wanted the last smack.

The girls got ready and went down for breakfast. Brandon greeted them in the dining room wearing an apron with flames on it that read "Hot! Hot! Hot!"

"Good morning," he said, spatula in hand. "We're serving up waffles with locally bottled maple syrup, sausage and bacon. Be ready shortly." He set down the butter dish and went back into the kitchen.

Wendy made herself and Kate a cup of coffee while Vivian dunked a tea bag in hot water. They sat down at the table and looked out the window at the lake.

"Y'all up for a walk after breakfast?" Vivian asked. "Maybe not up to Lucy standards, but still get us moving?"

Wendy nodded but Kate said, "I didn't sleep so good. I might want to take a nap after I eat."

"But we just got up!" Vivian noticed dark circles under Kate's eyes. "Why didn't you sleep?"

"I had a visit from my grandmother last night. She gave me a cryptic message."

"Oh, lord," Wendy said. "Two strange death dreams and now a visit from a dead relative. There's something's strange about this house."

Tracy walked in carrying a big plate stacked with waffles. "Hi, there. Who's hungry?"

Vivian hoped Tracy hadn't heard that. "I'm starting to think we're the strange ones, especially Kate with those dreams!"

"This dream didn't make any sense, so I don't know why it kept me up, but it did." Kate stabbed a waffle and put it on her plate before continuing, "I wrote it down." She pulled out an old receipt from her pocket. " 'Water and dirt make mud, but flames singe the heart. The book holds the key to the senior moment.' See. Complete nonsense."

Vivian politely waved off the waffles and spooned fruit onto her plate. Tracy fumbled the plate as she tried to put it down in the middle of the table. Vivian grabbed it and as she did noticed that Tracy's two middle fingers on her left hand were taped together. "Did you jam your fingers?"

"I tripped in the kitchen early this morning and bent them backward. Don't think they're broken. I've done that before and it sure hurts." She scurried toward the kitchen.

Vivian leaned across the table toward Kate and Wendy. "I wonder if that's true."

"She and Brandon don't seem to have the best relationship," Kate said. "Do you think he pushed her and she fell?"

"They sure did let each other have it last night," Wendy said, "but then there was the *boom-chica-bao-bao* going on."

Vivian snickered. "I heard that, too." She opened a yogurt and dropped three grapes into it. "That would be some pretty rough lovin'. Maybe it was an accident."

"I'd accidentally break a few of his fingers, and his face, if he did that to me," Kate said.

"Back to your dream, Kate," Vivian said. "What was it exactly? Let me see that note."

Kate repeated the message and handed over the receipt. "Best I can figure, she's talking about Brandon's first wife's drowning with the water and his second wife being buried with the dirt, but I don't understand the rest of the message at all."

"I agree with you," Wendy said. "What flames have we seen on this trip?" She took a sip of her coffee as Brandon walked into the room. Wendy spewed coffee everywhere, then coughed.

Brandon grabbed a couple of napkins and handed them to her. "You okay?" He patted her on the back.

She coughed a few more times and gave a thumbs up.

"We haven't had a guest croak on us yet. I'd rather you not be the first."

Vivian's eyes got big and she mouthed 'Oh my god' to Kate as Brandon set down a plate of bacon and sausage.

"How is everything?"

The girls all nodded their approval, no one able to say anything.

Vivian waited for him to return to the kitchen before busting out laughing. "There were some flames!"

Kate picked up a piece of bacon. "I actually like that apron."

Wendy blotted the coffee off her waffle. "He's awfully cheery for a guy who just received confirmation that his wife is dead."

"Maybe it's a relief to finally know for sure," Kate said. "I mean, he's been living in limbo for years."

"Unless he knew all along," Wendy countered. "It's not too late to check out, you know."

Brandon walked back into the room with a pitcher of milk. "I always like milk with my pancakes. Any takers?"

Vivian nodded yes.

Brandon poured Vivian a small glass of milk and set the pitcher beside her and walked out.

"Holy shit, he almost walked in at the wrong time," Vivian said. "Think he heard us talking?"

"He didn't act like it," Kate said. "Tracy's the one with broken fingers and bruises."

"If we're staying, we need to search this house," Wendy said. "Something strange is going on here. Two dead wives and a bruised and broken third? It ain't right."

Kate looked at her. "Do you think…?"

Wendy shrugged. "I don't know what to think. Brandon seems nice enough to us, but he was an ass to Tracy last night, and then what's with the other two wives?"

Vivian talked around her final bites of yogurt. "I can see an accident, like a drowning, happening, but the missing wife turning up dead and buried, that is beyond weird. We can't put Little Plum into jeopardy."

Kate shoveled another piece of sausage onto her plate. "Like I said, if I felt like we were in danger we'd be out of here. Something's strange, but I don't think we need to leave." She sniffed the air. "Y'all smell that?"

Vivian sniffed a couple of times. "All I smell is delicious maple syrup. This fruit's not cutting it."

Wendy pushed her plate away, alarmed. "It's smoke. Something's on fire!"

27

Vivian got up from the dining room table and looked outside. "No need to freak out, the fire's outside." She sat back down and polished off her milk. "I wish I could do that at my house. Instead I fill up a hundred bags. Seriously."

Eighty yards from the house, a big pile of leaves was smoking and flames licked up one side. Brandon walked out from behind the pile squirting lighter fluid on the leaves.

"Geez," Kate said, standing next to the window. "For a second, I was afraid the house was on fire. Old wiring, you know?"

Tracy bustled through the kitchen door again and picked up the breakfast dishes. "I'll be heading into town for a while this morning. Can I get you anything before I go? Brandon will be busy burning leaves and branches around the property."

The girls looked at each other, and no one said anything. Finally, Wendy answered, "We're good, thanks."

Tracy struggled to pick up their three plates plus the waffle platter and coffee cups, so Vivian pitched in and helped her to the kitchen with the dishes.

"Y'all usually burn leaves here?" she asked. "We just have to rake them into bags and they get picked up."

Tracy set the dishes on the counter. "They pile up this time of year, and if we don't keep up with them, they'd just about bury the house. No leaf-pick-up service around here. We just have to burn them. Safely, of course."

"That smell makes me crave s'mores."

"What are you girls going to do today?"

"Larson is taking us out on the lake later this afternoon in his boat. We're going on a walk around here for now, get some exercise."

"The smoke from the leaves can be pretty thick with all the piles we've got, but I have a couple of ATVs you can ride."

"Kate probably shouldn't ride those, being pregnant and all. We'll figure out something. Thanks, though." Vivian left the kitchen and joined Kate and Wendy upstairs.

Kate lay on the bed and Wendy had her laptop open, clicking away. Vivian walked to the closet and opened the door. "I know just the place to start the house search." She knelt down and tugged on the crawl space door. "I didn't see this until yesterday after Lucy took her suitcase." It didn't open easily, and Vivian fell back on her butt when it finally gave.

"What are you doing?" Kate walked up behind her and peered into the closet. "Oh."

Vivian looked through the door at a couple of boxes, some cobwebs and darkness. "I'm not crawling in there." She took a sniff. "Musty and full of spiders. No way."

"Me, neither." Kate smiled and rubbed her belly.

Wendy moved around Kate and stood behind Vivian. "Good find, Viv! Nobody has to go in there, I can reach the boxes. Let's snoop."

Wendy reached for the top of the two boxes and pulled it toward her. It moved easily but kicked up dust, making her sneeze. She got it through the door and set it on the empty luggage rack next to the closet. Then she grabbed the other.

Kate locked the door to both rooms. "I know Tracy's gone and Brandon's burning leaves, but just in case!"

Vivian coughed as she opened the flaps to the top box, then brushed off her hands before reaching in and picking up an old framed picture of a little girl riding a tricycle. Several more pictures of the same girl progressively aging were in the box, along with a porcelain-faced, blonde-haired baby doll. "I'm not picking her up."

"This old thing?" Kate asked, grabbing the doll. The eyes rolled back in the head, and Vivian yanked the doll out of Kate's hands and tossed it back into the box.

"Don't touch her. She's evil looking. You don't want to bring bad things to you and Little Plum!"

Kate laughed and reached for the doll again.

Vivian slapped at her hand. "I'm serious. She's creepy. Leave her alone."

Wendy picked up a picture of a girl skiing on a lake and took the cover off the back. "Says 'Mary Beth, age 14.' Looks like she knew what she was doing."

Kate reached in the box for a white, satin photo album trimmed in lace. A big puffy heart on the front read "Our Wedding Day." She opened the album and looked at several of the pictures, then turned it to show Vivian and Wendy. "Look at this."

Brandon and Mary Beth stood frozen in time, hand in hand, wearing tux and gown at a church altar. Her face was draped in a veil, and she carried a colorful bouquet of flowers. A brass candelabra with 12-inch tapers glowed behind them.

"Brandon looks so young," Wendy said. "Almost like a teenager."

"They both do," Kate said.

The girls flipped through the entire album.

"How long ago do you think this was?" Vivian asked.

Kate turned to the back where an invitation had been carefully laminated, surrounded by dried flowers. "Fourteen years ago."

"Wow, three wives and he's not even 40!" Vivian closed the album, and a plume of dust shot into her face.

Wendy coughed. "Yeah, and two of them are dead."

Kate set the invitation in the box, then closed up the remnants of Mary Beth's life. "I think it's sweet that he kept these, but I guess it's hard to just throw away your past loves and your wedding photos."

Wendy put the box back into the crawl space. "Yeah, but why here and not in a desk or cabinet or somewhere more normal?"

"And cobweb free," Vivian added, then sighed. "My guess is the second wife nixed it." She reached for the smaller box. "Let's see what we've got inside box number two." She easily peeled back the aged packing tape and opened the flaps.

Just as she reached her hand inside, a loud knock sounded on the bedroom door. She snatched her hand away, as if she'd been burned. "Oh, shit!"

Brandon's voice sounded outside the door. "Anyone home? I came to get the trash."

Vivian jumped up, grabbed the box from the luggage rack and threw it in the closet. Wendy started toward the door, just as a key went in the knob.

"We're in here, hold on a sec," Vivian said as she pulled a shirt off a hanger and tossed it over the box, then closed the closet door.

Wendy stood aside as Brandon walked in with a black trash bag. "I figured you girls would be out causing trouble somewhere."

Kate sat on the bed. "I needed a break after all that breakfast, but I think we're about to go on a walk around the lake."

"It's a beautiful day for it," Brandon called from the bathroom. "It's a little warmer than yesterday." He emerged with the trash bag. A black smear of soot was on his cheek. "Be sure to take some water. I'll be tending to the leaf piles if you need me."

"Thanks," Wendy said and followed him to the door, closing it behind him, then leaned against it and let out a sigh of relief.

"We almost got busted!" Vivian whispered. "Let's hurry so we can re-hide the evidence!"

Wendy tossed aside the shirt, grabbed the box from the closet, set it on the bed and opened it up. She reached inside. "Oooh, la la, what do we have here." She slowly revealed a black lace nightie with red trim.

"I'm guessing that's not Tracy's," Vivian said.

Kate reached inside and found a framed picture of a middle-aged woman, very pretty, trim with brown hair and riding on a horse. Another picture showed the same woman with Brandon standing behind one of those replica ship wheels that serve as great moneymakers for cruise photographers. It read "Majesty of the Open Seas."

"Definitely not Tracy," Kate said, putting aside the picture. She then picked up a black lace 4x6 photo album with red trim. "Look, it matches the nightie." She looked up at Vivian and Wendy with a mischievous smile. "Do we dare look inside?"

"You look," Wendy said. "If it's what I think it is, I don't want to see it."

Kate laughed and opened the album. It was Brandon and the woman standing on a white sand beach, turquoise water behind them. He wore a Hawaiian shirt, tan shorts and flip-flops, and she wore a strapless, peach dress and held a small bouquet of tropical flowers.

"This must be wife number two," Vivian said, staring at the woman's mouth, especially her lower jaw. Vivian felt the need to wash her hands again, but fought the urge. "She was pretty. Why would someone want to hurt her?"

"Maybe she turned out to be psycho, or was worth more dead than alive," Wendy offered.

The rest of the album was more of the wedding, Brandon and Rebecca feeding each other cake, clinking champagne glasses. One picture was of their hands, bouquet in the background.

"That diamond is huge," Vivian said, thinking back to the simple gold band from when she and Rick were married.

"This album didn't turn out the way I thought it would," Wendy said, "and I'm glad."

Kate flipped to the last page. "Hold your horses there." She showed them what she'd found. Rebecca was posing seductively in a black lace negligee. A white envelope lay opposite the last page so Kate opened it and pulled out more pictures. "Whoa! Naughty naughty!"

Vivian laughed. "I can see why he's hiding these pictures from Tracy!"

Rebecca's negligee had been tossed aside and Brandon had gotten full-body close-ups. Kate quickly shuffled through the rest, which became more and more intimate. Vivian wondered how they were able to get a picture of some of their more intricate poses.

Kate stuffed the pictures back into the envelope. "He's not a bad looking guy, but I've seen enough."

"More than enough," Wendy said and rubbed her eyes.

"I thought you weren't going to look," Kate said.

"I had to look after you were so excited about what you'd found. Then it was like a train wreck, and I couldn't look away. I'm going to have a difficult time looking at Brandon without thinking about, you know, *it*."

Vivian dug in the box and pulled out a folder that said "Northwestern Mutual" on it. She opened it and scanned the first page. "What do we have here?"

Kate looked over her shoulder. "Looks like $500,000 in a life insurance policy on Rebecca Holt."

"Who's the beneficiary?" Wendy asked.

"Who do you think? Brandon." Vivian flipped through more of the pages.

Kate tapped her finger to her lips. "Hmm, that's a decent amount of money, but it's not like Brandon could live forever off of that."

Vivian pulled out the next document and scanned it before handing it to Wendy. "You're the mortgage person, don't you look at this kind of stuff all the time on your clients' files? Am I reading this correctly with a balance of $2.9 million?"

Wendy took the investment statement from Vivian and looked it over. "Now this is something. Rebecca's full balance was $2,974,329.07. Getting close to an even three. A little more interest and she'd have been there."

Kate gave a low whistle. "Looks like Christine from the shop was right about her being rich. But where did she get that money?"

Wendy took the folder from Vivian and looked through more of the papers. She handed one to Vivian. "Read this. It looks like a will for a Roger White. I just ran across his death certificate, and it listed his spouse as Rebecca White."

"What did he die from?" Kate asked.

"Myocardial infarction."

"Heart attack," Vivian said. She'd had a will done after her divorce from Rick, but this was much more complex. She might not have a law degree, but she could figure it out. "Rebecca stood to inherit 100 percent of his estate, money, house, investments, but only if they didn't have any children. Do we know if they had any kids?"

"We didn't see any children in any of the pictures in her box," Kate said. "Did you find a will for her?"

"Ah," Wendy said and pulled another document from the folder. She sat on the bed while she flipped through it. "Doesn't look like she had any kids, and you know who her sole beneficiary was?"

"Lemme guess," Vivian said, but before she could answer...

Knock, knock, knock.

28

The girls were frozen for a second before Vivian snapped to and whispered, "Quick, let's get all of this back in the closet. Kate, look like you're resting."

"Just a minute," Kate called toward the door. "Who is it?"

"Me again," Brandon said.

Wendy and Vivian scrambled to get the papers into the box, and the box into in the closet. Vivian smoothed her shirt and fluffed her hair before opening the door. "Hi."

Brandon walked in. "I just came to get the towels. What happened to your walk?"

Vivian's phone rang, and she was glad for the distraction. She grabbed it off the nightstand and checked the display. Nicole.

Kate was lying down. She put her hands behind her head. "I just wasn't feeling up to it. The girls were nice enough to hang with me while I rested. I'm fine, nothing a little more bacon can't fix."

Brandon smiled and slowly looked around the room. He smelled of smoke. "Okay, glad all is well." He disappeared into the bathroom and soon emerged with the dirty towels.

"All is well, we're just chilling." Vivian sat on the bed next to Kate.

Brandon walked toward the door, then turned around. "There are makings for BLTs in the kitchen. Let me know if you'd like one."

"Thanks," the girls called as he slowly closed the door.

"Oh my god," Vivian whispered, hopping up and locking the door. "That was too close. Is he really working or just being nosy?"

"Nosy," Wendy whispered back and opened the closet door. "We need to put this stuff up exactly as it was and go downstairs. I think we found some good info, though."

"I really could use some bacon now that I think about it," Kate said, but then she closed her eyes. "Mini-nap first."

Vivian grabbed her phone. "That was Nicole who called. Let me call her back before we go down."

Nicole picked up on the second ring. "What are you doing today? I've found some good info. Do you have time to visit?"

Vivian looked at the clock. "Larson should be here in two hours to take us out on the boat. Can you come here?"

"See you in 20." Click.

They let Kate nap for 15 minutes, then the three headed downstairs. Kate helped herself to a BLT and offered to make one for the other girls but they declined. Vivian and Wendy sat out on the front porch while Kate made her sandwich and they waited for Nicole. They rocked and watched smoke billow from the piles of burning leaves around the property.

"Brandon's really got those going good," Wendy commented as he threw more leaves onto one of the stacks.

"It doesn't take a pyromaniac to burn leaves," Vivian said. "We used to burn trash at my grandmother's farm in Alabama. A little lighter fluid and a few matches, and you're playing with fire."

They rocked for a few more minutes before a car pulled into the drive and Nicole got out carrying a big chrome briefcase.

"Hey!" Vivian said.

"Hi. Are Brandon and Tracy here?"

"Tracy's not. Brandon's over there." Vivian nodded toward him.

Kate arrived at the screen door munching on her sandwich.

"I've been through my grandpa's files and have found some interesting stuff. I wanted to tell you about it, but in private."

Vivian opened the screen door. "Let's go in. I gotta see what you've got inside that ginormous chrome case."

They sat around the dining room table and Nicole pulled out several files. "My grandpa had notes on just about everyone in town. It took me awhile to sort through them and pick out some that are worth a closer look."

Wendy spread out the folders and read the labels. "Everyone in town? Are there a lot of creepy people around here or something?"

Nicole laughed. "No, he just liked to keep tabs on everyone's business. His theory was that everyone had a story and you never knew when it would become newsworthy."

"Good thinking," Vivian said and picked up a file. It read Jeremy Donaldson. She opened it and looked at several pages of handwritten notes in a bad scroll. She looked at Nicole. "I assume you can decipher this?"

"Grandpa wasn't known for his penmanship, but this file is on a student of Mary Beth's. She tutored him here at the house, and it was rumored they spent a lot of time together, like she took a special interest in him."

"Was something inappropriate going on?" Kate asked.

"From what I gathered, I think he had a crush on her, but she was just trying to help him. I talked to him this morning, stopped by his house since he keeps his shop there. He said they would stay after school and she would tutor him. Then Mary Beth drowned and he not only quit school but went off the deep end. He couldn't handle her death, and he left town as soon as he could. He worked on cruise ships, mainly in Alaska, and did that until his parents died in an accident a couple of years ago, when he came home."

Vivian had been flipping through the pages in the file while Nicole talked. She turned over the last page and caught her breath. "I've seen this guy. Why do I know him?"

Wendy leaned over and looked at the picture. "It's the locksmith who helped us at the trailhead the other day."

"That's him," Nicole said. "Jeremy inherited his parents' estate, but he still needed a job so he learned how to be a locksmith. He also wrote a couple of screenplays while he worked on the cruise ships, and he sold one of them, though I don't think it was for a lot. I asked him today if he was working on anything new, and he said he was almost done with a movie script."

"Interesting," Vivian said. "I've always wanted to write a screenplay. What's his about?"

"A student who falls in love with a teacher and they have an affair, but then she's murdered."

Vivian stared at his picture. "Wow. I've heard people write what they know. Maybe there was more to his affection for Mary Beth?"

Nicole shrugged. "I think so, and Grandpa didn't think the love was reciprocated. His notes are hard to read, but he clearly says Mary Beth seemed to be in love with Brandon."

"Scorned and rejected," Wendy said. "Not a good combo."

"What else did you find?" Kate asked. She picked up the thickest of the files, and the name read Mike Grimm. She set it upside down so she could easily flip to the back. She looked at the picture, then showed Vivian and Wendy. "We met him yesterday at the festival, right?"

"Sure did," Vivian said. "I liked his dragon paintings."

"He invited us to his studio," Wendy said. "Maybe we should go?"

"Do what you want, but you probably shouldn't mention Brandon," Nicole said. "Mike, Mary Beth and he have history all the way through school. Mike went to college at the University of Oregon where he evidently started drinking way too much and got into drugs. He dropped out and went to Portland, joined a grunge band, moved from couch to couch. He's been in and out of rehab several times. I know him to say hello, but not much else. I've heard he finally conquered his addiction and is clean."

Kate had turned over the last page in the file and started working her way backward through it. "That's great, but if they were friends, why shouldn't we mention Brandon?"

"Wait for it," Vivian said. "I can tell there's more to this story." Nicole was on the edge of her seat, drumming her fingers on the table.

"Mike moved home about a year before Mary Beth's death. One of the files Grandpa had is on a friend of Mary Beth's, a Suzy Fairlie, who says Mike spent a lot of time with Mary Beth once he was home. Brandon didn't like it, thought Mike wanted more than friendship, even though Suzy doesn't think Mike ever did anything of the sort to Mary Beth. Suzy says Mary Beth and Brandon had a big argument about it and Brandon forbid her to see Mike anymore. Things were strained between them for a few days, and then Mary Beth drowned shortly thereafter."

Wendy sighed. "What a sad story."

"It doesn't end there. One of the documents in the file is a police report and arrest record from when Mike came out here and attacked Brandon. He apparently inflicted some major damage. Mike told the police he was trying to beat a confession out of him, but Brandon said Mike was crazy and couldn't be reasoned with, like he was on drugs."

"Did Mike and Mary Beth ever date?" Kate asked.

"Not that I can find, but their families hung out together. I guess their moms were good friends, so they'd go snow skiing, boating, hiking, take trips, you name it. His affection was more brotherly when they were younger, but Grandpa thinks that changed about the time Mike came back. And Grandpa's notes say Mike never liked Brandon, thought Mary Beth could and should do better."

"Is that all on Mike?" Wendy asked.

"Grandpa just didn't like him much, thought there was something weird about him and that there was more to the story between him and Brandon. Mike always wears black, even turtlenecks and long pants in the summer. A lot of these notes are from Grandpa following Mike around town, just to see what he was up to. Grandpa didn't think Mary Beth's death was an accident; something wasn't picked up on the autopsy. He doesn't come right out and say it, but I think he was highly suspicious of Mike and that beating Brandon up for a confession was a cover-up attempt."

Vivian glanced out the back window to make sure Brandon was still outside. He was tossing a tree branch on the leaf pile. "But if he had feelings for her, why would he murder her?"

Nicole shrugged again. "Drugs and alcohol can do crazy things to people's brains, even after they're sober. Or maybe Mary Beth wasn't the intended victim."

"Is Suzy still around?" Kate asked. "I'd like to talk to her."

"Yes, she owns Tropical Fish, a fish store on the outer edge of town."

"We'll go talk to her," Vivian said to the girls, then picked up the next file on the pile, April Robinson. "Who's this?"

Nicole glanced at the file. "A fellow teacher, though they weren't friends for long. Or co-workers. Mary Beth caught April changing answers on the state equivalency test and reported her. April was fired and her teacher's license was revoked so she can never teach in the state of New York again."

"That sounds like motive for murder," Vivian said, knowing that test scores mattered in terms of school rankings and therefore funding, but cheating wasn't the way to go.

"Yep," Nicole said. "All the kids in her class had to retake the test."

"My mom is a teacher, and she would not tolerate another teacher who did that," Wendy said. "Mary Beth did the right thing, but it sucks that the kids had to suffer through the tests again."

Nicole flipped through the file. "Mary Beth certainly did the right thing in turning her in, but April was none too happy about getting banned from teaching. April went off on Mary Beth the day she got fired and made a lot of threats. Was it heat of the moment, or more than that since Mary Beth had ruined April's life?"

"No, actually, April ruined April's life by cheating," Vivian said. "Cheaters always lose in the end." *Like fuckin' Rick!*

Nicole tapped her fingers on the table again. "She really stands out to me as a suspect. The police haven't looked into her as far as I can tell. She made those threats, had her life in shambles, and Mary Beth dies shortly thereafter? Coincidental?"

A shadow passed across the table in front of Vivian and she looked up.

Tracy stood in the doorway, a concerned look on her face. She quickly wiped it away as she locked eyes with Vivian. "Having a nice time?"

29

Tracy walked in and glanced at the files spread out on her dining room table. "Hello, Nicole, good to see you," she said with a smile.

Nicole waved her hand around the room. "Hi, there, I love what you've done with the B&B. Very quaint."

"Thank you," Tracy said. "Can I get anyone anything? A little lunch? We have pimento cheese, lunch meat, peanut butter…"

Vivian was horrified Tracy had walked in on them but tried not to let it show on her face. *How much has she heard? If it's just the last part that Nicole said, then we might be okay. Try to act normal.* "You don't have to do that, it's a B&B, not a B&B&L."

"I don't mind," Tracy said. "I like to take care of our guests."

"Okay, you talked me into it. I'll just have a sandwich and some hot tea."

Wendy smiled at her. "I could use a pimiento cheese sandwich and a glass of water."

"I could use something stronger, but I'd better not," Kate joked and rubbed her belly. "I just had a BLT. Do you have something sweet back there?"

"How about some oatmeal raisin cookies?"

"Oh, yes, please, and thank you. With milk!"

Tracy looked at Nicole, smile still plastered to her face. "Anything for you? I made a batch of peanut butter cookies yesterday."

Nicole shook her head. "Hot tea sounds nice, thanks."

"Sure you don't want a bite?"

"No, thanks. I'm allergic to peanuts, so I'm pretty cautious."

"Oh, goodness," Tracy said and put a hand to her heart. "I'd die. I love peanut butter cookies!" She walked toward the kitchen.

The girls exchanged nervous glances before Wendy asked in a low voice, "Any other important people we ought to know about?"

Nicole slid a file to Wendy and another to Vivian. "Just these two, and I don't think it's much. A football coach who worked with Mary Beth at the school. Brandon and he had a falling out, a jealousy thing. Also, the town recluse, Otto Treadwell. Grandpa tried to talk to him about Mary Beth, thinking that even though Otto was quiet and odd, he might be more attentive than anyone realized and therefore might know something. Other than those two, there are a few sex offenders in town, but not many."

"Are the coach and recluse still around?" Kate asked.

"Coach Stubbs moved out of state years ago, and Otto passed away."

Vivian wanted to talk to Tracy and try to see how much she'd heard. "I think I'll go see if Tracy needs any help." She walked into the kitchen. Food was on the counters and sandwiches were in the process of being made, but Tracy was nowhere in sight. Brandon had set some groceries on a small kitchen table and was just walking in the side door with another armful. "Let me help you with those," Vivian said, reaching for a bag.

Brandon didn't release it. "That's okay, I've got it. You need something?"

"I was just coming to see if Tracy needed any help getting our lunch together."

Tracy walked in the side door drying her hands on her jeans, then grabbed a paper towel. Her grey sweatshirt sleeve was wet and she began to pat it dry. "Go relax with the girls. I can make a couple of sandwiches and cups of tea."

"I know this is bed and breakfast, no lunch and dinner included. Are you sure we aren't imposing? I don't mind helping."

"No imposition."

Vivian walked back into the dining room and whispered, "They're both in there."

Kate nodded. "Nicole was just telling us some ghost stories from around here. Great stuff, you gotta hear this one."

Nicole started over. "I haven't seen it, but lots of people swear it's true. Not far from here, a young couple, still in their wedding garb, left the reception and headed toward Canada on their honeymoon. They never made it. Their car went out of control and plunged into a creek. Both the bride and groom died instantly.

"People say they've seen the husband walking the road at night, searching for his bride, calling out to her. Others have seen the bride wandering the road alone, still wearing her bloody, torn wedding dress. People say she jumps out at cars, trying to make them crash. A few reported that they've glanced in their rearview mirror and found her crying bloody tears in the back seat, but when they turned around, she had vanished."

Vivian shivered. "I don't know if I want to be driving around here at night anymore!"

Tracy walked in with a tray loaded with sandwiches and drinks. "You

123

should be careful driving at night out here. If it's not ghosts, its deer, raccoons or the occasional bear." She set the tray down and then headed for the back door. "Enjoy."

"Thanks," Wendy said as the door swung closed. "Lots of strange and creepy stuff."

"No kidding," Vivian said and picked up her cup of tea. "And speaking of strange and creepy, what do y'all make of Brandon, Rebecca and the money?"

Nicole looked at Vivian with questions in her eyes, so the girls quietly filled her in on what they'd found in the crawl space.

"Wow, I knew he was loaded, but I didn't realize to what extent," Nicole said and then took a sip of hot tea. "Any idea what tea this is? It's different." She reached for the sugar and dumped some in.

"No idea," Vivian said, "but I like it okay. I use Sweet 'N Low."

Kate swallowed a bite of cookie. "Back to the money. It's certainly incentive to kill her, but their sex life looked exciting so it makes me think he'd want to keep her around."

"Maybe he got too rough, or just flat out abused her and accidentally killed her?" Wendy suggested. "He seems like a rough guy, and he bullies Tracy."

"He's definitely short-tempered," Vivian said, "but how did he accidentally kill her in the woods? What were they doing out there, getting *au naturel* in nature, or did he kill her here and haul her out there to bury her? How did no one see him? I'm not sure I buy the accidental death theory."

"Confirmation of Rebecca's death does make me question Mary Beth's drowning," Wendy said.

"And you can bet the cops have been questioning the same thing," Kate added.

"I'll see if I can find out anything from the sheriff deputies," Nicole said, then took another sip of tea. She made a face. "This takes some getting used to, kinda like Swiss chard or Brussel sprouts. It's an acquired taste."

The girls laughed, and then Kate told her about the message she'd received in her dream the night before. Nicole wrote it down. "No doubt she's talking about the murders. Do you have dreams like this all the time?"

"Nowadays, only when I'm on vacation."

Nicole closed her notepad. "Maybe the senior moment she's talking about is my grandfather? I'll see what I can come up with."

They talked about lighter subjects while finishing lunch, then Nicole started gathering her files. "I know you girls have a hot date with a hot fireman, and I've got a story to write on Ms. Pumpkin Patch getting arrested for drunk and disorderly last night."

"Uh oh, somebody might lose her prized carving knife." Vivian laughed.

"And the kicker, she was with 'Captain Carver' himself, one of the judges!"

Everyone got a big kick out of that.

"I'm going." Nicole closed the chrome briefcase and the girls walked her to the front door. "Have fun with your hose dragger." Nicole winked at Vivian as she stepped onto the porch.

Kate closed the door, then looked at her watch. "Larson will be here any minute. I want to pack a small bag. I'll meet you two out back in a few."

Wendy, a.k.a. the walking pharmacy, also wanted to take a few things, so she and Kate ran upstairs. Vivian rocked on the back porch, enjoying the crisp air. The smell of smoke blew her way, and it had her craving roasted marshmallows. She noticed Brandon and Tracy on the far side of one of the leaf piles in deep conversation. He clenched a fist before storming off toward the garage. Tracy stood still, staring after him.

Hmmm, wonder what that's about?

Kate and Wendy walked out of the house just as Larson cruised up to the dock in a white, older Bayliner deck boat.

"He's here!" Vivian yelled and hopped off the porch. She jogged down to the dock, trying to look sexy, skinny and athletic all rolled into one. *Don't be out of breath! Don't be out of breath!*

He waved and skillfully pulled alongside the dock.

Vivian pointed at the name of his boat, the Aqua Holic. "Nice," she said.

He smiled at her. "Hey, sexy, grab this line, will you?" He tossed her a thick, white rope.

I guess my jog was successful!

30

Larson hopped off the boat, grabbed the line from Vivian and tied off. His brown hair was windblown but he looked warm in jeans and a brown flannel shirt. "Hi, ladies, everyone looks ravishing today." He gave Vivian a hug, letting his hands linger at her waist. Then he took a step back. "You ready for some fun?"

"Mmm hmm," she said. "So you better deliver." She played with the button on his shirt.

He leaned down to her ear, nuzzling her neck a little. "Oh, I will."

Goosebumps broke out over her whole body.

He broke away and shook hands with Wendy, then Kate. "Do we need to get or do anything special for you, little Mama? I want to make sure you're taken care of."

Kate smiled and patted a bag she had packed. "Got everything I need right here." She took one more step and stumbled a bit. Vivian grabbed her arm and steadied her.

Kate looked down at the dock. "There's an uneven board here. Y'all watch out."

Larson took Kate's bag, helped them aboard and got them situated. He opened a hatch along the port side. "I doubt we'll need them, but lifejackets are in here. Anybody want one? Safety first!"

They all shook their heads no.

He pointed to a cooler in the bow. "I've got beer, a few sodas and bottles of water, along with grapes, sliced cheese and strawberries." He looked starboard to Wendy. "Crackers are in the compartment underneath you. And then I've got a surprise for later when we stop for our picnic."

"Wow," Vivian said as she sat down in the captain chair opposite him. "Fancy-shmancy. Were you a Boy Scout? Or a chef in another life?"

He grinned and fired up the engine as Brandon walked out of the garage toward the dock. "Hey, Larson! Where you taking these girls? Not party cove, I trust."

"I thought I'd cruise up to Moose Island," Larson shouted over the

126

engine. "Show 'em the hot spots."

Brandon gave the man nod. "Gotcha. Take good care of my guests. Have fun!" He turned and headed back toward the garage, not bothering to look at Tracy as he walked by her.

Larson untied the line and pushed off the dock, then put the Bayliner in reverse and slowly headed to the center of the lake. The yellow, orange and red of the trees reflected in the ripples of the water. Vivian wanted to reach over the side and touch it but instead got herself and Wendy a beer; she handed Kate and Larson bottles of water.

Larson set his in a cup holder beside the wheel. "Too bad it's not bikini weather. I'd take you three to Pulpit Rock. That, or we could at least ski or tube."

"What's that?" Wendy asked.

"Where we all go to cool off in the summer. Jump off the cliff, swim around."

"No cliff jumping for me these days," Kate said. "Not even in my younger days, but being hauled around the lake in a tube, that'd be fun."

"It's just nice to be out here," Vivian said and gave him her best smile, "with you." She was feeling flirtatious and a little naughty. He was adorable, single and lived far enough away, not to mention a *fireman*. How could this get any better?

"What's on Moose Island?" Wendy asked, then took a sip of her Moose Island Ale. "This is pretty good."

"In addition to being one of my favorite beers, it's an undeveloped island in the middle of the lake," Larson said. "There are two others, Buck and Hawk, but Moose is the largest and has a great camping spot where we can build a fire and cook an early dinner."

"I love a man who can cook," Vivian said.

Larson smiled and pushed the throttle down. He cruised around awhile, finally noticing the girls had all put on jackets. Wendy had brought Vivian's.

"Sorry about that," he said. "You're all probably used to 110-degree weather. I love the cold and the wind and forget other people don't."

"The cold? Really?" Vivian took a sip of her beer, set the bottle in a cup holder and stuck her hands in her pockets. "I would have thought you like the heat, being a fireman and all."

"I love the snow. I'm big into all the winter sports around here, but don't get me wrong, I love the heat." He winked at her. "But I worked this fire one time." His gaze drifted across the lake and he paused. "It was so intensely hot that I'm surprised my insides didn't boil."

"What happened?" Kate asked.

Larson pointed to his left. "That's Buck Island, quite a few nice homes on it." He rubbed his chin. "We got called to a fire in a two-story, wood-framed house that the homeowner tried to extinguish himself instead of calling 911 right away. By the time it got called in and we got there, the house was gone. We saved his cat, but even Sparky had burns on a couple of paws and singed fur. We had to give him oxygen." Larson shook his head and sighed as he steered left, going around the northern edge of the island.

The water was choppier and Vivian grasped the side of the boat to hold on. "I take it the guy didn't get out since you named his cat."

Larson looked over at her as she bounced along, grinned, then slowed a bit. "Shelter Straight is always rougher than the rest of the lake. Doesn't take long to navigate, though." He pushed the throttle down and got back to his story. "The homeowner, Derrick, was a single guy, a handyman, worked on everything from cars and tractors to kitchen sinks and houses. And he was a smoker."

"I feel a public service announcement coming on," Kate said and grinned.

"He'd done a few things for my parents over the years, and I even worked for him for a few months one summer as a teenager. I swear, he had every tool known to man. I had been in his basement a couple of times, and in addition to a ton of tools, I knew he had piles of wood, stacks of Sheetrock, paint cans, gas cans, car parts. He was down there, probably working on something, and a spark from his cigarette landed on a gas can. He was a four-pack-a-day smoker, and he drank a lot, too. Great guy if you could stand the smell of cigarettes, but he wasn't the sharpest knife in the drawer."

The boat bounced on a bigger wave, making Kate yelp. Larson slowed again, the current creating gentle rocks instead of the pounding slap just moments before. He looked back at her. "Sorry. You okay?"

She repositioned herself and gave him a thumbs up. "Just no more mega-bumps."

"So what became of Derrick?" Wendy asked as she redid her windblown ponytail.

"Instead of getting out of the basement, he pulled his garden hose inside and tried to fight it himself. There was so much crap down there to feed the fire, he never had a chance. The carbon monoxide got to him, and he passed out before he knew what hit him. Stupid mistake. The smoke always kills before the fire."

They rounded the southern edge of Moose Island and Vivian took in the scene across the lake. Geese were flying south in a V formation, and they reflected on the surface of the lake. Peaceful, except for the topic at hand. "How awful. He sounded helpful to have around."

Larson shook his head again. "He was, and he could have made it if he'd just gotten out of the house. Trying to fight a fire yourself is never a good idea. Call in the experts."

As they cruised up the right side of the densely covered Moose Island, Wendy reached for a bottle of water, then tried to hand one to Vivian, who waved it off and pointed to a beer instead. Wendy got her another and then said, "When I was a kid, the oven at our house caught on fire. Mom had left for work, and my brother and I were cooking biscuits. All of a sudden we smelled smoke. Simon was a quick thinker and grabbed the fire extinguisher Dad had hung by the garage door years before. He put the fire out, no problem, but the house stunk for days."

"I didn't know that. Way to go, little brother!" Vivian clinked bottles with Wendy.

"He's a pretty good brother. Saved the day there, worked on the car, drove us home from parties in high school."

"I did not contribute to his corruption." Kate laughed as Larson steered to the right, around the northern edge of Moose Island, and then pointed to a three-story log home. "That is exactly what I think of architecturally when I think of the Adirondacks."

"It's beautiful. We need to rent one of those next time," Vivian said, taking it in. "That way we can stay away from may-be-murderers."

Larson waved to a man sitting in an Adirondack chair on a balcony. "I see you've heard about Lake Placid's biggest mystery."

"Uhm, hello, we lived it, remember? I TOUCHED it, for goodness sake."

Larson grinned. "I know, but I'm glad. I might not have met you otherwise."

Vivian couldn't complain, he was right.

He changed the subject. "I love the great camps. Perfect way to spend a vacation."

"Camps?" Vivian asked. "I could fit three of my 2000-square-foot house in there."

"That's what we call them. Some of the houses date to the 1800s." Larson turned south and soon pulled up to a dock on the island.

He held on to the dock while also helping the girls out of the boat. Once Kate was on solid ground he handed her bag over. Vivian grabbed bags of groceries and Wendy helped him with the cooler. He set down his end of the cooler and opened his arms in a grand gesture. "Here we are, Hopping Bear Point. One of my all-time favorite camping places."

Vivian noted the dense foliage and the lean-to and wondered how many nights he'd spent out here wooing a woman. She figured this was where he took all of the ladies, trying to impress them with the boat, tales of fire-fueled tragedy and multiple…multiple Boy Scout badges. She felt a pang of jealousy but quickly dismissed it. It wasn't like she was looking for a relationship. But he was H-O-T hot, and she couldn't help wondering what an evening next to the embers, gazing under the stars, using body heat and friction to keep warm, would be like.

It'd be as blazing hot as lava!

She shook her head and snapped out of it. With the last man she'd "met" on vacation, things went awry big time, and with no warning. He was adorable, a good dancer, a good buttery nipple maker, and yet, the sex suckkkked. *Do not make that mistake again,* Vivian thought, looking Larson up and down. *He wouldn't suck, would he?*

They put their stuff down around the camp. The lean-to was a free-standing, rectangular log structure with three walls and a pitched roof. The open side faced the lake and had a short bench at the base that could be used as a bed. Visitors had carved initials, dates and all manner of randomness into the bench. The steeply pitched roof covered the back almost to the ground, while a shorter, slanted roof provided shade to the front.

A mound of rocks formed a fire pit in front. Vivian could imagine spending a cool night in the spring or fall out there, but forget it in winter. No way, José. Not this Texan.

A trail wandered off to the right, and Kate looked in that direction. "Do they have bathrooms around here?"

"Sorry, not that sophisticated," Larson replied.

"Little mama's gotta go. Be right back."

"I need to go, too," Wendy said as she and Larson positioned the cooler by the fire pit. She took off after Kate.

Larson got to work picking up kindling around the area and building a fire with the cord of wood he'd brought. Vivian opened them both a beer. She then got the goodies out of the grocery bag and made a few crackers with cheese, then dipped into the cooler.

"These are the best strawberries ever. They're so much sweeter than what I get at home."

Larson held a match to some kindling and looked up. "Thanks, grew them myself."

"I'm impressed. I would have been okay with Cheez Whiz, though. I'm an expert at decorating crackers with little swirls and flowers. My mad skills have made magazines, you know."

"And what would you have put on mine?" Larson asked with a grin, giving up on the fire for the moment and walking toward her, his eyes locked on hers. He wrapped his arms around her waist and pulled her to him. Tight.

He smelled fantastic, a perfect blend of sweat and sweet. "Hmmm, let me think. Something flaming for sure, Mr. Fireman." She pushed her hips into him, enjoying the hardness of his body. She let her fingers slowly drift from his neck to his shoulders to his arms. Oh my gosh, his arms. They were amazing.

He leaned down and kissed her, his hand reaching up and tickling underneath her breast.

"Mmmmm, yes," she said, letting the kiss linger, then going from his mouth to his ear. "Or something a bit naughtier. Maybe lower." For his cracker decoration, she was thinking an X, for X marks the spot.

Just then, Kate walked up. "Oh come on you two, I'm hungry. And without my husband."

Wendy popped out from around a tree, oblivious to the heat radiating from the non-fire. "Guess what? The trail markers here are UT burnt orange. The two we saw looked about as beat up as the ones on Haystack Mountain." She handed Vivian her phone, which showed a picture of an orange semicircle.

Vivian broke from Larson and looked at the picture, laughing. "I'll leave the hiking to other people. We've uncovered more than our share already."

"I'm with you," Kate said and sat on the bench next to the cheese and crackers. She scarfed down three with double cheese before she looked up and offered to make the others one.

They enjoyed the appetizers while Larson prepared the fire for their main course. He'd made grass-fed beef tenderloin shish kebobs.

"You are earning a Boy Scout badge, aren't you?" Vivian said, smacking him on the ass as he walked by with his 'bobs.

"I like to cook things over an open flame, what can I say?"

"I bet you do," Vivian said, then bit into a grape.

Suddenly, a loud boom sounded in the distance. She couldn't tell which direction it came from, but it couldn't have been far away. "I don't suppose that was some really big fireworks?"

Larson ran toward the shore. He peered at the horizon, looking for any indication of trouble in the sky. "I'm afraid not."

31

Larson ran to the fire pit and started stomping on the kindling that was lit. "There's a cloud of smoke south of here. I'm probably the closest responder and have to go check it out. Wendy, call 911 and report an explosion on the lake, just south of Hopping Bear Point. It looks to be on the southern end of Moose Island, or possibly on Buck Island."

Wendy got to dialing as Vivian threw the cold stuff into the cooler and Kate chunked stuff in the grocery bag. They were loaded on the boat within two minutes.

"Hold on!" Larson said as he pushed off the shore, then he landed behind the captain chair. He cranked the engine, pushed the throttle down and the bow of the boat rose out of the water, throwing the girls off balance, even though they were seated. He glanced over his shoulder. "You all right, Kate?"

She shouted, "Yeah," but didn't look at him, as she was looking at the dark cloud.

Vivian also had her head back, looking up. The cloud rose from the tree line, drifting east in the wind.

Larson steered south, following the coastline. The cloud loomed larger, and before long, the area where it had originated was visible.

"As I feared," Larson said, angling the boat toward shore. "Wendy, call 911 back and tell them there's a boat on fire at the Dillengers' dock on Buck Island and to send help."

The back of a 15-foot wooden boat was on fire, and it wouldn't be long before it spread to the dock. Not far away, a three-slip boathouse, a near-perfect replica of the house, stood dangerously close to the inferno. Vivian could imagine the fire racing down the dock to the boathouse, then catching the trees on fire and spreading to the house. The entire property would be engulfed. They needed help now!

Wendy did as told and Larson pulled up along the shore, about a football field away from the burning boat.

A man and a woman ran out from the trees nearby. "Holy shit! It just blew! Did you see that?" the man yelled.

"Is anyone hurt?" Larson asked. "Is there anyone else on the vessel?"

"We're fine. We weren't on it when it blew," the bottle blonde said. "It was just us, no one else." She looked to be in her early 20s and needed to take care of her roots. She wore a gray hoodie sweatshirt with a T-shirt underneath sticking out in places. Her matching sweatpants said "Pink" down the leg, and her black, lace bra was in her hand.

"I just finished restoring that boat. Dammit!" The guy kicked at the dirt and kept on cursing. He'd missed a button on the fly of his grease-stained jeans, and his long-sleeved T-shirt was on inside out. His brown hair was three weeks overdue for a cut.

Vivian took in their disheveled appearance and figured they had more to hide than setting the Dillengers' dock on fire.

"Is this your property?" Larson asked.

The guy turned around. "No, we just wanted to take a look around."

Another explosion boomed, though not as big as the first. A flaming piece of something impaled itself in the boathouse roof, igniting the shingles in a flash. Flaming pieces of wood were suddenly floating on the surface of the lake and strewn across the lawn.

The guy put his hands on his head. "Oh shit!"

Larson threw a fire extinguisher to the guy and hopped out of the boat. "Put out the debris on the lawn and try to keep the fire from spreading to the house." He tied a line to a big tree root along the bank and ran around the side of the boathouse.

The guy worked his way across the yard squirting at the bigger pieces of burning boat and stomping on a few smaller ones. Vivian couldn't see Larson, but soon a stream of water sprayed onto the roof.

"Is that lake water?" Wendy asked.

"They probably have a fire hose in the boathouse that pulls water from the lake," Kate said. "All this wood and no fire department right down the street, they need something to help in case of fire."

Bra Girl walked over to Larson's boat. "I can't believe this is happening. "Totally cray-cray, right?"

"Right," Wendy said, then faced the girls and rolled her eyes.

The girl looked at Wendy's water. "Do you have an extra bottle of water?"

Wendy reached into the cooler and handed her one. "What's your name? I'm Wendy, this is Kate and Vivian."

"Shawna," she said, then took a few gulps.

They all watched as the fire seemed to grow.

"What were y'all doing out here?" Wendy asked.

"I got my shift covered and Dale didn't have much going on at the shop, so we took his boat out." She waved her bra in the air as she spoke. "He just finished working on it, and it sounded like a fun thing to do. He said it was totally safe! I didn't know it was a lemon. I could have died!"

"Hope it was insured," Kate mumbled, only loud enough for Vivian and Wendy to hear.

Vivian choked back a laugh. "You said you got your shift covered. Where do you work?"

"At the Lake Placid Brewery. Dale's an auto mechanic." Shawna watched her guy squirt a stream of white foam onto a flame. "Now I wish I'd been at work instead of coming out here with that loser. He's a total jackass."

"Hope he's not your boyfriend," Kate said.

She shrugged. "I see him some, helps fill the void since I can't have the man I love." She took a deep breath and tapped her finger to her lips. "Yet."

Vivian was about to ask why not when two guys in a jon boat pulled up behind them. One, dressed all in black, jumped out and pulled the boat ashore. The other was head to toe in camouflage.

"What happened?" Camo asked, getting out of the boat with a fire extinguisher.

Vivian pointed toward distressed Dale, still shooting out mini-fires around the lawn. She explained what had happened.

 "We'll go help," Black said and they ran off.

A pontoon boat with Sheriff in big, black letters on the side raced toward the island, siren wailing. As it pulled closer, a third explosion sounded from the demolished vessel, shooting debris sky-high. A few pieces narrowly missed the pontoon as they fell into the lake.

Wendy looked at Shawna. "What's with all the explosions?"

"Maybe it's the cans of varnish that were still on the boat? He said he wasn't quite finished sprucing her up. Guess he doesn't need to worry about that anymore."

"How many cans were there?" Kate asked.

Shawna wrung her hands. "Just a couple. They were in my seat so I set them on the back bench."

Vivian turned her attention to the sheriff's boat. "Look who it is."

A stoic Deputy Brad Young was at the wheel. Beside him, Deputy Cheri Stokola sat in the co-captain's chair. She gave a quick nod to the girls as they pulled next to Larson's boat. Young cut the engine and jumped out to tie up to an exposed tree root.

"What happened here?" Stokola asked as she got out of the pontoon.

The girls and Shawna briefed them while the two sheriffs took in the scene. Dale stood by the house, Larson's fire extinguisher still in hand. Camo and Black from the jon boat were in the middle of the lawn, looking at a chunk of boat. All the debris on the lawn had been put out, but the boathouse fire roared. Though Larson was still spraying water on the roof, the flames were taking over.

The dock was ablaze, and flames were working their way toward the boathouse. The boat itself had sunk about halfway into the water. It wouldn't be long before everything was a total loss.

Stokola talked into her walkie-talkie, and someone on the other end said, "Be there in five. Out." Stokola turned to Young. "Let's go check on Larson."

They were halfway across the lawn when the boathouse roof cracked, then started to cave in. Embers flew in the air, and the spray of water onto the roof stopped. Larson ran toward the sheriffs, yelling at them to get farther away as a pine tree caught fire. Larson and Stokola ran for the boats but Young ran up to the house.

He grabbed Dale by the arm. "We need to get out of here until reinforcements arrive!" Dale dropped the fire extinguisher as Young led him to the pontoon boat and ushered him onboard. Larson motioned for Shawna to get onboard as well; she hesitated so Stokola guided her onto the boat. Larson and Stokola stayed onshore, next to their boats.

Another siren sounded and Vivian looked across the water to see a long, flat, white boat cruising in their direction. "Lake Placid Fire Department" shouted in big red letters on the side. One guy stood in the cockpit, earphones on, mic at his mouth. Another man sat on a bench seat in the back, black bag slung over his shoulder, and a third guy stood behind a red hydrant in the bow of the boat. They pulled in front of the boathouse, but at a reasonable distance, and water shot out of the hydrant onto the fire.

The fireman operating the hydrant sprayed water back and forth across the boathouse and on the dock. He didn't waste effort on the boat as it was now three-quarters of the way sunk. The spray of the hydrant had plenty of reach and could douse the nearby trees to prevent them from catching. The water wouldn't make it to the house from where they floated, but the velocity from the hose was fierce and Vivian had no doubt they could get closer and save the house if needed.

Kate sat back and crossed her ankles. "I like watching firemen work."

Wendy pointed to their boat. "The guy in the back's not doing anything."

"But he looks muscular and he's prepared, look at his black bag. He's ready to jump into action and save someone."

Stokola overheard their conversation and smiled. She turned her attention to Dale and Shawna, who sat across from each other in the pontoon. Neither looked happy. "Start at the beginning," she said to Dale. "How did the fire start?"

He looked up at her. "I just finished restoring that boat. Nothing was wrong with it. I just had her out a few days ago, ran her all over this lake with no problems."

"What were you doing here?" Stokola looked to Shawna.

"We just stopped here on the island to get out, walk a little. We didn't mean to burn anything to the ground."

Stokola looked from one to the other. Vivian thought maybe Stokola didn't buy it, but why would he blow up his own boat?

Dale slapped his knee. "There was nothing wrong with that engine. I'm a mechanic, for god's sake."

The two guys from the jon boat walked up. "There's something you need to see over here," Camo said.

Stokola followed them, along with Larson, to the middle of the lawn. Camo pointed at a piece of debris and made scissor motions with his fingers. Larson bent down and took pictures with his phone, then looked at Stokola and shrugged. They chatted for a while, examining the item from all angles before returning to the boats.

Stokola called Dale over to shore. He hopped off the Aqua Holic with ease, leaving the girls rocking in the water.

"This is a big mess we've got here," Stokola said, looking at him sternly. "Anybody hate you so much they'd want to kill you, Dale?"

32

W-w-what the hell do you mean?" Dale stammered at Stokola's words. "Nobody's got it in for me. I pay my debts and keep my nose clean. I'm not doing another stint in county. I learned my lesson after that first round of bullshit."

Stokola looked unmoved. Larson showed Dale the pictures he had taken with his phone of the blown-off boat part. "The fuel line was cut, look at the sliced line. It's too clean to have happened during the explosion."

Dale handed Larson back his phone. "I don't know who would have done this. My customers leave happy and I haven't pissed anyone else off — lately."

"Maybe you're not as good a mechanic as you think you are?" Larson said.

"Fuck you, hose boy. I'm not an idiot. There's no way I would have missed a slice like this. I rebuilt this engine and replaced everything, that hose included." He looked at Shawna.

She averted his gaze and focused on the fireboat. "I don't know anybody who'd try to kill him," she muttered.

Larson stuck his phone in his pocket. "I'll get these pictures to the arson investigator, but let's just be thankful you two weren't on the boat when it blew. With the fuel line cut and the vapors mixing with the heat of the engine, this could have taken two minutes or two hours. Miraculous. You two are very lucky."

Dale stared at the spot where his boat once floated. Vivian couldn't help but feel sorry for him.

The boathouse fire was almost out, and the dock was reduced to pilings. A few pieces of boat still burned on the water, casting a brownish orange glow as the sun set across the lake. That combined with the fall leaves reflecting in the water created an almost magical scene. Vivian imagined tiny fairies flitting around, waving their wands, turning everything a brilliant shade of orange and red.

"I could use a real restroom," Kate said to Larson. "Any chance we'll be leaving soon?"

"We've got this under control," Young said.

Vivian ran her hands up and down her arms. "It's a bit chilly, I need one of Tracy's hot toddies! Plus, Brandon promised us s'mores tonight."

Shawna snapped her head up and met Vivian's gaze. It was only a moment, but anger flashed behind her eyes. She turned and got off the boat.

What's with that? She got something against marshmallows?

Larson untied, pushed off, fired things up and turned the boat south. They cruised across the lake toward Turlington Farms B&B. The temperature had dropped at least 10 degrees, and Vivian's sweater was no match for the wind. She looked at Larson and envisioned him wrapping his muscular arms around her, whispering naughty nothings in her ear.

As they approached the dock Vivian saw two people in rockers on the back porch. "Is that Wendell and Mitzie? I thought they left."

Kate squinted toward the house. "It's not Wendell, that guy's bald, and even over the noise of the engine, we could probably hear Mitzie yapping from here." Kate concentrated a bit more. "Oh my gosh, I think it's Lucy! But wait… who's she with?"

Wendy made binoculars with her fists and shouted, "It's Pierre! I'd recognize that chrome dome anywhere!"

The girls had met Pierre LaRoche in Playa del Carmen on their first trip. He was the best friend of Jon Tournay, the soap opera star Vivian had spent a romantic evening with. His last, unfortunately. After returning home to Montreal, Pierre opened a gym with the money Jon had left him. Pierre was as big and buff as ever and still sported a Mr. Clean hairdo.

Kate clapped. "Yay, Lucy's back! But she's got some explaining to do."

"I expect she's got some sex-plaining to do," Wendy said.

Vivian bounced up and down in her seat, waving at them. "That slut! It's about time!"

Larson slowed to no-wake speed and cut the engine right before reaching the dock. He jumped out and tied up, then helped the girls disembark. Lucy and Pierre walked down to meet them at the shore.

Vivian hugged them both. "Hey, strangers, glad to see you!"

Lucy gave her a sheepish look. "Sorry about running off. I sorta freaked out." She hugged her again, then apologized to the other girls before introducing Pierre to Larson.

Vivian ran her hand down Larson's arm. "Y'all missed quite an adventure today. Larson saved the day." She looked up at him and smiled. "He's our fireman hero."

Larson shook his head and wrapped an arm around Vivian's shoulders. "I had Wendy call in the troops, and other than that, it was a group effort."

Lucy looked back and forth between them. "What happened? You all smell like burnt plastic, but I thought maybe that had something to do with the exhaust from the boat."

Larson's grasp slipped from Vivian's shoulders and made their way to her waist. He grazed her ass before casually lifting his arm to look at his watch. "I need to run, but how about we meet later? It's chili night at the Lake Placid Brewery. Let's say two hours?"

Vivian looked to the girls and Pierre, who all nodded. "See you there."

Larson leaned down and gave her a quick peck, then untied the line, jumped back on the Aqua Holic and headed out across the water.

Vivian's heart went thumpity-thump-thump watching him. She composed herself, then turned to Lucy and Pierre. "We'll tell you all about our fiery adventure inside by the fire. You know, since it's fitting."

They walked to the house and Pierre held the back door open for the girls. Everyone took a seat in the living room, but the fireplace was dark. Vivian stood in front of the hearth and threw a couple of pieces of wood on the grate. She picked up the box of matches just as a freshly showered Tracy walked into the room.

"I didn't realize you were back," she said. "I was just about to get the fire going." She took the box from Vivian and grabbed some newspaper. She stuffed it underneath the grate, struck the match and held it to the paper. "How was your day?"

"Exciting!" Vivian responded. "A boat exploded out on the lake!"

"Oh my gosh, that's terrible. Was anyone hurt?"

Vivian sat on the bricks and watched the flame consume the paper. "Thankfully, no. But it sounded like the fire could've easily started while they were on the boat. The couple probably would've been toast."

Kate grabbed a blanket off the back of the couch and draped it over herself.

"I want to hear this, but let me get you something warm to drink. You all look chilled to the bone. Be right back."

"So what have I missed?" Lucy asked.

Wendy, Kate and Vivian filled her in on the events from the day before, from the fall festival and the pumpkin drop to Mike Grimm and Nicole's grandpa's files, but Vivian didn't feel like she could get into a lot of details.

Vivian leaned toward Lucy's chair and said in a whisper, "We've found out some interesting info we'll tell you about later."

Lucy nodded.

Tracy walked into the room carrying a tray of hot cocoa and a bottle of Bailey's. Vivian smiled in appreciation.

"I'm so glad to be back," Lucy squealed.

Tracy handed out drinks, then sat next to Vivian and slapped her knee. "Okay, now tell me what happened today."

Vivian put a generous helping of Bailey's into her cocoa, stirred it, then told the story with the help of Kate and Wendy.

"Dale and Shawna are lucky to be alive," Kate finished.

"And unhurt," Wendy said. "It's a good thing they decided to go ashore for their, uh hummm, activities. Dale could've sustained a burned weenie."

Tracy's eyes got wide. "Excuse me?"

"Wendy!" Kate yelled.

"Oh, come on! He had his wiener between Shawna's buns when that boat exploded. She came out carrying her bra! And his pants were undone! You can't tell me you didn't notice."

"I noticed." Vivian grinned.

Lucy shoved her knee. "Of course you did."

Tracy laughed. "You girls are too much. I know Shawna. I'm glad she's all right."

"Do you know Dale?" Kate asked.

"Not very well. I used to take my car to him."

Brandon walked in carrying a bundle of wood and set it in a rack by the fireplace. She reached out and touched his arm. "But since Scooter Bill and I have been married, he's my mechanic now."

Brandon looked at Tracy. "He's not much of a mechanic, if you ask me. I'd never recommend him."

Tracy sighed and shrugged. "You're probably right, especially since his boat blew sky-high."

Vivian couldn't tell if Brandon's face was red from the heat of the fire or if he was upset by something, but she had an uneasy feeling. She finished off her mug of tastiness. "I'm going to go get cleaned up so we can meet my hot fireman."

Wendy stood. "I for sure need a shower, all this smoke smell in my hair. Yuck."

"Me, too," Kate said.

"We'll wait for y'all down here," Lucy said, squeezing Pierre's leg.

Vivian walked into her room and fell across the bed as Kate got into the bathroom first. For a pregnant woman, she moved quickly when it came to getting cleaned up. Vivian vegged out to the sound of the shower running and the comfort of knowing her friend was back. When her turn came, she was in and out of the shower in a hurry. Larson awaited.

Vivian, wrapped in a towel, walked to the closet for something semi-sexy to wear and noticed Lucy's bags weren't there. She went into the bedroom and double-checked, but nope, they were nowhere in sight.

She jumped into jeans, knee-high black boots with a low heel and a V-neck red sweater. She threw some mousse in her curls, hit them for two minutes with the blow dryer, threw on some powder, mascara and lipstick and was ready to roll.

The other girls were similarly dressed, Wendy in a brown sweater, jeans and her cowboy boots and Kate in black jeans and turtleneck, plus leather Clark's accented with a button on the side.

As the girls and Pierre walked down the front steps, Vivian bumped hips with Lucy. "Where's your luggage?"

Lucy looked at Pierre and grinned. "I'm going to be staying down the hall."

Naughty girl.

33

The girls and Pierre loaded up, with Kate serving as designated driver. They made their way down the long driveway of Turlington Farms and turned toward town. Wendy rode shotgun, and Pierre sat between Vivian and Lucy in the back.

Vivian stretched her right arm around Pierre's shoulder. "Catch us up, Pierre. How've you been doing in Canada? Been hitting the Canadian Club? The Molson? The Canada Dry?"

He ignored the beverage list. "You know I opened a gym a couple of years ago with the money Jon left me. I think he'd be proud. I just opened my third location and am scouting for a fourth in Toronto."

Wendy turned around and gave him a high-five. "That's awesome. Any plans to open a gym in the states?"

He looked down at Lucy and grinned. "I've been thinking some about it. I hear Denver is a nice place to live. And people are very active there."

"You could be Lucy's very own personal trainer," Vivian said. "Work on her stamina."

Pierre put his arm around Lucy's shoulders. "She has good stamina."

Lucy leaned over, putting her head in her hands.

Vivian laughed. "Man, I've missed you!" She kissed him on the cheek.

"I've missed you girls, too. I was so happy to hear from Lucy, you have no idea."

"Oh, we have an idea," Kate said.

"Okay, totally changing the subject," Vivian said. "We found a bunch of good stuff about Rebecca today in our closet."

The girls brought Lucy and Pierre up to speed on everything they'd discovered in the crawl space.

"So Brandon's worth millions?" Lucy asked.

Wendy nodded. "Millions."

"We found some interesting pictures, too," Vivian said.

"What kind of pictures?" Lucy asked.

Kate took a right onto Main Street. "Put it this way: We saw why

Brandon keeps that stuff hidden." She laughed and pulled into the parking lot of the Lake Placid Brewery. "I'm starving! I will probably eat a lot of chili tonight, maybe two servings, and I want extra beans."

"Little Plum needs some protein," Vivian said, getting out of the car.

Wendy shut the door and muttered, jokingly, "Yeah, but you don't have to sleep with her."

"My bed has room since Lucy has found other, more accommodating, accommodations," Vivian said and butt-bumped Wendy. "You could sleep with me."

"You snore. I'll take my chances with Tootie-loot Kate."

Pierre reached for the door handle. "This is more information than I wanted to know."

Wendy's phone chirped and she looked at the display, a flash of excitement was replaced by concern. "It's Nelson, I'll take this out here," she said and they all stepped to the side of the door. Wendy put it on speaker. "Hey, Wade."

They exchanged pleasantries and then Agent Nelson said, "I found the bio that your police officer in New Orleans did. It's definitely a cover for something, but I can't get into Jake's FBI file."

"So does that mean Jake has an FBI file?" Wendy asked. "Does, I mean did, I mean… does he work for the FBI?"

Nelson side-stepped the question. "It's going to set off alarms that I ran his name. I can't do it again."

"What about the phone?" Kate asked. "Were you able to get any information on that?"

"I can't access the info on the memory card," Nelson answered, "but I was able to trace that it was purchased in Bandera, Texas about seven months ago. It was sold by Cricket Wireless and paid for in cash. I don't have video footage to confirm who bought it."

"Bandera?" Wendy asked.

"Was Jake in the San Antonio area before he disappeared?" Vivian asked.

Wendy shook her head. "I didn't think so, but clearly I had no idea what he was up to."

Nelson signed off stating that was all the info he had and he couldn't look further as the suits would be bearing down on him for running the names of Paul Vaughan and Jake Stillson. If, by some chance, he could find out anything, he'd call.

Wendy sighed and hung up. Pierre gave her a shoulder hug and the girls joined in for a group hug. Kumbaya moment over, Pierre opened the door to the Lake Placid Brewery for the girls.

The brewery fit the typical Adirondack ambience of log construction and lots of stone. Vivian didn't see Larson, so they took a seat in the bar. The wall held a variety of bottles but also a ton of pictures in varying sizes. The bartender approached and tossed a coaster in front of everyone.

"What can I get for you?" she asked. What the short brunette lacked in height, she made up for in boobs. Her skin-tight tank top was out of season but showed off her bountiful bosom.

"Can you tell me about your home-brewed beers?" Pierre asked.

Bounty went through the list, describing and giving a few tastes. Everyone ordered a pint except Kate, who ordered a Coke.

"A little caffeine won't hurt," she said.

While they waited to be served and between glances to the front entrance, Vivian checked out the pictures on the back wall — couples, plenty of law enforcement, some firemen. She searched for Larson's face among the men, but the neon and Bounty the bartender kept getting in the way.

In one of the pictures she thought she saw a smiling Tracy, drink in hand, but with the distance, she wasn't sure.

Bounty set Vivian's Honey Rye Ale down on the coaster.

"Is that Tracy Holt?" Vivian pointed to the picture.

Bounty turned around and looked. "This one?"

"Yeah."

"She used to work here, before she got married." Bounty got back to her beer delivery, setting down Lucy's Ubu Ale. "There's another one of her over there." She pointed off to her right.

Vivian could see Tracy standing next to Brandon, Tracy wearing a white dress and veil, Brandon in a suit, both smiling, toasting the camera.

Kate had been in on the conversation. "Check 'em out. Interesting place for a reception, but then again, it's a pretty small town."

"Maybe the owner cut her a deal," Wendy said. "No wonder she knows how to make all those tasty concoctions."

Vivian didn't see any other pictures of the bride or groom, or any of Larson. She turned in the direction the bartender had gone and noticed Jeremy, the locksmith, down a few stools.

"Hey, there," she called and waved.

He smiled, stood up and walked over, checking out Lucy in the process. "I take it you haven't locked yourself out of anything lately."

"Negative," Vivian said, and Lucy added, "This is our friend, Pierre."

Jeremy's smile faded. After a few pleasantries, he turned his attention back to his brew.

It was never gonna happen, dude, Vivian thought, then she felt an arm wrap around her shoulders.

34

Larson landed a kiss just below Vivian's ear. "You look beautiful," he said, nuzzling her neck. "I could just have you for dinner. Forget the chili."

Vivian let that linger for a moment, then gave him a squeeze. "You don't look too shabby yourself."

Larson cleaned up nicely. Though his jeans and denim shirt were worn, they fit perfectly and accentuated all the right parts. She resisted the urge to run her fingers through the hair curling just above his collar.

He introduced them to his buddies Marty, James, Michael and Clay, who were also volunteer firefighters. Larson slapped Clay on the back and waved to James and Michael. "These two guys were on the lake today, but Marty stayed at the house flipping pancakes."

Marty flipped him off. "I was running the house. Don't make these girls think I'm a slacker like you."

"We know better than to believe a flipping thing this guy says," Vivian said with a wink.

"Let's go grab a table," Larson suggested and paid the tab as Bounty set it down. Pierre had grabbed for it, but Larson insisted.

They took a seat near a roaring stone fireplace.

Vivian grabbed a menu. "So what's good here?"

Larson scooted his chair closer and drew a deep breath. "You smell good." His fingers went up her neck and started playing with her curls. With his other hand he grabbed her menu and put it on the table. "You can't go wrong with the chili. Trust me." He squeezed her leg.

Oh lord.

The waitress took beer orders, then everyone ordered bowls of chili. They chatted for a while, talking about today's fire, but eventually the conversation turned to fire rescues.

The chili arrived and they dug in. Vivian liked it spicy, and this delivered. Her cheeks were flushed from the beer, her stomach warm from the chili, and she had a little warmness in her heart, though by no means was

145

she in love. Still, it was nice to be hit on.

James pointed with his spoon to Marty. "Any news on the journalist Evans and Tito took to the hospital?"

Marty set down his beer. "Betsy was on shift and I texted her but haven't heard back. They must be having a busy night in the ER."

"What journalist?" Vivian asked.

"The newspaper lady," Clay answered. "Earl's granddaughter."

"Nicole?" Wendy sucked in a breath.

He nodded and pointed his finger at her.

"What happened? Why is she in the hospital?" Kate pushed back her bowl.

"You know her?" Michael asked.

"We met yesterday at the festival and have sorta become friends," Kate said. "She came over to the B&B today."

"We can't tell you much because of privacy laws, but she sounded pretty bad," Marty said.

"Did she fall and hit her head or something? Car accident?" Vivian asked.

Marty looked apologetic. "I can't say, sorry."

"You may be able to visit her," Larson said and rubbed Vivian's arm. "Take her some flowers."

Vivian looked at the time on her phone, then at the girls and Pierre. "Let's run to the hospital. If we finish up now we can make it before visiting hours are over."

Larson gave them directions while they polished off their bowls and brews. The girls and Pierre got up to leave, saying goodbye to the firefighters.

Vivian rested her hand on Larson's shoulder. "Thanks for the directions. This night isn't turning out exactly as I'd hoped."

He stood and took her hand in his, entwining their fingers. "We've got a few more days. You have plans tomorrow?"

"I don't know what we've got going on tomorrow. Never know with these girls."

He grinned. "I'll be in touch." He leaned down and kissed her, letting his arms hug all the right places in the process.

She looked up at him, a bit dazed. "Okay."

Kate grabbed Vivian's arm and pulled her outside to the car, practically pushing her into the passenger seat.

"Okay, okay, I've snapped out of it," Vivian said.

Kate drove with care, but faster than usual. They swung by a grocery store and Vivian ran in and grabbed a bunch of fresh flowers, then they continued to the hospital. It was just after 10, and Kate found a front-row parking space. The main entrance was locked, so they trekked around to the ER.

Vivian walked up to the attendant behind the desk. Her name badge read Betsy.

She looked at Kate. "May I help you?"

Kate glanced down at her belly, then back to Betsy. "We're looking for someone who came through here earlier today. Nicole Jones?"

Betsy clicked around on the computer. "She's no longer in the ER, she's being admitted. Are you family?"

"No, but we just drove 300 miles to get here. Is there any way we can see her? Even for a few minutes?"

"She's in a holding unit, basically waiting for a bed, and she can only have two visitors at a time. I believe she may already have two back there."

"Can we swap places with one of them? Please, we've come all this way," Vivian said. "I just want to check on her. I won't stay long."

"Let me go see if they're okay with that," Betsy said, getting up.

She walked down the hall and swiped her badge onto the wall. The doors opened and she disappeared around a corner. Two minutes later she returned with a tall, light-skinned, African-American woman.

"Hi, I'm Kandace, Nicole's sister," she said, extending her hand. "Are you friends of Nicole's?"

Vivian introduced their group and explained how they'd met and seen her earlier that afternoon. "Is Nicole all right?"

"The doctor thinks she has E. coli poisoning. Her symptoms are consistent with it but they're running tests to confirm and rule out some other things. They're also checking with the health department to see if there have been any other cases recently. Right now she's severely dehydrated. They've given her medication to control her nausea."

"Poor Nicole," Kate said. "Do they have the fluid loss under control?"

Kandace shook her head. "At the moment I'd say no. You don't want to go back there; that's why I came out here."

"Does she have any idea where she got this?" Wendy asked.

"None. She had breakfast at home, and she had the same thing the day before. That was all she ate today so she has no idea what it could have been."

"When did she get sick?" Pierre asked.

"About 3 this afternoon."

"She was at the B&B late this morning but she seemed fine," Vivian said.

"Nicole said she was at Jeremy's house before she came to see us, remember?" Wendy said. "Did she eat anything there?"

Kate swiped a stray hair behind her right ear. "She didn't say."

"This is just awful," Lucy said. "Is there anything we can do for you or her?"

"I appreciate your asking, but no. She just needs to get better."

Vivian handed Kandace the flowers. "Please give her these and tell her we're thinking about her."

"I will. Nice to meet you all."

The girls and Pierre left the hospital. Kate drove the speed limit all the way to Turlington Farms. They said nothing for a long while, and Kate turned on the radio.

About three miles from the B&B Wendy spoke up. "I can't help but wonder if this wasn't accidental. Think about it. She starts looking into Mary Beth's and Rebecca's deaths and she suddenly gets sick? Alarm bells are ringing in my head."

"But who knew what she was doing besides us?" Kate asked.

Pierre had his arm around Lucy in the back seat. "Other newspaper people for sure. Perhaps you can talk to her tomorrow. Maybe help figure out how she ingested the E. coli."

Kate stopped at a red light. "I wish there was something we could do tonight."

"I have an idea." Vivian clicked off the radio. "But it's kinda illegal."

35

The light turned green but Kate kept her foot on the brake. Vivian pointed for her to turn left, though they were in the right lane. The car remained stopped.

Vivian looked up and down the street. "No one's coming. Go! We need to see who would want to hurt Nicole, and the best place to look for information is in her office. It's to the left. Let's do this."

Kate put both hands on the wheel but still didn't move. "Can't we get the key from her in the morning?"

"We need to look tonight," Vivian said and pointed to the left.

"How do you plan to get in her office?" Wendy asked.

"I haven't figured that out yet, but we'll know it when we see it."

"Small town, maybe she left the door unlocked?" Lucy suggested.

"Highly unlikely." The car behind them honked, and Kate pulled through the intersection, going straight. "I can't go to jail. I'm pregnant. Can you imagine? 'Excuse me, do you have a maternity prison outfit?' I want to help Nicole, but it will have to be with her consent and in the morning."

"But what if someone is trying to kill her?" Vivian pleaded. "Besides, they'll get you an extra-large, not maternity." She poked at Kate and giggled.

Kate was silent, but Vivian could see her brain in overdrive.

"Someone might try to sneak into her hospital room and finish her off. Security in the typical hospital isn't exactly Fort Knox. It's more like mall security. I bet I could sneak into any part of that hospital in the middle of the night, if I were a bad guy, and take out a patient, especially a defenseless, doped-up damsel in distress."

"Let's not test that," Pierre said.

Lucy patted Kate's shoulder. "I vote we go to her office, see what we can see. You can stay in the car if you want."

Kate sighed. "Why do I listen to y'all?" She made an illegal U-turn in the middle of the street, tires squealing.

Everyone screamed, even Pierre.

"You listen because you're a 1 percenter," Wendy said and laughed.

"A what?" Vivian asked.

"There's only 1 percent of the law she doesn't break, like the biker gangs."

"Geez, I don't think so," Kate said, turning right. "I'd much rather be part of the über rich 1 percent."

"It's because you really want to help Nicole and you, like I, suspect she's in trouble," Vivian said as they stopped with a jerk in front of the newspaper office.

All the lights were out in the brick building. Everyone sat in the car, unsure what to do.

Vivian continued. "And you bend to peer pressure. For that, we thank you." She started to get out, but Lucy grabbed her arm.

"How are we going to see anything in there?"

Wendy reached for her purse. "I've got a small handy-dandy flashlight in here. That'll help."

Pierre opened his door. "I'll check the front. If it's locked, I'll go around back, see if I can find a way in."

He ran to the front door and tugged, but it didn't open. He jogged around the corner of the building and was gone for a couple of minutes before returning to the car.

Vivian rolled down her window. "Any luck?"

"There's an old ventilation fan in the back. It's running slowly so I'd have to stop it, but I think there would be enough space for someone to squeeze through."

"Not it!" Wendy called.

"Me, neither!" Vivian yelled.

Lucy swatted at both of them. "Y'all haven't even seen it yet."

Wendy got out and held the door for Lucy. "We just ate chili. If I get squeezed I'm likely to squeeze out something myself. Nobody wants that."

"Fine," Lucy grumbled. "I'm having images of squeezy cheese. I don't want to see it come to life."

"I'll hold down the fort here," Kate said. "If I see anything suspicious or if someone shows up, I'll honk."

The group, minus Kate, went around back, and thankfully the lights were out behind the newspaper building. Vivian looked up and down the alley but didn't see anyone. They were relatively well hidden.

Pierre pointed to the fan. "I need to find something to wedge in there to stop it turning." He picked up a wooden pallet and set it underneath the fan, then piled two more on top of it. "This will help."

The fan was about nine feet up, in the middle of the brick wall. "Can we do this without breaking the fan?" Vivian asked him. "Or Lucy?"

Pierre shrugged. "Guess we'll see." He walked to the other end of the old building and around the corner. He came back with a log the length of his arm and the width of a mayonnaise jar. "This should do it."

"Where'd you get that?" Lucy asked.

"Wood pile at the house across the street," he answered, then said to Lucy, "I'm going to boost you up. Once you get inside, look for the fan switch and cut it off."

Wendy handed Lucy her flashlight. "May the Force be with you."

Pierre jumped onto the pallets and lifted the log. "You should take a few steps back, just in case." He adjusted the log in his right hand, getting a good feel for the weight distribution, then looked back at the girls. "Here goes nothing."

In one smooth motion he jumped up, then heaved the log with all his might, reaching up and slamming it between two blades. Bits of wood flew down onto Pierre and the pallets.

Vivian was impressed. The fan motor still hummed but the blades were no longer turning.

Pierre landed awkwardly on the pallets, which caused him to lose his balance. He fell back on his butt and winced. "Ouch."

"Wow!" Lucy said, reaching to help him up. "That was a Spider Man move if I ever saw one!"

Pierre shoved the pallets aside, leaned against the wall and laced his fingers together. "You ready, Spider Woman?"

Lucy looked up and down the street, not seeing any activity. She focused her attention and planted her right foot in his hands. "As I'll ever be."

Wendy and Vivian got on either side, just in case things went awry and she toppled.

Pierre gave Lucy a boost, and with Wendy and Vivian's help she managed to scramble her way up to where she had both feet on his shoulders, like a cheerleader, but the ledge of the fan was only to her chest. The fan's four-foot blades looked even bigger up close, and the ledge's 18-inch depth felt shorter.

I'm going to dive for it, Lucy thought. "Y'all be ready to catch me if this doesn't work! I'm going to pull myself in."

Pierre had his hand on the back of her thigh and was holding one of her hands. Vivian and Wendy had their arms outstretched, hands on the sides of Lucy's legs, helping steady her. "Don't worry, I've got you, babe," he answered. "I'll boost you up more when you're ready."

Lucy let go of his hand and put both palms on the edge. She bent her knees. "Okay, here we go. One, two, THREE!"

She pulled herself up, feeling Pierre's strength push her forward. She landed on the ledge, square on her tummy, next to the log holding back the blade. Because it was dark inside the building, she couldn't see down. She squirmed more onto the ledge and lay like that for a minute, letting her legs hang down and catching her breath.

Wendy and Vivian golf clapped from below.

"So far, so good." Lucy pulled the flashlight from her pocket and shined it into the warehouse below, looking for something to land on. An eight-foot table piled with newspapers was directly beneath her.

Crap, I have no other option.

She stuck the flashlight back into her pocket, then maneuvered herself through the humming fan, getting on her hands and knees. She yelled down, "There's a table below. I'm going to dangle from the ledge and drop onto it."

"Are you sure it's not too far?" Pierre said. "We don't want any broken legs tonight."

"I think it will be okay."

Lucy positioned herself sitting on the ledge. *How am I going to do this exactly?* She turned around and got on her knees, head between two blades. She began to scoot back, soon dropping her right leg over the edge.

Courage. Courage. Come on, Lucy, you work out six days a week. You can do this!

Then her left arm slipped forward, hitting the wedged log and moving it a tad. The fan blade moved toward her face, but the log held.

Not for long.

"OH SHIT!" she yelled, watching as the log spun free.

Lucy fell into darkness.

36

Lucy crashed onto the table inside the newspaper building feet first, but the papers were slippery, and her feet kept going, so she landed on her ass.

"Lucy! You okay in there?" Pierre yelled, panic in his voice. "Lucy? Are you all right?"

It took her a moment to shake off the fall. "Uhhhh, I think so." She did a quick check of body parts. "Yes, I'm okay." She slid off the table, doing another quick check as she stood. Everything seemed to be working.

She checked her pocket for the flashlight, but it wasn't there. She could make out the back door, two big pieces of equipment in the middle of the room and more tables along the wall. She looked at the table she fell onto and the newspapers she'd knocked everywhere. She got on all fours and crawled around, feeling for the flashlight. Not finding it, she crawled to the table and felt underneath.

Her fingers brushed the flashlight, rolling it just out of her reach. She bent lower and stretched her arm as far as it would go, barely touching the flashlight. She was able to roll it toward her and clutch it in her fist. *Finally!*

She stood and dusted herself off before clicking it on. The big pieces of equipment she had seen were the printing presses, and the tables along the wall held reams of paper, pens, manila folders and other office supplies. She shined the light toward the back door. *Let's hope there's not an alarm.*

She unlocked the deadbolt and turned the handle, holding her breath. She yanked the door open, ready to run should an alarm sound, but none did.

Pierre stepped in, placing both hands on her cheeks. "That was quite a ruckus." He slid his hands to her shoulders and down her arms.

"I proved white women can jump, but I also proved we can fall with the best of them."

She laughed, and the girls walked in.

"Nice job, Wonkita! I'm impressed!" Vivian high-fived her. "I couldn't have done that."

"You should have seen Pierre dodge that log!" Wendy said. "But all he

153

cared about was you. It's sweet."

Vivian took the flashlight from Lucy. "Unlike the Amazing Maize Maze, this bad boy's mine. I've been here before." She shined it around the room and tried to remember the layout of things from their visit yesterday. She could make out the doorway to the office.

They made their way around the printing presses to the door separating the printing area from the office. The windowless hallway was pitch black, so Vivian opened the door to the restroom and flipped on the light. She took a minute to let her eyes adjust before walking down the rest of the hallway to the office.

She saw the two wooden desks in the middle of the room and Nicole's desk centered in front of the window. A green banker's lamp sat on it, along with a cup full of pens and stacks of notepads.

"I'll start with Nicole's desk," Lucy said.

Vivian walked to one of the desks in the middle of the room and began opening drawers. Wendy picked up one of Grandpa's white file boxes. "I'll take this into the hallway and start going through it. We need to find Grandpa's heavy hitters list."

"I'll help you with that," Pierre said and picked up a second box.

Vivian pulled the middle drawer of the desk open and shined the light inside. Paper clips, pens, stapler, staples. She shut that and opened the top right drawer. Stationery. Next drawer, blank notebooks. Top left drawer held a stack of Lake Placid Brewery coasters. *What the heck?* The drawer below that was empty.

Vivian moved on to the next desk but didn't find anything significant. She walked over to Lucy, who was looking through a file.

"Anything good?" she asked.

"Brandon's file was on top of Nicole's desk. I think we need to take it back to the B&B with us. This sucker is thick, and we don't need to leave the light on long enough to go through it now."

"Good idea." Vivian looked around the room and saw Nicole's big, chrome briefcase beside her desk. "It's got locks, but let's see if we can put the file in here."

Lucy tried the latches, and they clicked open. She raised the lid and took out a pile of files. "April Robinson, Jeremy Donaldson, Mike Grimm, Tracy Holt."

"Tracy? What's in that file?" Vivian asked.

Lucy opened it and read a few pages. "She bartended at the Lake Placid Brewery and dated a guy named Scott Erickson. Says he was a plumber who took off to Omaha."

"What's in Omaha?" Vivian asked, baffled. *Why would you leave the beautiful Adirondacks for the Midwest?*

"He went to work for his uncle out there."

"This folder's different," Vivian said. "It's purple. And that's not Grandpa's bad handwriting. The folder itself looks newer."

"Maybe Nicole started this file?" Lucy said. She flipped through two more pages, then put all of the files in the case and shut it, careful not to change the combination on the locks.

Vivian opened the door to the hallway and shined the light toward the group in the restroom. "Any luck in there?"

Wendy poked her head out of the door. "One of these boxes was mostly random people, not much to the files. The box we're currently going through has a little bit thicker files, but I'm not seeing much of interest."

"Same here," Pierre said, "but honestly, I have no idea what I'm looking for."

Vivian walked into the office and pulled the lid off the last white box, shining the flashlight inside. The box was nearly empty.

She flipped through a couple of files. The names were in Grandpa's handwriting but Vivian didn't recognize any of them. *Is this his heavy hitters box?* She took them over to the briefcase. "Will these fit in there?" she asked Lucy.

Lucy popped the latches. "Yep." She stuck them in and closed it.

Vivian shined the flashlight around the room for a final look. "It couldn't hurt to take the rest of the files in this box. If Grandpa took the time to write it down and make a file, there could be something important."

Pierre picked up the half-empty box and walked toward the door to the hallway. "We've had lights on in here long enough. We need to go before someone calls the cops."

Vivian clicked off the lamp on Nicole's desk. They went back through the printing press area and hustled out the back door.

"How are we going to lock the door?" Vivian said as she walked out.

"No way to lock up without crawling through the fan," Pierre said.

"No way I'm doing that again," Lucy said.

Wendy tapped the box Pierre held. "We've got the important stuff here. There's not much to steal besides the one computer and the presses. I doubt that'll happen. I think our only option is to leave it unlocked."

"It'll be fine," Vivian said, even though she'd rather not. She didn't see any other option. "Nothing bad's going to happen. This is a nice, quiet town."

They walked to the car and found the engine off and the doors all locked.

Kate had her seat laid back and a forearm covering her eyes. She was fast asleep.

Vivian couldn't believe it. "So much for being our lookout!"

37

After tapping on the driver's side glass and waking up Kate, the girls and Pierre loaded into the SUV, files in the back, and headed toward Turlington Farms. Pierre had offered to drive, but Kate insisted she was fine. It had been a long day and not exactly the relaxing vacation Vivian had envisioned. She leaned her head against the back passenger door and started to nod off.

"That car is right on my butt," Kate said, pulling Vivian out of that sweet spot between consciousness and unconsciousness.

They were outside Lake Placid Village on a two-lane road lined with trees. Vivian turned to look out the back window and had to squint from the lights, which were high enough to shine directly into the back glass.

"What a jerk," she said. "I think it's a truck, probably a short guy since that is a big truck."

Wendy sat shotgun. "Are you going under the speed limit, Kate? Maybe you should go faster?"

"I'm going five miles over," Kate replied but pressed the gas pedal harder all the same. The headlights stayed just as bright and right behind them, keeping pace. "I wish there was a place for me to pull off and let him pass." She clicked on the high beams.

The road curved to the right but Kate didn't slow, just kept her hands at 10 and 2. The truck tapped their bumper, then backed off.

"Ahhh!" Kate screamed. "What the hell?"

"I'm calling 911," Wendy said just as a harder hit came. "Oh shit."

"I think they're trying to make us crash!" Kate screamed, just as the truck pushed harder against the back of the SUV, then backed off, revved the engine and steered slightly to the left.

"Hang on!" Pierre yelled.

The blow sent them into a spin. Everyone screamed. The lyrics to Josh Weathers' "Save Yourself" ran through Vivian's mind. *Go on and save yourself, baby!*

Kate tried to turn into it but the SUV careened off the road, crashing through the bridge railing, which caused the airbags to deploy.

The SUV plunged into the lake.

After the jolt of landing in the water, Vivian felt the weightlessness of the car as it bobbed. Cold water began gushing in through the doors, and the SUV started its descent into the dark waters.

"Crack the windows if you can!" she yelled.

"What?" Kate yelled.

"We need to equalize the pressure so we can get out."

Too late. The front of the SUV nosedived, the engine cut off and they lost power. Pierre turned in his seat and threw his legs up, kicking at the back driver's side glass. The window didn't give, so he kicked it again as more icy water poured in.

Kate fought with her deflating airbag, then pulled on her door handle, but it wouldn't budge. "Get me out of here!" She pounded frantically on her window. "My baby!"

"Kate, the pressure has to equalize before we can open the doors or bust out the windows," Vivian said, trying to sound calm, although she felt anything but calm inside. "It won't take much longer. We'll make it." *Let me be right.*

Kate leaned against the door, sobbing, and Wendy started pulling on the passenger's side door handle.

Vivian's panic rose as Pierre kicked at the window again. It didn't crack so he continued the pounding. With the headlights out, she had a difficult time seeing anything inside the car and couldn't see out at all.

The water rose to Vivian's stomach, and she knew they'd most likely die from drowning, although exposure would get them first if they could stay afloat that long. Pierre gave the side window another blow, this time breaking through. He delivered a few more swift kicks to the jagged edges.

"This is going to be tough, but as soon as the water is in here we'll be able to get out," Vivian said. "I saw it on 'Dateline' or something." Her legs were already freezing from the water. "Kate, it's going to be okay."

"Take a few deep breaths," Pierre said. "I promise, I'll get you all out of here."

It didn't take long for the water to reach the top. "Get ready!" he yelled. "I'm going to get Kate first. Then make sure Wendy is out. Lucy, you and Vivian stay together. Here we go!"

The water enveloped them. Pierre pushed his door open, then opened Kate's door. He took her hand and pulled her out, helping her to the surface. Then he dived back down and helped Wendy. She'd gotten her door open and was on her way to the top.

Vivian and Lucy were holding hands when they'd gone all the way under. After Pierre slipped out to get Kate, they started out of the car together, Lucy first, but their hands slipped and they lost each other in the panic.

Vivian swam out of the window and shortly surfaced. "Lucy?" she sputtered, coughing and swallowing lake water. "Lucy!"

"I'm here!"

"Kate?"

"I'm here with Wendy," she yelled.

Pierre grabbed Vivian's hand and pulled her toward the shore. "You can swim, right?"

"Yes. I lost Lucy." Vivian started crying. "I thought I'd lost Lucy." Her legs were numb from the freezing water, but she swam with every bit of strength she had. Thankfully the SUV hadn't flown too far out into the lake, and it was only a few strokes before she touched the bottom and dragged herself on shore.

The girls huddled together, hugging and crying on the small muddy beach, and made room for Vivian as she joined them.

"I'm going up to the road to get help," Pierre said and took off.

"Kate, how are you?" Vivian asked, drained.

Kate wiped her eyes and took a big breath while rubbing her belly. "I don't know. The airbag." She shivered.

"Help will be here soon," Lucy said, rubbing her hands up and down Kate's arms.

Wendy pointed to the guardrail they had flown through. "Thank god that was there. No telling how far we might have gone."

Vivian turned her attention to where the SUV had been. A few bubbles floated to the surface, then a burst came from the water and the chrome briefcase popped up.

"Grandpa's notes!" Wendy yelled.

"We might have ended up dead because of those," Lucy said.

"There has to be something important in his notes," Wendy said. "And we need to find it, so we can find who ran us off the road. Assholes!"

Vivian pumped her fist in the air. "Yeah! And they're going to pay for putting Little Plum in danger!"

"Yeah!" Lucy and Wendy said together.

Kate smiled a little and brought her knees up to her chest, or as close as she could get them. "I don't think Nicole accidentally ate something bad. This is related. Someone's got a secret and they don't want her, or us, finding it out."

"Kate, did you see anyone at Nicole's office before you conked out?"

"No, I don't remember seeing anyone."

Pierre showed up by the demolished railing. "Help is on the way. I ran to a house down the road and broke in to use the phone. I'm going to come down and help get you all get up here. It's steep, so we're going one at a time."

He trudged down and took Kate up first. Then Lucy, Wendy and Vivian last.

"I'm ready to kill whoever did this to us," he said as they used the trees as leverage to get up the embankment. "I was going to leave tomorrow, but now I'm staying."

Vivian almost lost her balance a couple of times; the mud didn't want to relinquish its hold on her feet. It was an arduous process, but they made it to the road.

The four girls sat on the side of the road and Pierre threw a comforter over them.

"I grabbed it off a bed in their house," he said. "Figured I could buy them a new one."

A cloud passed in front of the moon, and it was quiet except for the chattering of teeth. Vivian heard a car and then saw headlights coming around the curve. "Please let them be a Good Samaritan and stop."

"Amen to that," Wendy said.

Pierre jumped up and down and waved his arms. The car slowed and came to a stop, and the driver rolled down the window. Pierre bent to talk to the driver and pointed toward the lake.

"I'm so cold, I'm not sure I can take much more." Kate cupped her hands to her face and breathed into them. "This is where wearing a wetsuit and peeing in it could really warm you up."

"I refused to do that rafting in Colorado," Wendy said. "But I'd give it some serious consideration right now. I'm so cold I feel like my veins would break like glass if I extended my arms."

Pierre walked over. "Kate, they said you can come sit with them to warm up if you'd like. They don't care that you're wet."

"Oh, thank you!"

He looked at the other girls. "Sorry, only room for one. I'm going to run back down by the water and see if I can't get that briefcase."

"Be careful," Lucy called out, then looked at Vivian. "What would Bear Grylls say to do in this situation?"

"Strip down!" she answered and laughed. "By god, I might just do it!"

38

The wail of a siren cut through the night and lifted Vivian's spirits, so she decided to not get naked. The impenetrable cold was about to be a thing of the past.

A sheriff cruiser followed by an ambulance stopped, and two officers followed by two paramedics got out. They talked to the driver, who pointed toward the bridge and their group standing just beyond it. One paramedic stayed with Kate, and the other ran across the street toward them.

Another truck screeched to a stop coming from the other direction. Larson got out and joined the paramedic with the group as one of the deputies began putting flares around the scene.

"What happened?" He leaned down and put his arm around Vivian as Pierre appeared with the chrome briefcase.

"A truck ran us off the road. Pierre saved the day." She snuggled close to his warmth.

The paramedic was talking to Kate, asking her questions. Vivian watched as he opened the door to the car and helped her out. She walked with him to the ambulance, and he helped her onto the bench in the back.

Larson smiled at Vivian. "You sure know how to make a lasting impression. You're one woman I won't ever forget."

Vivian laughed and almost cried with relief but didn't take her eyes off Kate. "I do like to make a splash."

They laughed about that, and she told him about the truck that intentionally ran them off the road.

"That's unbelievable," Larson said. "And pretty damn frightening."

"What are you doing here?" Vivian asked.

"I was on my way home and heard the call on my scanner. I was close so thought I'd better stop." Larson turned his attention to Lucy and Wendy, and the other paramedic brought them each a blanket, Pierre included.

Pierre held up the briefcase. "Can we put this in your truck for now?"

"Sure thing, let me get this, you go get warmed up." Larson took the briefcase and put it in the bed of his truck.

160

Lights and a siren were seen and heard and a sheriff's car came into view moments later. The cruiser screeched to a stop and Deputy Stokola got out. She nodded to Larson and the paramedics as she walked toward the group. A second sheriff's car came around the curve and parked behind Stokola. Deputy Young slammed the door and bustled toward everyone.

Stokola's uniform looked like she had tossed it into the clothes hamper and then thrown it back on when she got the emergency call. She took out a notebook and pen, then looked at the girls and Pierre. "I'd say it's nice to see you again, but not under these circumstances."

Pierre introduced himself. Deputy Young, who had dark circles under his eyes, asked, "Can you tell us what happened?"

"We were on our way back to Turlington Farms," Lucy started.

"From where?"

She looked at Vivian, who answered, "The hospital. We had gone to see Nicole Jones."

Young looked back to Lucy, who continued telling the story with the help of Pierre, Wendy and Vivian.

"Can you describe the vehicle at all?" Stokola asked.

Vivian shook her head. "It was something high off the ground, like a truck. The lights shone into the back glass and not below, like a car's would."

Young looked at them. "Any idea why someone would try to push you into the lake?"

Vivian felt Lucy's eyes on her, but she didn't look her way. She didn't want to talk about the stop at Nicole's and the files. She didn't think admitting to breaking and entering was a good idea. "No," she answered, "no idea who would want to hurt us."

The paramedic who had been evaluating Kate walked up. "We need to get her to the hospital for an evaluation and an ultrasound. The airbag deployed and she's pretty shaken up. Her blood pressure is elevated."

Vivian's heart skipped a beat.

She nodded. "Thanks, Billy."

"I'm going with her," Wendy said to Stokola. "Buddy system."

Kate was moved off the bench in the ambulance, put on the gurney and strapped down.

Vivian wanted to cry.

Larson put his arm around her. "I'm sure it's just a precaution."

Wendy climbed in, sat on the bench and grabbed Kate's hand.

A sheriff's deputy closed the ambulance doors and patted them, indicating it was ready to roll. The ambulance took off, lights flashing but no siren.

Vivian shuddered as the ambulance pulled away. She couldn't believe one of her best friends was on her way to the hospital, her baby potentially at risk. The cold enveloped her, and she put her chin to her chest, staring at the ground.

"She's freezing," Larson said to Deputy Stokola. "Can't this wait?"

"How about we sit in the patrol cruiser?" Stokola said.

Vivian nodded, and they all walked over to her car and got in.

Stokola turned the heat on high and got back to business. "Has anything else strange happened to you since you found the jawbone two days ago?"

"Just the boat fire on the lake today," Vivian said, "but that didn't have anything to do with us. We just happened to be there."

Stokola nodded, then asked some additional questions, mostly about where they had been, if Kate had done anything on the road to tick someone off, etc. After about 10 minutes she said they could go.

"We'll get the car towed first thing in the morning, and we'll call you to come get your belongings." She paused. "Actually, we'll call the B&B, as I imagine your phones are ruined."

Lucy sighed. "That would be correct."

"Come on," Larson said and got out of the SUV. "I'll give you a ride. I promise to crank up the heater full blast."

Vivian wrapped her blanket tighter around her and shivered. "I need some heat, all right."

"Can we stop by the hospital?" Lucy asked. "I really want to get out of these wet clothes, but we should check on Kate."

Larson opened the back door of his truck. "I'll take you anywhere you need to go."

Pierre climbed in beside Lucy, and Larson started up his truck. He turned around in the road, squealing his tires, and headed back toward town.

"So what's in the briefcase?" he asked.

Damn! I was hoping he wouldn't ask.

When Vivian didn't answer immediately, Larson said, "Is there something else going on here I need to know about?"

What the hell, he didn't run us off the road. "We think Nicole was poisoned on purpose. We stopped by her office after we left the hospital and borrowed some files. I hope they're still legible."

"Why would someone poison her?"

Lucy and Vivian gave him the rundown on them looking into Mary Beth's and Rebecca's deaths. "We're not sure who could be behind all of this but we wanted to help."

Larson pulled into the hospital parking lot. "I've got some friends who work here, even someone in the ER. I'll go see what I can find and ask them to keep a special eye on Nicole. I won't mention any particulars, just that she

162

not have any visitors, that kind of thing."

They all walked into the ER, and the receptionist smiled at Larson. "You keeping my husband out of trouble?"

"That's a tough job, Betsy, you know that," Larson replied.

Lucy asked to see Kate, and Betsy gave them her ER room number and buzzed them back. Vivian and Lucy went to check on her while Pierre and Larson stayed in the waiting area.

The door to Kate's room was cracked so Vivian knocked as she gently pushed. "How's our Little Plum?"

Kate's color had returned, as had her pregnancy glow. She was wearing a hospital gown and was strapped to a fetal monitor that displayed a constant baby heartbeat. "The baby's just fine. The ER doc called the on-call obstetrician. He did an ultrasound and checked me from head to toe, literally. We're good." She tapped her tummy and smiled.

"Thank goodness," Vivian said and gave her a long hug. "I was so worried."

"Me, too," Lucy said and got her own hug.

"I called Shaun and told him my phone is kaput for now," Kate said. "I told him we'd probably get new ones tomorrow. I've got to call him back tonight, though."

Wendy sat in a chair beside the bed. "While the doctor was with Kate, I checked with the lady up front about Nicole, and she said they moved her to a room."

"That was pretty much what we thought would happen," Vivian said. "Larson is our ride tonight, and he said he'd swing by and check on her while we're here."

Another knock sounded at the door, and a nurse walked in with a clipboard. She handed it to Kate. "Looks like you're good to go, if you can please sign here. The doctor has provided instructions for care."

"What kind of instructions?" Vivian asked.

"He was afraid I might have some stiffness from the airbag. He gave me some meds, just in case. I'm okay, Viv."

"You be safe out there," the nurse said, removing the fetal monitoring wires and sticky patches from Kate's belly.

Kate scratched her signature and handed the clipboard back. "Thank you." She threw the covers off and looked at her wet clothes in a bag. "I think I'll just walk out in my gown."

Vivian looked at Kate, then at her waterlogged self. "Can I get one of those?"

The ER nurse brought Kate an extra hospital gown so she could wear it backwards and amply cover her derriere. She also brought a gown for

Wendy, Lucy and Vivian since they were still in their wet clothes.

"I don't think Larson wants my butt touching his seat," Kate said as she tied the strings in front and then slipped on her soggy Clark's.

It was all Vivian could do to keep from laughing at their appearance. Four girls in hospital gowns. She wrapped a hospital blanket around Kate as they walked to the lobby. "It's chilly out, you're going to need this."

Pierre waited for them by the door and did a double take but didn't say anything.

He probably wishes he had a gown, Vivian thought.

"Larson's outside." Pierre led the way as the automatic doors opened. Larson's truck was pulled into the emergency drop-off.

"How are we all going to fit in there?" Kate asked.

"It's roomy," Vivian said and bumped Lucy with her hip. "Besides, Lucy can sit on Pierre's lap."

Larson held the door for them and they piled in. "How's the baby?" he asked Kate.

She tucked the blanket around her and smiled. "Perfect. Did I miss anything at the accident site?"

"Not really," he said and pulled onto the road. He drove back the way they'd come and slowed as he approached the accident scene. The sheriff deputies were gone and the flares had burned out, but three construction barrels sat across the broken guardrail.

"Good thing my insurance deductible was met, since I couldn't have given the hospital a payment," Kate said. "I didn't even think about that when I called Shaun."

Larson handed her his phone and called her husband. As expected, he had freaked out about the accident but was calmer now knowing she and Little Plum were fine.

Kate handed the phone back to Larson and looked over her shoulder at the girls and Pierre in the back. "He was about to book the next flight here. I had to work hard to reassure him I'm fine and that we won't have any more issues."

Vivian patted her arm. "We'll be extra careful."

"I've been thinking," Kate continued. "Brandon has that big old SUV. Could it have been him who rammed us?"

"I don't think so," Wendy said. "The truck or SUV that hit us looked like an old Ford and had an aftermarket exhaust, which makes it louder than typical."

"I'm impressed a girl notices these things," Larson said, turning down the drive to Turlington Farms. "That is something you definitely need to tell Stokola."

"Way to be sexist, Larson," Wendy said, "but so you know, I have

Flowmaster exhaust on my Trans Am. Gives it the growl, so I just notice these things. If I heard that truck again, I'd know it."

"I'm going to point out every old Ford we see," Pierre said. "I'd like to crush whoever ran us off the road tonight."

Larson pulled to a stop at the B&B and ran around to the passenger door to help Kate out. He walked them to the porch and gave Vivian a hug goodbye. "I'll check on you tomorrow. Get some rest."

Pierre walked up the front steps with the briefcase. He clicked it open. "This thing wasn't completely waterproof. The papers are wet. What do you want to do with this tonight?"

"We can't leave it out here," Wendy said in a low voice. "We'll spread the files out in the bathtub or something, so the pages can dry."

Vivian reached for the door, but before she could turn the handle, it opened. Tracy stood in the entry in a bathrobe and motioned them in. She took in Kate's blanket and the hospital gown brigade. "My goodness, what happened to you? We were worried with it being so late."

"We had an unexpected dip in the lake tonight," Vivian said.

Tracy shut the front door and turned around. "Where's your car?"

Vivian fell onto the sofa, exhausted. "In the lake."

39

Day 5

Vivian awoke, sheets tangled around her and three pillows thrown off the bed. *What the hell?* Then she remembered the scattered images and funky dreams she'd had. She got out of bed and stepped around the files, making her way to the bathroom.

Wendy was at the sink brushing her teeth. "Mornin'."

"Mornin'," Vivian mumbled and picked up her own toothbrush. Her mouth was unusually dry so she cupped her hands under the faucet and drank some water before brushing. "How's Kate?" she asked.

"She got up, went downstairs for a bite, then got back in bed. I think she's still pretty tired."

"Yesterday was a really long day, and a bit on the treacherous side," Vivian said, squeezing toothpaste onto her brush, "but today will be better."

"It has to be. Today we will not wind up in, or on, the lake!" Wendy dried her face on a towel.

Vivian put her toothbrush into its holder and threw it in her toiletry bag. "We need to get new cellphones, but we can't do that until we get a new rent car. Maybe we can look through the files this morning, while Kate's asleep? Have you heard from Lucy or Pierre?"

"Negative, not one peep. Let me run down for a cup of coffee first. Be back in a jiff. Want anything?"

"I'm good, thanks." Vivian threw on jeans and a sweater, went back to the bathroom and put some mousse in her curls, then brushed her face with powder. Since Wendy wasn't back, she decided to go ahead and keep going with the makeup, something she usually didn't do. Ten minutes later she was done.

Wendy must have decided to eat breakfast, Vivian thought as she snapped open Nicole's chrome briefcase. She pulled out the top file: Brandon Holt. She perused Grandpa's notes, his handwriting now more familiar and easier to decipher, and took her time reading about Mary Beth's death.

Warm summer day, not a cloud in the sky. Brandon had been at work, but on his lunch break. No sign of forced entry to the house and no indication that anyone else had been there. Mary Beth had been known to go swimming in the lake by herself. Police didn't find any foul play, and the coroner didn't find anything suspicious. Her death was ruled an accident.

Vivian closed the file as Wendy opened the bedroom door. "Did you decide to get something to go with that coffee?"

Wendy quietly shut the door. "I went downstairs and didn't see Tracy or Brandon, so I went out back and tried to get in the garage. I wanted to see what kind of cars they have."

Vivian shifted on the bed, intrigued. "What'd you find?"

"Nada. The garage was locked up tighter than Queen Elizabeth's jewelry. Plus, the window in the side door was covered with a black curtain, so I couldn't see anything. I tried a few different ways to get in, but got nowhere."

"I hope they didn't see you sneaking around," Vivian said as she set Brandon's file on the bed. "Brandon could have been involved in Mary Beth's drowning. I remember passing the hardware store in town and it's not far from the house. He could've come home on his lunch break and done something. The neighbors are far enough away that he could've been here without being seen."

"I didn't see them around anywhere." Wendy took a sip of coffee. "In Kate's dream, Mary Beth's muscles froze up. What would cause that? Could Brandon have given her poison or something?"

Vivian tapped the closed file. "Good question. I don't know enough about poisons to know what would cause that. Know anyone we could ask?"

"Who's been poisoned?" Lucy asked as she stepped into the room. "I thought I'd come find out what was on tap for the day."

"Good morning there, little Miss 'Found Yourself a New Bed,' " Vivian said. "Don't you have a nice pink glow in your cheeks. Been sexercising?"

"Yeah, where is good ol' Pierre?" Wendy asked. "Did he need a rest?"

"Oh, stop," Lucy joked, bouncing up and down on the bed. "Do I really have a glow?"

"Heck, yeah, you do. Orgasms take years off your face," Vivian said. "I think they help with blood pressure, too."

"Hmmm," Lucy said, keeping her bouncing pace. "So what are y'all doing?"

Vivian picked up the next file on the pile, Jeremy Donaldson. "We're looking through these to find a killer, of course! But soon we'll be heading to town to replace our swimming cellphones."

"We also need to go talk to Mary Beth's friend, Suzy Fairlie, at the fish store," Wendy reminded.

Lucy peeked over at Jeremy's file. "I can see his issue with Mary Beth, unrequited love and all that, but what ties does he have to Rebecca?"

Vivian skimmed the file, not finding any relevant information other than what Nicole had told them the day before. "None that I can see other than their mutual husband."

Wendy dived into Brandon's file. She held up a newspaper article of Rebecca's death and a yellow Sticky Note. "This reads, 'Brandon = suspect?' " She picked up another piece of paper.

"Grandpa's notes say that after Rebecca died, he talked to people in the diner, men in the barbershop, even spoke to Amanda, Mary Beth's cousin who owns the You Name It store. Everyone thought Brandon had something to do with Rebecca's disappearance, and people in town also started wondering about Mary Beth's death, was it really an accident? That before Rebecca's death, everyone felt sorry for Brandon about losing his wife, but after he married the second so quickly and then she disappeared not too long after, folks thought he was involved in both situations. Grandpa agreed."

Kate walked into the room rubbing her eyes. "Everybody thinks he's in this up to his eyeballs."

Vivian gave her a smile. "Mornin', sunshine. How you feeling?"

Kate smiled. "I'm good. Had a little breakfast and a nap. I need to call Shaun. I think I should check in more often after last night. He was pretty freaked out."

"You want to borrow the B&B phone to call the rental car company and arrange to get another car?" Vivian asked. "Then we can ride into town and get new phones."

"I'm already on it," Kate replied. "The new rental should be here in 30 minutes."

Lucy looked at the files lying around the room and in the briefcase. "Let's each take a file and go through these while we wait. Then we're going to need to put these back into the briefcase and clean this place up. It looks like a tornado hit it."

Vivian scooped up the folders and paper on the bed, dresser and floor. It looked like her office at work, paper everywhere. She double-checked Jeremy's file in case she missed anything, but she hadn't. She set it aside, then picked up Tracy's purple folder.

It didn't take long to read the contents, as the only thing inside was a fluorescent green Sticky with a single question mark. She showed the girls.

"What the heck?"

Kate looked from Vivian's face to the big black question mark. "I guess Nicole has questions about Tracy. Or maybe she wants to ask her questions."

"Maybe Nicole thinks Tracy is next?" Wendy said.

Goosebumps broke out on Vivian's arms. "He is kind of an asshole to her." She shivered and set down the file and looked over Wendy's shoulder. "Anything interesting in April's file?"

"That Grandpa was a sly old guy," Wendy said. "He started keeping tabs on April as soon as news broke about the school testing debacle. He was in the school for an interview when April went off on Mary Beth and heard it all. The principal was walking him to Mary Beth's classroom when the shouting started." Wendy stopped for a sip of coffee and to turn the page.

"He said that on April's last day, she went across the hall to Mary Beth's room and screamed at her. The principal ran in and broke it up and told April to leave the campus immediately. Grandpa peeked into April's classroom and everything was scattered all over the floor and the desks were knocked over."

"Hurricane April," Kate said. "Does Grandpa say what he overheard?"

Wendy nodded. "He quotes her. 'You prim and proper goody-two-shoes. You got me fucking fired. Like you never changed a kid's answer to help him pass? One day fate is gonna kick you in the ass. Hard.' "

"That's incriminating." Vivian leaned against the dresser. "Anything else?"

Wendy flipped through a few more pages. "He followed her off and on for a couple of weeks. He suspects she keyed Mary Beth's car and threw a baseball through the principal's living room window."

"That's something," Lucy said, gathering up the pages on Otto, the town recluse. "People do the dumbest things."

Kate moved a file out of the way and sat in the chair. "Any connection between April and Rebecca?"

Wendy thumbed through a few more pages, then closed the folder. "Not that I see. She laid low. The last note said she started working at the Olympic Ski Jumping Complex."

Vivian put Tracy's file on top of Jeremy's and Brandon's in Nicole's briefcase, then picked up the contents of Coach Stubbs' file. She scanned the few pages and smirked.

"Listen to this. The football coach was known for being a little too friendly with some of the high school girls, including Mary Beth. Brandon quit midseason after finding out that the coach 'accidentally' bumped into Mary Beth so he could cop a feel. He had done that to a couple other girls and insisted it was accidental so nothing was done to him. Brandon didn't buy it and wouldn't play for him anymore."

"Not motive for murdering Mary Beth years later," Wendy said.

"Brandon was a key player, and they lost the rest of the games that season," Vivian said as she put the file into the white box. "But no, not motive for murder. If anything, you think he'd be after Brandon."

Kate opened her file. "Then why would Grandpa have him in the box of heavy hitters?"

Vivian looked out the window for the rent car. "Maybe we're missing some pages." She bent down and looked under the bed. She and Lucy had picked up all the loose sheets. "What do you have in Otto's file, Lucy?"

Lucy sat on the edge of the bed and opened the folder. "For a recluse, he knew a lot about the goings-on around town and evidently didn't always stay so reclusive. Grandpa used to see him sitting on a bench in Mid's Park on Main Street just watching people, so he'd join him and strike up a conversation. Looks like Otto had heard a good deal of the gossip about Brandon after Mary Beth's death, and even more after Rebecca disappeared. Some of the rumors were pretty far-fetched, like the one that Rebecca was already married and her husband showed up and took her home. Another was that she got amnesia and wandered off. This one is crazy — that she ran off with a bassoon player from Syracuse who was in town playing with the Sinfonietta in the summer. And, of course, there's always the aliens." Lucy gave Vivian a huge smile. "See, I'm not the only one who watches *The X-Files*."

Wendy looked at Lucy. "Where's Pierre?"

"In our room on the computer. He said he had to do payroll."

Kate held up a piece of paper from a file on the bed and waved it in the air. "Hey, guess who Mike Grimm is dating?"

40

Kate sat in the chair in Vivian's bedroom jostling a piece of yellow legal paper back and forth. "Guess, go ahead," she said to Vivian, Wendy and Lucy. "Take a big, fat guess. Guess who Mike Grimm is dating."

They looked at her.

"Uhhhm, Nicole?"

"No! April Robinson! The teacher Mary Beth got fired."

"Whoa," Vivian said. "What if they're in on both murders together? Conspiring?"

Kate set the sheet back in the file. "I can see why they'd want to murder Mary Beth, but Rebecca? If they killed her, we're missing the connection."

"It all links to Brandon," Wendy said. "There's no getting around it."

"True," Kate said. "I still think we should look into April and Mike today, though. Let's go see her at the Olympic Ski Jump Complex, then pay Mike a visit at his studio."

Vivian grabbed her jacket out of the closet. "I wanted to go see Suzy Fairlie at the fish store, so let's go there before we visit April."

A knock sounded at the door and Brandon called, "Girls, Deputy Stokola is here to see you."

The girls picked up the remaining files and threw them into the briefcase, then tromped downstairs to find Stokola in the living room chatting with Tracy, Brandon and Pierre. The conversation stopped when the girls walked in. Stokola had dark circles under her eyes but her uniform was clean and pressed.

"I brought all of the items that were in the car." She held up a clear plastic bag filled with the girls' purses. A little water sloshed in the bottom. "I just left the scene of the accident and thought I'd save you a trip to our office."

"Any updates on who ran us off the road?" Lucy asked.

"We just had the car towed out of the lake and will need to process it, look for paint chips, that kind of thing."

Tracy eyed the water in the bottom of the bag and reached for it. "Do you want me to take this onto the front porch?"

Stokola handed her the bag. "Sure. I need a minute with them."

Tracy shot Brandon a look, then grabbed the bag from Stokola and headed for the porch. Brandon walked out the back door.

Once they were out of earshot, Stokola turned to Wendy and Kate. "I need to get statements from you since I didn't last night." She pulled out a notepad and pen.

Vivian interrupted before the interview could get underway. "If I'm not needed, I'd like to get the stuff out of my purse. Get it drying out."

Stokola nodded. "I just need these two."

Vivian, Lucy and Pierre walked out on the front porch and found Tracy pouring the water in the plastic bag on her rose bushes. "I'll grab you some towels, be right back."

Vivian picked up her purse. "Let's see what the damage is." She pulled scraps of paper, gum, car keys, makeup and her wallet out of her orange leather purse. She uncapped her favorite lipstick and poured water out of the tube. "A stop to a drug store is in order, but I think my bag will be fine once the lining dries."

"I don't think I'm as lucky," Lucy said, going through her once silver and gray, now greenish-brown, leopard-print calf-hair Nancy Gonzales clutch.

Pierre nuzzled her neck and wrapped his arms around her waist. "I'll buy you a new one."

Vivian looked at the bag, though it wasn't her taste, and she knew it was expensive. "Be careful there, Pierre. She doesn't do knockoffs."

Lucy started to protest, but the sound of cars approaching stopped her. "That must be our new rental."

The cars pulled to a stop and a guy in a white dress shirt and black tie got out of a navy Jeep Grand Cherokee. "Hello. I'm looking for Kate Jameson."

"I'll get her," Vivian said and then went inside where Stokola was wrapping up. "The car's here."

Stokola shut her notebook and clicked her pen. "I'm done for now. I'll let you know if anything comes up or if we have any further questions." She headed for the door.

The girls went out front and Kate dealt with the rental car. Tracy had brought them towels and extra purses of hers for the girls to borrow. The selection was difficult as they were all ugly. Two resembled shag carpeting, one was purple corduroy, and the green leather on the third was so beat up, it was surprising there were no holes.

The girls threw their credit cards, cash and IDs into the ugly-ass purses and asked Tracy where to get new cellphones. She gave directions to an all-carrier one-stop shop and sent them off with a bag of cookies. They walked down the front porch steps to a shiny, navy blue Jeep Grand Cherokee.

Kate signed the paperwork and climbed behind the wheel. "I love that new car smell. This Jeep only has 1,400 miles on it."

Navigator Wendy got in the front seat and directed Kate into town and to the store that sold everything from batteries and alarm clocks to makeup cellphones. They planned to meet at the diner when each had a new phone in hand.

An hour later, Vivian set her new, hot-pink smartphone on the counter beside Wendy and pulled up the map app. "The fish store is on the way to the Olympic Ski Jump Complex." She looked at Wendy's French toast and told the waiter, "I'll have a plate of that."

"I didn't have breakfast," Wendy said as she slathered her plate in maple syrup. "Their brunch menu is kick-ass." She stabbed a slice of strawberry and toast and hummed as she ate it.

Vivian's new phone rang and a picture of Antonio with NOPD filled the screen. She picked up on the second ring.

"I've got some news on Jake's other cellphone."

"Let's hear it."

"My FBI contact was able to get the call history and is tracing the numbers. There was a lot of call activity and my guy's doing this on his own time, so it could take a while."

Vivian groaned inwardly. "Like weeks?"

"Could be a couple of months."

Now she groaned audibly. "That stinks but we understand. What about text messages?"

"There wasn't any text history. If there ever had been, it was wiped, but it seems odd he wouldn't have wiped the call history, too."

Vivian looked over at Wendy, who was sitting close enough to hear every word.

Wendy took the phone. "Thanks, Antonio, for helping. I appreciate it."

"You got it. I'll be in touch if I hear anything else."

Wendy set the phone on the counter. "Weeks or months. That sucks."

"Antonio will keep after him. He knows you need that info," Vivian said.

That didn't seem to cheer Wendy, and she picked up a magazine the patron beside her had left and flipped the pages. Vivian played with her new phone, waiting for her food.

They were finishing up just as Kate, Lucy and Pierre joined them. Kate sniffed the air and Vivian moved her jacket aside to reveal a to-go box. She opened it and held it out to Kate. "Two side orders of bacon and a slice of ham, just for you."

Kate laughed. "You're the best. I'll munch on it in the car."

They walked outside to the SUV, and Wendy consulted her directions before taking off. A short five minutes and one side of Kate's bacon later, she pulled to a stop in front of the fish store, but it was closed. A papier máché seascape, including a life-sized mermaid, decorated the front of the store.

"We'll have to come back tomorrow," Vivian said. "Cute display. I like the mermaid."

Wendy reversed and took NY73 to the Olympic Ski Jump Complex as Kate crunched her way through more bacon.

They took the fork to the dirt parking lot almost hidden by trees where a gate and small alpine building welcomed visitors. They drove to the gate and Kate rolled down her window to a teenage girl in black pants and royal blue polo with an Olympic emblem on the left breast pocket. Her brown ponytail stuck out of the back of her matching blue baseball cap.

"Hi, welcome to the Lake Placid Olympic Ski Jumping Complex, an icon of the 1932 and 1980 Olympics. Can I interest you in our Olympic Sites Passport? It gets you into all the sites as well as a gondola ride to the top of Little Whiteface Mountain and discounts on other items and activities. Here at the ski jump you'll take the chair lift up to the K120 tower where you'll get to tour the Nordic ski jumps themselves."

"How much is it?" Kate asked.

"Only $32, which is a steal compared to paying individually for the various venues."

"This may be the only one we get to," Wendy said.

"That's okay, it's good through next spring."

"We should totally do the gondola ride!" Lucy said. "I bet the view is amazing."

"Okay, I guess we'll take five."

Vivian reached into the borrowed purse and handed the girl the credit card and Pierre forked over two still-soggy twenties.

Lucy bounced up and down in the seat, in turn bouncing Pierre. "We are not leaving here without taking the gondola ride, and I'm riding with you!" She poked him in the arm.

"Well, all right then, I'll happily dangle by a thin cable and be carted up the side of a mountain." He smiled at her as she bounced. "With you."

The teen brought back five large, clear-plastic lanyards on black string, the credit card receipt and Pierre's change. Inside the lanyards were Olympic Sites Passport tickets, as well as a tiny brochure that looked like a real passport. Kate handed them out. "Don't lose this. It's our ticket to ride!"

Lucy and Vivian started singing the Beatles' "Ticket to Ride," and all five finished off with "but she don't care!"

They parked and hopped out, taking in the scenery. To their right three jump platforms towered over a pool, and rows of bleachers stood ready for spectators. A dirt path led to the ski lifts waiting to carry skiers to their jumps during snow season. A one-story, chalet-style building had a sign for the restrooms, gift shop and café.

"Let's try to to find April," Kate said. "And I need a pit stop before we go see the ski jumps anyway."

Wendy slipped her lanyard over her neck. "How are we going to do this?"

The four girls huddled together.

"I say we take the direct approach and just ask her," Wendy said. "Tell her we're staying out at Turlington Farms and want to know if we're sleeping in the same house as a killer."

"We can't do that. We've got to be more subtle," Vivian said. "Maybe we talk about the newspaper article or something."

"Ooh, I like that," Kate said. "Maybe she'll just chime in."

"That's what I'm hoping for."

They broke the huddle and Pierre held the door open. Kate made a beeline for the restroom while Vivian, Wendy and Lucy perused the Olympic-themed goodies. A woman in her late thirties sat on a stool behind the counter entranced in a *People* magazine. Her nametag read April. Her brown hair showed bits of gray around the roots and she wore the same blue shirt as the girl selling passports, but she had on khakis.

Vivian held up a fake gold medal and started swaying and singing, "I-I-I-I am the champion, my friend." She threw in a little air guitar. "And I-I-I-I'll keep on fighting to the end."

Wendy plucked the replica medal out of Vivian's hand. "All right, Freddie Mercury wannabe, we've got a job to do."

Vivian sighed. "Okay, okay." She moved to a rack of sale items, pushing the clothes hangers back and forth, and tried to sound inconspicuous. "So do we think Brandon is a killer? If we do, I'm NOT staying another night at Turlington Farms."

The woman didn't move, but Vivian saw her brown eyes flick their way.

"I agree," Lucy said, dangling more bait. "If I see the cops there again, it's over, we're leaving."

The woman slowly lowered her magazine.

Wendy set the hook. "That poor woman, drowned by her own husband, I can't believe it. And then finding the second wife's remains. Why is he not in jail?"

April was hooked so deep, she would have flopped herself on deck.

She stood up behind the register. "Are you talking about Brandon Holt?"

41

Vivian placed the sweatshirt she'd been contemplating back on the rack and walked up to the counter at the Olympic Ski Jump gift shop. "Oh, do you know Brandon?"

"I guess," April said. "Mostly I knew his wife."

"Which one?" Wendy asked. "He's had three."

April rolled her eyes. "Yes, I know. I used to teach with his first wife, Mary Beth."

"Are you still teaching?" Wendy asked.

"Oh god no, god no. I got so sick of those brats, I had to leave. I was done."

"Did you know Mary Beth well?" Lucy asked.

"Our classrooms were across the hall from each other. Brandon came up there a few times and went berserk. Yelling at her about finances. One time was after school and she was with that one kid, what was his name? The principal had to go in there and tell Brandon to leave. I think he might've been drunk."

"Do you think he was abusive?" Kate asked.

April shrugged. "I don't know, but she was a little too friendly with some of the students, in my opinion. Like that time I was just talking about, that student was hugging on her after Brandon left. She always had lots of students hanging around after school, especially the boys. But I shouldn't talk bad about her, she's dead." April did the Catholic sign of the cross.

"Any boys in particular?" Lucy asked.

"You didn't hear it from me, but I personally thought she might've been doing more than tutoring that one kid, what was his name? The hugger." April slapped her forehead. "Damn, I'm getting old. What was his name? He wound up becoming a locksmith."

"Jeremy!" Vivian yelled.

April looked at her like she was a loon. "Where'd you say you're from?"

Kate whisked by carrying a baby moose, tears in her eyes. "This is the sweetest thing I've ever seen. It's so gangly and ugly, yet so adorable. I have to have one. Little Plum needs it."

Vivian smiled and shrugged. "She gets emotional over stuffed animals. We think it's the hormones."

Kate put the moose on her shoulder and picked up a baby bear. "I need this, too." She laid them gently on the counter, petting each.

Wendy drummed her fingers on the counter. "So do you know for sure that Mary Beth and her student were, you know, working on extra credit?"

April rang up Kate's two new critters. "I never saw him sharpen his pencil in her sharpener, if that's what you mean. But they seemed to share a deeper connection than most teachers have with their students. It wasn't normal, just not normal." She looked at Kate. "That'll be $18.48."

Pierre stepped up and waved off Kate's credit card. "My gift to Little Plum."

Kate's eyes welled up again.

"Oh, geez," Vivian said. "Hormone attack, here we go."

April looked at Wendy. "You're staying out there at the B&B?"

"For now, yes," Wendy said.

"I've heard rumors that they found the second wife's remains out in the woods. How's Tracy handling that?"

"Do you know Tracy?" Lucy asked.

"I waited tables with her at the brewery after I left teaching. I was shocked she married Brandon after his first wife drowned and his second 'disappeared.' I should probably go out and check on her. She never was overly friendly, yet I had a soft spot for her. Seemed like she'd had a rough life, you know, never showed much emotion about anything."

"I heard her plumber ex-boyfriend ditched her for Omaha," Wendy said.

April laughed. "Yeah, that was the bottom for her. She really loved that guy, I guess. As much as she could love someone."

"How'd she hook up with Brandon?" Vivian asked.

"They grew up together, and then after number two disappeared, he started hanging out at the bar a lot and she got her claws dug in real deep. I saw the whole thing unfold, then I got hired on here. Next thing I heard, they were married. I think Brandon was so screwed up, so overwhelmed, he had no idea what he was doing. Everyone hated him."

Awkward silence.

"I imagine that was tough," Kate said, taking out her new moose and putting it next to her cheek.

April shrugged. "Reap what you sow. He was never a fan of mine, but I probably should run by and see Tracy. It's been too long."

"I bet she'd appreciate that," Wendy said. "She works hard, her breakfast kicks booty."

"I know I've packed on a few since I've been here," Kate said. "Check out this pooch!"

April cracked a crooked smile. "Yeah, I'll go for a visit."

"Let's hit the chair lift," Lucy said. "I'm riding with Pierre!"

"Maybe we'll see you out at the farm," Wendy said. "Take care."

"Thanks, enjoy your visit," April said as she sat back down and picked up her *People*.

The girls and Pierre hustled to the chair lift where a worker checked their passports, then helped them get on the chair lifts two by two. Vivian rode by herself since Lucy was with Pierre and they didn't want Kate to ride alone.

The breeze blew through Vivian's curls as she took in the serene mountainside. Little yellow and white wildflowers speckled the ground beneath her. The pine trees had been groomed well away from the jump areas. The ride didn't take long, and before she knew it an older gentleman yelled for her to lift the safety bar. She did, and he helped her off, scooting her to the right as the chair swung to the left and started back down the mountain.

Two large ski jumps towered in front of them. Between the jumps a sign displayed the Olympic rings and Lake Placid in red letters underneath. A cement tower stood behind the jumps.

"Let's go!" Lucy said, grabbing Pierre's hand.

A teenager greeted them at the elevator entrance. "Good afternoon, and welcome to the Olympic Ski Jumping Complex. Step right in."

He turned a key and hit a button. The doors closed and they began to go up. He started chatting about something, but Vivian couldn't hear anything.

Her ears popped just as the elevator slowed. The doors opened and they were inside the tallest of the jump towers. Pictures of past events hung on every interior wall, and windows lined the outside. Maps indicated what was in the view that went for miles: Whiteface Mountain, Lake Placid Village and Mirror Lake.

"Let's go out to the platform," Lucy said. "Hope no one is afraid of heights!"

They walked onto the deck with its 7-foot-tall chain-link fencing. Vivian stood at the edge and peered through a diamond-shaped square of fence. "Whoa. That's a LONG way down."

The adjustable platform was lined with wooden planks that dropped 120 meters.

"The sign says we are on the tallest structure between Montreal and New York City," Kate said.

"I believe it," Wendy said. "I'm having Sky Screamer flashbacks."

"Poor Astroworld is a goner now," Vivian said. "We spent many a summer day there. I had my first kiss on the gondola ride there."

"Meeeemmmmmorrrieeeessss," Lucy sang out, twirling around like she was Julie Andrews on top of a mountain.

"Wrong song!" Vivian yelled.

The door swung open and a family came out, so Lucy stopped, smiled nonchalantly and walked to the pay binoculars next to Vivian, nudging her in the process. "I know that's the wrong song, but it was more fitting."

They toodled around inside and out, looking at pictures and reading about the two Olympic Games that had been held there.

"I need a snack," Kate said. "Can we go?"

Wendy dug in her borrowed purse and pulled out a granola bar. "I brought this in case of emergency."

Kate took it gratefully. "Thank you!"

They piled into the elevator, and again, Vivian's ears popped as they changed elevation quickly. They took the same seating arrangements on the chair lift going down, and Vivian snapped pictures with her new phone, including a shot of Lucy and Pierre snuggling in front of her and a selfie. *I need to get more sleep! I have bags under my eyes!* She threw on her sunglasses and took another picture. *That's better!*

They hit the restroom and grabbed a drink before leaving. April wasn't in sight and another lady was behind the register.

They got into the SUV and Kate drove out of the gate and down the road toward Main Street. She cruised through town to Mike Grimm's studio, situated on the shore of Mirror Lake. The girls and Pierre got out and walked up to the door. A sign saying "Come around back" hung in the window.

The group found four tables set up with easels and canvases along the edge of the lake. A group of women ranging in age from 20 to 70 worked on replicating the original artwork. Mike looked very beatnik wearing all black, hand resting on his chin, as he walked behind the painters and stopped to give pointers.

"Welcome," he called and waved the five of them toward a table loaded with bottles of wine and a platter of cheese and crackers. "Join us for the Mirror Images painting class. I've got extra easels and canvases." He ran toward the back of the studio. "Get a drink. I'll be right back."

Vivian didn't want to stay for a painting class, but she knew they couldn't just barge in and start asking questions about Mary Beth and April. Her eyes landed on the shopkeeper from You Name It, Mary Beth's cousin, who had an empty seat and easel beside her. She nodded toward the cousin and said to Pierre and the girls, "This sounds like fun, we should stay."

Kate's gaze drifted over the group of lakeside painters and settled on the cousin and the empty seat beside her. "I'm in. I need something to hang in

Little Plum's room anyway."

Pierre groaned and took a step backward. Lucy hooked her arm through his and reached up to give him a kiss. He smiled as he leaned down to her. "You're going to have to make this up to me. It's insulting to my manhood."

Lucy's eyes narrowed. "We're here to gain information. You can tough it out." She laughed and led him to the table behind Vivian.

Kate and Wendy sat beside them and Mike ran out of his studio with set-ups for the girls and Pierre. Mike gave them instructions on getting started, and Kate immediately picked up her brush. She looked at the original artwork, a stormy sky, then started mixing colors and placing a few brush strokes across her canvas. Mike moved on, checking the other painters.

Wendy looked from Kate, to her plate of paint, to the original and back. She picked up her brush. "Here goes nothing."

Vivian grabbed a glass of white wine and settled in next to Mary Beth's cousin. "I bought some souvenirs from you a couple of days ago."

She glanced at Vivian. "I remember you. You had the snoring friend in the teepee. I see you're not dead yet. How are things going at Turlington Farms?" She put emphasis on Turlington.

"Going fine, Brandon hasn't tried to kill us." Vivian dabbed a bit of white into her black, then held out her hand and introduced herself. "What's your name?"

"Christine. How's that bitch Tracy treating you?"

42

Vivian could see how Tracy wasn't the warmest person and how the people in town wouldn't think too highly of her being married to Brandon. Turlington Farms survived based solely on tourists, not locals. She dabbed yellow onto her work of art, then turned to Christine. "She can cook, I'll give her that. She's fixed a lot more than breakfast for us."

Christine snorted. "She trapped Brandon, ya know. Not that I care, he deserves every bit of hell on this earth that's coming to him, but I don't care much for Tracy."

Vivian stopped working on her background. "What do you mean 'trapped'?"

"She said she was pregnant. They got married shortly thereafter."

"Oh no. Did she miscarry?"

Christine worked on her tree. "I don't have any proof, but if I had to guess, I'd say she faked it."

Vivian dabbed at her canvas, working on the stormy sky. She coughed a few times at Christine's statement. "That shouldn't surprise me, but it does. Wow. That's stooping low to get married."

Christine stopped painting and leaned in close. "Tracy wanted him since high school. I was two years behind them in school, and I remember. She was heartbroken when he broke up with her, took her a long time to recover. Then she started dating Scott, and she seemed happy."

"Who was Scott? The plumber who ran off to Omaha or wherever?"

Christine laughed and had a sip of wine. "The butt-crack-jeans plumber. He was never going to marry her. She eventually figured it out, and next thing you know, he moved off."

"Why wasn't he going to marry her?" Vivian asked, wondering what happened in Tracy's past to make her fake a pregnancy just to get married. She'd have to be pretty desperate. But then, in Vivian's experience, marriage was overrated.

"He slept with every girl who came along. Any opportunity that presented itself, boom, he was on it. He wasn't the kind you settle down with and raise a family."

Vivian lowered her paint brush, feeling sorry for Tracy. Being cheated on was the pits, and to stay in a relationship where that continually happened, she just couldn't imagine it. *That'd make me a bitch, too.*

Mike swung by and looked over Vivian's shoulder. Vivian worked on highlighting the leaves, then set down her paintbrush and picked up her wine. She had a sip and then another, and decided her tree highlighted by a blue moon was as good as it was going to get.

She clinked glasses with Christine. "To a job well done. Sort of."

Lucy showed off her painting, which did indeed look like a mirror image of the original. She set it down and picked up Pierre's painting. "A kindergartener could do better." She rubbed his bald head, then kissed it. "But you've got other talents."

Wendy rolled her eyes and showed them her painting. She didn't say anything. She didn't need to. What was supposed to be a tree didn't resemble a tree, and her blue moon was more purple than blue, and not quite round.

Pierre gave her a high five. "I see you're as talented as I am."

Wendy glanced at her painting and then back at Pierre. "I feel bad I wasted this paint and canvas!"

The group of ladies had started to get up and compare pieces, so the girls and Pierre made their way to Mike's studio. It was a one-room shop with a desk in a front corner and paintings lining the walls. Mike was in deep conversation with a fifty something bottle blonde who had her hand on his shoulder. He took a step back as he nodded toward his painting she was admiring.

"He looks like he needs saving," Kate said and wandered over. "Do you mind if I use your restroom?" she asked him.

He flashed a smile and pointed her in the right direction.

Vivian slowly walked past a couple of paintings that appeared to be a sequence. All were stormy skies with a non-descript person holding their face in an agonizing scream. She went up to Mike, who was still being held captive in conversation.

She lightly touched his elbow. "Sorry to interrupt. I'd like to find a painting for my son's room. Can you show me around?"

Mike's bright blue eyes sparkled, and he flashed a smile of relief. "Excuse me, Carrie." He walked to a closed door and pushed through it, waving to Vivian to follow. "I've got my tamer pieces back here."

Vivian followed him into the storeroom, where Mike had almost covered the walls with paintings of various sizes. Some resembled the stormy, screaming person, others were of vines climbing toward a dark sky, and others were of dragons big and small, scary and not so much, breathing fire and yet some with lopsided grins.

Wendy walked in. "Why don't you have more of these displayed?"

Mike shrugged and gave a grin, similar to his dragons. "I want to show off my best pieces and not clutter the front."

Vivian looked over his dragons. "These are really good." She took one off the wall, a dragon perched on a castle wall, its claws breaking into the rock, with a town in the distance. "I'll get this one for Ben. He'll love it."

Vivian turned to show Mike the piece she wanted, but her eyes landed on a painting just behind him and she couldn't speak. A chill went through her.

Tall evergreen trees lined a lake and reflected on the surface. The night sky twinkled with lights; fog rose up off the water. A woman shrouded in white floated in the middle of the lake, her face turned from the viewer. The stillness made it clear: She had drowned.

By now, Kate had joined them. "I noticed a framed picture in the hallway back there of you and a young woman," she said. "She's beautiful. Who is that?"

Mike glanced at the painting behind him, then smiled at Kate. "An old friend who passed away."

Kate returned his smile. "I'm so sorry to hear that. Were you close?"

Vivian cut her eyes to Wendy, who had also noticed the painting. Lucy and Pierre stepped into the storage room and Vivian looked at them, then to the wall behind Mike. Lucy sucked in a quick breath, then started coughing to cover it up.

Kate looked back and forth between Mike and the painting of the drowned woman. "Is this painting of your friend?"

"Yes, it's how I envisioned Mary Beth."

The small storeroom seemed to close in on Vivian. She needed out of there, and away from Mike. She held up the painting for Ben. "I want to get this, because uhmm, we need to go. How much is it?"

Mike turned from Mary Beth's painting to Vivian. "I'll give it to you for $30. Let me get my Square and ring you up."

He walked out of the room and Vivian mouthed to Pierre and the girls, "Oh my god, it's Mary Beth."

Mike walked back in and looked at his visitors. "Is everything fine in here? You seem like you've seen a ghost."

Vivian handed him her credit card. *I wonder if I'm doing business with a killer.*

Pierre led Lucy and Kate out of the small room and Wendy lingered in the doorway as Mike swiped Vivian's card. Thankfully, the Square reader worked on the first try.

183

Mike had Vivian sign the receipt on his phone with her finger and said, "I hope your son enjoys the painting."

Vivian shoved her credit card into her purse and walked toward the door. "Thanks, I'm sure he will." She walked into the main gallery and toward the front door where Pierre, Lucy and Kate stood waiting. "We gotta get back, see you around."

Mike looked at everyone, then back to Vivian, eyebrows raised in question. He tapped his right index finger against the side of his leg. "Sure. Float – I mean swing on by anytime."

43

V ivian practically fled Mike Grimm's gallery, glad to be out of there, especially since night was falling. His demeanor was odd, and the painting of Mary Beth's drowning had unnerved her. Kate unlocked the door on their rental, and once they were all safely inside, Vivian said, "Did y'all see that painting? Can you believe it?"

Kate started the engine. "Grandpa was right to be suspicious of Mike. That painting was eerie. It could be his way of bragging about what he'd done."

Pierre rode shotgun for a change and turned to Kate. "Why wouldn't he have that painting in the main gallery where it's more visible?"

"It might upset the locals," was all Kate could say.

"He'll never sell that painting," Wendy said. "He doesn't need to have it displayed in the main gallery. He knows where it is. I bet he goes back there and looks at it a hundred times a day."

Vivian shivered, not liking the idea of Mike getting pleasure from killing Mary Beth. She glanced at the time on her phone. "We're supposed to meet Larson in 30 minutes at Lake Placid Brewery. Why don't we head on over there, unless anyone has another stop to make."

No one did, so Kate, now an expert with directions in town, drove them to the brewery. She parked and turned off the car. "Could April be in trouble dating Mike?"

Vivian opened her car door. "I think we need to talk to Larson. He's local and might have a good perspective on all of this."

The girls and Pierre walked into the rustic Adirondack building and grabbed a long table off to the side of the bar. Everyone had a beer except Kate, although she said she'd like one at this point. The group went over possibilities and potential suspects until Larson arrived.

He sat on the bench beside Vivian and greeted her with a kiss. "Good to see you."

She squeezed his leg and left her hand there. "I'm glad you're off tonight so we could get together."

His smile faded a bit. "I'm on call, but let's hope our citizens don't start any fires tonight."

The waitress came by to take Larson's order, but her smile faded when she noticed Vivian's hand on his leg. He ordered a cup of hot tea since he was on call, and the waitress quickly returned and set the cup down with a clatter.

Vivian waited for her to walk off before turning her attention back to Larson. "Speaking of Lake Placid's fine citizens, we'd like to talk to you about a few of them."

She and the girls explained how they'd been looking into things since finding Rebecca's jawbone. They told him about Grandpa's files and that they didn't think Nicole had accidentally gotten E. coli poisoning. They also told him about their suspicions on Brandon, Jeremy and Mike Grimm.

Larson shook his head when they mentioned Mike's painting of Mary Beth. "He's definitely eclectic and he's been a smart-ass his whole life. I'm not sure anyone missed him while he lived in Oregon." Larson fiddled with his empty cup of tea, the waitress hadn't been by in a while. "A killer — " His phone emitted three high-pitched beeps. He glanced at the screen and threw $5 on the table. "Crap, there's a house fire. I've got to go."

"Can I go with you?" Vivian asked and flashed a smile. "I'd love to see you in action."

Larson leaned over to give her a kiss and paused. "Sure, but you've got to stay in my truck." He picked up his $5 and threw down a $20.

Vivian turned to the girls and Pierre. "I'll text y'all the address on the way."

Larson tugged at her elbow and they hustled out the door. He didn't waste time with chivalry, just clicked the locks and had the truck started and in gear before she had even closed the door. "Buckle up," he said as the tires squealed and they took off.

He slowed down at a red light, then blew through it once he knew it was safe. He gave Vivian the address to the fire, which she texted to Wendy.

"I don't know the situation yet, so it is imperative that you stay in the truck unless I tell you otherwise." He took a right and they were in a cute neighborhood. "I don't want anyone getting hurt." He paused. "Though I wouldn't mind having to give you a little mouth to mouth."

He screeched to a stop and threw the truck in reverse. "Dammit! Missed my turn." He wrenched the wheel to the left at the next intersection and put the truck into drive again.

Vivian rubbed his shoulder. "I'll behave."

Larson turned onto a street lined with cars, a fire truck, two cop cars and an ambulance. Emergency lights lit up the night, and the smell of smoke intensified as he drove closer to the fire.

Finally, Vivian saw it. In addition to the billowing smoke, the house gave off an orange glow. A large tree in the front yard was burning, too. Larson pulled to a stop a hundred yards away, grabbed his gear out of the back seat and got dressed.

"This looks pretty bad," he said through the open door as he pulled on his boots. "We could be here awhile."

"I can leave with the girls, but I'd like to watch the action for a bit," Vivian said, taking in the scene. Hoses ran from the fire truck to the yard. One fireman stayed at the truck, and two more held the hose while another sprayed water at the base of the flames.

"Any idea whose house it is?"

"I'd say whoever is in the back of the ambulance," Larson said. He gave her a final warning to stay put and ran off, helmet in hand.

Vivian watched him run down the street to the fire truck. *Mmmm, mmmm, good.* As he got out of sight she turned her attention to the ambulance. Sheriff deputies Stokola and Young stood at the back, talking with someone in the bay. Stokola was writing on her notepad. Just then, a navy blue Grand Cherokee zoomed past her, Kate at the wheel.

Vivian shoved open the door and jumped out, then ran after them, waving her arms. "Here I am!"

BOOM! An explosion on the side of the house sent debris sky high. Vivian watched in horror as a burning piece of something flew onto the street, landing right in front of the SUV. Kate slammed on the brakes but couldn't stop in time. She drove over it, where it caught the undercarriage on fire. Kate pulled to the curb and stopped, but no one moved to get out.

They don't know there's a fire under the car!

Vivian ran to the Jeep. "Get out! Get out!"

Wendy rolled down her window. "What's wrong?"

"THE CAR IS ON FIRE!" Vivian screamed.

Four doors flew open, and Kate, Wendy, Pierre and Lucy scrambled out.

The smell of gas reached Vivian's nose just as there was a loud pop. "Run! Run!"

WHOOSH!

44

Vivian kept running, knowing their rental was toast. Burnt toast. Lucy passed her, as did Pierre, and she glanced to her left and saw Kate and Wendy. They ran all the way to the ambulance, which was on the other side of the burning house.

Vivian ran up to a fireman. "Our car's on fire!" She pointed down the street to the once-blue SUV with flames shooting from it.

"What the hell?" The fireman grabbed his shoulder-mounted walkie-talkie and blurted out some orders. Soon after, several firemen began uncapping a fire hydrant down the street, closer to the SUV. Before they could get the water going, flames had spread to the car interior. A loud hiss accompanied the first cascades of water hitting the flames.

Kate leaned against a tree, her borrowed cross-body purse drooping in front of her.

Deputy Young checked on her. "I'm fine," Kate said, then coughed. "I just need to sit down."

"Let's get you out of this smoke," Young said and walked her to the passenger door of the ambulance. He yelled over to one of the EMTs, "Hey, Charlie, this one might need some help." He opened the ambulance door and nudged Kate into the cab. "I'll be right here if you need me."

Vivian and Wendy walked over to her.

"I'm okay, really," Kate said. "I'm going to call the car rental company and let them know what happened." She closed the ambulance door and gave a thumbs up.

Vivian's curiosity got the best of her and she walked around to the back of the ambulance where an EMT was busy inside. She peeked inside the bay for a clear view of who occupied the stretcher.

A semiconscious April Robinson lay strapped to a gurney, her face covered in soot. An oxygen mask covered her nose and mouth, and she groggily moved her head from side to side. Beside her, Mike Grimm sat in a tight space, holding her hand and stroking her hair.

He looked up and locked eyes with Vivian just as the EMT slammed the bay doors and scurried around to the driver's door.

Kate got out of the passenger's seat and the ambulance took off, sirens blaring and crossing paths with a third fire truck making its way onto the scene.

"You feeling better?" Pierre asked her.

"I am. I think with the smoke and the running, I just got winded."

"Let us know if you need anything, little mama."

She nodded.

"What'd the rental car company say?" Lucy asked.

"Put it this way — it's a really good thing we got the additional insurance."

Deputy Cheri Stokola walked up, a look of wonder on her face. "What on earth are you guys doing here?"

They explained how they'd been with Larson when he got the call and that Vivian wanted to watch him in action.

"You know, with his hose," Vivian said.

Wendy stepped over a hose that ran to the front yard and rolled her eyes. "This is a little more action than any of us bargained for. That was the craziest thing. One second we were all looking at the house fire and, next thing you know, we were almost on fire. That's our second rental, you know." She gave Kate a smile. "You might get blacklisted."

"I don't think they'll ever rent to me again."

Vivian gave Kate a shoulder hug. "I'm so glad y'all got out of there in time. Close call." She turned to look at their SUV. Though there hadn't been a huge explosion, the vehicle was still on fire, and now it was waterlogged. Totaled.

Two firefighters from the second truck dragged a hose over, setting up on the other side of the house. They had made progress on the SUV, but the house fire still raged, even though there were now eight hoses on it.

A large, dark shadow emerged from the front of the house carrying a hatchet.

I feel like I'm in a movie, Vivian thought, admiring the tall figure.

Larson swung the hatchet down by his side and walked up to Vivian, looking better than ever in his fireman get-up. He flipped the shield up on his mask. "What's this I hear about a car on fire down the street?"

"It's not yours, don't worry." Vivian gave him a toothy grin.

He raised his eyebrows. "Then what, may I ask, are you doing out of it?"

"Kate had a wee-bit of an accident in the rental. A piece of debris flew underneath the car and whammo, the SUV burst into flames."

Larson tilted his head back, as if he was looking for a shooting star. "Keys are in my truck," he said, grinning. "Take it back to Turlington Farms,

189

but please, don't take it for a plunge or do anything that will catch it on fire. I'll have one of the guys drop me by for it. Leave the keys in it, I'll be late."

"Are you sure you want to let us borrow it?" Vivian asked. "I can't make any promises. We seem to be dooming cars left and right."

"Yes." A drop of sweat fell from his brow. "Perhaps you should let Pierre drive. I've got to get back to this. Please be careful." He winked at her and brushed his gloved finger under her chin, then lifted the hatchet back onto his shoulder. "See you later."

She couldn't help but smile and wish he was sweating for carnal reasons. She turned to the group, fanning herself and feeling a little dazed. "Let's blow this fireworks stand."

They walked to Larson's truck and squished in. Pierre climbed in the driver's seat and Kate rode shotgun. The other three climbed into the extended cab, and they made their way out of the neighborhood and back toward Turlington Farms.

"Smells like a barbecue in here," Kate said. "I'm getting hungry!"

Everyone cracked up, but they did make a pit stop at a convenience store to get her a sandwich and bag of chips.

"Just what I needed," Kate said, sinking her teeth into a roast beef sub.

Pierre pulled into the drive and parked behind the house, leaving the keys as instructed. As they got of the truck, lightning streaked above the lake, followed by a roll of thunder.

"I'm going to sleep good tonight," Wendy said. "I love the rain."

"Me, too," Kate said, then yawned. "I wish I didn't need a shower."

"We smell like a slab of sizzling shish kebab," Vivian said. "Now I'm getting hungry."

Once inside, Kate hit the shower, Vivian the kitchen, Lucy and Pierre the porch swing, and Wendy the couch.

Vivian found a leftover biscuit and grabbed the butter and grape jelly. She was punching the buttons on the microwave when Tracy shuffled in wearing her robe and blue slippers. "Sorry, did I wake you?" Vivian asked.

"Nah, I needed some water." Tracy grabbed a glass from the cupboard, then turned around. "What's that smell? Do you smell it?"

Vivian nodded. "Yeah, I smell it. I'm surrounded by it. It's me."

"What? What are you talking about?"

A crack of thunder shook the house and raindrops, pelted the awning over the back porch.

"We were with Larson when he got a call about a house fire and went to check it out."

"I thought that was his truck outside."

"That's a whole other story. Our rental burned to bits when Kate ran over some debris, so he let us borrow his truck." Vivian dipped her finger into a drop of spilled jelly on her plate.

"Oh my gosh, it burned?"

"Yep. It's toast on wheels. Kate already called the car rental company."

"Is everyone all right?"

"Fit as a fiddle. We just smell like s'mores."

As Vivian picked at the crumbs of her biscuit, Tracy started to leave.

"Oh, the fire we went to, it was someone you know," Vivian said. "We actually met her today at the Olympic complex. April Robinson."

Tracy turned around. "April?"

"Yeah, we told her where we were staying. She said she might come see you. I'm guessing she didn't make it by."

"No, she didn't. So it was her house that burned?"

Vivian nodded. "It's a pile of rubble by now."

"Was she home?"

"I saw her in an ambulance. She looked...well...like she got lucky."

"Wow," Tracy said. "Thanks for letting me know." She turned back around. "G'night."

" 'Night."

Vivian rinsed her dish and put it in the sink. She called around the corner to Wendy, "Hey, whatcha doing?"

Wendy had tears in her eyes.

Vivian sat down next to her. "What's wrong?"

"Oh, you know, just thinking about Jake with the car fire."

Vivian could have smacked herself in the forehead. She hadn't even thought about Jake and his burned out car in Las Vegas. "Oh my gosh, I'm sorry."

They were quiet for a moment.

"But just remember, it wasn't him. He's still out there, we just need to find him."

Wendy sniffed, then wiped a tear off her cheek. "Yeah, I know. And I do feel like he's out there. It's just hard, you know."

Vivian nodded. "You need anything?"

"Nah, I'm about to go up and de-smoke myself."

"Me, too."

Wendy took a deep breath. "You go ahead. I'll be up soon."

"You sure? I don't mind hanging out."

"No, no, it's okay."

"Okay, g'night." Vivian went upstairs, stripped down and took a 20-minute shower, enjoying the hot water and the thick steam building up in the bathroom. It felt good in her lungs versus the harsh smoke they had been around earlier.

She dried off, then slipped on a T-shirt and boxers. She looked around the room, at the files scattered about. They actually looked a little more organized. *Maybe Tracy came in and cleaned up.*

She picked up the top folder from a pile on the dresser. Coach Stubbs. She slipped into the sheets and opened it up. Nothing unusual that she could see, which made her wonder why there was a file on him at all. She got up and searched around, looking for dropped pages. Anything that would explain more about his connection, if there was any, in Mary Beth's death.

She yawned and laid the file on the nightstand. She clicked off the lamp and snuggled down in bed, concentrating on the gentle raindrops tap-tap-tapping against the window. It didn't take long before she had slipped into a peaceful slumber.

45

Day 6

Vivian rolled over, pulling the covers off her head. She smelled smoke but snuggled her pillow and yanked the covers up over her eyes. She lay there for a beat before it hit her. *Holy crap, smoke!*

She threw back the covers, jumped out of bed and ran into Kate and Wendy's room. "Fire! Quick, get out of the house!" She sprinted toward their door.

Wendy pulled a gray sweater out of the dresser and sniffed. "That's bacon cooking."

Kate walked out of the bathroom wrapped in a towel. "Applewood smoked, I'd say."

"Could be hickory or maple," Wendy said. "I see that on the packages in the store sometimes."

Vivian paused, doorknob in hand, and took a breath. "I must still have smoke in my sinuses after yesterday. Either that or I'm losing it."

"Or both," Wendy said with a smile then walked into the bathroom and closed the door.

"I'm starved," Kate said and pulled on a pair of yoga pants. "Join me for breakfast? Smells delicious!"

Vivian laughed and went back to her room. "Yeah, yeah, I'll get ready quick."

Before the girls could leave the room, Wendy's phone rang. The words "Wade Nelson" lit up the display.

"Good morning, Agent Nelson," Wendy said, putting him on speaker.

"Morning," he said. "I had a visit yesterday from the higher-ups. I knew running Jake's name and the passport name would set off some bells, but I didn't expect the deputy director in my office."

"That sounds serious," Wendy replied.

"I don't know what Jake was up to, but it involves a higher pay grade than mine. I'm sorry, but I can't look into this any further. You need to stay out of it, too."

Wendy's shoulders sagged and she looked at the floor. "Did you reach out to Antonio Robichaux?"

Nelson hesitated before answering. "I did and I've talked to his agent friend. He's in the IT Applications and Data Division but not much higher up the food chain than I am. He doesn't need to be looking into this, either."

Wendy sighed. "He was able to get the call history, but Antonio said it will take him weeks to thoroughly analyze it."

When Nelson didn't respond, Wendy said, "Thanks for taking this as far as you could."

"You got it," Nelson answered. "If there's any other information I come across, I'll get in touch. Take care, and Wendy — "

"Yeah?"

"I'm really sorry." Click.

Wendy set the phone on the bed and stared at it. "I hope Antonio's friend comes through for us because it sure doesn't look like Nelson will. He's not my knight in shining armor."

Vivian felt awful that Nelson could not, or would not, do anything else. "I'll call Antonio today, see if he has any other ideas."

Kate's tummy rumbled, so she, Wendy and Vivian followed the bacon smell into the dining room where they joined Lucy and Pierre, who were almost finished eating.

"Tracy and Brandon made a feast this morning," Lucy said as she set down a bottle of maple syrup. "There's enough for 20 people, easy."

"Are they expecting more guests?" Vivian asked.

Pierre shook his head. "They haven't said. Tracy's just in a really good mood and is cooking like crazy."

Tracy bustled through the dining room door carrying a plate of pancakes. "Oh good, you're up. We've got pancakes, Belgian waffles, regular waffles, hash browns, biscuits, eggs poached, fried or scrambled, white and wheat toast, a variety of fruit, oatmeal, sausage, bacon, and... there's something I'm forgetting."

"Grits?" Wendy asked.

Tracy's face remained serious as she set the pancake plate on the sideboard beside the waffles. "Oh dear, I need to add those to my grocery list."

Kate looked at the variety of food. "Who did you make all of this for?"

Tracy patted Kate on the arm. "You guys, of course. I thought you'd be hungry after yesterday."

Vivian tried to hold back a laugh and grabbed a plate. "I'll do my part to make sure it doesn't go to waste."

The group did their best, but plenty of food was leftover. "I hope Brandon's hungry," Pierre said. "I can't eat another bite."

Brandon walked through the dining room on his way outside and shook his head. "Now she's baking a cake. It'll be cookies next."

"What's gotten into her?" Wendy asked.

"I've only seen her like this a couple of times. I'm not sure what it is, but it's best to just eat and say thanks. We'll take some of this to the neighbors later." He pushed open the back door and hopped down the steps.

Vivian threw her napkin beside her plate. "I want to go call Larson, check up on April." She stood and mouthed "upstairs."

"I'm going to sit out back," Pierre said. "Enjoy the morning." He leaned and whispered into Lucy's ear loud enough for Vivian to hear. "And see what our chef whips up next."

Lucy giggled and gave him a peck on the cheek, then went up the stairs after the other three girls.

The door to the bedroom firmly shut, Vivian dialed Larson. "Hi, there. You'll be happy to know your truck made it here safe and sound last night."

"That's a relief," he said, sounding groggy.

"I take it you were up late last night."

"Stayed at the house for another three hours putting the fire out, then stomped around, dousing hot spots."

"How's April doing this morning?"

"I heard she's out of the woods, but she'll have one hell of a headache. She should get discharged today."

"Does she remember what happened?"

"I haven't heard her side of the story and I don't know if the police have talked to her yet, but she's got quite a knot on her head. She might have passed out from the carbon monoxide and other gases in the fire and hit her head as she fell."

"Any idea how it started?"

"The arson investigator was out there at the crack of dawn, and the report is that the gas to the stove was on but the pilot wasn't lit. Dan, one of the investigators, found candle wax on the fireplace mantel. He suspects she had a couple of candles going and that once the fumes from the stove reached those, kaboom! The explosion spread the fire instantaneously but the force was focused higher up and not across the floor, so April wasn't badly burned or killed."

"She's really lucky. I wonder why she left the gas on."

"You're asking the wrong guy. People bump knobs and turn them on, forget things. Who knows?"

"Have you heard if Nicole has been discharged?"

"If I had to guess, she's probably still admitted. My friend Marty is going to drop me by there to grab my truck, but I'd like to see you tonight. Lake Placid Brewery about 9? I can't get free until then."

"Sounds good, see ya then." Vivian relayed the information to Lucy, Kate and Wendy. "Let's go see Nicole and maybe we'll even see April. I feel so bad for both of them."

"We should get April a $100 Visa gift card," Kate said. "She's going to have a lot of rebuilding to do with losing everything in the fire. That would help with some clothes at least."

"We can use money from our Getaway Girlz trust fund," Wendy said. "But first we need a replacement car. Again."

Kate groaned and called the rental car company. The operator told her the new SUV should be there within the hour. "We need to get cleaned up, then let's go sit on the porch while we wait. And I may grab a snack for later."

Vivian smiled at her. "And by snack, you mean bacon."

Kate stretched and stood. "I'll put it on a biscuit at least."

They all laughed and took turns getting ready and threw on their usual brisk weather wear: jeans and sweaters.

Finally ready for the day, the girls joined Pierre on the back porch. Lucy quietly filled him in on what they'd learned about April and Nicole. Just as she was finishing, Brandon walked up, hammer in hand.

"I heard about your car. That's unbelievable."

Vivian didn't feel right telling him their plans, so she said, "Our car will be here shortly and we thought we'd go for a drive, maybe to Saranac Lake or to Lake George, see a little more of the Adirondacks."

He opened the back door. "Nice day for a drive. Steer clear of any bodies of water or fireballs." He went inside the house but popped his head out the door a minute later. "Your new car is here."

The girls and Pierre met the rental car employee in the driveway. He handed Kate the keys and a clipboard. "I need you to sign the new rental agreement and check whether you'd like additional insurance."

"That's a big, fat affirmative," Kate said, signing the form. She handed him the pen and clipboard. "We'll try not to destroy it."

46

Kate got behind the wheel of the bright red SUV and everyone else piled in. "Viv, why don't you call Nicole, just to make sure she's not home yet." She took off down the drive of Turlington Farms.

Nicole answered her cellphone on the fourth ring with a weak, "Hi, Vivian."

"Hey, Nicole, you okay? We're going to come see you."

"I'm getting better, but I'm still in the hospital."

"We'll pop in. We may check on someone else while we're there — April Robinson."

"What's she doing in here?"

"That's a whopper of a story," Vivian said and filled her in, then said, "We're almost there, see you in a few minutes."

Kate pulled into a CVS so Wendy could buy a get-well card for April and the gift card. She got back into the car and pulled out a card with the cartoon image of a newspaper headline that read, Get over it already! "I thought we ought to take Nicole a card, too."

Kate pulled into a parking space at the hospital shortly thereafter. She looked at the two-story building. "We've been here way too much on this trip."

They made their way to Nicole's room. Kandace, Nicole's sister, let them in. "Good to see you all."

"You, too, though we wish it was under different circumstances," Vivian said and handed Nicole her get-well card. Dark bags hung from Nicole's eyes and her skin seemed to have aged overnight. New wrinkles lined her laugh lines. "So what's the plan? When are you getting out of here?"

Nicole looked at Kandace, then back to Vivian. "I probably would have gone home yesterday — I'm basically over the E. coli poisoning, they've been pumping me full of fluids —but I went into anaphylactic shock yesterday afternoon. It was bad."

Kandace huffed from her chair in the corner. "She almost died."

Nicole dismissed Kandace's comment with a wave. "You were quick to

197

call the nurse. I was already in the hospital so the chances of me actually dying were slim."

Vivian leaned against the windowsill. "What happened?"

"Tracy came to see me, said she felt bad I'd been at her house and got sick. I think she was trying to feel me out, see if I thought her hot tea was what made me ill. I don't know what I had that was contaminated. I'm going to throw out all of the food at home."

"Your food has already been tossed," Kandace said. "Mom and Charbra did it. But it's that woman's fault you almost died, I'm telling you."

"Kan—." Nicole started to answer but Kandace cut in.

"That bitch ate a peanut butter and jelly sandwich right before she came to visit. Wasn't that nice?"

Kate snapped her fingers. "Didn't you say you were allergic to peanuts?"

"That girl waited around while they got Nicole's reaction under control and then told the nurses that she hadn't even thought about it," Kandace said.

"You don't believe her?" Wendy asked.

Kandace looked at Nicole. "I can see where if you're not allergic to nuts, you wouldn't think about it. But…"

"You didn't like her from the start," Nicole said.

"I sure as heck don't like her now."

Nicole sighed. "I know, and she's not exactly my favorite person, either."

"She seems all right to us," Lucy said. "We've determined that Tracy might not be in the best marriage. We think Brandon's mean to her, maybe a bit rough, too."

"Great, now I feel bad for talking about an abused woman," Nicole said.

Vivian looked at her. "Don't feel bad, you need to feel better. Let us tell you about our last couple of crazy days."

The girls filled her in on their adventure on, in and around the lake two days ago and the house fire the night before.

"I'm never traveling with you girls," Kandace said, shaking her head.

"I'm glad to see you are all in one piece." Nicole tapped on the bedside railing. "I've heard rumors Brandon and Shawna had a little something something going on. I was in the bar at Lake Placid Brewery a couple of weeks ago and he was there flirting with her. She gave him a hug when he left that lingered a little too long. Did she say when she started seeing Dale?"

"It sounded like it was new," Wendy said. "But Brandon might not've liked it just the same."

Nicole laughed, but sounded weak. "You can't call it cheating when you're married and your girlfriend goes out with someone else."

Vivian gave her arm a gentle squeeze. "We'll go so you can rest. If we don't see you before we leave tomorrow, let us know if you ever get to the bottom of Mary Beth's and Rebecca's deaths."

"You got it. Take care. Enjoy your last day of vacation."

The girls and Pierre said goodbye and headed to the nurse's station. Before Vivian could ask where April's room was, Jeremy walked out of a room down the hall and closed the door behind him.

She tugged on Kate and Lucy's sleeves. "Quick! Y'all take Pierre and go talk to Jeremy, take him down to the cafeteria."

"Talk to him about what?" Lucy asked. "And why?"

"I have an idea. Y'all need to keep him distracted," Vivian answered. "Wendy and I are going to go break into his van, see what we can see."

"We're gonna do WHAT?" Wendy asked.

"Just trust me!"

47

Kate looked at Lucy and Pierre. "We can talk to him about his movie script, say we've written one and does he have any advice, that kind of thing."

"That's good," Pierre said. "It'll keep him talking, but what's our movie about in case he asks?"

Kate smiled. "A pregnant lady who gets run off a bridge at night into a cold lake and the whoop-ass she brings to the guy who did it to her."

They walked toward Jeremy, who had just hit the down button on the elevator. Lucy gave him a big smile.

He recognized them and nodded as they all got on the elevator. "You aren't locked out of your car again, are you?"

The elevator doors closed.

Wendy turned to Vivian. "What's our plan? I don't know how to break into cars."

"We need a supply room, STAT." Vivian grabbed Wendy's arm and pulled her down the hall. She read the cards on each room listing patients by last name. When they came to one that wasn't marked, Vivian tried the handle and it popped open. She stuck her head inside.

"Grandma?" She saw shelves of supplies. "Jackpot! Come on! Don't turn on the light."

Wendy looked both ways in the hall, then tucked herself into the room and closed the door. "Now what?"

"Remember how Jeremy had that blow-up thing that he put between the window and the door frame? I was thinking we could try and copy that with an IV bag and tubing."

"And why are we doing that?"

"Just to see what we find. You never know."

Vivian clicked on her flashlight app and began searching the shelves. Bedpans, pillows, boxes of latex gloves, hospital gowns and bandages lined the shelves directly in front of her.

Wendy stood on the bottom shelf, trying to pull down a large box. She stretched up and inched it to the right. Then she slipped, shoving the box off the shelf and into an IV pole, sending it crashing into the wall.

Both girls froze and held their breath for several seconds. Vivian didn't hear any footsteps running their way and no one opened the door to see what happened, so she kept up the search.

Wendy opened the box and pulled out a couple of empty 250-milliliter IV bags. "Score! But now we need the lines." She flung that box back and opened another. "We're in business. Let's get out of here!" Wendy stuffed the goods into her purse.

"We need a wire coat hanger to grab the lock," Vivian said, opening the door. "Coast is clear."

She and Wendy walked out, trying to look innocent.

A hospital bed emerged from a doorway down the hall carrying a fragile-looking older man. A transportation tech pushed him toward the elevator. "Here we go, Mr. Weaver." the tech said.

"I'll check in here," Vivian said and snuck into the room. In a small closet near the bathroom she found a white plastic bag that said "Patient Belongings." A single white, wire hanger hung from the foot-long rod. Vivian grabbed it and scurried out.

Wendy gave her a thumbs up, then they casually walked to the stairwell and hurried down to the first floor and made their way outside. They scanned the parking lot, which was full.

Wendy pointed off to the right. "That's it, I think."

They hustled down the closest row of cars, then cut over several rows before crouching beside Jeremy's locksmith van.

"You ready?" Vivian said.

"I guess." Wendy got the IV bag and tubing from her purse and connected them. She handed the open tubing end to Vivian. "Finally, a good use for all that hot air! Your idea, you blow. I'll pop the lock."

Vivian laughed and unrolled the tubing. Wendy did another look around and, not seeing anyone, shoved the coat hanger between the glass and molding on the passenger side door. She took the bag and slid it through the crack.

"Time to huff and puff and blow that bag up!" Wendy smiled at Vivian, then went back to looking around.

Vivian blew. It was easy at first but got more difficult as the bag filled.

"More!" Wendy encouraged.

Vivian kept at it, covering the end of the tube between breaths so as not to lose the air already inside.

"Almost there!" Wendy said, peering down at the lock. "I just need a little more leeway!"

Vivian gave it all her might and the window pulled apart enough for Wendy to hook the coat hanger on the lock.

"This is going to be tricky," Wendy said as she slid the hanger toward the lock. She got the curved end of the wire on the far side of the lock and pulled, but the hanger slipped off. She tried several times before the lock moved even a little.

"Geez, its 55 degrees outside and I'm sweating." She took a break to wipe her brow and make sure no one was watching before concentrating again on the lock. It took two more tries, but it finally flipped the other direction.

Vivian and Wendy both let out a breath they'd been holding and Wendy pulled on the door handle. Vivian was ready to run off, but no alarm sounded.

"He's a locksmith and he doesn't even have an alarm on this thing?" Wendy said. "That's just silly." She climbed in over a pile of trash in the front seat and moved to the back. "Look at all the stuff back here."

Vivian had to step over mounds of junk in the floorboard but managed to get in and shut the passenger door. The back of the van's left side had three rows of shelves containing blue bins filled with a variety of boxes. Four black toolboxes sat on the floor under the bottom shelf.

On the right side, a large, red toolbox had been bolted to the floor, and a thick piece of plywood was attached to the top. It acted as a work surface, and a gray key cutting machine sat on it. The tidiness and organization of the back was in stark contrast to the disaster in the front where years' worth of receipts, fast food wrappers, coffee cups and gloves, you name it, now lived.

"I probably should've asked before we broke in here," Wendy said. "But what exactly are we looking for?"

Vivian rifled through the blue bins and boxes. "Anything to do with getting Nicole sick or starting April's fire. Accelerants, perhaps, or a petri dish where he's growing E. coli. Or lock picking tools. I think April was attacked and either knew her attacker and let him in or someone was able to unlock her door."

Wendy looked at her like she was crazy. "Petri dish? You kidding?"

"I don't know! Kind of. But we're here so start searching."

Wendy pulled open the top drawer on the red toolbox. "I don't think people just carry around batches of E. coli. However, there could definitely be something growing in all that crap on the floorboard."

"It doesn't look like he's big on using a trash can," Vivian said, looking through one of the black toolboxes on the floor.

"Why would a locksmith need Goo Gone?" Wendy started reading the back label of a nearly empty bottle.

Vivian closed the lid on the toolbox and shoved it back into place. "I have no idea. Maybe lock picking gets sticky and he needs to get gunk off his hands."

"This stuff will start a fire. The label says it contains petroleum distillates and to avoid use around heat, sparks or flames. This bottle isn't all that big. April might not have noticed if Jeremy had it in his pocket."

"You'd probably need more than one bottle to get a good fire going." Vivian looked around the back of the van. The edge of the carpet in front of the left back door was tucked underneath itself. Vivian pulled the corner of the carpeting toward her and it lifted, revealing a rectangular piece of plywood. She pried it up and found a black leather pouch crammed in the space. "Check this out."

Wendy handed her a roll of blue shop towels. "I don't know if you should touch that with your bare hands. We've left fingerprints all over the van, but it would probably be best not to leave any on that."

Vivian used two of the blue paper towels to unzip the case. Tucked into pouches were flat, long-handled, stainless steel tools, all with different shapes on the end. One looked like a mini-saw, another had three waves, another had a sharp curved tip, and yet another had a more gradual curved tip.

"I think I know a lock picking set when I see it," Vivian said. "Let's take it! We can get into Brandon's garage, see what he doesn't want us to see."

Wendy put back the shop towels and Goo Gone. "I'd love to get into that garage, but I don't think we should take anything from this van, especially that. We don't know Jeremy's involvement yet. What if he's the one who set April's house on fire and he used those? We need the sheriff to find them."

Vivian sighed and zipped the pouch back up. "Have you looked through everything in there?" She nodded toward the red toolbox.

"Yes, so I guess I'll risk my health and wade through the cesspool up front to check out the glove box."

Vivian opened the pouch, snapped a picture of the toolset with her phone, then put everything back into place as Wendy maneuvered up front. "Anything interesting up there?"

"I'd say so." Wendy moved aside so Vivian could see what she was pointing at.

A handgun.

48

D on't touch it!" Vivian squealed to Wendy as they crouched in Jeremy's locksmith van, staring at a gun.

"I'm not going to touch it!" Wendy said. "I've been on enough vacations to know what I should and should not touch!"

"I know, I know."

"None of our ladies were killed with a gun, so this doesn't mean he's our guy," Wendy said. "But it is an interesting find. Other than that I've found a Nickelback CD and a roach."

"Ewww!"

"A marijuana roach, not the flying insects we grew up with in Pasadena. I also found a roll of quarters and a pair of dirty underwear."

"Gross."

"Tell me about it. I started to reach into the glove box and then thought better of it. Glad I found a pencil in the console and poked around with it." She used the pencil to move items on the passenger's seat. "I bet his house is just as disgusting, and if so, there's no telling what Nicole came into contact with there."

Vivian turned to look at the disaster, but she saw four familiar figures walking their way and panicked. "Time to go!" She shuffled to the back, unlocked the door, cracked it open just enough to squeeze through and jumped out while Wendy crouched down and locked the passenger door, then locked the back door and hopped out, too.

They ran behind a big truck parked beside the van, then squatted low and ran up the row toward the hospital. Vivian stopped to catch her breath beside a minivan.

"Oh my god, I just knew he was going to see us. He was looking right at us."

Wendy peeked around the back glass. "He's standing beside his van with Pierre, Lucy and Kate. They must have done a good job keeping him distracted. I don't think he saw us." She turned to face Vivian. "What's that in your hand?"

Vivian looked down at a stainless steel pocketknife. "I don't know."

"You little thief." Wendy took it from her and pulled open one of the blades, except it wasn't a blade. "Oh my, it's a — "

"Lock picker thingy!" Vivian said and clapped, then snatched it back from Wendy. "It was an accident."

"Accident, my ass." Wendy smiled at her.

After Jeremy drove off, they walked out from behind the minivan. "Yoo-hoo!" Vivian called to Lucy, Pierre and Kate. "Way to keep him busy!"

"That guy loves to talk about himself," Pierre said as the group met. "He could have gone on for hours if he hadn't gotten a call."

"He's got an interesting story," Kate said. "We asked him about Mary Beth, and he seemed to really love and respect her."

"I thought he was going to cry," Lucy said, shaking her head. "His affection seemed legit."

"He could still be a killer," Wendy said, "but after seeing his van, I don't want to see inside his house."

"Y'all find anything?" Lucy asked.

Wendy shook her head. "Not really, but he had a gun in the glove box."

"I'd say that's something," Pierre said. "But I can see why he carries one. There's no telling who or what he comes across in his business."

Vivian turned toward the hospital. "I picked up a little something." She showed them her lifted lock pick. "Let's go see April."

The girls and Pierre went inside and up to April's room. Kate knocked and slightly opened the door. "Hello," she called softly.

Mike Grimm pulled the door open all the way and walked into the hallway. His black turtleneck and black slacks were rumpled but didn't smell of smoke. The large cup of coffee in hand and circles under his eyes told the story of a sleepless night.

"April is finally resting a bit," he said. "They kept her up all night because of the concussion." He pulled an imaginary piece of lint off his shirt. "She made me go home to shower and change, said the smell of my clothes was too much."

"How's she doing otherwise?" Lucy asked. "Will she get out today?"

Mike touched the bandage on his forearm. "The doc's going to see how she feels when she wakes up. If she feels okay and isn't dizzy, they may let her go."

"Did you get hurt in the fire?" Pierre asked, checking out Mike's bandage.

"It's not so bad. I had a few minor burns. This one was the worst, covers most of the back of my hand, but I should heal up okay."

"Does April remember what happened?" Wendy asked.

Mike shoved his uninjured hand into the front pocket of his jeans. "I've been over it with her several times and the police did, too, but she doesn't remember much. She sure doesn't know how she hit her head. She said there was a knock at the door and she went to answer it, but she doesn't remember who it was or if she let him in or anything. Next thing she knew, she was waking up in the ambulance."

"She is so lucky," Vivian said.

Kate shifted from one foot to the other. "This may be a weird question, but do you know if April knows Jeremy Donaldson?"

Mike looked perplexed. "Who?"

Lucy imitated turning a key in a lock. "A local locksmith. He was a student at April's school years ago. Drives a big white van with red letters on the side."

Mike's eyes lit up. "I've seen that van around town. April will say hi to former students she runs into, but I don't know if she knows him or remembers him from school."

Kate reached into her purse and pulled out the envelope containing the Visa gift card. "Here's a little something for her. Let her know we stopped by and wish her well. Good luck to you both."

Mike took the envelope and said goodbye as he stepped back into the room. The girls and Pierre took the stairwell down to the first floor and went out to the parking lot.

"What do you girls want to do next?" Pierre asked. "Anyone else we need to interrogate, any other cars we need to break in to, anything like that? Or are we actually going to take that drive to Saranac Lake or Lake George?"

Vivian bumped her arm into his. "Watch it, mister." She couldn't help but feel disappointed at where their leads had taken them. "I don't feel like we're any closer to figuring out what happened to Mary Beth or Rebecca than we were three days ago, and now Nicole's gotten sick, we've been run off the road, and April's house burned down."

"Don't forget our car burning to a crisp last night and the boat explosion the day before," Wendy said. "Good grief, who's the pyromaniac around here?"

Kate hit the clicker and unlocked the doors on the SUV. "After talking to Jeremy, I don't think he had anything to do with Mary Beth's or Rebecca's murders. He didn't even know Rebecca. He did have some weird love thing with Mary Beth, but I think that's all it was."

"He could be a really good actor and is hiding something," Vivian said, clicking her seat belt. "Maybe he knows who did it."

"Hmmm, but why not tell the police?" Kate started the car but didn't put it into reverse. "And I don't see why he would have it out for Nicole or April."

Wendy piped up from the back seat. "He could've made Nicole sick to keep her from looking into him and tried to kill April because she knows something. She taught at his high school, she has to know him. She could for sure know a lot about his and Mary Beth's relationship."

Kate shook her head. "I'm not feeling it."

"I was definitely wondering about Mike Grimm murdering Mary Beth after seeing that painting yesterday," Lucy said. "But what involvement would he have with Rebecca? And he seems to love April. Surely he wouldn't try to burn her up."

"I think he's just an odd guy, always wearing black. And he says weird things sometimes," Kate said. "But where does his path cross Nicole's? Why make her sick?"

Pierre laid his arm on the back seat around Lucy's shoulders. "People get sick all the time. Maybe Nicole actually just got sick. You know, just ate or drank something bad."

Kate backed out of the parking spot. "It's too coincidental that she got sick when she started diving back into her grandpa's files. I think someone got her sick on purpose."

"Who knew besides us that she had his files?" Wendy asked. "Jeremy might've wondered about it since she talked to him, but otherwise she only talked to us out at Turlington Farms."

That struck Vivian. "She talked to us at Tracy and Brandon's house. Tracy came in! Maybe she overheard and told Brandon."

Lucy grabbed Wendy's arm. "What if they're in on this together! That could help explain the randomness of the crimes. Drowning, burying someone, E. coli poisoning, running us off the road, arson."

Vivian turned in the front seat to look at Lucy. "You might be on to something there. A husband and wife duo of sex, drugs, murder, mayhem, porno and pyromaniacs."

"Drugs? Porno?" Kate questioned.

Vivian shrugged. "Ehhh, okay, so those are a bit of a stretch, but what a headline!"

Kate drummed her fingers on the steering wheel as she pulled up to a red light. "I feel like we're missing something. I don't think we check out tonight. We can play it cool for one more night. If they don't know what we know, we'll be all right."

"I chatted with Brandon while you girls were upstairs this morning," Pierre said. "He and Tracy were going to be around the house today so I'm afraid there's not much snooping we can do."

"Which is a shame," Wendy said, "because I feel like there's more good stuff to find. There was great stuff in our closet, and I bet he's got more important info hidden. And I still want to look in that garage, dammit!"

Kate turned right. "I want to go on the hike again. I feel like I need to see where Rebecca was buried. That's where I missed something."

"What can you possibly find?" Lucy asked. "The sheriff's crime scene people were all over the area."

"I don't know, but I've got a strong feeling that's where I need to start the search over."

"I wore my Kate Spade moccasins," Lucy said. "I can't hike in these, they're suede, they'll get ruined."

Vivian couldn't think of any other leads to follow up on. "You're going to have to take your chances, Lucy. I think we go on the hike. Kate needs her peace of mind, and with us leaving tomorrow, this is the last chance we'll get." Vivian kicked a foot in the air. "I'm in my hiking boots. I'm in!"

Lucy sighed. "Fine, but our trust fund might owe me a pair of shoes."

Wendy crossed her ankle over her knee and hit Lucy with her tennis shoe. "I didn't dress as fashionable as you, but I'm ready for action in these babies!"

"I'll give you a piggy-back ride through the mud," Pierre said to Lucy and squeezed her hand.

49

"A re you sure this is a good idea?" Lucy asked Kate as the group started up the trail. "Your shoes don't look slippery, but your Clarks won't hold up to the streams we have to cross, or the mud. Besides, we didn't bring any water or snacks. What if you get hungry?"

Kate kept marching. "I'm not worried about it, and you're not getting out of this. These women came to me in my dreams seeking help. I have to see this through. It torments me."

Lucy sighed and trekked after Kate, being careful where she stepped. "I don't like coming out here unprepared. We need water in the CamelBak at least."

Vivian leapt across a small stream, the ground squishing under her feet as she landed. "And snacks."

Kate followed, then reached into her jacket pocket and pulled out a Ziploc bag. "Who said we don't have snacks?" She bit into a bacon biscuit sandwich and offered the bag to everyone else. "Anybody?"

Vivian wanted a bite but decided Kate needed it more. Plus, she didn't have any water. She'd be thirsty and there was no way she was going to drink out of the stream — deer pee, bear pee, porcupine pee. "No, thanks," she said to Kate, and they got back to hiking.

As they went up in elevation and moved further and further away from the car, Vivian hoped they weren't going to regret this impromptu hike.

The trail was easier to follow since the sheriff and crime scene techs had trampled a better path, and before long the adventurers reached the area where they had picnicked four days prior. It was also the area that started it all — where Austin had brought them the human jawbone.

Lucy stopped a few feet from the bank. "There's still not a good place to cross. We're going to have to splash through." She looked down at her shoes, now covered in mud. "Sorry, Ms. Spade."

"I'm sure she'd love to sell you another pair," Vivian said, then looked at Kate. "You sure we need to go to where Rebecca was buried?"

"Absolutely. Whatever I'm missing, that's where I'll find it." Kate splashed across without hesitation.

Lucy took the lead and picked up the pace. "Let's get this over with. My feet are freezing already."

They made it to the dry streambed and the tree where Rebecca had been buried. More of the roots were exposed, and Vivian wondered how the tree hadn't fallen. One strong gust of wind and it might, she figured.

The group spread out, searching the vicinity, but Kate walked straight to the tree. She crouched down and held onto a couple of roots while peering underneath.

Wendy walked up to her. "Getting any vibes?"

Kate shook her head.

The crime scene techs had turned the ground in a wide radius but Kate picked up a stick and sifted the dirt just the same. So did Wendy, and Lucy and Vivian came over to help. Pierre walked around several trees, inspecting the trunks.

After a few minutes of digging through the dirt, Vivian looked at Kate. "Anything?"

"No, the techs probably found whatever there was to find, but I still feel like there's a piece of information that will link this whole thing together. I just have to find it."

Pierre walked over, inspecting Rebecca's tree. He started at the bottom and worked his way up, finally looking above his head. "Something is carved up there."

About 9 feet up, Vivian could see the outline of a heart with something scratched inside. "I'm too short to make it out."

"Boost me up," Lucy said to Pierre.

He bent down and she climbed onto his shoulders, then he stepped closer to the tree.

"What do you see?" Kate asked.

Lucy ran her finger over the carving. "It's very faint, but a heart."

"Take a picture with your phone," Wendy said, craning her head back to try and see it.

"Good idea," Lucy said and pulled her phone out of her pocket. She snapped the picture and Pierre helped her jump to the ground. They high-fived, and he kept his hand going and smacked her on the butt.

"I'd like to see you in a cheerleader outfit." He winked at her.

"Oh stop."

"Let's see the pic, Miss Rah-Rah-Sis-Boom-Bah," Vivian said, laughing. The group hovered around her phone and Kate drummed her finger on her lips. "What's it say inside the heart?"

"I think it's says SB plus T, but it was hard to tell," Lucy said.

Kate took the phone. "There's something familiar about it."

"Was it at the lean-to on Moose Island?" Vivian asked. "There were lots of things carved into the bench there."

"I saw that there were carvings, but I didn't pay any attention."

"At Lake Placid Brewery?" Lucy offered.

Kate shook her head. Wendy ventured, "At the Olympic complex? There was a post at the base of the mountain that had markings and stuff. Maybe you saw it there?"

"No," Kate said. "That's not it."

They threw out a few more ideas, but nothing jogged Kate's memory.

Vivian shrugged. "T could stand for Tracy, but what about SB? B for Brandon, but why the S?"

Wendy studied the picture again. "The legal documents we found in the crawl space all had his name as Brandon. I don't remember if there was a middle initial, but there definitely wasn't an S in front of Brandon."

Kate glanced at the picture, then up at the mark on the tree. "This is the key. We have to figure out what it means." She gave the phone to Lucy. "Let's get back to Turlington Farms. I want to see those papers again." She took one last look at the tree before setting off at a brisk pace down the hill.

As they hiked along, Vivian asked, "What was Tracy's boyfriend's name, the guy who ran off to Omaha? Scott or something like that?"

"We need to check in Grandpa's file. He had it in there, but that sounds right," Wendy said as they splashed through the big stream again.

"What was his last name?" Pierre asked as he helped Lucy across. "Start with a B?"

"I have no idea," Kate said. "I can't remember."

No one else could, either.

The hike down the mountain was much quicker than the hike up, and they made it to the car without incident and without having any idea what SB stood for. Kate fired up the SUV and pulled onto the haunted road. Sun low in the sky, no ghosts were visible or popped up in the crowded back seat.

"Maybe the S stands for a nickname," Pierre said as they cruised down a hill.

"Ehhh." Kate made the turn off of Highway 86 a little too fast, squishing everyone to the right.

"Scoot your booty over," Lucy said to Pierre and thumped him in the ribs.

"Holy shit!" Kate screamed and slammed on the brakes. "That's it!"

Vivian's head jerked forward and back, and her heart hammered. She looked out the windshield for something in the road. "What is it? What?"

Kate pushed the accelerator down, shot the car forward, gravel kicking up behind the tires. "Scooter Bill!"

50

Vivian grabbed her oh-shit handle and held on tight as Kate picked up the pace of their SUV. "Scooter what?"

Kate turned down the lane for Turlington Farms, again too quickly, leaning everyone to the left. "Tracy called Brandon that a couple of times, and now I remember where I saw that carving. It's on the dock behind their house. One of the boards isn't flush with the others, and I tripped on it when we went out on Larson's boat. I looked down and there it was. A heart with SB+T scratched inside. It looks almost identical to the carving on the tree."

Vivian's head spun, and not only from Kate's driving. "Scooter Bill plus Tracy. My gosh, it's Brandon!"

"He left a mark at each spot where he murdered his wives," Lucy said. "The tree for Rebecca and the dock for Mary Beth. Have y'all seen that marking in the house anywhere? Is Tracy next?"

"He's a serial killer and we saw him burning the leaves, he's good with fire," Wendy said. "You think he tried to kill April by burning down her house?"

"But why after all this time?" Kate asked. "That doesn't make sense. Maybe her fire is unrelated."

Vivian looked out the windshield as they pulled up the drive. The normally cheery yellow house with white gingerbread trim now looked foreboding. "I really don't know if we should stay here tonight."

"We have to get our bags," Kate said and smoothed her hair. "We need to remain calm so Tracy and Brandon won't know anything is off."

"What are we going to do with this information?" Wendy asked. "We don't have any proof Brandon is the murderer, and the police never found any wrongdoing on his part in either death. It might be a hard sell."

Kate tapped her fingertips together in her lap. "Pierre, you go find Brandon and keep him away from the house. We need to look around."

"Where are we going to start?" Vivian asked.

"Where all secrets are kept, of course, in the attic," Kate said.

"The access door to the attic is at the end of our hallway, but..." Lucy hesitated. "Don't we need to leave this to the cops? What do we expect to find?"

Kate opened her door and got out. "I'm not sure, but we've got to start somewhere. These women are counting on us."

The group got out of the SUV and walked into the house. The smell of baked goods greeted them as they walked to the dining room. A three-tier cake covered in white fondant icing and decorated with yellow, orange and red icing leaves sat in the center of the table. Chocolate cupcakes topped with orange frosting and two plates of cookies completed the spread.

The water stopped running in the kitchen and Tracy walked into the room drying her hands on a towel. Her apron was splattered with red food dye, and she had flour on her face. Her eyes were bloodshot. "Welcome back. You have a nice drive today?"

Vivian tried not to let the shock of Tracy's appearance show. "We sure did." She gestured to the table. "I see you've been busy."

Tracy shrugged. "Since it's your last night I wanted to show our appreciation for having you as guests. Your stay hasn't been the most relaxing, and I wanted to try and end it on a better note."

Kate picked up a cupcake. "Mmmm, thank you, we appreciate that."

"Is Brandon around?" Pierre asked. "I have an old radial arm saw at home and wanted his thoughts on what I should do to fix it, or if I should just give up and buy a new one."

"He's chopping wood behind the garage." Tracy picked up a knife and cake server. "Anyone like a piece of Italian cream cake?"

"I hate to mess up your cake, it's so pretty," Vivian said.

Tracy sliced into the top tier.

"But since you've started, I'd love a piece."

Tracy smiled as she gently set a huge piece on a plate.

Maybe it was Tracy's bloodshot eyes, or maybe it was the splatter of red dye on the apron, but something in her smile sent a chill down Vivian's spine. "I think I'll take mine to our room if you don't mind." She looked at the girls, imploring them to get the message.

Wendy looked at her, then at Tracy. "Me, too. Being in the car all day makes me tired. Whew!"

"I'll stick with the cupcake for now," Kate said, then headed toward the stairs.

Lucy passed on the baked goods and went upstairs while Pierre went outside in search of Brandon.

Vivian walked in as Kate pitched the cupcake in the trash. "You think she's the one who got Nicole sick with the E. coli?" Kate asked.

Vivian scraped her cake into the trash, too. "I don't know. She's been feeding us for days and we haven't had any issues, but something isn't right here."

"She looked a little crazy," Wendy said, dropping her plate into the trash.

"She is a little crazy to cook and bake like she did today," Lucy said. "That cake looked like a wedding cake. All that was missing was the bride and groom on top."

Vivian looked out the window and could see Pierre helping Brandon with the wood. "What if she's in on this with him and the abused spouse is just a front?"

Kate joined her at the window. "Let's hold off on that until we can look through the attic. I'm willing to bet Brandon has more things hidden up there he doesn't want Tracy to find."

Lucy opened the bedroom door and peeked out. "Coast is clear, let me go try the attic door." She crept down the hallway and tried to turn the knob to the attic but it was locked. She hurried back into the room. "Now what?"

"We've got to get in there," Kate said.

Vivian smiled and pulled Jeremy's lock pick set out of her purse. "No problem!"

51

Vivian walked as quietly as she could down the dark hallway outside her bedroom to the attic entrance. Lucy stationed herself near the top of the stairs. Kate and Wendy stayed at their bedroom door looking ready to dive inside if needed.

Vivian twisted and tugged on the attic door handle. She had no idea how to use Jeremy's lock pick set, but she figured this old door couldn't be too complicated. She opened a blade that was as curved as a treacherous road. She pushed it into the hole on the doorknob. She twisted it left and right, but nothing happened. Jammed it in pretty hard. Still nothing.

"Tick tock, tick tock," Lucy whispered.

"I'm working on it!" Vivian whispered back. She tried the blade with the gradual curved tip and slid it through the small hole in the door handle and started jiggling. She heard a small click. "I think I got it!" She turned the handle. "Open sesame," she said and pulled the door open.

Lucy, Wendy and Kate tiptoed down the hall toward her. Vivian clicked on the light and started up the narrow staircase. The boards creaked under her feet, sounding like an alarm going off with each step. She reached the landing and couldn't see much, given the dim, bare bulb in the middle of the attic. The mustiness got to her, and she coughed several times.

Wendy popped up behind her. "Thank goodness I brought this," she said and clicked on her flashlight. "It's small but powerful."

The attic was about the size of one of their bedrooms except they could only stand up straight in the middle; otherwise the pitch of the roof was in the way. The floor was unfinished, and a small, dirt-caked window faced out toward the garage. Dust floated through the beam of light as Wendy moved the flashlight across the room, displaying the handiwork of generations of spiders.

"Over there," Lucy whispered, pointing to the right.

Two sets of old suitcases shoved in a corner had boxes stacked beside them. An old floor lamp, drapery rods and a twin-sized mattress leaned against one wall. The only items not completely covered in dust were five boxes in various sizes marked Christmas decorations.

The girls crept over and Wendy handed the flashlight to Kate, who peeked inside a long rectangular box. "Christmas tree," she whispered, then moved on. The other four boxes were as marked, no surprises except the last box contained a framed picture of Brandon and Mary Beth, arms around each other, in front of the snow-covered house, which was decorated in white Christmas lights.

"They could've used this as their card. Sad." Kate put everything back exactly as it was. "Now what?"

Lucy walked toward the mattress. "Think there's anything hiding behind it?"

"Let's see," Kate said and walked close to it.

Lucy pulled the mattress from the wall, then quickly set it back, kicking up a cloud of dust. Kate covered her face, coughed and moved away. Lucy stepped back and ran into the floor lamp, knocking it over.

Vivian held her breath, listening for footsteps. After what felt like long enough, she turned to Lucy. "Be careful!"

"Sorry!"

"Let's hurry," Kate said and picked up the first of three small suitcases.

Nothing was found except an empty tube of toothpaste, some bobby pins, a couple of hotel-sized complimentary soaps and a white sock.

"That just leaves those," Vivian said, hunching over to get to the last stack of boxes. She pulled back the flaps on a medium-sized one. The light from the bare bulb wasn't enough to see what was inside. "Kate, can you come over here with the flashlight?"

Kate stood beside her and shined the light in the box. "What in the world?"

Vivian reached for an item wrapped in tissue paper and carefully unwrapped it. A cow wearing a party hat and covered in confetti was sitting on a birthday cake holding a little sign that read Happy Birthday To Moo. "Cute." She picked up the next item wrapped in tissue and discovered a Hawaiian-themed cow figurine with sunglasses, lei and grass skirt.

Wendy came around the other side of the box. "My mom collects these Cow Parade things. They could probably sell these on eBay for a little bit of cash."

Vivian sifted through the rest of the box but the only occupants were bovine. Vivian handed the box to Lucy, who moved it out of the way. In the next box were old dishes. Lucy moved that to the side and pulled at the shipping tape on the next box, trying to open it. "I can't get it."

Kate reached into her pocket. "Here, I've got the car keys." She punctured the tape and put the key back.

Vivian opened box number three revealing four royal blue books with Lake Placid High School on the spine spanning 1992 to 1995. "Yearbooks."

She opened the front cover on 1992. The inscriptions were to Brandon, and Vivian read them aloud. "Brandon, I've had a crush on you since third grade and I'll always love you, signed Regina."

Kate pointed to an inscription in the corner. "Brandon, you suck, Mark." She picked up the 1994 yearbook and started flipping through.

Lucy grabbed 1993. "This was Brandon's, too." She flipped through it, pausing and laughing at some of the outfits.

Wendy picked up 1995. "This is weird." She held it up for the other girls to see. "No inscriptions. Nothing."

"Maybe since it was his senior year, he didn't want it signed?" Vivian said.

"That's usually when you *do* want it signed," Lucy said.

Wendy flipped through the first few pages as Kate peered over her shoulder, then went back to the junior yearbook.

"Let's check our key players," Vivian said and looked up Mary Beth Turlington under the freshman class. Nothing written by her picture, so Vivian scanned the whole freshman class for Tracy's picture. It was a small class and didn't take long. One small heart was under Tracy's name in blue ink. "I'm guessing Brandon hearted Tracy. Y'all look them up, too."

"What was Tracy's maiden name?" Lucy asked.

"Browne."

Lucy quickly found the page. "Whoa, she had some '90s bad hair."

Vivian looked over. "Indeed."

"There's a little heart under her picture," Lucy said, "so I guess he still 'hearted her' their sophomore year, too."

Vivian watched as she flipped to a smiling Mary Beth, then Brandon.

In the middle of the book Lucy landed on the football team's page. "Aww, they were cute." There was Brandon in uniform and Tracy in a cheerleading uniform standing side by side, holding hands. Lucy read the inscription. " 'I'll love you forever, Scooter Bill.' "

"So they were together their freshman and sophomore year. That's a long time when you're that age, and a big deal," Kate said.

Vivian closed the book she was holding. "I'm ready to get out of here. This is getting us nowhere."

Wendy flipped to Tracy's senior picture, but there was no heart or anything written so she turned the page to Brandon's picture, but again, nothing. "Let's check out Mary Beth," she said and turned the page, then gasped.

"What?" Vivian came over to see.

In the place that should have held Mary Beth's senior picture were deep, black, ballpoint pen scratches. The page was deeply grooved. Her name had been scratched out and "Bitch" was written in its place.

"I have the feeling this isn't Brandon's book," Wendy said as she turned to his picture. Surrounding it was a giant heart inscribed with SB+T in red ink.

Kate drew in a quick breath. "Oh my god, it's not Brandon that's the killer, it's Tracy. We've got to get out of here!"

They threw the books down, not bothering to close anything up, and followed Kate down the steps.

She pushed on the attic door. "It won't open!"

"Let me try," Vivian said.

Kate scooted out of the way. Though the handle would turn, the door wouldn't budge. "What the — oh my god, is that smoke? It's smoke!" Smoke billowed under the attic door and crept around the edges. Vivian touched the handle again and could feel it getting hotter. "Holy shit, the house is on fire!"

52

Vivian banged on the door to the attic as smoke began filling the small staircase. "Help! Help! We're in here!" She tried the knob again, but no go. She, Wendy, Kate and Lucy were trapped.

"Help!" All the girls yelled, banging and shoving on the door.

The smoke started getting thicker so Vivian pulled her sweater up over her face and indicated they should do the same. "Kate, get back upstairs. Wendy, go with her. Lucy, let's try to break open this door."

"No, let's stay together," Wendy yelled. "Buddy system. We can't get out that way anyway."

Vivian looked at Lucy, who nodded. They all four turned and ran up the narrow staircase.

Once in the attic, Wendy ran to open the window, but it wouldn't budge.

"Watch out!" Lucy ran toward the window, floor lamp in hand like a javelin. She let it fly and the glass shattered, letting in fresh air, just not enough of it. Smoke now poured through the floorboards and attic walls.

Kate coughed several times and looked around frantically. "This is a balloon frame house. This attic will be engulfed in minutes, especially if this started on the second story."

Vivian's eyes burned as she looked around the attic again, just in case she had missed something, but there was no other way out. "We've got to get through the window." She ran over to it and looked below.

The pitch was steep, but if they could crawl down the roof of the second story, they might be able to swing over the side and drop down. Anything was better than burning alive. "Pierre! Pierre! HEEEEELLLLLLPPPPP!!!!"

Vivian turned away from the window. "Lucy, go first so you can help Kate. And see if you can get Pierre's. He and Brandon need to catch Kate."

Vivian moved out of the way and looked at Kate, who had one hand pulling her shirt above her mouth, the other wrapped protectively around her belly.

Wendy held onto Kate's arm and, between coughs, said over and over, "It's going to be okay, we're going to get out of here."

Lucy knocked the few remaining pieces of glass out of the frame and then crawled through the window.

Kate stepped up, ready to go next, and Lucy reached for her hand. "Don't cut yourself on the glass," Lucy yelled, helping Kate steady herself.

Kate looked inside the window at Vivian and Wendy. "The shingles are hot, hurry!" She turned and sat on her butt, scooting down after Lucy.

Wendy looked at Vivian.

"You go," Vivian said. "Go! I'm right behind you!"

Wendy didn't hesitate and carefully but quickly got out the window. She dropped to her butt and followed after Kate. Lucy was already at the edge.

Vivian started to crawl out, then remembered the senior yearbook. She hesitated for a second before deciding to go back for it. Flames now lapped up the steps and on the wall around the door. Vivian held her breath and ran to the boxes.

The flames provided a little light, and she was able to make out the books through the haze. She grabbed three, hoping 1995 was among them.

"Vivian!" she heard Wendy screaming from the window. "VIVIAN! Hurry! Let's go!!"

Vivian fell to her knees, her eyes and lungs burning. She crawled toward the direction of the window, pushing the books in front of her. *Audrey, Lauren, Olivia, Ben. Audrey, Lauren, Olivia, Ben.* After the agonizing crawl, she reached the window and popped her head outside, needing oxygen.

"I'm here, I'm here," she coughed, then shoved the three books outside.

"You scared me! Come on!" Wendy yelled, grabbing the yearbooks and chunking them off the roof.

Vivian threw herself out of the window, not realizing how steep it was. She landed with a thud, then began rolling down the roof. She tumbled over and over, unable to stop.

"Viv!" Lucy yelled, lunging for her as she approached the edge. She grabbed Vivian's sweater and pulled, which was enough to stop her momentum, but they were both perilously close to going over.

Vivian righted herself, rubbing her eyes. "I can't see anything."

"That may be a good thing," Kate said, looking at what lay below.

Wendy joined them at the edge. "Holy shit."

"I'm jumping down," Lucy said. She dropped one leg over the edge.

"Be careful, Lucy!" Vivian yelled. Their bloodshot eyes locked for a moment before she dropped down, dangling from the roof's edge.

Pierre came running from near the lake just in time to see Lucy hanging from the second story. Brandon was behind him.

An old truck crashed through the door of the garage and raced off down the drive. Brandon had to jump out of the way to avoid being hit.

"There goes Tracy!" Wendy yelled, then turned her attention back to

Lucy. "Hang on, Lucy, here comes Pierre!"

Pierre made it to the porch and underneath Lucy just as her grip slipped and she fell.

"Kate, you're next!" Wendy said.

Kate was sitting on the ledge, feet dangling over the side. "I can't!" she screamed.

"You have to!" Pierre yelled up at her. "We'll catch you, I promise."

Lucy yelled to her from the ground, "Do it for Little Plum!"

Kate was bawling.

"Do it like Lucy did," Vivian said. "Turn around and drop down."

Wendy and Vivian helped Kate turn, then helped her balance as she got ready to go over.

"You've got this," Wendy said. "Nothing bad is going to happen."

Kate screamed as she dropped over, kicking her legs wildly. Both Vivian and Wendy held her arms as she dangled.

"Kate, look at me," Wendy said. "On three you've got to let go. Pierre is down there."

Kate closed her eyes. "Okay. Okay. I can do this."

"Here we go," Wendy said. "One, two three!"

Kate dropped, screaming a scream Vivian would never forget. *The scream of a mother afraid for her child.*

Pierre held Kate close as she sobbed into his chest. Lucy ran over and helped Kate get away from the house so Pierre could catch Wendy. She dropped to the edge like Lucy and Kate had, dangling from the second story.

Brandon and Pierre stood below, ready to catch her. Suddenly, the edge she was holding crumbled and gave way. She dropped awkwardly to the side as Vivian watched from above.

"Wendy!" Vivian yelled.

Brandon shifted to the left, reaching for her, but her knee hit Brandon in the jaw and her boobs wound up in Pierre's face. Part of the porch railing fell and they all landed with a thud. Brandon definitely softened the blow, and Wendy was able to stand and join Lucy and Kate.

Tar from the shingles had begun to melt and stick to Vivian's hands, and smoke was pouring from the window and all areas of the roof.

"Okay, Vivian, you're up." Pierre clapped his hands and held his arms out for her.

Vivian had never been so happy to see two men waiting on her. She shifted around, getting on her knees, then dropped the first one over.

Audrey, Lauren, Oliva, Ben. Audrey, Lauren, Oliva, Ben.

Crash! The roof collapsed.

53

Sparks swirled around Vivian as the second-story roof caved in and she fell. Pieces of the house flew everywhere; one hit her leg before it hit the ground in a spray of embers. The kids' faces flashed before her eyes, and she knew they'd miss her.

Before she could scream, strong arms caught her. She, Pierre and Brandon tumbled to the ground in a heap, Vivian on the bottom.

The men out of the way, Lucy poked Vivian in the face. "Viv, Viv, can you hear me? I think she's unconscious."

The cracking and roar of the fire blared in Vivian's ears. She opened her eyes and sucked in a few lungs-full of air. "I'm not unconscious," she responded, still trying to catch her breath. "I'm waiting for my fireman to give me mouth to mouth."

"They're almost here," Lucy said, relieved. "My god, girl, you've got nine lives."

Vivian sat up. "Meow." She took a deep breath. "That was scary!"

"Get back! Get back!" Brandon yelled as more of the roof started to crumble.

Lucy helped Vivian up and they all backed away from the house.

"Where are the yearbooks?" Vivian asked between coughs. She spotted one close to the broken off porch railing.

Lucy dashed to pick it up.

Brandon got the other two and looked at Vivian in bewilderment as she took the books from him.

"I'll explain later."

A siren wailed down the driveway and red, flashing lights shone through the trees.

"How did the house catch on fire?" Brandon asked.

"Was that Tracy in the truck?" Kate asked, wiping at the tears running down her cheeks.

Brandon looked at Pierre and the girls. "Yes. What the hell is going on?"

Vivian looked at the yearbooks. Thankfully, 1995 was among them. She turned to Mary Beth's senior picture and showed it to Brandon. "Tracy killed her. And probably Rebecca, too."

Brandon's eyes were wide and he shook his head. "No. No way. Mary Beth drowned and the police are looking into Rebecca's death. Tracy didn't kill them."

Wendy pointed down the driveway. "Tracy almost ran you over just now, and I'm pretty sure that was the truck that ran us off the road."

"No, I don't believe it."

Vivian pointed to the heart with SB+T beside Brandon's yearbook picture. "This is scratched into the dock behind your house, and it's also on the tree Rebecca was buried under." Two fire trucks had parked in the driveway, and Vivian had to yell to be heard over them. "She called you Scooter Bill, right?"

Brandon ran his hands through his hair, then pulled on the ends. He looked from the fire truck to the house.

Six firemen jumped off the trucks and unrolled the hoses. Larson, in full gear, ran up to Vivian and the group. "Is anyone in the house?"

"Everyone's out," Vivian said, indicating herself and the girls.

He held her by the shoulders and looked her in the eyes.

Vivian was a sooty mess, her blonde hair frizzed out and her blackened face streaked with tears. "I'm mostly okay. I was hoping for mouth to mouth."

Larson smiled at her and shook his head. "You're one hot mess." He turned serious, back to business. "Kate?"

"I need to get away from the smoke, but I think I'm fine," she answered.

Larson glanced at the house, then back to the group. "Where were you in the house when the fire started? Any idea what happened?"

Lucy explained how they'd been locked in the attic, crawled out of the window and then on the roof. "Pierre and Brandon caught us when we jumped and Vivian fell."

A Mustang and a sedan pulled to a stop behind the fire trucks and two more volunteer firemen got out and put on their gear. They ran to the trucks and started helping the others. An ambulance raced down the driveway and screeched to a halt.

Larson ushered them all farther from the house. "As you learned the hard way last night, debris can go a long distance."

The group walked behind the fire trucks and the paramedics hustled over.

Larson handed Vivian, Wendy and Kate off. "This one took quite a spill and this one's pregnant. They all jumped off the second-story roof."

"Check her first," Vivian said, pointing to Kate.

Two sheriffs cars stopped. Deputies Stokola and Young got out. "Is anyone in the house?" Young asked.

"Not anymore," Pierre said.

"What happened?" Stokola asked.

"Tracy happened," Lucy said. "She set the house on fire and blocked the attic door so we couldn't get out. She tried to kill us, then took off in their truck."

"She just drove off?" Young asked Brandon.

The flames reflected in Brandon's eyes as he watched the bed and breakfast burning. He dropped to his knees, head in his hands, and began to cry. "Yes."

Pierre stepped up. "She tore out of here like a bat out of hell and almost ran over Brandon and me. You need to catch her."

"What's the color and year?" Young asked, hand on his walkie-talkie.

"Black, 1977, GMC Sierra 4x4," Brandon answered quietly.

Young called dispatch. "She's suspected of arson and 4 counts of attempted murder."

Vivian sat on the bumper of the ambulance. "We think Tracy killed Mary Beth and Rebecca." She still held Tracy's senior yearbook and showed them the heart with SB+T by Brandon's picture. "She calls Brandon Scooter Bill. This same inscription is on the dock behind the house, and it's on the tree at Rebecca's grave."

Brandon took the yearbook and opened to the page with Mary Beth's scratched-out picture. Then he shoved it away, looking even more depressed and upset. He cleared his throat and wiped at a tear.

"Mary Beth had celiac disease. If she ate wheat it could cause cramping in her muscles, but she was beyond careful with her diet. I've thought about it and thought about it, and to me, it has to come back to the celiac disease. She must have eaten something with wheat in it. Please don't tell me Tracy did this to her. Please."

"Sorry, Brandon." Vivian looked away from him, upset to see him cry. The fire was completely out of control. Not a good day for Brandon Holt.

Stokola turned to Brandon. "Do you have any idea where Tracy would run to? Any place she'd hide?"

Brandon sniffed and stood up. "No idea, but she does know all the back roads. I think she'd stick to those."

"Hearing this makes me wonder if Tracy slipped something into Nicole's hot tea the other day and that's what made her sick," Vivian said. "She said it tasted funny. I had a cup of tea, too, and it was fine so I assumed Nicole just didn't like the taste."

Wendy nodded. "Tracy might've overheard something. We still had the files in the house. Damn, they're burned to a crisp now."

The Talking Heads song "Burning Down the House" popped into Vivian's head, which had begun to pound behind her eyes. "I think I need an aspirin."

Larson had her follow his finger with her eyes, then he shined a small flashlight in them.

"You should probably come home with me tonight and let me do a more thorough examination." He grinned. "Just to make sure."

Her heart and parts further south fluttered at the prospect. She nodded. "That sounds like a very good idea."

54

Day 7

Vivian heard water running. She stretched and slowly opened her eyes, taking a look around in the daylight. Larson's bedroom was pretty much what she expected.

Flat-screen TV across the room, a large oak dresser, a bookshelf piled high with *Sports Illustrated*, a couple of classics and a dictionary. She pulled the plaid flannel sheets up under her arms and rolled onto her side, fluffing her hair behind her on the pillow trying to look pretty and peaceful all at once. She checked for sleep in her eyes, then heard his footsteps and couldn't help but smile as she played possum.

"I see someone is awake." Larson sat on the bed and stroked her blonde curls. "Good morning."

She opened her eyes. "What do you mean? I smile in my sleep all the time."

"I bet you do."

She ran her fingernails up and down his muscular biceps, then smoothly transitioned to his thigh, playing with the hem of his boxer-briefs. "You know, you could make me smile a little bit bigger this morning." She let her fingers slide upward.

"Haven't you had enough yet?"

Vivian laughed at that and tucked her fingers underneath his waistband, then tugged. "This girl is from Texas where we like things bigger and better. You've got both, now get back in here."

He let his underwear drop to the floor. "Is this what you're looking for?" he asked, showing off his "bigger," then slid underneath the covers, covering her body with his. His warmth and strength enveloped her and he kissed her passionately, letting his tongue linger. He smelled amazing, a mix of Irish Spring and sex.

He moved from her mouth, kissing and nibbling down to her neck, then nuzzled her breasts but didn't stop there. That's when he really got going with the "better."

Two hours later they both were glowing from their morning romp. The covers and pillows were thrown all around the bed, and Vivian's head was hanging over the side.

"You're pretty flexible," Larson said.

"All those years in dance class, at least I have that to show for it. Not sure I should tell my parents that's where their money went."

He laughed and stood up. "It's almost 10, and we're supposed to meet the combustion crew at the diner in 30 minutes. What time is your flight today?"

She groaned. "Around 3."

"You can borrow one of my shirts for breakfast, so people don't think the diner's on fire, but then after that I suggest you hit one of the shops in town." He reached for her hand and helped her sit up. "Want to hop in the shower?"

"Are you going to be there?"

"What do you think?"

"Then heck, yeah."

They jumped in his tiny shower, taking turns with each other's backs and other hard-to-reach places. He had two-in-one shampoo and conditioner, which her hair did not like. She needed more moisture for the curls, but it was the only option. She looked under the sink and found some hair gel, squeezed it into her palm, then ran it through her wet hair.

Larson carried a clothes basket into the bathroom and pulled out Vivian's freshly laundered clothes. "I'd rather see you naked, but you're going to need these."

"I'd rather you see me naked, too!" Vivian laughed. "Thanks for washing my super sooty, stinky duds, I was dreading putting these on."

"I couldn't let you go home like that."

She got dressed, then Larson wrapped a flannel shirt around her shoulders. "You're going to need this, too. It's chilly out." He snuggled into her neck. "Mmmmm."

She didn't want to mess up the moment, but they were already 15 minutes late to the diner. "We better go."

"Yeah, we better."

They got in his truck and headed to town. The others had stayed at the Crowne Plaza, which was within walking distance of the diner.

Larson found a spot on the street and they hustled inside, finding Wendy,

Kate, Lucy and Pierre already eating.

"Good morning," Vivian chimed as she sat down and picked up a menu.

"Sorry, we were starving," Kate said, taking a bite of a strawberry-smothered waffle.

"No worries. We overslept," Vivian said and buried her head behind her menu.

She and Larson ordered, and pretty soon everyone was sitting back, full and happy.

"I see you've already been shopping," Vivian said to them.

"Pierre treated us since everything we had is now ashes." Lucy squeezed his hand. "And he gave us some cash for the trip home."

"I have my wallet and keys," Pierre said, "but lost my new Philipp Plein sneakers."

"Uh oh," Vivian said. "You don't have an expensive shoe habit like Lucy, do you?"

He smiled and shrugged. "I might have splurged on those."

"We ran to a five and dime last night," Wendy said. "Not high falutin' but we picked up some sweats to sleep in and a few toiletry items. I needed contact solution like nobody's business. My contacts were practically glued to my eye balls."

"Then this morning we found a little boutique that opened at 10 and made the clerk very happy," Lucy added. "Probably met her day's quota in the first 30 minutes."

"Larson had everything I needed," Vivian rumpled his hair. "He even washed my clothes for me."

"I'm kinda digging your lumberjack-lady look," Kate said. "It's very Lake Placid."

"It's cool outside and I needed his flannel shirt to keep warm."

Pierre paid the tab and Larson threw down a tip. "What time are you heading to the airport?" he asked.

"My, Viv's and Kate's flight is at 3," Wendy said. "Lucy's not until 3:40. We probably need to head to Albany around 12:30 so we can return our perfectly intact, beautifully undamaged rental."

"Third time's the charm," Vivian said, but then she thought about everything they'd lost in the fire. "Aw, my souvenirs I bought for the kids. And how are we going to get on a plane with no ID?"

"At least we won't have to check bags." Lucy laughed.

"I'm serious! What are we going to do?"

"You'll probably get an extra pat-down," Larson said, then winked. "You'll like it, I'm sure." He pulled a couple of twenties out of his wallet and shoved them in Vivian's front pocket. "Here's some travel money, don't let them grab your cash when they pat you down."

The group ran in and out of stores on Lake Placid Village's Main Street, getting souvenirs and a secret group gift for Kate's baby.

At 12:20 they hiked uphill to the Crowne Plaza and began their goodbyes.

Pierre hugged Vivian tight. "I wish you the very best, Vivian. I'm happy to see you so happy."

"Thanks, Pierre, that means a lot. I'm so grateful you were here for Lucy, and for us. We might be in a much different condition if it weren't for you."

He smiled and kissed her on both cheeks. "Until next time." He turned to Lucy and scooped her into his arms. He kissed her like he might not see her again, or at least for a very long time. She kissed him back just as passionately.

"Get a room!" Wendy shouted.

Vivian laughed and ambled up to Larson. "So I guess this is it for now."

He nodded yes. "Keep in touch." He put his arm around her waist, then kissed her gently. "And stay out of trouble."

"Never," she whispered.

The four girls climbed into the rental and waved goodbye as they headed down the hill. They hadn't gone two blocks when Wendy turned around from the front seat.

"This may sound morbid, but I'd like to run by the B&B. You know, maybe check on Brandon."

"Why?" Vivian said. "He was kind of a jerk."

Wendy shrugged. "He wasn't the nicest guy I ever met, but I feel sorry for him. He lost two wives at the hands of someone who supposedly loved him. Talk about betrayal."

"We probably should go by and ask about insurance taking care of our stuff," Lucy said. "I lost four pairs of expensive shoes in that fire, and by god, somebody's paying for that."

Kate took a right, pointing them in the direction of Turlington Farms. "Okay, but we can't stay long. We don't want to miss our flights."

229

55

As the girls pulled up to the bed and breakfast, a man in khakis and a white shirt carefully stepped through the rubble snapping pictures while another man in navy pants and a polo shirt took notes. The blackened remains of the house provided stark contrast to the bright, sunny day.

A few singed rose bushes outlined where the front porch used to be, and the yard was a muddy mess. The garage was still standing and looked untouched. The right side door was up and Brandon walked out.

Vivian was surprised. "I guess we should get out and say hello." She opened her car door.

Kate grabbed her door handle. "You mean, goodbye?"

Vivian felt so bad for Brandon. She gave him a hug. "How you doing?"

"Called the insurance company. The adjuster should be here any time." He hitched his thumb toward the guy walking through the rubble. "That's Dan, the arson investigator, and John, the fire chief."

"Where are you staying?" Wendy asked.

"We — " he stopped for a second. "I have a garage apartment. It will do until I can rebuild."

"Are you going to reopen the B&B?" Kate asked.

"I think it's what Mary Beth would want me to do." Brandon cleared his throat and looked away. After a moment he looked back at the group. "I'm going to do things a little differently, though. I'm going to hire the help, not marry them."

The tension broke, and Lucy laughed. "Speaking of, any news on Tracy?"

"I've already talked to deputy Stokola this morning." Brandon shook his head. "Tracy was caught in the middle of the night at the Canadian border. She had a bag of cash and a U.S. passport with a fake name."

"Where did she get the cash and passport?" Lucy asked.

"I have no idea," Brandon said. "She must have had it stashed here in the house."

"Did she get booked for murder or attempted murder?" Wendy asked. "It should be four counts of attempted for sure." She looked at Kate. "No, make that five!"

"Six if you count Pierre when she ran us off the road into the lake," Lucy said.

Brandon looked at Kate and nodded. "They're holding her on suspicion of arson and attempted murder. That's why the arson investigator was here at first light. They're getting enough evidence to book her. She hasn't said a word since she was taken into custody."

"Any chance she'll go down for drowning Mary Beth and killing Rebecca?" Vivian asked.

"I doubt she'll ever confess, and I don't know how they'd prove it," Brandon said. "The best we can hope for is she goes to prison for what happened here last night." He rubbed Vivian's arm. "I'm sorry she did that to you."

Vivian grabbed his hand and gave it a squeeze. "It's not your fault. She's nuts."

Brandon shoved his hands in his pockets. The fire chief and arson investigator said goodbye on their way to their car. "It was arson," the investigator said. "I'm fairly certain we've got enough proof to nail her."

The fire chief looked at the girls. "You are all lucky to have escaped."

Brandon watched the men leave, then turned his attention back to the girls.

"Best of luck to you," Wendy said and extended her hand.

The girls took turns wishing him well and got into the rental.

"I don't know if we'll ever be back," Vivian said, "but I hope something good can come from all of this."

Kate looked at the smoldering house. "It already has. Two women have found peace because their murderer is behind bars. Even if she's never tried or convicted, the world will know this story now and what truly happened. Come on, Girlz, let's go home."

Epilogue

Vivian's four-day-old cellphone buzzed on her desk. She read the display, not recognizing the area code. "Hello?"

"Hey, Vivian, it's Nicole."

"Nicole, hi! How are you?"

"Fully recovered and back at it."

"That's great to hear." Vivian put her on speakerphone, then stood up and closed her office door. "So what's up?"

"Just wanted to see if you had any comments on Tracy being indicted on arson and attempted murder. Not only do they have the fire investigation, but they pulled evidence off the truck she used to try to run you girls off the road."

"Wow, I hadn't heard that." Vivian drew doodles on her giant desk calendar. "All I have to say is that Tracy needs serious psychological help."

"Anything else you'd like to add? This is front-page stuff."

"Not really. We trust she'll get what she deserves."

"Okay." Nicole's voice trailed off and Vivian heard the clacking of a keyboard.

"I saw your fireman the other day," Nicole said after a moment. "He had a very cute, red golden retriever hanging out of the side of his truck, enjoying the wind whipping around his ears."

"Larson adopted Austin!" Vivian smiled.

"He said he's going to take him out any time they have a search and rescue because he's got the nose that knows."

They laughed and chatted for another minute, but then Vivian's desk phone rang.

"That's my work line. I better grab it."

"Okay, take care, Vivian. 'Bye."

"Goodbye," Vivian said, then grabbed her desk phone. "Vivian Taylor."

At first she didn't hear anything. "Hello? Hello?"

"Viv," Wendy cried. "Oh my god!" she wailed.

"What is it? Did the police find Jake?" Vivian's eyes teared up, and her heart sank. "Should I call Ali to come be with you?" Ali was Wendy's good friend in Houston who was supposed to be her maid of honor.

Wendy sniffled and took a deep breath. "No, Ali doesn't need to come over, but we do need to get to Vegas. Soon."

"Why? What'd you learn?"

Wendy started crying again. After a minute, she was able to speak. "Jake was up to something … something bad."

Vivian grabbed a tissue and wiped a tear. "We kinda figured that. I mean, with the passport and money. So let's go to Vegas, figure all this out."

"But Viv, it's much worse than we thought. Jake was involved with the mob."

Lea, Johnell, Angela and Robbyn in Lake Placid.

Handy dandy back seat bar.

Pumpkin dropping!!

Lea hiking and showing off her baby bump.

Robbyn getting a bear back scratch.

The Getaway Girlz in Upstate New York!

Acknowledgments

As always, we must begin with and thank our all-time fav Getaway Girlz, Lea Bass Rogers and Angela Wenk. May our vacations be many, our laughs, unending, and our wine glasses always filled. Now let's go to VEGAS BABY!

And special thanks to our other Girlz, Laura Trujillo, Christine Moreno, Ellen Rink, Vikki Shelton, Stephanie Surendran, Christina Judge, Alicia Jenkins, April Cicarello, Beth Zimmerman, Janet Neff and Linda Pugh. You ladies provide more funny fodder than you'll ever know! Love ya, girlz!

To John Dycus – our word and fact checker, occasional tisker, but most of all, biggest supporter. We'll try to keep your adrenaline racing for many books to come!

A special thank you must always go out to Janet Neff, PR helper and promoter, party thrower and pool provider, and the most amazing friend any set of Girlz could ask for. And a big high-five to Mr. Bill. Those candied bacon deviled eggs are the bomb.com!

Thank you to our two photographers – our husbands! You braved the elements (and heights) to get the perfect shot.

We've gotta give a big shout out to our beta-readers! Thank you to Jackie Meeks, who sped-read and, as always, made our story stronger. And to Stephanie Surendran, who also put in a rush job, but was still as meticulous as ever. And, to Tom Hill, who has time to speed read since he's now retired. Way to go Dad!

We have to thank our numerous experts who helped make our story authentic – Brian Simons for his law enforcement input and gun knowledge, Sarah Simons her medical brain, Cheryl Mc Intyre for her knowledge of ghostly and ghastly Upstate New York stories, Mike Joiner for his fantastic fireman information, Jeramy Daugereaux for lock picking knowledge – if we hadn't known you since 1st grade, this might make us nervous!

Our favorite restaurants around Fort Worth continue to hook us up with great happy hours, fantastic service, yummy food, free electricity for our laptops and most of all, friendly faces. Special thanks to Chuy's who not only supports us in great drink specials, but hangs our books on their wall.

We love music and we love Josh Weathers – you keep us wanting more with every song. Please come back – we know it's in your soul!

Johnell wants to thank…

Thank you to my loving, kind, generous and adorable husband (yes, I did say husband!) After knowing each other for 34 years, I guess it was time for us to take it to the next level, and what a level it is! The past year and a half was made even more amazing because you were in it. I must also thank all six of these growing, rambunctious, fantastic kiddos. Danielle, Sadie, Cayce, Cameron, and newly added, but loved just as much, Austin and Alison. Thanks for always being such good Barnes and Noble buddies and for not complaining too much when I have to do my book thing. Just keep remembering...college fund!

I also want to thank Robbyn – you're doing a GREAT job with sweet Ashley, our youngest Getaway Girl! She's amazing, like her mom! And thanks to Dave who keeps that sweet girl while we're writing! Appreciate ya!

Robbyn would like to thank…

My husband, David. Thanks for taking care of the sweet girlie while I'm working. And for putting up with the late nights!

Congratulations to Johnell and Big Lou! I'm so happy for you and wish you many years of happiness! - R

About the Authors

The women behind Joan Rylen are Johnell Kelley and Robbyn Foster, friends since kindergarten. They grew up in Pasa"Get Down"dena, Texas, a suburb southeast of Houston. From Brownies to high school band, these girlz have stuck together through thick and thin...marriages, divorces, births, deaths and of course, destruction.

Their annual girls' trips with two other good friends were the original inspiration for *Getaway Girlz*. Johnell and Robbyn are the authors of three books in the Getaway Girlz series and have plans for many more. They can be seen around Fort Worth, Texas, writing in bars and having an all-around good time.

Johnell and Robbyn hope to inspire women, whether they're 21 or 91, to stay in touch with old friends and take getaways of their own. There's nothing like a good friend who knows all your stories-the ones so crazy you can't make them up, and loves you anyway.

Watch for the next book in the Getaway Girlz series:

LAS VEGAS
VENGEANCE

Available 2015

www.getawaygirlz.com

facebook.com/getawaygirlz

twitter.com/joanrylen

youtube.com/getawaygirlz